# NOTHING

# BUT

# THIS

# NOTHING BUT THIS

a love story

## Natasha Anders

Montlake
Romance

Published by Montlake Romance, Seattle
www.apub.com

Amazon, the Amazon logo, and Montlake Romance are trademarks of Amazon.com, Inc., or its affiliates.

ISBN-13: 9781542094412
ISBN-10: 1542094410

Cover design by Caroline Teagle Johnson

Printed in the United States of America

*For Oliver, the best little writing assistant I could ever have asked for. Fly high and free, my precious angel.*

# Prologue

*This party blows.* The words flitted through Libby Lawson's mind—not for the first time that evening—as she propped up a wall and watched people who were really no more than casual acquaintances talk too fast, laugh too loud, and hook up with careless abandon.

This wasn't Libby's usual scene. Not that she had a usual scene. Her work as a sous-chef at a tiny but exclusive restaurant in London's Soho kept her much too busy to attend many parties. But a few of her colleagues had insisted on dragging her out to some media mogul's rooftop on her one free night of the week. And then had immediately abandoned her.

Libby had no real clue whose party this was, and, after being hit on by several random drunk guys—and one drunk chick—she was about ready to make a discreet exit.

Her feet were killing her; she wasn't used to the stilettos her flatmate had convinced her to wear. Libby was all about practical footwear. Why anyone would want to wear four-inch spikes on their feet was beyond her.

She ran disinterested eyes rapidly over the gathering of slightly too perfect people and froze when her gaze met a familiar dark, brooding stare.

*Greyson Chapman?* Recognition, shock, and awareness immediately sizzled through her body and froze her on the spot. *God*, talk about a blast from the past.

Even more startling was the fact that when he looked up and met her eyes, he seemed to instantly recognize her. Meeting his serious gaze felt like a jolt of electricity shooting through her entire body. He maintained eye contact, and she shoved herself away from the wall and waited as he pushed his way through the throngs toward her.

As an impressionable teen, Libby had always been fascinated by Greyson's dark mysteriousness. By comparison, everyone else she knew—including his twin—was an open book. But Greyson had intrigued her with his silences, his brooding, and his emotional distance from even those closest to him. She had followed him everywhere, until he had called her a stalker and told her to back off. At fourteen to his eighteen, she had retreated, humiliated beyond bearing to have her crush talk to her like that.

He'd gone to Yale in the United States soon after that confrontation, and she had continued with her life. Seeing him only rarely on his returns home for the holidays. And then not at all when she'd gone off to culinary school.

"Olivia." His dark, deep voice sent a shudder of intense familiarity through her, and her nipples beaded instantly.

She had always felt that awareness around Greyson, but he had never seemed to reciprocate.

"Greyson."

"Let's go." He held out his hand to her, and she stared at it for a long moment before taking it with a quirk of her lips. His warm, dry, much-larger hand folded around hers, and he tugged her toward the exit.

She was wobbly on the unfamiliar heels but managed to keep up all the way down to his chauffeur-driven luxury car.

He paused to say something to the driver, but Libby and Greyson didn't speak to each other until they were in the back, side by side, concealed from the driver's eyes—and all other curious gazes—by tinted windows.

"You're beautiful," he said, wasting no time as his eyes trailed over her body and face. Leaving her with goose bumps, aching nipples, and an unfamiliar hot, heavy wetness between her thighs.

*Beautiful?*

Her throat was dry, and she felt dizzy as she tried to orient herself to this new reality. A reality within which Greyson Chapman thought she was beautiful. She swallowed several times before she felt confident enough to speak.

"You're not too bad yourself," she croaked. His lips tilted at the corners as he continued to stare at her with predatory intent. God, what the hell was *this?* He had never before stared at her with such overt desire in his eyes.

She was wearing a silky black halter-neck jumpsuit with a plunging back. The flowing pant legs and the four-inch heels made her appear much taller than her actual height of five feet seven. Her black, wavy hair tumbled wild and free down her back and framed her face. She had tried to make an effort and knew she looked good tonight, but still, she didn't think she looked that different from the Olivia Lawson whom Greyson had known and ignored for most of his life.

He was wearing a tuxedo—much too formal for the rooftop party—and it was nearly midnight, which meant that it couldn't possibly have been his first event of the evening. She discreetly sniffed the air, wondering if he was a bit inebriated. She smelled nothing but the fresh, masculine scent of the probably exorbitantly expensive aftershave he used and a faint whiff of tobacco smoke.

God, he looked amazing. His strong jaw was dark with stubble. And his lean, austere face, so similar to—and yet so very different from—that of his twin brother, Harris, was as beautiful as she remembered. He had perfect, bow-shaped lips; a sharp, arrogant nose; deep-set, dark-blue eyes that could pierce your soul set between thick, lush eyelashes; and straight dark brows. His black hair was conservatively cut, with a side part. Short and no nonsense. Even as a boy he had never seemed interested in having it longer or more stylish.

As she watched, he lifted one of those elegant, capable hands to his bow tie and tugged at it, loosening it and unbuttoning the top button of his crisp white shirt. Making him look almost roguish.

"Have you eaten?" he asked.

"Not really."

"I hear you're doing very well for yourself," he continued, surprising her again. She had never really thought he'd given her more than a moment's consideration in the years since she'd seen him last.

"I'm doing okay," she said, her eyes on his lips. There was a wicked curve to the bottom lip, and she wanted to taste it. She licked her own lips in reaction, shocking herself. His intense eyes followed the movement of her tongue avidly. Like a cat watching a mouse.

"Your parents have retired," he said softly, and she frowned, not really sure why he'd bring that up.

"Yes." Her mother and father had been his family's cook and chauffeur, respectively. Libby had grown up in the Chapman house. She had happily played with the twins as a child, at first totally unaware of the huge social and economic gap between her and the boys.

"Good." The purring satisfaction in his voice startled her.

"Good?"

"That means I can do *this* . . ." He reached out, cupped her nape beneath her fall of hair, and tugged her toward him. He turned so that he was facing her, and as she watched in fascination, his eyes drifted shut. He tilted his head and slotted his mouth over hers in a hungry, all-consuming kiss.

It was unexpected but so, *so* good. She moaned, her hands going to his chest and then burrowing beneath his suit jacket and around his back. She wriggled closer and opened her mouth to allow him entry.

He didn't waste any time, his tongue swooping in and laying waste to any semblance of reservations or common sense.

Before she knew it, she was straddling his lap, her mound grinding against the huge erection surging between his thighs. He had her halter undone and her small, braless breasts exposed to his eyes, hands, mouth, tongue, and teeth.

Libby wasn't very experienced, but this felt like the most natural thing in the world to her. This was Greyson; she'd known him forever. She had wanted him for nearly as long, and now he was here, seemingly from out of nowhere. He was holding her and kissing her and touching and caressing her. She was on fire with need and lust for him, and she couldn't see any reason why she couldn't have him.

He was the one who called a halt to things, releasing her lips with palpable reluctance while he fumbled with her halter top, tying a clumsy knot at the back of her neck. She winced when he caught a few strands of her hair in the knot, and he muttered an apology. He dropped his hands to her waist and lifted her from his lap to place her on the seat beside him.

"Greyson," she moaned, embarrassed by the naked pleading she heard in her own voice.

"I know. I'm sorry. But we're here."

*Here?*

"Where?" she asked blankly.

"I told my driver to bring us back to my hotel."

"That's assuming a lot," she said huffily, gradually coming back to her senses and a little irritated by his cheek. Typical Greyson, always getting what he wanted.

"Too much?" he asked, looking both arrogant and uncertain at the same time. How was that even possible? "Should I ask him to take you home?"

She swallowed audibly and folded her arms over her chest, trying not to react at the slide of the silky fabric over her swollen, sensitive nipples. He looked rather out of sorts himself; his hair was mussed, his tie completely off, his top four shirt buttons undone. And she knew he was still hard, could see it in the hunch of his back as he tried to find a comfortable way to sit.

"Olivia?" he prompted her, and she shook herself.

"Do you have food up there?"

"We can order room service," he promised.

*Don't overthink it, Libby.*

"Okay," she said cautiously, feeling like she was about to step out of the car and fall down a crazy rabbit hole. He didn't smile—his expression barely changed at all—but she could tell from the flare of his eyes and the sudden hitch of his breath that her response pleased him.

Libby and Greyson lay sprawled on their backs, staring up at the ceiling, chests heaving after their third energetic bout of lovemaking of the evening. Libby curled up on her side and rested her head on his corded biceps. She trailed a finger down the center of his chest, toward the sexy indent of his belly button.

"That was fun," she said, dropping a kiss on his well-defined pec. The muscle twitched beneath her lips. His arm curled around her back, and his long, elegant fingers combed through her tumble of dark, wavy hair.

"It was good," he agreed, and she smiled. Greyson Chapman would never use a frivolous word like *fun*. She had often wondered if he even knew how to have fun. He had always been so quiet and serious. She had known him her entire life, and she couldn't recall once hearing him laugh out loud.

She knew he was surprised by the fact that she'd been a virgin; many of her friends and acquaintances would have been as well. She wasn't shy, or prudish about sex, and she'd had no noble objectives of abstinence before marriage. She had simply been busy and too distracted by her studies and then work to bother with the opposite sex. She had been much too exhausted most of the time to concern herself with dating and often wondered how others found the time to manage a successful career along with a healthy relationship.

She couldn't believe she had so meekly done his bidding tonight. Following him out of that party like an eager little puppy. She hadn't given it a moment's thought, and she wondered: Had she reconnected with Greyson at the restaurant instead of a party, would her work have taken precedence as it had on so many other occasions? Or would the end result—them in bed together—have been inevitable? She tilted her head to look at him, and yes, she had no doubt at all that she would have been in this exact same position, regardless of where or when they had met again. She would probably have followed him right out of the restaurant at the merest haughty crook of his finger.

It was a humiliating realization. She was still such a giddy girl when it came to Greyson.

She had stayed in contact with his brother, Harris, of course. They texted and called each other often. He was one of her dearest friends, and she couldn't imagine not maintaining contact with him. But she had lost track of Greyson. He was literally the last person on earth she'd expected to see tonight. So very far away from his home in Cape Town.

And while she would never in a million years have believed they'd wind up in bed together, there had been a sense of inevitability to their union. This man, who had avoided her at all costs and had never so much as looked at her after her sixteenth birthday, was now her lover, and it was incredibly surreal.

"The condom broke," he pointed out gruffly, and she pushed herself up onto her elbow to look down into his remarkably unperturbed face.

"Did it?" She wasn't particularly concerned; she knew how fastidious Greyson was about his health. And pregnancy was highly unlikely, considering she had finished her period just a few days before.

"Yeah, the first time."

"I'm not on the pill," she said, and he shrugged before stretching and yawning languorously.

"You were a virgin," he said after his long, catlike stretch, his voice completely lacking inflection.

"I was. No time for lovers."

"You want to get married?" he asked.

"Eventually," she responded, baffled by the question.

"I meant to me." His voice was still ridiculously nonchalant, and Libby huffed an incredulous little laugh.

"Don't be preposterous," she said dismissively, curling up against his chest as one of his hands dropped to her butt cheek and squeezed.

"I'm serious."

She lifted her head again and met his sleepy blue eyes curiously.

"Why?" she asked, entertaining his silliness for the moment. Greyson wasn't one to really make jokes, but this couldn't be anything other than a jest.

"Why not? We've known each other for years. And we're *clearly* sexually compatible. I have to settle down at some point, and I think we'd be good together."

Marriage. To Greyson.

For a moment she allowed herself to fantasize. Once, long ago, she had dreamed of just such an eventuality. To have ownership of his heart and his body. To allow him the same over hers. She played that out in her mind for a moment. Imagining the life they'd build together. He would finally allow her into the dual fortresses of his heart and mind. She would know his every secret, understand what made him tick. And she would use the knowledge to make him adore her as much as she had once adored him. As she could so easily come to adore him again. It was a heady little fiction. And she knew it stemmed from the vestiges of her long-ago adolescent crush.

Her current reality was exciting and surreal enough without adding to it with ridiculous fantasies.

Besides, he couldn't possibly be serious.

"I don't need a husband," she pointed out, feigning insouciance with a roll of her eyes. She thought about that broken condom. Was that where this was coming from? And what if—against all odds—she was pregnant? She wouldn't *have* to marry if she was, but it would be better. She stared at his beautiful, stern features for another long moment and acknowledged that she still felt that absurd pang of excitement mixed with desire, awareness, and fascination when she looked at him. She deliberately forced those emotions aside. Hating how vulnerable they made her feel.

"Fine, what about dinner, then?" he suggested idly. "Tomorrow night?"

"I'm working."

"I know. I meant afterward."

"That'll be after midnight."

"If you prefer, we could call it a midnight snack?"

"All right." Her response needed absolutely no thought. There was no way she was going to deny herself the pleasure of his company. The chance to spend time with him and get to know him better.

He smiled. A small lifting at the corners of his mouth; his pleasure wasn't evident on his lips so much as in his eyes, which lit up in an expression that could only be described as delight.

"Fantastic." His free hand dropped to her other butt cheek, and he squeezed appreciatively, moving her until she was straddling him. "Are you sore?"

"It's not too bad."

"Good," he purred. "Now kiss me."

# Chapter One

*Present day*

"Where's Greyson?" Libby moaned. Her brother-in-law, Harris, smoothed her hair back from her damp forehead.

"He's on his way," Harris promised, and Libby sobbed as she reached for his hand and squeezed painfully. She hated that Greyson wasn't here. She had tried to ignore the first signs of labor, denying reality because she couldn't quite believe she would be doing this without her husband.

Harris was like a brother to her. Her child's uncle. But he wasn't enough. Greyson needed to be here.

Why had he abandoned her when she needed him most?

"I want my husband."

Harris made soft soothing sounds. He was trying his best, but Libby wasn't in the right frame of mind to appreciate that right now.

"I know, Bug. His plane landed an hour ago; he'll be here soon."

"He doesn't want our baby." The pain was coming almost constantly now. But her admission hurt her so much more than the physical discomfort of labor. A soul-deep, gut-wrenching acknowledgment that had been gnawing at her for months.

"That's nonsense." Harris's voice was crisp and matter of fact. He sounded so confident that Libby could almost fool herself into believing him. "Of course he does. He's just been busy."

"No. I can tell. He's so disinterested, he hates us both . . . I know it." She was incoherent and irrational in her pain. All she knew was that she was about to have her first child, and her husband wasn't with her. He wouldn't be there to see his son or daughter come into the world. She had known something was wrong—had known it since she'd first announced her pregnancy—but she had used the same excuses Harris was now employing. Greyson was busy, he was under stress, he was traveling a lot . . . so many excuses. None of them true.

All rational thought fled when the pain changed, became deeper, more agonizing.

"Not long now," the doctor advised. "You're fully dilated, Olivia. Time to push."

"I can't; he's not here yet. He's going to miss it."

"It's okay, Bug," Harris comforted her gently. "He's trying his best to get here, and I know he'll be gutted to miss it. Do you want me to get your mum?"

Libby was barely able to focus on the question, but she shook her head.

"You know she's squeamish." She gasped, her hand tightening around his fingers for a few moments as she rode out another swell of pain. "Tina here?" Tina was her best friend and had attended half of her birthing classes with her. Harris had attended the other half, filling in for his always-absent brother.

"She's on her way, but I don't think she'll get here in time." This baby definitely wasn't wasting any time. Libby had always heard that first births took a long time, but this was a very hasty affair. Barely six hours had passed from the first contraction to now.

"Then you're the guy," she told Harris with a grimace of pain, and he nodded, his grip on her hand tightening.

"Well, you heard the doctor, Bug. Time to push."

She didn't want to. How could she? A father needed to see his child come into the world. But in the end the overwhelming need to push overruled all else, and Libby did what instinct dictated.

Hours later, after the initial excitement of showing her baby off to her parents, her in-laws, and Tina, Libby woke from an exhausted sleep and blinked into the gloom of the room. It took her a moment to orient herself, and she tensed when a confused glance to her left confirmed her husband's presence. His face was grim as he stared off into the middle distance. Completely identical to Harris but so unmistakably Greyson.

"Did you see her?" Her voice was hoarse, and she absently noted that she was thirsty. His eyes shifted to hers.

"Yes." His voice was curt, displaying absolutely no emotion.

"She looks like you."

"Does she?" Still in that horribly cold voice.

"I think so."

"Then she looks like Harris, too, doesn't she?"

"I suppose so," she said, a bit baffled by the fact that he felt the need to point that out. "I missed you. I wanted you to see her come into the world."

"Shit happens," he said with a dismissive shrug, looking like he had not one single regret at missing such a momentous occasion.

"I asked you not to go. I told you I was due soon."

"And I told *you* it couldn't wait. Ten million dollars disappeared; I had to get to Perth to figure out what the fuck was going on down there."

"Harris could have gone," she pointed out. In fact, Harris *should* have gone. As the CFO of the Chapman Global Property Group, he was the obvious choice to deal with an embezzlement problem. In fact, she was sure that any of their executives could have handled the problem without either of the Chapman brothers getting directly involved.

She licked her dry, chapped lips, desperate for a sip of water, and was about to ask Greyson to pour her a glass, but his icy indifference made her hesitate.

*He doesn't want to be here.*

It was obvious in the tense set of his jaw and the bleak coldness in his elusive gaze. He sat stiffly, his shoulders straight and his spine barely touching the backrest of the chair. Greyson had always been a little unapproachable, but this was something else entirely. This was a stranger. A man who looked like he had never touched her with any tenderness or passion. A man who looked like he barely knew her and didn't much care to.

His gaze shifted and made contact with hers, and in a moment of absolute and stunning clarity, she understood that this man—her husband—*hated* her. The knowledge stole her breath, and she gasped, her eyes flooding with tears at the shocking revelation. She had never fooled herself into believing that he loved her, but she'd always thought he liked her or at least had some measure of fondness for her.

"What's wrong?" he asked, likely in response to her tears. His voice was as indifferent as the rest of him, and she knew he didn't care what her answer would be.

"I-I was thinking . . . we never discussed names," she prevaricated hastily, needing a moment to gather her thoughts and emotions. His brow kinked, the only expression he ever allowed himself. "What should we name her?"

He shrugged. The gesture was disdainful and disinterested at the same time.

"You choose."

"But . . ."

"Name her whatever the fuck you want," he snapped, the ice cracking and allowing her a glimpse into the terrifying darkness lurking beneath. The profanity shocked her, as Greyson rarely swore. Harris was the earthier of the two and could swear up a storm at the slightest provocation. Greyson had a great deal more restraint than his ten-minutes-younger brother.

Libby struggled to push herself up, and he didn't move a muscle to assist her.

"Okay, Greyson, what the hell is your problem?" she wheezed, after—with a great deal of difficulty and indignity—managing to lift herself enough to feel less vulnerable.

"Not sure what you mean."

"You know exactly what I mean," she snapped, folding her arms over her chest and wincing a little when she brushed against her over-sensitive nipples. They would be bringing the baby in for a feeding soon. Before, she had been excited for Greyson to witness that, at least, since he had missed so much else, but now she no longer knew what she wanted. All she knew was that she had to figure out what was going on, and soon. They couldn't continue like this. "You've been cold and distant and not the slightest bit interested since I told you I was pregnant. And I want to know why!"

He smiled . . . if one could call it that. A frigid, joyless baring of teeth that looked terrifyingly sinister on his gorgeous face.

"Because it doesn't interest me. None of this interests me, not you and *not* your child. I was hoping you'd come clean, but I see you'd just happily continue with this ridiculous charade if I allowed it."

"What are you talking about?" Her voice dropped to a hoarse whisper, and suddenly her thirst felt uncontrollable. She desperately wanted that water, needed it, focused on it to the exception of all else. Because it was so much better to concentrate on her raging thirst and the currently unobtainable water than it was to look into her husband's hate-filled dark-blue eyes. She didn't want to hear what he had to say—she knew it would be ugly and hurtful and would finally damage what was left of their relationship beyond repair.

"Hello, Mummy . . . look who's awake and hungry!" A cheerful voice sliced through the oppressive tension like a machete, and Libby jumped. Greyson shifted his hostile gaze toward the doorway, where a nurse was wheeling a crib into the lavish private hospital room. The woman's eyes were trained on the tiny, pink-wrapped bundle in the crib, which thankfully allowed Libby a moment to regroup and plaster a smile onto her face.

The smile became genuine when the pleasantly rounded, apple-cheeked middle-aged nurse lifted the infant and gently handed her over to Libby. Avoiding Greyson's intense stare, Libby kept her focus on the adorably scrunched-up face of her gorgeous daughter.

"Hey there, sweet thing, are you hungry?" she asked gently. "Oh my God, you're *so* beautiful." The last was breathed reverentially as she unwrapped the folded blanket and once again took inventory of those perfect little fingers and toes, that delightful button nose, the pair of confused milky-blue eyes, and the tuft of black, downy hair on a perfectly round little head. Libby would have to say that this was probably *the* most perfect baby that anyone had ever birthed *ever*.

She tried to share a smile of delight and wonderment with Greyson and found him glowering at their tiny daughter like she was a strange and particularly unattractive species of insect. Libby hugged her baby close to her chest, immediately feeling the overwhelming urge to protect her from the borderline hostility she saw in her husband's eyes.

The nurse was bustling about, helping Libby sit up a little straighter, elevating the hospital bed so that her back was supported.

"Do you need help feeding her, or do you think you can cope?" the woman asked brightly, and Libby shook her head, her eyes on the baby, who was already starting to root against her chest.

"I think we'll be fine."

"Congratulations, Daddy." The nurse finally acknowledged Greyson's brooding presence, and her bright smile dimmed a bit when she received nothing in response. "Um, so I'm Sister Thompson. Press the call button if you need me."

She cast another uncertain look at Greyson before leaving.

Libby concentrated on her baby's needs, because that was so much better than dealing with Greyson right now. She unbuttoned her pajama top and gently directed her daughter's seeking mouth toward the nipple. The infant latched on greedily, and soon the room was filled with nothing but the sounds of her suckling and contented little snuffles.

Libby couldn't stop touching her, brushing her thumb over the baby's downy cheek, then the silken fluff of her black hair, the barely there brows, and her sweet nose, which looked like it would eventually take Greyson's perfect shape. She lifted the warm, sweet-smelling bundle slightly so that she could drop a kiss onto her brow.

"You need a name, sweetheart," she whispered against the soft skin of her baby's head. "What about Clara?"

She deliberately chose a name she knew Greyson hated, wanting some reaction from him. Something that would show that he cared. If he protested against the name, at least she'd know he was interested, that he wouldn't want his daughter named after his and Harris's much-despised childhood nanny.

But he said not one word, and she lifted her eyes to his face. He was staring at the baby, his gaze hooded and his expression blank.

"Greyson?" she whispered, wanting him to look at her, to tell her what was wrong. He lifted his eyes, and all that frigid hostility came flooding back. She started shaking, feeling that ice settle into her bones.

"I'm going to get some coffee," he said abruptly, shoving himself out of the uncomfortable-looking chair. It looked too small for his massive frame. Strange how that worked: Harris was the same height and size as Greyson, but she hadn't feared for the chair's immediate future when he'd been sitting in it earlier.

Greyson always seemed so much larger than life. At least he did to her. He had always been the one she'd been drawn to, even when they were kids. He'd been the broody twin, the one who would nurse a grudge and seethe in silence for hours. Harris had been, and still was, the complete opposite. His temper would boil over, and he'd have a good old rant and then go back to being his jovial self in very short order. The twins were as opposite as night and day when it came to temperament.

Growing up, Libby had always been fascinated by Greyson's mysterious silences. Harris had never interested her in the same way. Four years younger than the brothers, Libby had known the twins her entire life but had never been a part of their social circle. Even though she had attended the same private school they had—a stipulation in both her parents' employment contracts—she had never really belonged. Only Martine—Tina—Jenson, also ostracized from the twins' glamorous clique of friends, had befriended her.

Libby and the twins had played together at home, of course, but when the boys had reached their teens, they had started hanging out with their social equals, had attended parties and events that nobody had ever bothered inviting Libby to. Harris had happily given her the details her voyeuristic, envious heart craved, and she would listen breathlessly and gawk at the pictures on his phone.

At twelve she had taken to following Greyson around, happy to watch him while he sunbathed at the pool, content to sit a few meters away while he studied in the garden, satisfied to gaze at him while he ate whatever quick snack he had mooched off her mother. Surprisingly, Greyson had allowed that to go on for a couple of unhealthy years before seemingly getting sick of her. Which had led to the lowest, most humiliating point of her relationship with him. She could still hear the disgust in his voice when he'd flat out called her creepy and commanded her to stop "stalking" him.

She shook her head now at the ridiculous child she had been. Libby had left for culinary school four years after the boys had gone to college. She had set aside her childhood infatuation with Greyson Chapman and had instead focused on building a reputation as a pastry chef.

She had dreamed of opening her own dessert bar and had worked brutally long hours in the kitchens of some of the top restaurants in

Paris, Rome, and London, striving to achieve that goal. Until eleven months ago, when all of that forward momentum had come to a grinding halt. Two months after meeting him again, she had found herself married and—as she would later discover—pregnant. Or maybe that was pregnant and married. She had never been entirely sure of the timing. But this little one had been born just over nine months after their rushed wedding.

Maybe Greyson felt trapped, forced into a life that he'd never really wanted. But he had pushed for the marriage. They had seen each other every night for two months after that rooftop party, and he had mentioned—sometimes practically demanded—marriage every single night of their "courtship." If nearly two months of constant sex—and little else—could be considered a courtship.

Libby had finally caved because her infatuation had returned with a vengeance, and it had felt more intense with sex thrown into the mix. It had started to feel perilously close to love. And because he had made her feel so damned special, with his slavish attention to her every little need, both in bed and out, she had wondered if he was verging on feeling the same way about her.

She thought back to those first few months of marriage. Everything had seemed fine. She had been dazed by the speed of their nuptials, and they had been dealing with parental disapproval on both sides—the only one who had seemed truly happy for them was Harris. And despite her relative inexperience, the sex had been off the charts. Even though her entire life had been devoted to her craft, without much time for intimate relationships, Libby had known that what she had with Greyson was rare and uniquely intense.

When Libby had discovered that she was pregnant, she had thought they could actually make something of their marriage. It hadn't been planned and had definitely put her career on hold, but Libby had been ecstatic at the thought of a baby.

Greyson had not been as thrilled.

But she had expected his attitude to change, soften perhaps, as her pregnancy advanced. Instead, he had retreated further and further from her. Leading to today. To this moment . . .

Where it appeared that her husband hated her.

And their baby.

He returned ten minutes later, by which time the baby had been fed and burped already. Libby was staring down at her beautiful daughter raptly when Greyson reentered the room. She looked up and held his eyes for a brief moment before allowing her gaze to travel over his face and body. There were circles under his deep-set, dark-blue eyes, giving his handsome face a gaunt appearance. He looked absolutely exhausted; his strong jaw was blue with stubble, and his thick, silky black hair stood up in tufts. He had clearly agitated it with his fingers, as he was wont to when he was stressed or tired. He was wearing a gray, pin-striped, Dior three-piece suit, but half of his pale-blue shirt hem was untucked and hanging over the front of his waistband, his tie was askew, and as she watched, he tugged his jacket off and threw it over the back of the visitor's chair, rolling up his sleeves to reveal his tanned, corded forearms. She loved his arms and hands—they were so strong and capable. In the beginning, she had often lain wrapped in those arms, running her fingers over the veined ridges on his hands.

She couldn't remember the last time she had done that. They hadn't been that close or intimate in months.

His cool gaze dropped to the baby's sleeping face.

"Would you like to hold her?" she asked, her voice low, and his eyes snapped up to hers. Something resembling horror roiled in those dark-blue depths.

"She's asleep, I don't want to disturb her." The panic in his tone melted her heart—he was terrified. Greyson probably had the same reservations and doubts she had about being a good parent. Why hadn't she realized that before? It was easier for her to adjust and to love this little stranger thrust so suddenly into their midst. She had carried the baby under her heart for months. Greyson hadn't had that luxury. He probably just needed a chance to develop the same bond with his daughter.

"You won't," Libby reassured him gently, tilting the precious bundle toward him. "Meet your daughter, Greyson."

He stiffened, his face closing up tighter than a fist, while the panic in his eyes transformed to something close to revulsion. No, this was not the usual first-time father fears. This was something else.

"Greyson? What's going on?"

"I know she's not mine, Olivia," he said, his voice emotionless, his face frozen into a mask of indifference . . . but his *eyes*. So much hate and rejection.

It distracted her so effectively that it took a second for his words to sink in. And when they did, she didn't react, didn't move, didn't do anything but stare at him for an endless moment. She understood the words but couldn't quite fathom the meaning. She broke down the statement and tried to restructure it in a way that would make sense. Because currently, it was all wrong and couldn't possibly be what he had meant to say.

"I'm sorry, I don't understand," she finally admitted, wondering if she was developing some kind of aphasia. Hearing things wrong. It could happen. A complication of childbirth. For a second the possibility seemed so real—more real than what she'd actually thought she'd heard—it terrified her.

"I can't have children," he said, still in that terribly controlled voice. Libby continued to stare at him, completely confused. What was he saying? She shifted her gaze to her baby and then back up to his face.

Did he mean that he didn't want children?

"What?"

"For fuck's sake," he snapped impatiently, finally losing some of that control and shocking her again with his language. "Drop the act, Olivia! I'm infertile, and I don't know whose fucking kid that is—or maybe I *do*—but I know for sure that she's not mine."

These words were real; she wasn't imagining them or hearing him wrong. He was actually saying these truly reprehensible things.

"You're not infertile," she said, her voice faint. "Of course you're not. We just had a baby."

"*You* have a baby. I have a cheating wife trying to foist another man's kid off onto me. And I'm sick of this sham."

"I don't understand."

"Olivia, stop this. I'm exhausted—I just don't have the energy for your games, and I refuse to pretend anymore."

"If you thought this was all a pretense, a lie, why didn't you say something before now?" she asked. Her voice lacked heat, sounding as confused as she felt. What was this? Yes, he'd been absent and disinterested during her pregnancy, but she hadn't ever considered that *this* was what was churning away just beneath that perpetually moody surface.

"I was hoping you'd both just admit it and release us all from this fucked-up situation."

"We *both*? Who's the other party in this scenario?"

"We can discuss this tomorrow; I'm tired. I'm heading home."

"*No!* You can't just leave after these ridiculous accusations!"

"You can't deny it, Olivia. The fact is I'm infertile, and you just had a baby. So there's no way in hell that child is mine."

"You're going to regret this, Greyson," she predicted, the shock and hurt fading a bit to be replaced by absolute fury and indignation. She welcomed those emotions; they made her feel less vulnerable, less fragile . . .

"I really don't think so, Olivia. My only regret is not ending this farce sooner."

"I'll never forgive you for this," she promised, her voice hushed.

"I'm not the one who needs forgiveness here." His voice was grating and seemed to scrape across her sensitive nerve endings, leaving her feeling lacerated and raw. He picked up his jacket, draped it over the crook of his arm, and moved toward the door.

"If you leave now, don't bother coming back." She wasn't going to let this hateful, cold man anywhere near her child ever again. He didn't deserve to be her father.

"Don't worry, there's no chance of that," he said with a humorless little chuckle before giving her his back and striding from the room.

Libby kept her dry, burning eyes glued to his departing figure. Hoping for some sign that he had doubts . . . or regret. One look back. Anything.

But he left without hesitation, and she sagged back in bed, her hold tightening on her defenseless sleeping baby.

*Don't look back!*

Greyson kept his eyes fixed forward. He refused to give her the satisfaction of looking back. All these months . . . willing her to just own up to her deception. Wishing both of them would afford him the respect of admitting to their disgusting infidelity.

He hated what they had done to him. Hated that he hadn't been able to find the words to confront them about it.

Hated *them*.

He had waited for one of them to admit to the affair, hoping he wouldn't have to confront them. But neither of them had said a word. They had allowed this day to come. Allowed their baby to be born and expected Greyson to just . . . what? Be her father?

He wasn't sure when the affair had started. They had always been close. Always been *such* good friends. It had grated . . . how often Greyson had come home to find *him* there. So comfortable in Greyson's home and so at ease with his new wife.

Greyson strode blindly toward the elevator. He was grateful to find himself alone in the metal cubicle once the doors slid shut. He leaned back against the wall and gripped the railing so tightly his palms hurt.

He longed to get home. Longed to close himself off from the world and break something. No. Break *everything*.

He thought back to the moment he'd absolutely known they were cheating. That day he had seen them having lunch together in an exclusive restaurant. Heads bowed; talking, laughing, whispering . . . so clearly delighted to be in each other's company. Neither of them had ever been that easy in his company. They hadn't seen him, and he hadn't approached them. When he had asked her over dinner what she had done that day, she had lied to him. Blatantly lied. Said she'd had lunch with Tina.

Of course they were cheating on him. Why the fuck else would she lie about having lunch with Harris when she saw him all the time?

The elevator dinged open, and he blindly strode out and toward his car. He climbed in but didn't start the vehicle; he merely sat behind the wheel, staring blankly out at the almost-deserted basement parking lot.

Greyson hadn't confronted her about the lie, but that was when he had started retreating. His and Harris's birthday had been just a few days after that . . . but, knowing that she would feel obligated to celebrate the occasion with him, he had fabricated a two-day business trip on their birthday weekend. He had hated the thought of playing nice with her and Harris. Had absolutely despised the idea of pretending that everything was fine when his life was falling apart at the seams.

After his return from the unnecessary trip, she had presented her news to him like it was some bizarre belated birthday present. He vaguely recalled her nattering on about wanting to surprise him with the news on his birthday. But in the shock of the moment, he hadn't been paying much attention to anything else she'd had to say. Greyson had loathed the idea of that baby. Of everything it represented.

The baby was here now. And he was shaken to the core by how very much he had found himself wishing that the lie Olivia had concocted was the truth. He had watched, unseen for a few moments, while she had breastfed the baby. And had wished—desperately wished—*he* had been the one to give her that child.

Harris had given her the one thing Greyson never could. And seeing how happy she was with that baby in her arms made him feel even more inadequate than he had when he had realized that she'd been unfaithful to him. He had never made her that happy. *Could* never make her that happy.

When Harris returned half an hour later after a pleading phone call from her, Libby simply burst into tears. Harris's appearance—so painfully identical to her husband's—finally pushed her over the edge.

"What's this? What's wrong, Bug? Is the baby okay?" he asked, all concern, as he wrapped her in his arms. It took a while for her to get the story out, and by the time he managed to decipher exactly what it was she was saying in between the sobbing and stuttering, he had dropped his arms and was staring at her with an incredulous, infuriated expression on his face.

"Wait, are you telling me my idiot brother doesn't believe that the baby is his?" he asked, searching for complete clarification. And a fresh stab of hurt and humiliation hit her as she nodded.

"What the fuck?" Harris muttered beneath his breath and shoved his hands into his trouser pockets. He glared at the floor, shaking his head, obviously as confused by this as she was.

"H-he says he's infertile," Libby whispered, plucking a tissue from a conveniently placed box on the bedside table and blowing her nose messily. "I don't understand this at all. I swear to you, I haven't slept with anyone else."

"Libby, I wasn't even thinking that," Harris promised, and his resolute faith in her made her resent Greyson's lack of trust even more. "Look, we'll get to the bottom of this, okay? There has to be some kind of misunderstanding."

"No misunderstanding at all. Your brother's an asshole, and I'm ending this disaster of a marriage as soon as I can."

"No. You can't do that. Just give him a chance to fix this."

"Harris, what does it say that you're here fighting for his marriage while he hasn't even bothered to touch his own child? Don't you get how completely bizarre that is? I don't care about his reasoning—we never should have married. I don't know why he pushed for it in the first place."

"I thought maybe it was because of the pregnancy," Harris confessed, rubbing a hand over the back of his neck.

"Initially, I did too. The first time we slept together was . . ." She hesitated, blushed, and then rolled her eyes at her own stupid embarrassment. "It was my first time. *Don't ask,*" she forestalled him, lifting a hand when Harris frowned and looked like he was about to comment on that. "I was celibate and not on anything. He used a condom, but it broke. He didn't seem overly concerned about it, but immediately after that he mentioned marriage. I figured it was because of the broken condom; I mean, before that night I had always believed that he felt nothing but indifference toward me. I brushed it off . . . but he kept asking. Even when it became evident that I wasn't pregnant after that first mishap. I know I should have refused his proposal, but he made it seem—ugh, you know Greyson—he made it seem so *logical.* Like I'd be silly not to agree to his proposal.

"I hesitated at first, but the way he was—*we* were—together . . . it felt like something more, something *real,* was developing between us. It felt like a fairy tale, and I was a complete idiot for allowing my past infatuation to color my decisions. I bought into the ridiculous happily-ever-after fairy tale. I foolishly thought that maybe he harbored similar rose-colored visions of the future. I expected this perfect life with this perfect man, but it was nothing like what I imagined it would be. He worked long hours; he rarely confided in me or spent time with me. I mean, you saw what he was like, those evenings he'd come home while you were visiting. He'd be so surly and uncommunicative. Barely a hello before retreating to his study. We had our moments, but they were few and far between, and nonexistent after I told him about the baby.

"I was such an idiot. I was blinded by my own lust and infatuation. I think, realistically, I *knew* marrying him was a mistake. I knew I was being stupid, but I thought he liked me, that maybe he could love me. I can't believe I actually thought we had a plausible reason for marriage. Hindsight tells me I was grasping at straws."

She shook her head. Disgusted that she had been so stupid at the ripe old age of twenty-six. Stupid and embarrassingly naive.

"Now he says he can't have children, and I-I'm just so *confused*. I don't know why he pushed for marriage. I don't know what he wanted or wants from me. All I know is that he seems to hate me. And I think—I'm sure, after tonight—I hate *him*."

"I know he's been a moody bastard lately," Harris said. "More so than usual. He wouldn't talk to me and has been picking arguments for no reason, but he wouldn't fucking tell me what the problem is. But there must be something else going on. Let me talk to him and see what's going on in that head of his. Don't do anything rash until you've heard back from me."

"Rash? I'm sorry, nothing I do now will be *rash* . . . he spent the last seven months thinking the absolute worst of me. He never let on, he made me believe that we had something real . . ."

Only he hadn't. Not really. The first two months of their marriage hadn't been perfect, but she had told herself they needed to get used to each other, used to married life. It had felt like the start of something potentially good. But now, looking back on that promising beginning, she realized that it had only been sex. Lots and lots of really hot sex. The times not spent in bed, he'd been at work, and they had rarely had any meaningful conversation.

Libby had always known that he was naturally reticent; Greyson had never been one to let anyone—even his own twin—close. He was buttoned down and closed in. She had figured it would take time for him to get used to the idea of having her around, having a mate he could share his thoughts and feelings with.

And then the last seven months, after she'd announced her pregnancy, had been completely joyless and frigid, without even sex to foster the impression of closeness. Now that she thought back on it, she considered all those moments she had spoken to him about the baby, consulted him—despite his blatant lack of interest—on nursery decor, urged him to consider names. She remembered the missed ob-gyn appointments, that first ultrasound test (the one Tina had attended with her), and the scary fall after which she'd started spotting. Her parents, Tina, Harris—even her less-than-friendly mother-in-law, Constance, for heaven's sake—those people had been there for her. Greyson hadn't.

Not once.

And Libby had made excuses, while her husband had barely bothered to offer a single one. He was busy; it was a difficult time of transition in the company, with new contracts, old contracts, business meetings/trips/dinners . . . she'd only been fooling herself. He had *never* shown an inkling of interest in her or the baby.

Their marriage had ended with a positive pregnancy test, and she hadn't even realized it was dead until now.

"Look, just give me some time to get to the bottom of this. You know how Greyson can be. He never says what he's really feeling . . ."

"Oh, believe me, there's absolutely no doubt about his real feelings, Harris. He looked at us like he hated us. He looked at my baby like she was the most repulsive thing on the face of this earth. I won't have him anywhere near us ever again."

"Libby . . ." Harris ran a frustrated hand through his hair. He kept it a little longer than his brother did, but the gesture still reminded her of Greyson, and Libby fought back a pang of pure agony as she understood that she would never see her husband again. That the man she'd thought she knew, thought she loved, had never existed beyond her imagination.

"I'm going there right now," Harris said decisively. "I'll be back later. Don't worry, Bug. We'll get this straightened out."

Frustrated that he wouldn't listen to her, didn't understand, Libby just stared at him, refusing to respond. He would have to see for himself.

Harris squeezed her shoulder and dropped a kiss on top of her head. He hesitated for a moment, looking like he wanted to say something more, before leaving without another word.

Libby blinked back tears as she watched him leave and then dragged out her phone. She scrolled through her contacts before finding the one she needed. The one person she knew she could rely on, who would have her back without question.

"Tina? I need you. Please, can you come back? It's urgent."

# Chapter Two

The loud, obnoxious knocking took a while to register. Greyson, completely wiped after his long journey, had come home and—going against the cardinal rule of combating jet lag—fallen into bed, succumbing to sleep almost immediately.

He hated personal confrontation. Professionally, he had a reputation for being an aggressive go-getter. But he liked keeping things neat and tidy in his personal life. He didn't do ugly scenes, which was why he had allowed his farce of a marriage to continue for so long. It had felt like a kick to the groin when Olivia had so smugly announced her pregnancy, looking at him with that bright, sunny smile, her face expectant, while she waited for him to fall all over himself at the prospect of that baby.

The faithless, cheating bitch. He should have ended this months ago. But he had hoped she and her lover would decide that they were better off together and do the deed for him.

But today, when she had so proudly tried to introduce him to his "daughter" . . . he shook his head. Her absolute gall had sickened him. Who knew? Maybe she *didn't* know which one of them was the father. Greyson didn't much care what her reasoning was . . . all he knew was that it wasn't him, and now that she knew the possibility of

Greyson being the dad was zero—and understood that he knew about her infidelity—she could go and play house with Harris.

The pounding at the door continued, and Greyson grunted before levering himself out of bed and making his way to the front door of the huge penthouse apartment in the V&A Waterfront in Cape Town that he had shared with Olivia these last nine months. He had given the maid the night off after getting home, ignoring the woman's excited congratulations.

He dragged the front door open and grunted when Harris stormed into the apartment, slamming his shoulder aggressively against Greyson's as he shoved past him.

"What the fuck, Greyson?" his brother seethed.

Greyson bristled, offended that his brother *dared* invade his privacy like this. What was he doing here? Was he here to apologize? He could take his fucking apology and shove it up his ass. Greyson would never forgive him for what he had done.

The thought of Harris touching Olivia, kissing her, stroking her . . . seeing every part of her. It was enough to make Greyson feel physically ill. All his life he'd had to compete with his fucking brother. They'd shared a womb, and despite being born first, Greyson had been the weaker of the two babies, constantly plagued by ill health throughout his childhood because Harris had taken the lion's share of nutrients in vitro.

And of course, Harris had been the more confident, popular twin. Loved by everyone. Adored by the masses. He and Olivia had been attached at the hip throughout childhood, and maybe the reason Greyson had allowed her to trail after him for so long when she'd hit puberty was because for *once* in his life, someone—no, not just any old someone, *Olivia*—had found him more interesting than his brother. Seeing her again, touching her, *loving* her . . . he had been primitively and possessively thrilled to discover that he had been her first.

She had been his alone, and he had fucking loved that. But it had taken mere months before Harris had ruined that for him. Taken *her* from him.

He stared at his brother, loving him yet hating and resenting him so much at the same time it was almost physically impossible to bear. He wanted Harris gone.

*Now.*

"I'm knackered, Harris," he said. And immediately despised himself for once again defaulting to the simpleton who could never say exactly what he felt.

"You're an asshole, that's what you are. You've just had a beautiful daughter, so why the hell are you here and not by your wife's side?"

"Always ready to fight the good fight for your little 'Bug,' aren't you?" The words tumbled from Greyson's lips, bringing with them months—no, *years*—of resentment, fury, and envy. "What the *fuck* were you thinking, Harris? Did you think I'd just accept this, like some weak little patsy? Did you think that I'd never find out? That you could just do whatever the hell you pleased while I'm left to deal with the consequences of your actions? Just like ten years ago, when you left me to clean up your mess." He paused for a moment, watching his brother flinch as his verbal blow landed. He felt a moment's sick guilt for bringing it up, but he needed Harris to know that he wasn't going to stand for this. They would both happily have left Greyson to raise that child as his own. He knew it; it was the only thing that made any kind of sense to him. If they had wanted to change the status quo, they would have done so by now. They hadn't, and that told Greyson that their plan was for him to play father to their child while they continued their twisted affair without any blowback from either family.

"We're not discussing that," Harris said, still ashen with shock after Greyson's previous statement. "We're talking about your abandonment of your wife and child."

"That's not my child," Greyson stated matter of factly. He felt a weird, almost perverse triumph at being able to fling that truth down between them. "I had mumps when I was nineteen. I'm sterile." The doctor had been brutally frank on what he thought Greyson's chances were of ever conceiving a child. Greyson had made peace with that fact long ago. He didn't think he was cut out to be a father anyway. At least that's what he had always told himself to soothe away the pang of masculine inadequacy he had never dared to acknowledge before discovering that his wife had conceived a child with his brother.

His words made Harris pause, a confused frown wrinkling his brow, before he shook his head. "Of course she's your child," Harris practically shouted, looking beyond frustrated with Greyson. "She even has your fucking birthmark on her thigh."

Greyson knew to which birthmark Harris was referring, a port-wine stain neatly shaped into a crescent that resembled a C. His grandmother had often joked that the Chapmans sported their own brand. He hadn't known that the baby had the same birthmark, but his stomach sank as his brother's words laid that last, lingering doubt to rest.

"I'm not the only one with that birthmark." His lips barely moved as he forced the words out.

Harris's jaw dropped at that statement, and his eyes widened and then narrowed. He moved so swiftly that Greyson barely had time to react—one moment they were eye to eye, and the next Greyson was on the floor, staring up into his brother's livid face.

"You bastard." Harris's voice was quiet. Greyson didn't recognize this silently seething man as his usually irascible brother. Harris looked furious and hurt and betrayed. And that pissed Greyson off. If anyone should feel betrayed here, it was he.

He leaped to his feet, unfamiliar fury clawing at his throat as he fought the urge to raise his voice. To shout and use his fists as his brother had just done.

"*I'm* the bastard?" he asked, his voice wobbling a little as he fought to control the wave of absolute rage that crashed through him. "I'm not the one who fucked his brother's wife."

Harris drew back his fist again, but Greyson's well-honed reflexes kicked in, and he easily sidestepped his brother's punch, shoving the man in the same move. This time Harris was the one who went sprawling to the carpet.

"Greyson." Harris's voice was hoarse with emotion as he glared up at Greyson from the floor. "You're my brother. I love you. But I don't know if I'll ever be able to forgive you for this. I had mumps too. I got the same fucking doomsday speech from Dr. Crowe. Not that I cared much back then, but I always had it in the back of my mind I'd go for a second opinion eventually. When I was ready to have kids. If you believe you're infertile, then you have to believe I am too. So where did that baby come from? I know it wasn't from me. I would *never* touch Libby. She's your wife! How the hell could you think I'd do that to you? How could you think *she* would do that to you? The girl has been crazy about you for years. *Why?* I don't know. You've never deserved her."

"And you think that you do?" Greyson asked distractedly, the heat gone from his voice as his brain attempted to process his brother's words. He tried to cling to his righteous anger, but all he could think about was the time he and Harris had both been laid low with mumps. They had always gotten ill at the same time. When they were kids, their nanny, Clara, had complained that they were doing it deliberately to make her job and life miserable.

He'd never considered it before, because Dr. Crowe had had separate discussions with them at the time. They'd been young adults and as such, for the first time, had been afforded the dignity of being treated as individuals rather than a single entity.

He and Harris had never discussed it, and he had never really thought about it. Hearing that he couldn't conceive hadn't meant much to his nineteen-year-old self. The thought of having children hadn't even occurred to him at that age, and the news hadn't really bothered him much. He had never considered that Harris would have received the same news.

He had never doubted Dr. Crowe's prognosis. Never thought to get a second opinion. What if . . .

He shook his head violently.

*No.*

No what-ifs.

If he could conceive, if that child was his, then he had just fucked up so badly that there was no way of ever recovering from it.

But . . . *what if* . . .

He felt his breath catch in his chest. He met Harris's eyes. His brother still looked pissed off. More than that . . . he looked broken.

"You and Olivia have always been close," Greyson pointed out softly, knowing that he was clutching at straws now.

"We're friends," Harris said icily.

"But I saw you . . ." The words sounded weak even to Greyson's ears, and they tapered off for a moment as he thought about that day. In the restaurant, the smiles, the laughter . . . the *intimacy* of it.

"Saw us?" Harris pushed himself up from the floor and stood in front of Greyson, refusing to meet his eyes.

"At the Glass Lounge one afternoon about seven months ago. You looked . . ." Greyson paused, his brow furrowed and his stomach roiling in sick confusion. Why wouldn't Harris look at him? Harris never had qualms about meeting anyone's gaze. The only time he avoided eye contact was when he was trying to disguise his emotions. When he was trying to hide how badly he was hurt. Greyson cleared his throat before continuing. "You looked cozy. And Olivia straight up lied to me about your lunch. Why would she lie about lunching with you?"

Harris seemed to shake himself out of his funk, finally lifting his hooded gaze to Greyson's.

"That's it? Fucking lunch?" He practically spat the words. "That's your proof? Your reason for ignoring your wife, rejecting your child, and . . ." He stopped abruptly and shook his head. His face twisting with emotion.

"Not only lunch," Greyson said, his voice thready and lacking conviction. Everything that had seemed so damned certain just ten minutes ago now felt as insubstantial as the morning mist. "She lied. Why would she lie about it?"

"Because she wanted to surprise you on our birthday." Harris's eyes slid from his again. His words emerged on a stiff monotone, his voice lacking its usual verve. "She told me she had an announcement to make and wanted the evening to be special. She didn't give a rat's ass that it was my birthday too . . . she was too focused on making sure the night would be perfect for you. We met that afternoon to discuss how I was supposed to distract you, keep you away from the apartment until she had everything set up. Only you weren't around to distract, were you? You flew out to London for the weekend without any kind of warning.

"You want to talk about cleaning up someone's messes? *I'm* the one who had to fucking tell her you had left without a word. I'm the one who had to go to your apartment and inform your wife that you wouldn't be there to see how beautiful she looked for you. Or how much work she had put into preparing the perfect meal for you . . . you should have seen that place. The fairy lights, the candles, the flowers. I'm the one who had to see the devastation on her face and then watch as she forced it back to make yet another excuse for your sorry ass. You took a stupid little white lie and used it to destroy your marriage. *And* your relationship with me."

"Harris . . ." Greyson's attempt at communication stalled right there. He couldn't find the words. He didn't know what to say, what to believe.

Where to go from here.

A birthday surprise. She had mentioned something similar when she had told him about the baby. But by that time he had already decided that she was not to be trusted. That she was a lying, cheating bitch who didn't deserve his attention. And then she had told him about the baby, and it had frozen him inside. Iced over his every emotion . . .

Harris finally met his eyes, and Greyson sucked in a harsh breath as he saw the suspicious sheen in his twin's gaze.

*Fuck!*

He opened his mouth to apologize, but the words were inadequate. His brother's sincerity wasn't in doubt. And if Harris wasn't the baby's father, the birthmark left only one other viable candidate.

His stomach felt like it was about to revolt . . . and then it did.

He barely made it to the bathroom on time. And when the bout of extreme self-disgust had waned enough for his gut to settle, he made his way back to the living room.

Harris was gone.

Leaving Greyson with nothing. And nobody.


"He actually *said* that?" Tina asked, her voice a study in horror and disbelief. After Tina had returned to the hospital in record time, Libby had taken one look at her friend before succumbing to a fresh bout of tears. The entire sordid story had tumbled from her lips in stops and starts while Tina had listened to the halting diatribe in shocked silence. Libby knew she had to be a complete mess, her face swollen and wet from all the tears she had shed.

"Yes. I have to get out of here, Tina. You have to help me," she begged.

"Of course, but . . ." Tina shook her head, looking uncertain.

"No buts," Libby interrupted defiantly. "My husband just told me I doesn't believe our child is his. There are no buts here; I'm leaving him."

"That goes without saying," Tina soothed, always loyal. "But I'm not sure you can leave the hospital just yet."

"I can. Both Clara and I are healthy enough to leave." Libby had asked the doctor earlier, and while the man had advised against it, when pushed he had acknowledged that keeping them there overnight was just a precaution.

"Clara?" Tina asked, her eyebrows rising.

"Yes. I've decided to name her Clara." Libby knew that her decision to name her baby that had stemmed from a place of defiance and pettiness. If Greyson wanted no part of his beautiful daughter, then he had absolutely no say in what Libby chose to name her. She knew, given his disinterest earlier, that he probably didn't give two damns about what she named the baby anyway, but she still felt a surge of satisfaction in knowing that the name she'd chosen was nowhere near anything Greyson would have wanted.

"It's a pretty name," Tina said sincerely, and Libby sagged back onto the bed, feeling exhausted and heartbroken.

"Look, I'll make a deal with you," Tina said quietly, reaching out to take one of Libby's hands into hers. "Spend the night in hospital, and I'll take you anywhere you want to go tomorrow, okay? It's best for both you *and* Clara."

Libby lifted her free hand to cover her eyes and sobbed, tears seeping from beneath her palm and running down the sides of her face to soak the cushion beneath her head. She hated this. Hated how lost and afraid she felt.

"I don't understand why he's being so cruel." God, she sounded truly pathetic. She hated that too. She loathed how weak he had made her. Tina didn't answer, merely squeezed her hand comfortingly.

"We'll get you discharged first thing in the morning, okay? It's nearly midnight now anyway, and I'm sure they're going to kick me out soon. Do you need anything before I go?"

Libby shook her head, completely incapable of suppressing her sobs.

"Oh, Libby," Tina whispered. "I wish I could make this go away, I honestly do. Do you want me to speak with Greyson? See what's going on?" Tina tended to avoid the Chapman brothers, so her offer to speak with Greyson was really sweet. Libby lifted her hand from her eyes to meet her friend's concerned gaze.

"No. It's fine. Harris has already said he was going to talk with him about this. Against my wishes, I might add. He's trying to fix it. It can't be fixed. I won't forgive Greyson for this."

"Prick," Tina muttered under her breath, and Libby wasn't sure if she was referring to Greyson or Harris. She had never really told Libby why she so despised Harris when she had once worshipped the ground he walked on. "I'll pick you up first thing in the morning, okay? You'll stay with me. Unless . . . I mean, do you want to stay with your parents?"

Libby shook her head, dislodging even more tears onto her wet cheeks. "No. I can't. Their flat was bought and paid for by the Chapmans. I don't want anything to do with that family or their filthy money right now."

"Of course."

"I mean, my parents earned their retirement gifts, and I'm happy for them. But . . . I don't want to feel beholden to those people. I can take care of myself and my child. I don't need them." Libby's voice was strained and nasal with tears but still held a firm note of defiance and anger.

"I get it," Tina soothed. "You can stay with me until we figure out the rest, okay?"

"I need Clara's things," Libby cried, feeling totally despondent as she recognized that she couldn't sever all ties completely yet. Not until she got everything she needed for her baby.

"Don't worry about that. I'll take care of it," Tina promised.

Something was wrong with this fucking whiskey. It wasn't doing the job. Greyson glared at the nearly empty bottle bitterly before taking another swig from it, hoping that this time it would have the desired effect of wiping the image of Olivia's tearful face from his memory. The liquor barely burned on the way down anymore, and he paused for a moment, giving it time to work, and then swore when he saw her face, clear as day. The confusion, followed by horror, and then an emotion that he had refused to acknowledge as pain at the time. Instead of dulling his senses, the whiskey was giving him clarity that he would rather not have. The pain and confusion on her beautiful face hadn't been an act; he could see that now.

The absolute loathing that swiftly followed had also not been faked, and that memory more than any other drove him to finish the bottle before reaching for another.

There was banging coming from the front door, and he swore, resenting the intrusion.

"Fuck *off*!" he yelled in response to the thumping, but the intrusive asshole was persistent, and the banging only got louder. Swearing even more, he slammed the bottle of alcohol down onto the coffee table, staggered to his feet, and stumbled to the door. Apparently, the whiskey had succeeded in screwing up his motor skills if nothing else. He flung the door open and experienced a moment of sheer, unadulterated joy when he saw his brother standing there.

Could it be that Harris had forgiven him for the unforgivable?

"I'm here for some of Libby's things," Harris said, his grim face and voice immediately dispelling the notion that his brother was there to offer him absolution. It took a moment for the words to sink in, and when they did, Greyson felt dread rising from the pit of his stomach.

"Why?" he asked stupidly, and Harris rewarded the question with an irritated glare.

"She'll be staying with Tina for a while."

"Not with you?" Was that really his voice? It sounded thick and slurred. Fucking whiskey. Leaving his brain as sharp as the proverbial tack while apparently negatively impacting every other aspect of his body.

"No, Greyson. Sorry not to confirm your disgusting and offensive suspicions about us, but no, she won't be staying with me. I would be happy if she did, mind you . . . but apparently she'd rather not be around someone who looks like *you* right now."

Greyson took the hit; he deserved that and much more. But it still stung like a son of a bitch.

"She can stay here. There's plenty of space," he said, knowing even as he said it that it was a ridiculous idea.

"Are you fucking joking? Why would she stay *here*? After everything you've accused her of?"

"I could move out."

"Look, I haven't even spoken with her. Tina called me."

Greyson took a moment to absorb that information. "She did?" Martine Jenson quite understandably hated his brother's guts. For her to voluntarily call him was a big deal.

"Yeah, Libby doesn't want to speak with me, either, right now." Harris fought hard to keep the hurt out of his voice, but even in his less-than-sober state, Greyson could tell Harris was bothered by that.

*Jesus.* He had cocked things up so badly there was very little chance of ever setting them to rights. He knew that. Months of seething resentment and anger, of treating his wife poorly. Of avoiding his brother and scrutinizing the man's every interaction with Olivia through a haze of distrust and poisonous suspicions. Every smile, every touch, every comment between them filed away carefully for further inspection and then added to the growing list of reasons to detest them for betraying him.

He shook his head and came back to the present when Harris brushed by him and headed toward the nursery that Olivia had so lovingly decorated while always asking for—but never receiving—his help or advice.

"Can you pack a bag for Libby? I don't want to go through her things." Harris threw the question over his shoulder as he entered the nursery. Like Greyson needed any more proof that his brother and wife were *not* lovers. A man who had been intimate with a woman would think nothing of packing a bag for her.

Greyson reluctantly made his way to the bedroom he had shared with Olivia during the first two months of their marriage. Repulsed by the notion that she had allowed another man to have sex with her, he had made up some bullshit excuse not to sleep with her after she'd announced her pregnancy, and he had unofficially moved in to the guest bedroom. He had recognized her confusion at the time but hadn't really given a rat's ass about it. Now, as he entered the bedroom and inhaled the lingering traces of her perfume, he imagined her falling asleep here every night. Alone and wondering why he had abandoned her.

He knew she hated him now. But it couldn't possibly be as much as he hated himself. This was such a mess, and he could see no way out of it.

*Fuck.*

# Chapter Three

"I don't understand why you won't move in with us," Stella Lawson, Libby's mother, said quietly as she gently rocked a contentedly snoozing Clara in her arms. "We have the extra room; your father's just using it for storage right now. We could have you and Clara settled in no time."

It was a familiar refrain, one she had heard from her mother, father, Harris, and even her in-laws. It seemed that everyone wanted Libby and Clara to move in with them. Everyone, that was, except Greyson, who had not contacted Libby in any way, shape, or form since that last fraught exchange in the hospital. Nobody dared mention him around Libby. The one time her mother had hesitantly brought up the subject, Libby had very coldly informed her that the topic was not up for discussion.

Harris was the only one who never bothered to drag her into any forced discourse about her marriage. Something in him had changed after the night he had offered to chat with Greyson. He had never reported back on the conversation; clearly it hadn't gone as he had anticipated, and he had instead helped Tina move some of Libby's clothes and a lot of spare baby paraphernalia into Tina's flat. Which in itself was a notable feat, since Tina and Harris could barely tolerate each other under normal circumstances. Having them set aside their differences to help Libby move had been significant.

Libby had moved out without fuss and fanfare, and she hadn't seen her husband since that awful night three weeks ago.

"I'm sorry, Mum, I wish I could stay with you, but you know I want nothing from the Chapmans."

"It's a bit late to say you want nothing from the Chapmans when you married into that family, my girl. And just so we're clear, it's not the Chapmans who are offering right now, Olivia. We're your parents, and while *you* may think this place is a handout, it's our home, and we worked damned hard for it," her father's stern voice interjected, and Libby shut her eyes, gathering herself to meet the man's gaze. She hated the disappointment she frequently saw in those brown depths of late. Her father had always been so proud of her, and his disappointment stung like a whip. Libby hated knowing that she had let him down. He had never approved of the marriage, stating that a man like Greyson would make a terrible husband.

Her father had never been fond of Greyson. Harris, yes. But Greyson was cold and unapproachable and, according to her father, had never been good enough for Libby. An opinion that she was sure would have surprised the very high-and-mighty Greyson Chapman, who thought he was God's gift to the fricking world.

"I don't think of this place as a handout," Libby muttered, ashamed that her father thought she felt that way. "I really don't. But *you* worked for it. I didn't. And I don't want to live here. Not right now. Not right after . . . everything."

"Roland, leave the child alone. We've always encouraged her to make her own decisions; we can't make this one for her. Are you happy staying with Tina?" her mother asked astutely, and Libby hid a grimace. Truth be told, she *wasn't* happy living with Tina.

The woman had been her best friend since they were teens. Tina had spent a great deal of time around the Chapmans and their friends when they were kids but, like Libby, had never really fit into the group. She had been a couple of years younger than most of the others in the group and had always flitted on the fringes of that clique. In the end, the lonely girl had befriended Libby, despite the fact that she was two years Tina's junior. The age difference hadn't mattered; both girls had desperately needed the friendship. They had been firm friends ever since.

Because Tina was older, Libby had always valued her opinion on everything from hair and clothes to the seemingly hopeless crush Libby had had on Greyson. Despite Tina's natural shyness, she had always seemed so glamorous and perfect to Libby. Libby had envied her gorgeous red hair and silky-smooth skin, as well as the breasts and curves she had started to develop very early on in her teens. Libby had remained flat chested and boyishly slender throughout her adolescence, and that situation had only marginally improved in adulthood.

Tina's future had once seemed so assured. She was intelligent and had had medical school firmly in her sights. She had just seemed to have it all: brains, beauty, and the sweetest personality. She had always been there to listen and offer advice. And Libby had considered herself so lucky to have her as a best friend.

But somewhere during Tina's gap year after high school, the wheels had come off. Medical school had fallen by the wayside, and over the last ten years, she'd aimlessly drifted from job to job. Libby wasn't sure what had happened, and maybe she should have delved a little deeper, but she had been abroad a lot and crazy busy with her own studies and career. She'd been confident Tina would work it out.

Especially since Tina had always seemed so happy and self-assured whenever Libby had spoken to her over the years. They had remained close, despite the physical distance between them. But now, despite that closeness, Libby inexplicably felt like an unwelcome intruder in Tina's home.

It wasn't anything overt, but Tina seemed so distant. She was always out late and left for work early. She barely looked at Clara, and that more than anything was what bothered Libby. She didn't expect everybody to automatically love her baby, but *damn it*! Clara's father had already rejected her, and now her de facto aunt, Tina, who had given up half of her living space for Libby and the baby, had barely even touched Clara.

Libby wasn't sure what the hell was going on, but she was sick of this weirdness coming from the people who were supposed to love and treasure Clara. Maybe Tina was feeling cramped in her own home . . . which was why it would be best if Libby left. Before things got too strained and started to *really* hurt her longest-standing female friendship.

"That's why I'm here today, actually," Libby said in response to her mother's question. Her voice was hoarse. "Uh . . . remember Chris? My mentor in Paris?"

"You mentioned him a few times. The model?"

"Yes."

"What about him?"

"He owns a charming little café, and he has offered me a job as his second."

"That's lovely." Her mother beamed happily. "We could look after Clara while you're working, of course."

"It's not that simple," Libby said before clearing her throat. "It's on the Garden Route."

Her parents both stared at her in silent dismay, and her mother's rocking motion sped up slightly.

"That's a six-hour drive," her mother gasped, her voice strained.

"I know. But it's, like, only an hour by plane," Libby pointed out with forced cheer.

It had taken her a long time to decide that this was what she wanted. The distance would be hard, but she needed it. She needed that physical space between her and Greyson, even if he didn't seem to care where in the hell she and Clara actually were. And she needed an entirely clean slate, a fresh start in a new town, where she could begin her life with her beautiful baby. Some place where she didn't feel like she was encroaching on someone else's space. Somewhere she could finally regain her independence after her ridiculous brain fart of a marriage.

"I need this, Mum," she said, meeting her mother's golden-brown gaze, so similar to her own. "I hate moving so far away. But I really need this."

"Who will help you? With her?" her mother asked, her eyes dropping to the baby's sleeping face, and Libby's eyes flooded. She would miss her mother's proximity, the immediacy of any counsel, solicited or otherwise. Constance, too, had opinions on what was best for Clara, how to hold her, burp her, feed her. Both grandmothers had their own ways of doing things, and while their advice wasn't *always* welcome, they were doing what mothers did best, filtering their knowledge down to the next in their feminine tribe. It was invaluable, and Libby would find a way to maintain it, but for now, more than that . . . she needed to find herself again. Needed to find her own voice as a mother.

"We'll be fine. And you're just a phone call or a Skype session away."

"Roland." Her mother's voice was imploring as she diverted her gaze to Libby's father, obviously hoping he would find a way to talk his daughter out of her decision. But Libby's father stared at his daughter for a long moment, his stern, attractive features searching as he assessed her face.

"She'll be fine, Ma," he said with a decisive nod. "Let the girl figure it out for herself."

*Three months later*

"You don't have to move out, you know?" Chris said, crunching into an apple as he watched Libby neatly fold Clara's tiny clothes and pack them into the huge suitcase spread open on the unmade double bed.

Libby had really enjoyed reconnecting with her friend and mentor, Christién Roche. She would have been an idiot to pass up the chance to work with Chris again. So she had happily escaped to Chris's beautiful forest cottage on the Garden Route three months ago. She had been even happier with the comfortable amount of physical distance the move had put between her and Greyson. A former model, Christién Roche had strutted his stuff on the catwalk and in magazines for years before going to culinary school. Libby had met him while doing an internship in Paris five years ago, where he'd been the pâtissier at a well-known Michelin-star restaurant.

The man was a creative genius, and for some reason known only to him, he had given it all up to open a tiny coffee shop in the Western Cape of South Africa. The place had been running for four years and was only now starting to build a reputation as a quality restaurant. Chris barely advertised and was wholly dependent on word-of-mouth referrals. It was starting to work, as patrons loved the idea of eating at a hidden gem of a restaurant that only they and a few others knew about.

"I know that," Libby said in reply to the tall, gorgeous man's former statement while offering him a small smile. "But Clara and I are cramping your swinging bachelor lifestyle. We've imposed enough, and I'm excited about the new place. And you know I can't commute between your place and Riversend every day. It's a forty-minute drive."

Chris made a rude sound and waved his hand dismissively. "I do not know why you have chosen to buy that house. It is . . . how do you say? A dump. Not fit for you and this precious bonbon!"

"I like the town, and I know the house needs work, but I'm looking forward to fixing it up."

"It will take more than some paint and the crack filler to fix that place up."

Libby bit back a smile at the awkward turn of phrase. Chris's English was generally excellent, but occasionally words like *Polyfilla* defeated him.

"I know that commuting to and from Riversend every day could be a nightmare in that piece-of-shit joke you call a car. But this means you should change cars," he pointed out. These were all familiar arguments; he had been against the idea of her buying that house from the start. Libby had filled out the paperwork two months ago. The transfer deed had been finalized just the week before, and Libby would be moving out of Chris's place today.

But her extremely handsome Congolese friend with the dreamy accent was not too crazy about the fact that she was leaving. He had taken her and Clara in without reservations, had asked few questions about her marriage, and had gone completely gaga over the infant. Which was a bit shocking, as Libby didn't think Chris had ever really been near a real, live baby before. He was a completely doting uncle and spoiled Clara rotten.

"There's nothing wrong with my car, Chris."

"It is in worse shape than that dump you want to live in," he argued, holding up a finger and glaring at her. "I do not understand why we cannot continue like this. You can work here, and there is ample space for Clara."

"You don't really need me, you know that," she muttered. He had a small but highly competent staff at his restaurant. Employing Libby had been a favor, and they both knew it. Especially since she could only work part time while Clara was so tiny. The arrangement was fine for the short term, but it had never felt permanent to Libby. She wanted to settle down and build more of a career. Working for Chris would be too limiting: because of the nature of his business, there was absolutely no room for growth for Libby.

"I'll be putting Clara into day care; they have an excellent kin-dergarten—which offers a phenomenal infant day care service—in Riversend. I've loved working here, and I owe you so much, Chris. But it's time for me to find my feet and establish a secure future for myself and Clara. Besides, MJ's offers an exciting new opportunity for me."

"A fast-food restaurant. You will waste your exceptional talent at a fast-food restaurant." He practically spat the words, and she grinned wryly. He could be such a snob sometimes.

"It's hardly a fast-food restaurant. It's a family restaurant, with a decent and varied menu."

"I know this place. The menu has not changed in twenty years."

"How do you know that? You've only been here for four years."

"How I know is not important. I do not understand why you want to be a grill cook at some diner with a mediocre menu."

"I won't be the grill cook. I'll be revitalizing the menu. Tina has big ideas for the restaurant."

Tina had first seen the restaurant when she had brought Libby and Clara to stay with Chris three months ago. It had been a long drive, and Libby could easily have flown, but she hadn't wanted to risk taking her four-week-old baby on a plane. Tina, despite her emotional detachment while Libby and Clara had been living with her, had seemed hurt that they were moving out and had eagerly suggested a road trip.

They had stopped in the tiny, picturesque town of Riversend and had enjoyed a meal at MJ's. Shockingly, Tina, who had been direction-less for so long, had fallen in love with the faded establishment and immediately claimed that she had to have it. Said it was fate since she had the same initials. Never mind that she knew absolutely nothing about running a business. But Tina had inherited a huge amount of money from her paternal grandfather and had more than enough to purchase and revitalize the restaurant. Upon purchase, she had offered Libby a partnership of sorts: free rein to run the kitchen as she saw fit and license to create the new menu and focus on experimental desserts, while Tina ran the business end of things.

Libby sometimes wondered if Tina had bought the place just so that she, Libby, could have something to fall back on. Which would be exactly the kind of impulsive, impractical, mad thing one could some-times expect from Tina. She hoped Tina wouldn't be that foolhardy, but Libby wasn't going to leave her best friend to manage a restaurant without her help. Not after everything Tina had done for Libby and Clara. Besides, MJ's had potential, and she was sure she and Tina could help it succeed.

Libby hoped working closely with Tina would fix whatever was broken in their friendship as well. Things had been rocky and uncertain since she had moved out of Tina's flat. They were treading on eggshells around each other, and Tina still seemed a little hesitant around Clara. But this venture felt like a chance for them to rediscover their bond and possibly reinvent their friendship.

It also presented a massive opportunity for Libby. She could be her own boss and create a signature menu. She'd have time to experiment with desserts—her true passion—and really turn the place into a buzzing premium eatery. She could barely contain her excitement at the thought of how much this could change her life. She loved that she could feel excited about her career again. For too long the only emotions she'd had associated with it had been regret and loss.

She had been going through the motions at Chris's café. But with MJ's, she felt a thrill whenever she considered the potential, what it could mean to her as a chef, to Tina as a burgeoning businesswoman. How much independence it could give them both.

And it didn't hurt that the town was gorgeous. The perfect place to raise Clara.

"Tina is giving the restaurant a face-lift. She's rebranding, changing the menu, and redecorating. MJ's is nearly unrecognizable now."

Chris muttered something unsavory beneath his breath and offered her a rueful smile.

"If this will make you happy," he conceded begrudgingly, "then I cannot stand in your way."

*Make me happy?* Libby wasn't sure what it would take to make her truly happy again. But this shot at independence, a second chance at the career that she'd so willfully abandoned for a man who felt nothing for her, was a good start. She returned his smile, fighting back the ever-lurking melancholy, and put down Clara's tiny onesie to hug the man who had gone from fun acquaintance to invaluable friend in just three short months.

"You've been such a wonderful friend to me, Chris. I can't tell you how much this has meant to me."

"It has been my privilege, *ma petite*," he said into her hair. "You deserve happiness. You and my precious Clara bonbon both deserve it. I will visit all the time. I do not want Clara to forget her *oncle* Chris."

"That will never happen," she promised and gave him one more huge squeeze before resuming her packing.


"Ugh, this place is falling apart, Libby," Tina said, wrinkling her nose as she took in the house Libby was in the process of moving in to.

"It just needs a bit of TLC," Libby disagreed, her eyes running around the tiny living room and kitchen as she mentally cataloged all the work that needed to be done. Instead of feeling overwhelmed, she had a renewed sense of purpose. She was optimistic about this house, about the future. While she had this to focus on, she didn't have to think about Greyson. About the divorce papers she'd had drafted up. The ones she had shoved into Clara's nappy bag and tried to dismiss from her mind.

"I got it at a fantastic price," she said. It had taken nearly all of her savings and a small loan from her concerned but supportive parents, but Libby considered it money well spent.

"Yeah, I can see why." Tina opened up the kitchen faucet and winced when the pipes groaned and slightly brown water spluttered from the tap in spurts rather than a steady stream. "You and Clara should at least move in with me until you have most of this sorted out."

"Then we'd be living with you indefinitely." Libby laughed.

"I don't see a problem with that."

"You will when she wakes you up at night again," Libby said, and Tina smiled slightly in return. Her eyes dropped to where Clara's baby seat had been placed on the scrubbed-down kitchen counter, before hastily darting away.

Libby wanted to ask her. She really did, but something painful and desperate in Tina's eyes stayed her tongue. She had once believed she and Tina had no secrets from each other, but this was something huge and potentially emotionally destructive, and with everything else she had to deal with right now, Libby let the moment pass. She wasn't proud of her own cowardice, but at the same time, she felt resentful that Tina had put her in this position.

It had been hard not to miss Tina's reaction to Clara during those first four weeks when they had shared a space. She had happily helped Libby with everything else but had never offered to hold the baby, or change her, or do anything that involved direct interaction with Clara. It was abundantly clear that her friend—who had once considered becoming an obstetrician—was not comfortable around Clara. But Libby had given Tina's behavior a little more consideration after moving in with Chris. The other woman had given up her home to a constantly crying newborn and her emotionally wrecked best friend. With everything going on, of *course* it must have been difficult for her to adjust. Clara was older now, starting to develop a distinct personality, and she was a complete delight to be around. Libby felt certain that with their situation being less fraught, Tina would finally have the opportunity to enjoy Clara. It would just take some time.

"We'll be okay, Tina. The bedroom is fine, so's the bathroom . . ." Well, it would be if she could just get the freaking plumber to come and sort out the pipes. But the guy was proving hard to pin down. Libby was tempted to google the solution and try her hand at plumbing. But she knew that would only exacerbate the problem.

Libby had painted the bedroom and scrubbed it from floor to ceiling a week ago, after the transfer had been completed. She'd bought a single bed for her, and happily—thanks to Harris and Tina—Clara had a crib and anything else a baby could possibly need.

Also, her parents sent way too many clothes and toys. Spoiling their first grandchild the only way they currently knew how. As did Greyson's parents, in addition to Harris, Tina, and Chris.

Libby felt overwhelmingly guilty about excluding her parents and about the fact that she knew Harris and his parents would like more of a presence in Clara's life. Harris had been trying to arrange a visit for months, but Libby tended to avoid his calls, keeping their correspondence limited to text messages instead. Sending him pics of her life and her baby every day. She knew that Harris was concerned; he kept asking if she was all right, to which Libby only ever responded that she and Clara were both okay.

Constance and Truman Chapman had visited them while they were staying at Tina's. That had been predictably awkward. But the older couple had lavished attention on Clara, clearly enamored with her. After Libby had moved to the Garden Route, Constance had messaged her once only, a tersely worded missive asking if she and the baby needed anything. Libby had politely thanked her and told her they were both fine. It hadn't deterred them from sending *numerous* care packages.

Greyson, of course, hadn't attempted to call or text her. Not once. And though she told herself that she didn't care, that still hurt like hell.

Greyson had been strictly rationing himself. No more than one look a day. It was all he deserved. As such, the innocuous-looking manila folder remained firmly closed and tauntingly perched on the edge of his desk. *He* had put it there, of course; having recently discovered a masochistic bent within himself, he had placed the folder just within eyesight, perfectly straight, its edges not touching any other piece of stationery on the large walnut desk. He couldn't open it yet. Not for another hour.

His phone chimed, and he glanced at it and shut his eyes for a moment when he saw his brother's name on the screen. He knew what it would be. It was all Harris sent him these days, outside of business emails. His brother, ever the opposite of Greyson, had recently discovered a sadistic inclination within *himself*, and Greyson was the one and only person on whom he chose to practice that tendency.

Every day. Just one text. With an image attached.

He swallowed and reached for the phone. The folder would wait, per his ritual. But this could not. He inhaled deeply, held his breath, and opened the text.

The breath escaped on a shuddering sigh as he stared into bright eyes and a gummy, dimpled smile. Again, that instant gut punch he felt every time he received a new picture from his brother.

*Clara.*

The name brought a grim smile to his lips. Olivia had chosen it to spite him, of course. And he couldn't blame her. That one soft little jab didn't come close to what he deserved. Besides, he found that he didn't mind the name at all anymore. Whenever he thought of it, this was the face that came to mind.

He didn't ask from whom Harris got these pictures; Greyson knew Olivia was sending them to his brother. But he also knew that she hadn't really spoken with the guy since she'd left. Depriving both Harris and Olivia of a friendship that had meant so much to them: yet another fault that could be placed at Greyson's door.

He stared at the image avidly, his finger tracing the soft curve of one chubby cheek. She was getting so big. He added the picture to the album he had titled *Clara* and flipped through the four months' worth of photos slowly, working back from today's to the first one he'd received from Harris about a week after Olivia had walked out of the hospital and his life. The angry, wrinkled, wet face, mouth open, gums gleaming as she cried. The picture broke a piece of his heart, as it did whenever he saw it. He knew she was probably crying because she was hungry or needed a nappy change, but every time he looked at the photo, he ached to pick her up, to cradle her as he should have that first day, to protect her, love her, and soothe her.

But he had thrown that privilege away. Had tossed her and Olivia aside without once considering the consequences. Always so certain he was right.

He had failed as a husband, and he had failed as a father . . .

He shook his head in self-disgust.

*A father.*

All these years of feeling less than whole. Of feeling somehow lacking. All because he had been too damned proud to go for a second opinion. Because going to another doctor—to a fertility specialist—would have made it seem important to him. Would have made him look like he cared. And he hadn't wanted to care.

No. That was wrong . . .

He hadn't wanted anyone to *know* that he cared.

His worst fear—unacknowledged even to himself—was having the belief that he was incapable of doing something so fucking basic reinforced. No kids for him. No grandchildren for his parents. No niece or nephew for his brother.

And no child for his wife.

He should have gone to another doctor once Olivia had agreed to marry him. He should have checked. But he had been too damned proud, too afraid of failing again. He hadn't had to check. He'd thought he already had all the answers.

His wife was pregnant? She must have cheated. That had been his answer, his universal fucking truth.

He shook his head again, choking back a bitter laugh.

He hadn't just failed as a husband and as a father . . . most importantly, he had failed as a man.

Once he had believed that his supposed infertility made him less of a man. But this, his treatment of Olivia. Of Harris . . .

*Of Clara.*

That was what made him less of a man. That was where he had fallen down.

He buried his face in his hands and longed for a drink. But he was rationing himself there as well. No more alcohol.

Drinking himself into a stupor would in no way make him the better man he was striving to be.

He lifted his head and glanced at his watch.

Twenty minutes to go. His eyes fell to the folder again. He could no longer fight the urge to open it. And while he knew he didn't deserve this fix, he was too weak and selfish to resist it.

He reached for it, opened it carefully, and stared down at the latest collection of photos his investigator had sent him. The man was old fashioned and paranoid—he never emailed information. Instead, every week, he brought his latest update straight to Greyson's office.

The folder remained on Greyson's desk, and every day he allowed himself a glimpse into Olivia's life. Today was special, because there were new pictures, updates, and anecdotes about how she was doing. He knew he shouldn't be keeping tabs on her, knew it was invasive and that he had absolutely no right, but he told himself he was watching out for her. Making sure she was doing all right.

He exhaled on a shuddering sigh as he stared down at the two-dimensional pictures. They didn't do her justice. She was so beautiful. He was happy to see she was putting on some weight again. She had looked positively gaunt those first couple of months. But now her wavy black hair was glossy with health, and despite the encroaching cold, wet winter weather, her perfect brown skin had a sun-kissed golden glow to it. He knew it was warm and silky to the touch.

Like so many other Capetonians, Olivia was of multiracial descent, going back several generations. She was exotically beautiful and had always fascinated him with her big, luminous light-brown eyes; her heart-shaped, generous mouth; and her slender athlete's body. He'd hidden that fascination, of course; she was the only daughter of long-time family employees and had grown up in the Chapman house, and Greyson wasn't going to be *that* guy.

It had felt wrong to want her, and he hadn't acted on his attraction until he'd seen her at a party more than a year ago. She had been so independent, talented, smart, and absolutely gorgeous, and added to the fact that her parents had retired the year before, he hadn't been able to resist her. They had fallen into bed that very first night, and it had stunned him to discover she was a virgin. It had felt *right* to offer her marriage. He had pushed for marriage, and it had soon become all he could think about. All he wanted.

He should have told her about his belief that he couldn't have children; he knew that. It was a fucking huge betrayal of trust to go into a marriage without telling the other party that you were unable to have kids. But he had wanted her—it had been crazy and irrational. He'd wanted to keep her in his bed, and the only way he could see himself doing so guilt-free was by marrying her. He'd had a vague idea that he'd somehow find a work-around to the humiliating "sorry, can't have kids" conversation, and then before he knew it, she'd been telling him she was pregnant, and he had been fucking *livid*. He had watched her every move afterward like a hawk, hoping she'd reveal the identity of her lover to be anyone other than Harris. But the only man she'd been close to was Harris. Always fucking Harris. His brother and Olivia had always been tight. Always laughed and joked and talked . . . it hadn't been that much of a stretch to imagine they'd taken that extra step toward intimacy.

Greyson swallowed the nausea the mere thought of Harris and Olivia *together* still had the power to produce.

The possibility had once seemed so damned *real* to him.

But he really should have known better, considering his brother seemed to harbor complex and intense feelings for someone other than Olivia. But Greyson had been irrational. The emotion he'd experienced had felt perilously close to jealousy. But that was ridiculous; he couldn't be jealous. No woman, not even Olivia, was worth feeling jealous over.

And yet . . .

### One year ago

The flowers were a little over the top. And uncharacteristic. Greyson pensively glared at the huge bunch of pale-pink peonies and seriously considered tossing them down the trash chute once he reached the penthouse.

But he wanted to do something nice for Olivia . . . he had been working full on in the month since their rushed wedding, and he'd been home late and gone early most days. He had stayed in London much too long while trying to win over Olivia. Two months. He had allowed too many minor tasks to lapse, and he'd been playing catch-up for a few weeks. In addition to that, something fishy was going on in one of their Australian branches, and he was working hard to figure it out. That meant staying in the office late to make conference calls with their Oceania Division VP.

Until he knew exactly what was happening, he was keeping it under wraps. Harris knew about it, of course, but Greyson wanted to be certain his suspicions were correct before he handed the matter over to his brother, the CFO. He knew he should have allowed Harris to take over by now . . . but the company was Greyson's responsibility, and he liked to run a tight ship.

Today was the first time in weeks that he was home in time for dinner, and he wanted to surprise Olivia by treating her to a romantic meal at one of her favorite restaurants and lavishing some attention on her. He hadn't seen much of her lately, and he . . .

He huffed a short, incredulous laugh as he turned the realization over in his head for a moment: he missed her.

He stepped out of the elevator, a smile tugging at the corners of his mouth. He glanced down at the flowers again; it was a stupidly romantic gesture. But he wasn't going to toss them down the chute. Peonies were her favorite flower, and he wanted her to have them. He wanted her to know that he had bought them with her in mind.

He opened the front door to their penthouse apartment, his entire body tensing in anticipation. He was excited to see her. He would apologize for his neglect and promise that things would get better soon.

The apartment was silent. No music or noise from the television. Just the loud, ominous ticking of the huge grandfather clock. Olivia had once told him it reminded her of—how had she put it?—*every horror movie ever*. The memory made him smile. She always made him want to laugh or smile with her offbeat observations and unintentionally funny insights.

"Olivia?" His voice bounced off the walls; the apartment was too large and sparsely furnished. Shortly after moving in, Olivia had told him the penthouse felt cold and unwelcoming, and he had suggested she redecorate. He wanted her to feel at home. And it wasn't like he felt any particular connection to the stuff in here.

She had recently started looking at color and fabric swatches. And the coffee table in the living room was now laden with decor magazines.

Greyson wandered from room to room, hoping to find her in one of them, but he could tell that the penthouse was empty. Immensely disappointed, he moved to the huge chef's kitchen—the one place in the penthouse Olivia truly appreciated—in search of a vase for the flowers.

He was just placing the filled vase on a side table when the front door swung open and his laughing wife stepped over the threshold. Harris was with her, his face alight with amusement as he held something aloft above his head while Olivia tried to grab it from him.

"No way, Bug," Harris was saying, his voice wobbly with amusement. "You ate most of the others, this one is mine."

"You don't even like chocolate that much," she replied with a pout, and Harris grinned at her before deliberately popping whatever it was he was holding—chocolate, presumably—into his mouth.

"I like *this* chocolate," he said, his voice muffled by whatever he was chewing. He looked up, spotted Greyson, and swallowed before smiling. His teeth were still covered with some chocolate. "Hey, Greyson . . . settle an argument. Would you say turkish delight is the most hideous thing they could possibly put inside a chocolate? Or . . ."

"Pineapple," Olivia finished for him. A smile lit up her lovely features as she bounced toward Greyson and planted a happy kiss on his lips. "You're home early."

"I, uh . . ." Greyson wasn't sure what to respond to. The chocolate thing or her observation about him being home early? Instead he settled on, "I don't care for chocolate."

"Philistine." Olivia wrinkled her nose at him. But her smile deepened. She stood on her toes and gave him another kiss. "We were just about to have some Thai takeout and watch a *Say Yes to the Dress* marathon. Joining us?"

"Wait, you said we could watch the football," Harris complained. "I'm not watching that dress show, Libby."

"And I'm not watching a bunch of guys aimlessly kicking a ball around for ninety minutes."

"You always do this. You always lure me in with these false little promises, and then we wind up doing whatever the hell you want."

It was the Harris-and-Libby show, and as always Greyson felt relegated to merely an observer.

"I brought some work home," he fabricated quickly, never sure where he slotted in when they were in their best-buddies mode. Olivia looked a little disappointed but unsurprised, and she wrapped her arms around his waist and gave him a hard hug. His arms closed around her instinctively, and he relished the warmth of her slight body against his, the smell of her skin and her hair. She was intoxicating.

The hug ended too soon, and she stepped away after one last lingering kiss.

"We'll be in the den, watching *something*," she said with a roll of her eyes. "Join us if you need a break, okay?"

He nodded, and she brushed a loving hand over his jaw.

"If I send you an SOS text, come and save me from whatever ridiculously girly show she's forced me to watch, okay?" Harris muttered in an aside to Greyson. The latter forced a smile and nodded curtly.

Greyson watched—eaten up with resentment and disappointment— as his brother draped a casual arm around Libby's shoulders and steered her toward the den.

Neither of them so much as glanced at the flowers on the side table as they walked right by.

### Present day

Greyson shook his head, impatient with himself for allowing the disturbing memory to intrude on the already unpleasant present. So many nights he had come home hoping for some one-on-one time with Olivia, only to find Harris—or sometimes Tina—there. Tina he didn't mind, but to find Harris there so often . . . he made an involuntary sound at the back of his throat. Greyson now recognized that the sour emotion churning away at his gut every time he had seen Olivia and Harris chuckling over some incomprehensible joke had been jealousy. He had been wildly jealous over their easy familiarity, the camaraderie, the casual touching.

The jealousy had eaten away at him, had made him irrationally suspicious. It had allowed him to completely lose sight of reality, to color his view of the two of them. By the time he had spotted them in that restaurant, he had been more than ready to believe the absolute worst of them.

Four fucking months since he had seen Olivia last. Since he had grudgingly looked at the infant he now accepted was his child. It was too long, and he couldn't stand the thought of another four passing without seeing them. Worse . . . of years passing. Of never seeing Olivia again and never getting to know Clara.

The thought was beyond bearing.

Before he could overthink it, he swiped his screen and brought up his brother's number. He and Harris very rarely exchanged personal calls anymore. Except for the pictures Harris sent him every day, they kept things strictly business between them. But Harris needed to hear his decision. Greyson owed his brother that much, at least.

Harris replied almost immediately.

"Yeah?" The man's voice was curt and unwelcoming, but that didn't deter Greyson. His decision had been made the moment Harris had sent him that first picture so many months ago. It had just taken him this long to summon up the guts to do what he knew needed to be done.

"I'm bringing them home."


"Nobody's coming," Tina lamented, agitatedly chewing on her thumb-nail. Libby tugged her shorter friend's hand away from her mouth.

"They'll come," she said confidently, even though nerves were gnawing at her stomach. It was MJ's grand relaunch, and they'd opened the doors half an hour ago. Opened the door to crickets.

Not the queues they'd been hoping for. Libby had expected the place to be packed, especially on a Friday night. She'd hoped curiosity, if nothing else, would have them come in to check out the place. The staff, which they had kept largely intact, stood around uncertainly.

"People here are really old fashioned," Thandiwe, a college student home for the holidays, offered. The young woman had worked for MJ's throughout her teens, always part time. She was one of their best servers and had helped train the new staff members. "MJ's has been something of an institution in this town, and maybe they think you've messed with tradition or something?"

"But when I first arrived in town and ate here, people were complaining about how the menu never changed and it would be nice to have some variety," Tina pointed out.

"Yes, but they've been saying that for years." Thandiwe shrugged. "I think they enjoyed complaining about it. But it was familiar, and they loved it. I'm sure people will come. Give it time. It's this or Ralphie's"—the local pub—"and everyone knows the food is mostly terrible at Ralphie's. Once they've sampled the new menu, they won't know what to do with themselves."

Thandiwe excused herself and went to chat with some of the other waitstaff. After what looked like a terse exchange, they all scattered in different directions, immediately looking a lot busier than they had just moments before.

"You sent notice of the reopening to the district paper, right?" Libby asked Tina. The paper, *Riversend Weekly*, circulated on Thursdays and usually contained job opportunities, advertisements for local businesses, and news about town events.

"Yes, of course," Tina said, and she lifted her phone and swiped at her screen. She seemed to be looking for something. "I . . . it has to be here. I sent it on Monday."

"Did you check the paper?" Libby asked, not liking how this was going. Tina shook her head, a frown marring the smooth lines of her forehead.

"I forgot to pick up a copy. I meant to get one, but it completely slipped my mind. But I sent it—" She paused, her eyes glued to her phone screen, and the sick dread in her expression did not bode well. "Crap."

"Tina?" Libby prompted her, not really sure she wanted to know. She could guess anyway.

"It didn't send. I don't know why it didn't send," Tina said, sounding horrified.

"Oh, Tina." Libby tried to keep the censure from her voice, knowing that her friend probably felt terrible already, but this was bad.

"I should have double-checked," Tina said. "I'm sorry, Libby. First the banner and now this."

Tina was referring to the huge, festive banner they had both designed to announce the relaunch, which hadn't arrived on time. That, along with a few hundred flyers to circulate around town and the ad in the paper, represented their entire promotional plan for the relaunch. But Tina had given the graphic design company the wrong dates. The banners and flyers, which promoted their opening-week specials, would only be arriving next week. At which point they would be about as useful as nipples on a man.

There was usually some amount of organized chaos around the launch of a new restaurant, but this was worse than usual. Everything had gone wrong at the eleventh hour. Nothing was going according to plan.

"It's okay." Libby tried to appease her friend, even though she was horribly disappointed. "People are coming in; it could have been worse."

Tina shook her head. Her hand lifted to her mouth, and she started gnawing on her thumbnail again.

The door tinkled, and a couple ambled in. The two were holding hands and chuckling, but they stopped abruptly and cast surprised looks around the near-empty restaurant.

"Hey. You're open! That's fantastic. Where is everybody?" the woman—Libby recognized her as one of the childcare workers at the kindergarten—asked.

"Apparently resistant to change," Libby said with a bright smile, focusing on business. An answering smile lit up the woman's pretty face.

"Hello, we haven't officially met. I'm Lia McGregor. You're Clara's mum." She walked toward Libby, dragging the handsome blond man behind her.

"Olivia Lawson. Please call me Libby," she said, taking an immediate liking to her. She held out her hand to the slightly older woman, who took it and shook enthusiastically.

"Really lovely to officially meet you. This is my fiancé, Sam Brand."

"Nice to meet you," the man said, also taking Libby's hand. He had a wicked smile and an English accent, if she wasn't mistaken.

"This is the restaurant's new owner, Martine Jenson. But everybody calls her Tina," Libby said, gesturing toward her friend, who acknowledged the couple with a slightly austere smile, as was her habit with strangers. Tina didn't befriend people easily.

Lia McGregor seemed to have no such problem. She was still smiling warmly, and her eyes brightened at Tina's name. "Ooh. You're an MJ too? That's perfect," Lia enthused.

She continued chatting cheerfully, and Libby watched Tina closely during the exchange. Her friend, never one to immediately warm to new people, still looked distracted and anxious. But Libby knew that this time Tina's anxiety did not stem from being forced to chat with strangers. She could tell that Tina's mind was still on the unsent email. Libby couldn't understand how Tina could have made such elementary errors just before their opening weekend. They both had so much riding on this restaurant, yet now—at the most crucial time—Tina seemed to be mentally and emotionally imploding.

And that terrified Libby. Unlike Tina, she didn't have wealthy parents and an inheritance to fall back on, and she couldn't help feeling a simmering pang of resentment at the other woman's seemingly careless attitude toward her responsibilities. Libby needed Tina to recognize that she had staked Clara's future on this restaurant. This could *not* become yet another one of Tina's failed "projects."

She feared that Tina was crumbling beneath the pressure, and she wasn't entirely sure how to make things right. She only hoped Tina would find a way to cope. If she couldn't, then they were both doomed to lose much more than just a business. Libby wasn't sure their friendship would survive such a catastrophic loss. Not when she had left a stable—if unremarkable—job to do this with Tina. If it were just her, she would be able to brush off such a loss and move on, but she had a baby now, and *everything* she did was for Clara.

The evening wasn't the disaster they had feared it would be. But it wasn't the capacity crowd they were hoping for either. Still, it was a busy and tiring night for both women. Libby tried to maintain focus, but it was hard when she knew Clara was in Tina's office in the back, with a young sitter they had found online. She was trying to gradually wean Clara off the breast, planning to pump milk for bottle feedings—a necessity—at day care and then to continue with breastfeeding in the evenings. She wanted to maintain a stable routine for Clara. But she felt incredibly guilty about it, as her original plan had always been to breastfeed for at least six months before even thinking of weaning. She hated losing out on those last two months. But in this case, head had to overrule heart.

At least she still had the evenings, and tonight she popped in occasionally to cuddle and breastfeed her baby and to make sure both Clara and her teenage sitter were comfortable and happy.

The sixteen-year-old girl, Charlie Carlisle, had been frank about the fact that she'd never sat for an infant before, but Libby had been desperate and had liked the no-nonsense teen immediately. Still, it made her feel better to know that they were close by.

At the end of the evening, Libby was relieved to call it a day. She knew Tina was disappointed by the turnout and wondered—not for the first time—how much money her friend had put into this venture. Tina had been secretive about the finances, telling Libby to focus on creating the mouthwatering, inventive dishes that Tina was sure would put MJ's firmly on the map as a premium eatery.

Their new friend Lia McGregor and her immediate family had lavished the food with praise. But most of the other locals who had ventured out had been stingy with their feedback. Time would tell if word of mouth would generate new business and if the people who had come out tonight would turn into regular patrons. Come summer, tourists would flock to the seaside town, and there would definitely be an uptick in business then. But Tina and Libby knew that the only way the business would survive was if the locals took to it. Or they would go belly up before next winter.

Once the last of the patrons had left and the kitchen staff had the cleanup under control, Libby joined Tina in her office. Charlie was still there, putting her e-book and phone into a tattered denim backpack.

"Thank you for all your help tonight, Charlie." She smiled at the pretty girl, found her purse, and dug through her wallet for the payment.

"She's a darling, Mrs. Chapman. I enjoyed taking care of her." Libby winced inwardly at the name, wishing she'd thought to introduce herself as Libby Lawson to Charlie. Now she was stuck with Mrs. Chapman, which was aggravating when she would rather not acknowledge the fact that she'd ever been married.

"Please, call me Libby," she said hastily. "Clara seems to like you. How often do you think you would be available to sit?"

"I can sit most weekends. School nights will be a bit more difficult because I have swim practice after school, followed by studying and homework."

"Of course." Libby smiled, swallowing down disappointment. She wasn't sure what to do about the weeknights. She had to be at the restaurant from ten thirty to three for the brunch and lunch crowd and then back by six thirty for dinner service. The early shift was fine because Clara spent those few hours in day care. But evenings would be a problem. She needed to find a nanny . . . but the cost was prohibitive.

Libby paid Charlie, and the girl beamed happily.

"Do you need a ride home?" Libby asked.

"Oh no, my brother, Spencer, is waiting for me."

"Spencer is your brother?" Spencer was Lia McGregor's good-looking but intimidatingly big brother-in-law. The man had hovered around his heavily pregnant wife, Daffodil, all night. The woman in turn had rolled her eyes and good naturedly teased him about his overprotectiveness. Libby envied the woman her doting, concerned husband. And couldn't help but compare how the man was around his wife with how absent and disinterested Greyson had been throughout Libby's pregnancy.

She forced the bitter memory to the back of her mind and focused on the girl. Spencer and Daff had been introduced by their first names only, so she hadn't made the connection that they might be related to her babysitter. Charlie was biracial, and with her dusky skin and soft dark-brown curls, the familial relationship wasn't immediately apparent. But now she could see the resemblance: the girl had her brother's emerald eyes, shy smile, and dimples. But she was very petite, while her hulking brother was huge.

"Yep. He's a little overprotective; he'd never allow me to walk home or even use Uber. I mean, we have, like, two Uber drivers in town, and Spencer knows them both, so I don't know what his deal is." She rolled her eyes, clearly finding this bit of brotherly tyranny tiresome. Libby hid her smile and nodded.

"Best not to keep him waiting any longer," she said, and the girl nodded.

"Thanks again, Mrs. Chapman. Same time tomorrow night?"

"Yes please." Libby nodded, and the girl bent over the crib to gently stroke the sleeping baby's head.

"Sweet dreams, Clara. See you soon. Night, Mrs. Chapman. See you, Tina."

Tina—who had been silently staring at her laptop throughout Libby's exchange with the teen—looked up and waved as the girl flounced out in that carefree manner only teens seemed to possess.

"She's sweet," she said in reference to Charlie, dragging her reading glasses off and pinching the bridge of her nose tiredly. "God, I'm knackered."

"Me too." Libby sank down in the chair opposite her friend. "How did we do?"

"Just about broke even tonight," Tina said with a tight smile.

"It'll get better," Libby reassured her—mentally crossing her fingers in hopes that her words would prove to be prophetic.

Her friend nodded with an unconvinced smile. "It has to."

"Tina, how much did you spend on this place? Renovations and rebranding included?"

"My inheritance more than covered it," Tina said with another tight smile. "It's fine. It's just . . ."

"Just what?" Libby prompted her when her friend stalled in midsentence. She hated feeling like Tina was hiding something from her. Libby knew that she had been too involved with her own life and concerns to pay more than cursory attention to her friend's behavioral changes before now, but it was becoming more and more apparent that something was very wrong with Tina. And had been for a long time. It made her once again second-guess her decision to go into this business venture with Tina. But it was too late for regrets, and she could only hope this worked out, despite whatever was going on with her friend.

"This is the first thing I've done," Tina said. "The first meaningful thing, and my parents are just waiting for me to fail. I know it. They think that I'm a total waste of space. Their flighty daughter, who could never keep down a job, trying to run a restaurant. Without any qualifications whatsoever."

Self-doubt reflected in the woman's pretty sea-green eyes, and Libby shook her head. She felt abruptly terrible about all her earlier uncertainty regarding Tina's commitment to the restaurant. In a moment of revelatory clarity, she understood that Tina was absolutely terrified of failing. Libby had judged her too harshly earlier; Tina wanted this to work, but it wasn't easy for her. Libby, with her past experience in the restaurant business, had simply expected Tina to immediately get everything right, when that was a near-impossible ask for even an experienced restaurateur.

Looking at her miserable friend, she mentally readjusted her expectations and dialed back her impatience. Reassurance and support would get both of them a lot further than criticism and doubt.

"Stop it," she commanded the morose woman sitting across from her, and the distant look faded from Tina's eyes as she focused on Libby again.

"Stop what?" she asked blankly.

"Allowing what your parents think of you to influence the way you think about yourself. You can do this, Tina. We can both do it."

Tina scrubbed both hands over her face and allowed herself another deep sigh before lifting her eyes to Libby's again. "Yeah, we just need to figure out a way to get all those previous customers back. If the townspeople really are as stubbornly loyal to the old MJ's as Thandiwe thinks, then I'm not sure how to lure them back."

"Look, it's only the first night. They have to drive thirty minutes to get to another halfway-decent, affordable family restaurant. Or leave their kids at home and go to Ralphie's for limp fish and chips or stale burgers. Soon, desperation for a good night out, more than anything else, will have them coming back."

"Maybe." Tina nodded, again looking completely unconvinced.

"Definitely. And Daff said she'd help us with some marketing." The woman was the marketing-and-promotions manager for her husband's three huge sporting-goods stores and had promised to work up a marketing strategy for MJ's while she was on maternity leave. Her husband hadn't been too pleased with that, but Daff had complained of being bored at home.

"It seems like a lot to expect from a total stranger," Tina said skeptically.

"I don't know about you, but after five minutes with those sisters, I feel like I've known them for years."

"Yeah, they're pretty nice." Tina, being Tina, still looked doubtful.

"More than nice." *Warm* and *welcoming* were the words that sprang to mind when Libby thought of the sisters. And immediately affectionately familiar. It was hard not to like them. Tina nodded again. Her eyes were troubled, but she didn't say anything more on the subject.

"Come on, let's go home and get to bed. We have another long day tomorrow," Libby said, and Tina ducked her head, powered down her laptop, and tucked it under her arm; she then slung her bag over her shoulder. Libby packed up the baby bag and gently gathered her contentedly sleeping baby into her arms.

The kitchen staff had left, and the building was eerily quiet as Tina did a walk around the restaurant to make sure everything was off and in place. It looked amazing. The staff had done a wonderful job of cleaning up. The decision to keep them had been a sound one.

Libby watched as Tina took one last, lingering look around and smiled at the glimmer of pride she saw in her friend's eyes. The place looked beautiful, a far cry from the shabby interior of before, and Libby experienced her own surge of pride at everything Tina had accomplished here. Her good taste was evident in everything from the furnishings to the tableware to the new color scheme. Tina may have made a few crucial mistakes this weekend, but *this* was something she had done exceptionally well.

Libby hoped, for both their sakes, that the townsfolk would start supporting MJ's, because it would be a shame for all of this work to go unappreciated.

"You sure you don't want to stay at mine tonight? I mean, does your shower even work?" Tina asked as she stood beside her car and watched Libby secure Clara in the car seat.

"I managed to get it working this morning. The water was cold, though." Libby shuddered at the thought of another cold shower, but she was determined to tough it out. It was her home, for better or worse. She was going to make it perfect . . . and she'd appreciate it more after all the initial trials and tribulations.

Tina had a small semidetached house just a few minutes away from the restaurant, but she had driven to work because of the heavy rain that morning. Libby's house was a little farther away, closer to the beach.

Tina nodded and got into her car. She rolled down the window and watched until Libby was safely in her own car. They both started up their vehicles simultaneously and drove in opposite directions.

The house was shrouded in darkness when she got home, and she cursed herself for not remembering to at least leave the porch light on when she left for work. Her place was a little out of town and quite a distance from the next-closest house. A security system was another item on her very long to-do list, but until then, she had to remember to do things like leave lights on. She didn't just have her own safety to consider anymore.

It was going to be enough of a struggle negotiating the cobbled path to the porch while lugging a baby carrier, baby bag, and her own huge purse. Having to do it in the dark would be much worse.

She considered leaving Clara in the car while she dashed inside to switch on some lights, but the thought of leaving her baby in the gloom was disturbing, and she decided to leave the baby bag and purse instead.

Decision made, she unclipped Clara's carrier from the car seat and hooked it over the crook of her arm. She was gratified when the baby didn't so much as whimper, and she grabbed her house keys and phone, switching on the device's flashlight to light the way. There was an overgrown garden between the carport and the path to the house, and she ducked and weaved her way through there—shuddering at the possibility of spiders—before thankfully setting foot on the path.

She screamed when a huge figure loomed ahead of her in the darkness.

"I have Mace!" she lied in a high-pitched voice after her scream petered out. Clara immediately started crying.

"Libby, it's me." The deep, dark, instantly familiar voice that resounded into the black night was unwelcome, to say the least. Libby screamed again, the sound rife with frustration instead of fear this time.

"*Stop* that, for God's sake. You'll have the neighbors out to see what all the fuss is about."

"Good, let them come," she said, hearing the near hysteria in her voice and not caring. "Let them call the cops. You're trespassing, and I want you gone. *Right now!*"

She gently rocked the carrier, trying to bring the baby's crying under control. She lifted her phone light directly into his pale face. He winced when the light hit his eyes, and she felt a petty surge of satisfaction at the morsel of discomfort her gesture had brought him.

"We need to talk."

"I have absolutely nothing to say to you."

"Libby, please."

"Why are you here? *How* are you here? Who told you how to find me?"

There was a long pause as he continued to grimace in her general direction, his eyes slits to protect himself from the light.

"I have money and resources. I've known where you are for months . . ." He hesitated before continuing, "For four months, to be exact."

"Well, then *why* are you here?"

"Can we discuss this inside?"

"I don't want you in my house."

He compressed his lips in that way he had when he was trying to refrain from speaking his mind. An expression with which she was much too familiar. It used to bother her back when she cared about what he was thinking. He opened his mouth as if to say something, then changed his mind and swallowed back the words.

Oh, wasn't he just the model of restraint tonight? Well, Libby had no such reservations and felt a sense of complete liberation when she unleashed the torrent of resentment and fury that had been roiling away just beneath the surface for much longer than the four months since she'd left him. A lot of her anger had been tamped down during her pregnancy, when he hadn't offered a single word or gesture of support. The excuses she had made on his behalf . . . she was disgusted with herself for not speaking up sooner. But now he was here, in the flesh, and she could finally let him have it. With both barrels.

"You're a vile, disgusting excuse for a man, Greyson. I want nothing more to do with you. I don't want my baby within a hundred miles of you. And even that seems too close. I don't want you here, contaminating our lives with your toxic presence. You don't get to come here and . . . and . . . whatever the hell *this* is. I don't know what you want, I don't *want* to know what you want. I want you *gone*."

"Libby, I understand why you feel that way. But I thought . . ."

Clara's crying was escalating, and Libby's rocking increased agitatedly.

"Yes, I know. Thought you were infertile, right? And I'm supposed to—what? Feel sorry for you? Understand your cruelty? *Forgive* your cruelty? Am I to take it that you've had that paternity test done? You know she's yours, am I right? Is that why you're here? Because let me tell you, mister, you have no moral right to my child—I will not allow you access to her just because you now believe you're her father."

"I haven't had any paternity tests done."

That made her pause, but not for long.

"I don't care," she decided. "I *don't* care. Go away. Back to your diamond-encrusted ivory tower. Leave us alone. We don't need you."

"I know you don't. But . . . maybe I need you?" The soft voice, the hesitation, and the actual words all combined to add fuel to an already-raging fire. Oh man . . . seriously? He was going to play *this* card?

"Greyson Chapman doesn't need anyone. You're an island, with your own government, your own wealth, and your own natural resources. You need us as much as you need more money, which is not even a little."

"That's not true." He tugged at his already-loosened tie. She had only seen him this disheveled and out of sorts once before. And that was on the day he'd so thoroughly renounced both her and his own child. The memory made her jaw clench until her teeth ached, and she fought back the urge to scream yet again.

"I've been consulting with a divorce lawyer," she said, forcing calmness into her quivering voice. Clara's cries had become near shrieks, and she needed to get rid of him so that she could take care of her baby. "You'll be served papers very soon. Sign them."

"Libby, I know I fucked up," he said softly. She could see sweat beading on his forehead and in the stubble above his beautifully curved upper lip. He was incredibly pale and looked thinner than when she'd seen him last. His suit—usually immaculately fitted—looked too roomy on his broad, loose-limbed frame.

"This was more than a fuckup, Greyson," she said. "You spent seven months hating me, resenting me, thinking I was a cheat. *Seven* months! My pregnancy wasn't the easiest—I needed you. And you were never there. And the worst thing was I made all these stupid excuses for you. I didn't see the truth until it was too late. You hated me, hated my baby . . . because you thought she was someone else's, while thinking that I was a conniving, cheating slut."

"I thought . . ."

"Yes, yes." She waved her free hand impatiently, the cell phone light bouncing wildly in the dark before coming to rest on his face again. "Infertile. And yet when I announced my pregnancy, instead of doubting your original diagnosis, you just immediately assumed the worst of me. Maybe, just *maybe*, you should have had yourself retested instead of instantly thinking that the woman who was a freaking virgin before you charmed your way into her bed cheated on you. Within just weeks of our first time."

"I have a lot to make up for."

"Let me just stop you there. You have nothing to make up for, because there won't be any 'making up' here. We're done. In fact, I'm not sure we ever started. Our marriage was a farce from beginning to end. I see that now. Please leave. I have to get *my* baby in out of this cold."

She put deliberate emphasis on the possessive pronoun.

"I have nowhere to stay," he said softly, and she laughed at that bit of nonsense.

"A man like you always has somewhere to stay, Greyson."

"The hotel is fully booked."

"And you assumed what? That I'd let you stay *here*? Don't be ridiculous." She shook her head and stepped around him, bracing herself in case he chose to touch her. But he let her pass without any interference, and she released a tense breath as she continued on her way to the front door.

She unlocked the door and stepped inside with a relieved sigh. Instead of switching on the porch lights as she'd originally intended, she twitched the lacy curtain over the door's glass panel aside and watched as he stood there for another long, endless moment. Just staring at the front door. Finally, he scrubbed a weary hand over his face, and his shoulders slumped as he slowly turned around and walked down the darkened path toward the parked car that she hadn't even noticed as she'd driven up to her house. She would have to be more vigilant in the future.

Her phone buzzed, and she looked down. It was Tina. She was tempted to ignore the call, desperate to calm her agitated baby down, but curiosity got the better of her.

"Hello?"

"Be warned," her friend's breathless voice said urgently. "The Twisted Twins are in town! Harris just showed up at my door."

He *had*? Why was Harris in town? Was he here to offer support to his douchebag brother? And why go to Tina first?

"I know," Libby responded. "Greyson was just here."

"Fuuuuuuuuudge! What did he say?"

"I don't care what he wanted to say," Libby said defiantly. "I told him to shove off and never come back."

"Good girl," Tina said firmly.

"Why was Harris there?" Libby asked curiously.

"Ugh, I'll tell you tomorrow. I'd rather not go over all of that again right now."

"Okay. Sleep tight."

"Are you okay, Libby?" Tina asked, her voice brimming with concern. "Do you need me to come over?"

The offer brought tears to Libby's eyes, and she blinked them away impatiently. These moments of unwavering friendship meant the world to Libby, but Tina confused her. How could someone be so kind and considerate one moment and then completely flaky and unreliable the next? She never knew if she was going to get her best friend or some other version of Tina. The version who didn't want to be around her baby and who couldn't be trusted to do the simplest of tasks. Tasks imperative to the survival of their business.

Sometimes it felt like she was surrounded by unreliable people. The only one she could truly rely on to be completely consistent was Harris. And even that usually dependable relationship was floundering a bit after everything that had happened between her and Greyson. Even though he hadn't said as much, she knew that Harris's loyalties had to be split between her and Greyson. And that had to be placing a great deal of strain on him as well as their friendship.

"I'm fine," she assured Tina quietly. "Just going to get the munchkin changed and into bed. See you in the morning."

# Chapter Four

Greyson settled behind the wheel of his luxurious rental car and swore long and hard. He had flown up to the Garden Route. In the company helicopter, with his brother sitting in aggrieved silence across from him. Harris had already been seated on the chopper by the time Greyson had boarded and had proceeded to ignore him on the short flight over.

Greyson resented his brother's intrusion but at the same time couldn't really blame him for coming. He knew the other man's actions were a pointed indication of his loyalty toward Olivia. Greyson understood he had lost any semblance of allegiance from Harris, but having the other man there and squarely in Olivia's corner stung. A lot.

And then when Harris *had* deigned to speak to him, it had been to offer unsolicited advice. Greyson had ignored him, not needing to be reminded—yet again—of how much better Harris thought he knew *his* wife. Harris had advised him to proceed with caution, and Greyson had chosen to go straight to her house. Preferring a no-nonsense approach.

But of course he had scared her, lurking in the shadows like a stalker. After four months apart, he had been desperate to see her. To see Clara. And both had welcomed him with screams of anger and dismay.

"Shit." The word contained little heat, laden instead with weariness and disappointment. He dug out his phone and did a quick search of local hotels and B and Bs, his eyes occasionally drifting back to the still-dark outer facade of Libby's ramshackle old house. The place had a large, overgrown garden, full of thigh-high sedges, bottlebrush bushes, a couple of bare apple trees, and assorted other fynbos plants. The rest of the space was wild with weeds.

The building looked old and drafty, like the next strong gust of wind could blow it over. He had seen pictures of it, of course, but it was much worse seeing it in person. He hated that she lived in that house. Wanted to swoop in and drag both her and Clara back home where they belonged.

"Motherfucker," he swore again, a frantic internet search later. The word was ugly and unfamiliar on his tongue. He didn't like using profanity, finding it base and unnecessary. Words could excoriate without the speaker resorting to the lowest common denominator, as Olivia had so succinctly proven earlier. He preferred to use the barest minimum of words required to get his point across. He had never felt comfortable getting caught in any type of extended personal conversation with people. Unless it was business related, he never quite knew what to say. Small talk was meaningless, and he had never gotten the knack of it. Only with Olivia had he ever felt remotely able to overcome that social stumbling block.

Lately, he found that resorting to a good old-fashioned swear word now and then proved quite satisfying on occasion. This wasn't such an occasion. No amount of swearing would alter the fact that there was no accommodation available for miles around. Not in this town and not in any neighboring towns.

He dropped his head back against the headrest, tempted to just curl up and go to sleep right here . . . but he knew it was just a matter of time before Olivia called the cops on his stalkery ass.

He groaned and covered his face with one hand, his phone still clutched in the other.

"Damn it." The words were milder—more familiar and completely resigned. He lifted his hand from his face and brought up his brother's number.

He stared at it for a while before pushing the call button. Harris answered almost immediately.

"Yeah?"

"There are no vacant hotels, motels, or guesthouses in this fucking town," he said gruffly. Yet another coin for the swear jar. This was getting too easy.

"Libby didn't welcome you back with open arms, then?" Harris asked smugly, and Greyson's jaw clenched as he sought to control his surge of temper. When he didn't respond to Harris's question, his brother asked, "What did you think was going to happen, Greyson?"

This time his hand clenched into a fist on his thigh. Harris sighed. He sounded tired.

"I rented a flat," Harris murmured, and Greyson sagged in relief, recognizing the quietness in Harris's voice as an acquiescence that Greyson damned well knew he didn't deserve. "It has two bedrooms. You can have the spare room if you want. But the place is small, so you're going to have to resign yourself to seeing more of me than you'd probably like."

Greyson's eyes drifted back to the house. The interior lights were still off, but he knew she hadn't gone to sleep yet. She was probably watching and waiting for him to leave. He heaved a long, heavy sigh. He'd barely caught a glimpse of Clara. She'd been distraught, and he'd been to blame for that. Not exactly father-of-the-year material.

He needed to stay. He had to clean up the mess he had made. Had to be a father to the child he'd never believed he could have. And . . . if he was lucky enough, perhaps he'd even have another chance to be a decent husband to the wife he had so callously tossed aside.

"Where?" he asked and listened carefully as his brother gave directions to the place he'd had the foresight to rent, while Greyson hadn't thought beyond, *Must get to Olivia. Must see Clara.*

Greyson had always prided himself on being an intelligent man, but of late he'd shown a marked lack of anything resembling brainpower.

Greyson parked his car beside his brother's rented 4x4 and glared at the exterior of the shabby house in front of him. From what he could tell, the building had been divided down the middle to create two dwellings. It wasn't much better than Olivia's house. But at least this one was a rental. His brother had rented the one on the right. The one on the left was dark and possibly empty. Greyson would call the landlord in the morning to see if he could rent it. A much more tolerable solution than sharing a space with his pissed-off brother.

He shook his head and thought of the pub he had driven past on his way here. He could use a stiff drink. But his fast-growing dependency on alcohol after Olivia had left had scared him, and he had stopped cold after a seemingly endless three-week bender. He couldn't remember much about that time and preferred not to dwell on it now, but his weakness had appalled him. And he was abstaining just to prove he could.

He got out of the car and grabbed his suitcase before making his way up the rickety porch steps. He didn't bother to knock, knowing the door would be unlocked, and strode into the house with what he hoped was much more confidence than he felt.

Truth be told, he wasn't at all sure how the hell this situation with his brother was going to work.

He cast his eyes around the interior quickly, assessing and finding it extremely lacking.

"This place is a hovel," he said and then winced inwardly at how arrogant he sounded. Perhaps not the most grateful of openers, considering his brother was doing him a favor.

"Yeah, well, you don't get to be choosy. The smaller room is yours. There may be some clean bedsheets in the linen closet in the hallway."

Greyson frowningly looked at the door Harris was pointing at. "I'd hardly call this a hallway." The place was tiny, and even at the best of times, he didn't think he and Harris would ever have been capable of getting along in such a confined space. God, he *really* hoped the place next door was vacant.

"Make yourself comfortable," Harris said, choosing to ignore Greyson's unintentional criticism, even though Greyson could see the flare of annoyance in his brother's eyes. "I'm off to bed."

He turned to walk away.

"Why did you come?" Greyson couldn't resist asking. He knew, of course, but he needed to hear Harris verbalize it.

His brother stopped and turned to face him again. "Libby. She seems happy here. Settled. You're going to destroy that happiness if you insist on . . ."

To hell with this. Harris and Olivia might be the "best of friends," but considering how much that friendship had intruded on his marriage, maybe it was time people started to remember that Greyson was her husband. Even if he didn't quite deserve the title at the moment.

"It's really none of your business," he interrupted Harris coldly, and the other man sighed, the sound harsh with impatience.

"You know that's not true," Harris argued. "Contrary to what you may believe, Libby is like a sister to me. I care about her well-being."

"But I'm your *brother*." Greyson couldn't quite keep the bitterness from his voice. Olivia's and Harris's loyalties had always seemed stronger toward each other than to Greyson, and he had always resented that. "You should care more about mine."

Harris laughed in his face at that, the sound containing equal amounts of genuine amusement and incredulity. And honestly, who the hell could blame him?

"Yeah?" Harris said, his voice still brimming with bitter amusement. "I think you lost the privilege of being called *brother* when you accused me of fucking your wife and fathering your child."

"I'm reconsidering my opinion," Greyson acknowledged stiffly, feeling a surge of resentment at his brother's words. His brother, who had spent more time with his wife during the first two months of their marriage than Greyson had. A situation that would have tested any sane man. But he forced that resentment back and kept his voice cool as he continued, "I acknowledge that I may have been hasty and unfair in my accusations."

"Big of you," Harris said sardonically. "So I can expect an apology soon, then?"

Greyson knew his brother deserved an apology—because no matter how much time Harris had spent with Olivia, Greyson should have trusted him. Trusted them both. Harris and Olivia had always been friends, and maybe if he had said something about how he felt, things wouldn't have escalated the way they had. But he didn't quite know how to say sorry for something so completely unforgivable. And God knew if he couldn't apologize to his brother, he didn't stand a chance in hell with Olivia, because she deserved more than apologies. She deserved nothing less than to have him standing in front of her barefoot on broken glass, begging for her forgiveness. And even that wasn't enough.

Not for the first time, the daunting task that lay ahead of him nearly made him turn tail and run. Or head for the closest bar, where he could drown his fear and anguish with more alcohol.

He was such a coward. A *fucking* coward. He blinked and tried to focus on the here and now with Harris.

"Is that what you want, Harris?" he asked, keeping his voice soft and controlled. "An apology? Will that fix everything? Make it all right again?"

Harris tilted his head and watched him for a long moment as he considered his question. Eventually he shook his head, and Greyson's heart sank.

"I don't know. But it's a step in the right direction." Harris watched him expectantly for a moment, but Greyson, never very good at expressing emotion, could find nothing further to say. Harris's face reflected cynicism and exasperation, and he shook his head before walking away, retreating to his room.

Greyson's shoulders slumped, and he picked up his bag. Best to get some sleep. He was going to need to keep his wits about him and his energy up. God knew he had an uphill battle ahead of him.

Libby couldn't fall asleep. She tossed and turned for hours, hating that she was allowing Greyson to upset her this much. She groaned and sat up in frustration, throwing the bedcovers off and pushing herself out of the bed. She crossed the short distance between her bed and Clara's crib and checked on her baby. It wasn't time for her feed yet, and she was sleeping peacefully, sprawled on her back, one chubby little arm flung up over her head.

Naturally Libby tried to sleep when Clara slept, but that was proving impossible tonight. She ran a frustrated hand through her bed-mussed hair and shuffled her feet into her fuzzy slippers. Then she padded into the kitchen and put the kettle on the stove top. Maybe some chamomile tea would help her relax enough to get some sleep.

She stood in the kitchen, impatiently drumming her fingers on the cracked Formica countertop closest to the gas stove while she waited for the kettle to boil. The wind was howling, and rain lashed against the kitchen window. A vicious stormy night, perfectly suited to her mood.

The kettle finally boiled, and she dropped a tagged tea bag into a mug before pouring hot water over it.

She dunked the tea bag in and out of the water in a restless up-and-down motion while she stared out into the black night. She didn't know what she was going to do about Greyson. She wasn't foolish enough to believe he would leave her alone, now that he was here. He would want to see Clara. He wouldn't be here if he didn't believe the baby was his. What had changed his mind was anybody's guess, especially since he'd said he hadn't had any paternity tests done. She refused to be curious about whatever the hell motivated him. All she needed to do was maintain her resolve to not allow him any leeway.

He didn't deserve it. And more to the point, she and Clara didn't deserve to be treated like second-class citizens *finally* good enough for his notice. In hindsight, so many things bothered her about their hasty marriage.

The secrets more than the distrust.

If he had truly believed he was infertile, he had married her without once considering how she might feel about possibly never having children.

Selfish bastard.

She thought back to the first time he had proposed. That should have been a strong indication of what she was letting herself in for. She had laughed it off at first, but after just six weeks, she had been unable to resist him. Stupid. So stupid.

Libby shook herself and stared down at her forgotten tea. She had been so lost in her memories that the tea had gone cold and the bag was completely submerged. She clicked her tongue and tossed the cold liquid down the kitchen sink. She briefly contemplated making another cup of tea, but Clara started fussing and then crying.

"All right, sweetie," she called, making her way back to the bedroom, where she lifted her crying baby into her arms. "Mummy's here. I know you're hungry."

She sniffed and grimaced.

"And stinky. Let's make you comfy first."

She deftly changed Clara, keeping up a soothing stream of nonsensical chatter throughout the process. Her concentration drifted as she went through the now-familiar routine, her mind still caught up in the past.

She and Greyson had seen each other exclusively for two months after that first night together. In London on business, he had extended his stay as long as he could while he wined, dined, and bedded her every day without fail. She had gone on the pill, and he hadn't used condoms again after that first night. They hadn't explicitly spoken about birth control, but she'd assumed that he expected her to be on the pill, since he hadn't bothered with condoms after their obligatory talk about sexual medical histories.

Now, of course, she knew the rat had simply assumed he couldn't have children and hadn't told her. No need for condoms when you thought you were shooting blanks. When she thought of how often he had spoken of marriage, pushing in that noncommittal way of his, she just about wanted to blow a gasket and punch something.

How could he in good conscience have gone into a marriage with her without disclosing something so vital about himself? She wasn't sure how she had gotten pregnant while on the pill, but she surmised that she had conceived shortly after their rushed civil-ceremony wedding. It had been a chaotic period, with them traveling from London back to Cape Town; she must have missed a day.

Thinking Greyson could not have children probably wouldn't have affected her decision to marry him. Career driven, Libby hadn't been immediately concerned with having children. Sure, a few years down the line she would definitely have wanted a couple. But she would have been happy to adopt if he had proven infertile.

All that was moot now anyway. Clara was here, she was beautiful, she was loved and wanted. At least by her mother. It just astounded her that Greyson hadn't immediately doubted his doctor's diagnosis after she had announced her pregnancy.

Libby had foolishly allowed herself to become more and more infatuated with him during those two months. Falling in lust, then like, and then love with him.

*In love.* With a man who had never truly told her anything about himself. Now when she looked back on those first few weeks, she could so clearly see herself believing that infatuation and intrigue were something more. Something real.

She had known nothing about him. Sure, she knew him intimately, knew what he liked in bed . . . but again, that was just what he *liked*. She had never been certain if he *loved* it or was blown away by it. He was great in bed. She had never found his performance lacking, but she didn't think he'd ever truly lost control of himself. Not even when he'd been buried inside her and at his most physically vulnerable.

If anything, that was when he was most guarded. As if he couldn't bring himself to let go and truly trust her with his body, heart, and mind.

Their marriage had been so flawed. But she had fooled herself into thinking it was real.

She shook her head, rocking gently back and forth while she listened to the soothing sound of her baby suckling contentedly at her breast. Libby was finally getting her life back on track; there was simply no place in it for Greyson and the emotional upheaval he would create.

Greyson woke up just after dawn. His head was throbbing, and his eyes felt gritty from lack of sleep. His entire body ached, the bed was ridiculously lumpy, and the room smelled rank, like something had crawled into the walls and died. His first order of business was to find a better place to stay. If not the place next door—which he doubted was an improvement on this flat—then somewhere. *Surely* this hole-in-the-wall town would have more to offer in the way of accommodation. In Greyson's experience, opportunities always presented themselves at the right price.

He sat up and stretched, trying to get the kinks out of his muscles. Maybe he'd go for a jog. Or to the gym. He had spotted one last night. Above the large sporting-goods store. He muttered a mild curse word beneath his breath when he remembered that he hadn't packed any gym clothes. Maybe he'd just buy something at the same store.

He got up, and his toes curled on the sticky, cold linoleum floor. *God.* It felt disgusting beneath his bare feet. He had only packed dress shoes. Not exactly appropriate for wearing around the house. He picked his suitcase up and dropped it on the bed, scrounging around for a pair of socks. He was an organized packer and found a pair almost immediately in the left-hand, lower side of the suitcase, where he always kept his socks and underwear. He tugged them on and tested them on the floor. Still gross, since the fuzzy cotton stuck slightly to the floor with each step he took. Nevertheless, it was better than having his bare feet on the revolting surface.

He didn't bother closing his suitcase again, instead opening his bedroom door and sucking in a bracing breath when a wall of cold air hit him. He was wearing long pajama bottoms and a T-shirt, his usual sleeping apparel, but it was no defense against the frigid cold of this place. He could see his own breath, for God's sake!

There was no sign of Harris, but the coffee maker had some coffee already brewed, and he made his way to the machine and gratefully poured himself a mug. He had his phone out, checking his messages, when he took the first sip and nearly spat it all over his screen.

"Damn it!" he muttered, glaring into the mug. The thick, black witch's brew was bitter and practically undrinkable. He scowled as he thumped the mug back onto the cracked kitchen counter.

He could hear voices coming from the patio. Harris's and a lighter female voice. He tilted his head as he tried to figure out why the voice sounded familiar.

*Martine Jenson.* Why would she be here? And why would she and Harris be speaking? As far as Greyson knew, Martine hated his brother. Justifiably so, considering what Harris had done to her when she was eighteen. There was no reason for them to be speaking . . . unless . . .

Could it be about Olivia? If it was, Greyson felt that he should be privy to said conversation.

He strode confidently to the door and dragged it open, his head turning to the swing on the right, where—shockingly—his brother and Martine sat side by side, deep in an amicable and intimate-looking conversation.

The amicability faded the moment the woman caught sight of him. She gasped, and her entire body tensed.

"What the hell are *you* doing here?" She turned her fierce glare on Harris and rephrased the question. "What's he doing here?"

"He needed a place to stay," Harris said, and Greyson took exception to the note of apology and pleading he picked up in his brother's voice.

"Good morning, Martine," he greeted her pointedly. She ignored him, keeping her eyes on Harris like Greyson didn't exist, and that just got his back up further. He did *not* appreciate being ignored.

"And you're letting him stay with *you*? After everything he's accused you of? After what he did to Libby and Clara?"

Harris had told her about that? Greyson immediately felt both defensive and unbearably mortified. Did that mean Olivia knew too? For some reason he'd never considered the fact that Olivia might know about his initial assertion that Harris was Clara's father. The thought of Olivia knowing about his awful accusation made something inside him shrivel up into an ugly ball of shame. How could he face her after that? Accusing her of cheating in the first place had been horrible enough. Falsely accusing her of cheating with *Harris* was unforgivable.

"He's my brother," Harris was saying, still sounding apologetic and defensive. And worse, ashamed. He was *ashamed* to have Greyson as a brother. That felt truly awful. "You can't hold that against me, Tina."

"Trust me, that's the *least* of the things that I hold against you, Harris," Martine said venomously, and Greyson wasn't so mired in his own self-pity that he didn't feel that blow on behalf of his brother.

91

Harris leaped to his feet. "For God's sake . . ."

Martine held up an imperious hand, halting whatever Harris had been about to say in its tracks. She got up, too, and regally swept from the porch, still not bothering to even acknowledge Greyson, before slamming into the other house.

Well, at least now Greyson knew what she was doing here. She lived next door. He wondered if Harris had known that before moving in here.

Convenient . . . for Harris. But super inconvenient for Greyson. No moving in next door, then.

*"Fuck!"* Harris swore vehemently as he made his way back toward the doorway, where Greyson still stood rooted to the spot. His face was a mask of anger and resentment as he slotted his hands over his hips and glared at Greyson. "You had to fucking choose that moment to come out, didn't you? She was actually *talking* to me for once."

He shoved past Greyson back into the house and thumped around in the kitchen for a short while before slamming his way into his room.

Greyson tilted his head back and stared at the corrugated metal of the porch roof, hating everything about this damned place and situation. He heard Harris leave the room and make his way to the bathroom, and after a few moments, the ancient pipes protested as the shower turned on.

Greyson sighed, feeling utterly exhausted. His life was a colossal mess of his own making, and he wasn't sure he possessed the ability to fix it.


Harris left soon after his shower, without saying another word to Greyson. Greyson puttered around the house for a while, going through kitchen cabinets in search of something to eat. All he found was a bottle of cheap red wine, one that he contemplated opening for an uncomfortably long time before shutting the cabinet door again, and a dried-up

orange from God knew when. After fastidiously getting rid of the desic-
cated orange, he aimlessly wandered around the tiny house looking for
something to do. He heard Martine's door open and shut at about nine
thirty when she left, presumably for the restaurant, and imagined that
Olivia would be on her way there too.

He wondered where Harris had gone and was tempted to message
his brother to ask. But he knew the man wouldn't reply. The recognition
of that fact made Greyson feel a little lost.

And a lot lonely.

Greyson had never before felt lonely, and it had taken him a beat
or two to even identify the curious emptiness in his chest as loneliness.
He took a shower, the water lukewarm after Harris's shower earlier, and
then walked around in underwear and socks for a while, reluctant to
drag on one of the many suits he'd brought along with him. They were
all carelessly flung over the back of the rickety chair in his room, still in
their garment bags. Unusual for him. He didn't like disorder. He had
briefly toyed with the idea of unpacking his suitcase and hanging up
his suits, but . . . an unfamiliar apathy, mixed with the belief that he'd
probably be moving from this house soon, kept him from doing so.

Still, he couldn't walk around in his underwear all day long, and
he definitely couldn't wear a three-piece suit in this tiny beach town.
Harris's bedroom door was ajar, and his duffel bag lay open on his bed.
After staring at the bag for a long time, Greyson determinedly strode
into his brother's room and rifled through his stuff.

The sportswear the other man had brought felt soft and a lot more
wearable than Greyson had ever thought possible. Before he knew it,
he had dragged on navy-blue sweatpants with a matching hoodie and
a pair of his brother's scuffed trainers.

He felt odd. Unlike himself . . . but curiously light and free.

He dragged his hands through his hair and considered his options.
For a brief moment he toyed with the idea of going to MJ's. Talking
to Olivia.

But he knew it wouldn't go well. He needed to know what to say to her, and right now he didn't have a clue. And after comprehending that she might know about his accusations to Harris . . . the thought of facing her was daunting.

In the end he withdrew to his room, shoved his suitcase to the floor, and curled up on the bed. He retreated into sleep mere minutes later.

# Chapter Five

It was a quiet lunch service, and while that was bad for business, part of Libby appreciated the easy pace because it allowed her kitchen staff to get into a comfortable working rhythm. A few of the cooks were left over from the former kitchen staff, but Libby had chosen her own sous-chef, butcher, and fish chefs. They had had a few trial runs earlier that week, practicing prep for some of the dishes Libby had created for the new menu, but nothing could really prepare a team for working together in an open kitchen for the first time. There had been a few hiccups last night, but because it had been a slower night, they had been able to smooth out the wrinkles, and they were running more efficiently today.

As head chef, Libby had creative license over the entire menu and made sure her kitchen ran like a well-oiled machine. They were getting there, and she was more than happy with her team.

They were halfway through lunch service, and Libby—whose passion lay in confectionaries—was in her happy place, at the dessert station. She turned to pick up her piping bag and froze in her tracks. For a heart-stopping second, she thought the tall, dark, gorgeous man standing staring at her with a tentative smile on his lips was Greyson.

But the crooked nose, so unlike Greyson's, and the loose-limbed relaxed stance, nothing like the rigid, military precision of her husband's posture, quickly identified him as Harris.

"Hey, Bug. I've missed you."

"Oh my God, Harris." She choked on his name before happily walking into his arms. He enfolded her in a bear hug, lifting her off the ground in the process.

"I've missed you too," she said into his shoulder, her voice muffled. They stood wrapped up in their embrace for a moment, happy to reconnect after such a long and emotional absence. Libby pushed at his chest after a few self-indulgent moments more, and he let her go. She wiped her damp cheeks with the backs of her slender hands and cast a self-conscious glance around the kitchen. The rest of the staff were pointedly keeping their heads down.

"What are you doing here?" she asked, her voice pitched low.

"The waitress said it would be okay if I popped in to say hi."

"Not in the kitchen, *here* in Riversend."

"I wanted to make sure my brother toed the line and didn't hurt you again."

She compressed her lips before looking around for Agnes Ngozi, her second.

"Agnes, continue prepping for dessert, please. I'm stepping out for a few minutes. Send for me if you need anything."

"Yes, Chef," Agnes responded in her usual unruffled manner. Libby appreciated the woman's calm demeanor; it projected an air of serene confidence that was invaluable in a busy kitchen.

Libby hooked her arm through Harris's and tugged him back into the restaurant.

"Where are you sitting?" she asked, and he led her to his table, where they sat down together. Libby rested her chin in her palm and stared at her brother-in-law for a moment, a soft smile on her lips.

"I'm really happy to see you, Harris, but you didn't have to follow him here," she said quietly, and he lifted and dropped his broad shoulders in a quick movement.

"I know, Bug, but more than you, I wanted *him* to know that I have your back. What did he say to you last night?"

"He didn't have the opportunity to say much of anything. I let him know that I wasn't too thrilled to see him." She sat up straight with a heavy sigh, her hands dropping to the table in front of her. She restlessly toyed with the silverware. "Harris, I don't want you to interfere."

"What?"

"You heard me," Libby said, her resolve deepening. Her marriage to Greyson was over—that was a given—but Clara complicated matters. The fact that he was here spoke volumes as to his intentions. He wanted more. Libby wasn't stupid; she knew that that "more" was probably Clara, or at least some kind of contact with her.

Libby needed to decide how much, if any, access she would grant him. Right now she had the upper hand; she could negotiate from a position of strength. But it would be best if she and Greyson figured this out without any external interference. She was only grateful that this "negotiation" would take place on her turf. She knew her husband well enough to know that he hated not having complete control over his environment and emotions. He was out of his comfort zone here, and she wanted that. She wanted him wrong footed.

Libby would have *loved* to deny him any and all privileges regarding their daughter; it was what he deserved. But realistically she knew that once lawyers and courts got involved, he would be allowed to be a part of their daughter's life, regardless of Libby's personal feelings on the matter. It would be best for Libby, for *Clara*, to find a solution that favored them rather than Greyson. And the best time to do that was now, while she had the upper hand. And she knew she did. She had seen it in his hesitation last night.

She had had a lot of time to think about what she wanted last night, and she knew the best thing for her and Clara was to allow him to be a part of the baby's life. No matter how much she hated that prospect.

That didn't mean she was going to make it easy for him.

"If the look on your face is anything to go by, my brother is in for a tough time."

"I can handle him," Libby said with a lot more confidence than she felt. "Thank you for being such a good friend, Harris."

"You kidding me, Bug? You're like my baby sister! There's nothing I wouldn't do for you."

"Would you like to say hi to your niece?"

"*Would* I? Does a duck cluck?"

"Not really," Libby said with a chuckle as she got up and led the way to the office.

"You know what I mean," he said, sounding disgruntled, and she laughed as she opened the door to the tiny back office. She halted when she saw Tina at her desk, and her mouth dropped open in surprise. She hadn't seen Tina in front, but she hadn't really expected to see her friend in the office. Not in the middle of the lunch service.

Tension seemed to come off both Harris and Tina in waves, and Libby winced inwardly at the awkward situation. Tina had attempted to talk to her earlier about Greyson, but Libby hadn't been prepared to answer questions about her estranged husband's unexpected appearance in town yet. It had completely slipped her mind that Tina had mentioned Harris coming around to her house last night, and now she wondered what that had been about.

Nothing good, if the atmosphere in the office was anything to go by.

"Tina," she said awkwardly. "I thought you'd be on the floor."

"I had to do some accounting," the other woman responded softly, immediately angling her laptop screen downward, which made Libby doubt the veracity of her friend's words.

"Harris wanted to say hi to Clara," Libby said, and Tina's lips lifted in a sickly imitation of a smile, her already-pale features almost ashen.

"That's nice." Tina's voice was faint and lacked any semblance of sincerity. Libby shifted her gaze to Charlie, who was watching everyone with lively curiosity in her pretty green eyes.

"Charlie, this is my brother-in-law, Harrison Chapman." Harris, who had been watching Tina intently, seemed to shake himself, and he offered Charlie a fleeting smile before focusing on Clara. His face was alight with tenderness.

"God, she's gorgeous," he said, sounding almost awed. "The pictures didn't do her justice. She's bigger than I was expecting."

His hands left his pockets, and he reached for Clara, who was asleep in her foldaway bassinet. He paused before touching her and looked at Libby uncertainly.

"Can I . . . is it okay if I hold her?"

"Of course it is, Harris," Libby said, lifting her sleeping baby herself and carefully handing her over into her uncle's strong, capable arms. He hugged her close and began to rock her. Libby felt a pang of regret that she had denied him this for so long. *Harris* hadn't repudiated his niece—he shouldn't have been punished for Greyson's mistakes. Neither should his parents. Or *her* parents, for that matter.

She watched as Harris whispered soft little nothing phrases into Clara's ears. He nuzzled and kissed and cuddled the baby, clearly in love with his niece, and Libby couldn't keep the smile from her face. She instinctively glanced at Tina, wanting to share the sweet moment with her. But she was shocked to see anguish and something close to hatred burning in her friend's usually gentle sea-green eyes as she stared fixedly at Harris. Her eyes were shining with unshed tears as she surged to her feet, rocking her desk chair with the violent motion.

"I have to get back to work," she said, her voice trembling, and Libby shook her head, alarmed by Tina's reaction.

"We'll be out of your hair in . . ."

"I'll see you later, Libby," Tina interrupted. She fled from the room, leaving a shocked silence in her wake.

Harris murmured a vehement curse word beneath his breath. Clara was starting to fuss, and Libby, still stunned by Tina's reaction, absently took her baby from him.

"Uh. I should get back to work," she murmured, and Harris gave Clara another kiss on her cheek.

"Right," he said, his voice filled with patently false cheer as his eyes drifted back to the door through which Tina had just exited. "And I'm starving, so I'd better get back to my table. I'll be in town for a while, Bug. I promise I won't interfere, but I need a vacation, and this is as good a place as any to hang out for a short while. Besides, I want to spend more time with my niece."

He gave Libby a quick hug and left abruptly. Libby's eyes dropped to where Charlie was very pointedly reading her e-book, obviously trying to mind her own business.

Tina's baffling behavior was becoming a real concern. She had tried to talk to her friend about Harris, about her strange behavior around Clara, and now she was starting to think Tina wasn't being honest about exactly how much buying and relaunching MJ's had cost her. While she gently rocked back and forth, humming softly to the contented baby, she tilted her head back and hated how much she resented whatever it was that Tina was going through. She felt selfish and hateful, but she really didn't want to have to deal with Tina's dramas in addition to her own stresses right now.

"Your mummy is a terrible best friend, sweetie," she whispered against Clara's soft hair, keeping her voice low so that Charlie wouldn't hear her. She would try to talk with Tina after the lunch service. Try one more time to discuss whatever was bothering her. Libby owed it to their friendship to try and figure out whatever the hell was going on with the other woman.

She gave her baby one more cuddle before handing her to Charlie and heading back to the kitchen.

Greyson was jerked out of a sound sleep by the sound of an engine idling and then stopping outside. He blinked blearily at his phone and was shocked to see that it was close to twelve fifteen in the afternoon. He had been asleep for nearly three hours. It was unusual for him to sleep during the day, and he felt groggy and out of sorts.

He yawned, stretched, and crawled out of bed like an old, arthritic man. He stood waiting in the living room, but when he heard no tread on the porch stairs, he frowned, wondering if he'd imagined the sound of the engine. He strode to the front door—wincing because he'd forgotten to put his shoes back on—and swung it open. He stepped onto the porch, surprising Harris, who was standing beside his 4x4 staring at Martine's front door. The other man's head turned toward Greyson, and his eyes widened.

"Greyson." His name emerged cautiously from Harris's lips as he slowly climbed the patio steps. Approaching Greyson as one would a wild animal. "You okay?"

He came to a standstill in front of Greyson, and damned if his nostrils didn't flare slightly as he inhaled discreetly.

*Shit!* Harris thought he'd been drinking. How mortifying. Yet another embarrassment brought about by Greyson's appalling lapse in control after Olivia had left. Harris had been aware of Greyson's fleeting entanglement with substance abuse. And Greyson hated that his brother knew about his weakness. But he knew that he owed Harris for taking care of the business and protecting Greyson's reputation during that time.

He swallowed down the humiliation and pretended not to notice Harris's concerned gaze sweeping up and down his body and face.

"Where have you been?" Greyson asked gruffly.

"To Knysna for a new mattress and then to the restaurant . . . to see Libby and Clara."

Greyson forced down the swell of bitterness at that revelation. The knowledge that Harris was free to see *his* wife and child whenever he wanted, while Greyson himself hadn't even been allowed much more than a glimpse of Clara last night, burned like fucking acid. He kept his face expressionless, batting away the urge to ask Harris how Olivia was today. He knew his reappearance in her life had come as an unpleasant and unwelcome surprise. But he didn't want to panic her or upset her. He just wanted to figure out a way forward from here.

"There's no food in the house," he said instead, and Harris's eyebrows lifted almost to his hairline. Not hard for him, when his hair was a shaggy mess that fell almost to his brows anyway.

"So go and get some groceries," Harris said, and Greyson blinked. Somewhat arrested by his brother's words.

*Get groceries? What?* To say shopping wasn't Greyson's forte would be understating it. He couldn't actually recall ever setting foot in a grocery store in his life before.

"Maybe later," he mumbled quickly. He closed multimillion-dollar deals every day of his life; he could damned well buy a few groceries. He turned back toward the house, and once inside, Harris's shocked voice broke the silence between them.

"Greyson, are you wearing my clothes?"

Greyson turned to face Harris again before casting a glance down at his body. He'd forgotten he was wearing Harris's stuff and couldn't tell if his brother was pissed off about it or not. Harris looked mostly confused and a little stunned.

"It was the closest thing available. I haven't unpacked my bag yet." More eyebrow lifting from Harris, and Greyson barely refrained from childishly rolling his eyes.

"You look like crap," Harris said, and Greyson fought hard to keep his expression neutral and his resentment from showing.

Of *course* he looked like crap! His life was in shambles, his wife hated him, and he hadn't even held his child yet. Did everybody just assume Greyson was fine with that? He wasn't *fucking* fine! Why the hell should he *look* fine?

"Fantastic," he said, resorting to facetiousness and self-directed humor. "Nice to know I look like I feel."

Harris stared at him like he'd never seen him before.

*Now the fuck what?*

"What?" he asked, swiping at his nose for good measure. "What's wrong?"

"Nothing. I just thought you'd completely lost the ability to laugh at yourself is all."

Of course he'd thought that. Nobody really understood Greyson. Some days he barely understood himself.

"Yeah, well, when your only options are laugh or—" *Cry?* Greyson couldn't believe he'd been about to say that. He clamped his mouth shut and cleared his throat uncomfortably. He directed his eyes down to the floor, not wanting to see his brother's reaction to that revealing lapse.

"Anyway, when your options are shit," he awkwardly rephrased, "it's best to choose the path of least resistance."

"So what are your plans, Greyson?" Harris asked, his voice surprisingly gentle, and Greyson's gaze swung upward to meet his brother's intent stare. "What do you intend to do here?"

*Get them back,* was his instinctive first thought. But he knew that that was easier said than done.

Lunch service was in full swing, and the kitchen staff had a natural rhythm going. Libby was ecstatic with the way her team was working together and was happy to loosen the reins for a bit to let them do their thing while she focused on desserts for the rest of service. She was absorbed with that when Ricardo, the restaurant manager, walked into the kitchen looking completely flustered.

"Chef Libby, a word, if you don't mind."

Irritated with the interruption, Libby glared at the man before nodding to one of her underchefs to take over with desserts, not wanting to disturb Agnes, who was overseeing the rest of the kitchen. She led Ricardo toward the walk-in freezer, where it was less busy.

"What's wrong?" she asked with barely leashed annoyance.

"We're running out of napkins."

"*What?*" she asked in disbelief. Interruptions were irritating. Unnecessary interruptions pissed her the hell off. "Ricardo, take that kind of stuff to Tina. Unless we have a complaint about the food, there's absolutely *no* reason for you to be back here."

"That's just it—she's not here, and I can't reach her."

Libby stared at him for a long, uncomprehending moment, and he shifted awkwardly from foot to foot. Ricardo, a handsome, debonair, compact figure of a man who generally exuded competence, looked wholly uncomfortable.

"She's not here?" Libby repeated slowly, not quite understanding. "*Tina?* Tina's not here, is what you're telling me right now?"

"Yes, Chef," Ricardo said with a nod. "She left about forty minutes ago. She seemed upset."

Forty minutes ago? Just after Harris had dropped by the office.

"And you tried calling her?"

"She's not answering," Ricardo said.

"Okay. I'll try her; maybe she's on an errand or something. Meantime, you figure out what to do about the napkins. You're the manager—I'm sure you'll find a solution."

"Yes, Chef." He turned away, and Libby followed him out and headed toward the office. Charlie looked up from her books with a quizzical smile, Clara fast asleep.

"Hey, Mrs. C. Clara's fine. Sleeping like . . . well, like a baby," the girl said with a soft laugh.

Libby nodded distractedly. Her eyes went to her baby's sweet, peacefully sleeping face for confirmation before tracking around the office in search of some clue as to why Tina wasn't there. "Did Tina say where she was going?"

Charlie's eyes looked troubled at the question, and she shook her head. "I think perhaps Ms. Jenson just needed a little quiet time. Clara was crying and resisting the bottle. She was hungry and a little cranky. And it took a while to settle her down and get her to feed. I would have called you if she fretted too much, but she eventually took the bottle with less fuss than last night."

"Tina left because Clara was crying?" Libby asked flatly, and Charlie's eyes widened in alarm.

"I mean, I thought maybe she was just stepping out for a few minutes, but she's been gone awhile. So maybe she had something else to do?"

"Maybe," Libby said absently, not wanting the girl to think she'd caused any trouble, but seriously, what the *hell*? This arrangement was not going to work if Tina bailed every time Clara cried. Which, now that Libby thought about it, Tina had been doing since Clara's birth. She glanced at Tina's desk and noted that the woman's laptop was still there.

"Okay, thanks, Charlie. Did you get some lunch yet?" she asked, her mind still working overtime; she barely heard Charlie's affirmative response. She smiled down at her peacefully sleeping baby and stroked her head with a gentle finger.

"I'll see you girls later, okay?" she said, and Charlie nodded, her eyes back on her textbooks.

Libby exited the office and dragged her phone from her smock pocket, brought up Tina's number, and called. It went straight to voice mail. As did the next three calls.

This was definitely *not* cool. How could she just walk out in the middle of lunch service? And *what* was her problem with Clara?

The more Libby tried to reach Tina, the more pissed off she got. Where the hell are you? she texted. No response.

She shook her head and shoved the phone back into her pocket. Yesterday, when Tina had looked so vulnerable and terrified, Libby had been willing to give her the benefit of the doubt. But it was really hard to continue making excuses for her when she pulled shit like this. Tina might not give a crap about this business, but Libby had a kitchen to run and didn't currently have time for whatever was going on with her friend.

Greyson had stopped by a men's apparel store for some casual clothes before coming to the sporting-goods place. It was massive, with every kind of sportswear and equipment one could possibly need or desire.

He wandered from aisle to aisle, piling his cart full of any comfortable-looking outerwear that took his fancy, before finally heading to the checkout. When he got there, he noticed that the place seemed uncommonly empty. He had dismissed any attempts of help from the salespeople, preferring to browse without interruption, and now he noticed that none of them were around anymore. And there didn't seem to be any other customers either.

There was one checkout counter open, and it was manned by a huge guy, who topped Greyson's six feet and three quarters of an inch by about two inches. But it was more than just his height that made him massive; he was powerfully built, and Greyson, who was by no means a slouch when it came to fitness, felt like a twig compared to the guy.

"Hey," Greyson muttered while he unloaded his goods onto the counter. "Where's everybody?"

"We closed about half an hour ago. Staff's gone home. Half days on Saturday."

"How long have I been here?" Greyson asked, startled by that information. He was pretty certain the place had been open when he'd walked in. Of course it had; how else would he have gotten in?

The other guy's mouth twitched slightly. "About forty minutes."

Greyson stared at him in disbelief. "You should have said something."

The man shrugged in response to that. "No harm done." He sorted through the many items Greyson had offloaded onto the counter but didn't comment on the—now that Greyson looked at it—ridiculous amount of sportswear.

"Uh, I noticed you have a gym."

"Hmmm," the man rumbled, his eyes on his task.

"Do I need a membership card or something?"

The guy's piercing green gaze lifted to Greyson's. "Moving to town?"

"Not really, but I may be here awhile."

"Spencer Carlisle." He held out his hand, and Greyson, bemused by the unceremonious introduction, took his hand in a firm handshake. Since the store was called Carlisle Sporting Solutions, this guy had to be the owner.

"Greyson Chapman," he responded with equal brevity.

"A flat fee will cover three months."

"How many visits?"

"Unlimited."

Greyson nodded. That seemed like a good deal. "I'll come by on Monday to sign up. Do all the other businesses in this town close at one on a Saturday?"

"Grocery store and hardware store will be open for another couple of hours." He finally finished ringing up and bagging the mountain of clothes and whistled appreciatively at the final total.

Greyson handed over his card, and once their business was complete, he nodded at the man. "Thanks for staying open."

"Worth it," Spencer said with a quick grin. He didn't appear to be a man of many words, which Greyson could appreciate. "Where are you staying?"

Greyson told him, and the man winced. "Place is a dump."

"I know."

"My sister-in-law's house is available for rent."

"I didn't see any other vacant places when I was looking for short-term rentals."

"Word of mouth only. You interested, contact the vet, my father-in-law."

Oh, Greyson was definitely interested. He couldn't wait to get out of that hovel and now wondered if Harris had chosen it solely because Martine lived next door.

"Sounds great. Thanks. I'll see you on Monday."

The man nodded and unlocked the front door to let Greyson out.

It was bucketing down by now, and Greyson dashed for his car, dumping his packages with the other pile of shopping in the back. After he pulled away from the curb, he headed downtown, then cruised slowly past MJ's, hoping to catch a glimpse of Olivia. He seriously considered going inside to talk to her again.

He shook his head and drove to the grocery store instead. He passed the hardware store on the way, and a plan started to formulate in his head.


Tina wasn't there at the start of dinner service either. Now more concerned than angry, Libby tried to reach her again. She couldn't leave to go check on Tina, so she kept sending increasingly anxious messages.

Finally, just after seven, her phone rang, and she was relieved to see her friend's name on the screen.

"Tina? What the hell? Are you okay? Where are you?"

"Hey, Libby. I'm so sorry. I came home to do some work, and I fell asleep. My phone died, so I got none of your messages until now."

Libby drew in a deep, calming breath at her friend's response. Her friend's *lying* response. How could she have gotten any work done when her laptop was still in the office? And she'd been *sleeping*? Sleeping while they worked through two services without her? What in the actual—?

"Charlie told me you left when Clara wouldn't stop crying," Libby said, inserting some serious frost into her voice as she finally reached the end of her tether.

"I need to . . . I'm sorry. I needed to concentrate."

Libby squeezed her eyes shut at that response. Hating the way it made her feel. The resentment, anger, and hurt. Clara had already been rejected by her own father. Tina purported to *love* the baby, but this didn't feel like love to Libby.

"I'm sorry I left," Tina continued when Libby swallowed back the angry words she longed to toss at the woman. She felt like a protective mother bear with a wounded cub. She wasn't prepared to subject her baby to any further negativity. "I'll be right over. God, this is so . . ." Whatever Tina had been about to say faded into nothing, and the silence hung awkwardly between them for another beat.

"I'll see you soon." Libby knew she sounded cold, but she wasn't prepared to pander to any more of Tina's weird behavior.

"Fifteen minutes," Tina promised before disconnecting the call. Libby shook her head and shoved her phone back into her pocket before focusing her attention back on her kitchen. It was up to her to make up for Tina's complete lack of professionalism. She wasn't sure what she was going to do, but she knew she could no longer have her baby around Tina's negative energy.


She was busy garnishing a dark chocolate mousse when she heard Tina's timid voice coming from behind her nearly twenty minutes later. Libby's head snapped up, and she pinned her so-called friend with a cool look before calling Agnes over to step in, interrupting whatever lame apology Tina had been in the middle of uttering.

She was blindingly furious and strode toward the back doors that led to the alley, not bothering to check if Tina was following her.

Two of the busboys were sneaking a smoke, and since she hadn't authorized the break, she glared at them angrily. They both paled, apologized, and rushed back inside, leaving the two women alone in the well-lit alley.

"I'm sorry about earlier," Tina said, and Libby folded her arms across her chest, unimpressed with her words.

"Having Clara in the office is clearly not working," she said, cutting to the chase and choosing to ignore Tina's apology. "I'm trying to find another solution."

"No. Libby . . . that's not necessary. I just . . ."

"Tina, it's not fair that you have to work with a crying baby in your space."

"And it's not fair that you have to move your infant daughter to a place where you won't be close to her. We can make this work. It's only day two. We'll all get used to the arrangement."

She was saying all the right things, in the sincerest of voices, but Libby was not buying it.

"Like you got used to having us staying with you that first month?" she asked pointedly, and Tina looked stunned by the question.

"I . . ."

"It's obvious you're not too fond of babies, Tina," Libby interrupted firmly, refusing to soften at the utter devastation she saw in Tina's eyes. "And that's okay . . . but I'd rather have Clara around people who love and enjoy her."

Tina reeled back as if absorbing a blow and sucked in a harsh, stunned breath. She blinked rapidly, her green eyes bright with tears.

Libby nearly apologized, but she bit back the words. She had a baby to consider now, and Clara's needs would always come first.

"I do love her," Tina whispered, looking utterly devastated by Libby's words. But how could Libby believe her when Tina had never shown any indication of love or affection for Clara? Instead, she had gone out of her way to avoid being in the same room as the baby.

"It's not just Clara," Tina admitted quietly. "It's all babies, Libby. I can't be around them."

Was that supposed to make it better? It didn't; it made it so much worse. And it merely served to confirm Libby's belief that the woman she considered her best friend found being around her baby a burden. Which was so hard to believe, since Tina had once seemed to adore babies.

"What happened to you?" Libby asked angrily. "You wanted to be an obstetrician, for God's sake. And now you can't even stand to *look* at my baby."

"I *do* love her," Tina said, looking like she was trying to convince herself more than Libby. "She's beautiful."

"It's okay, Tina," Libby said dismissively, needing to get away from the woman and this conversation as quickly as possible. Because it was *not* okay. She didn't understand this. She *wanted* to understand it, but unless Tina chose to be more forthcoming about what had happened to her, Libby feared their friendship was teetering on the brink of disaster.

She stood for a moment, hesitating, as she stared into her friend's devastated face. She felt herself softening in the face of all that misery. She teetered on the brink of begging Tina to confide in her, to talk to her and explain what was going on. But she knew that the middle of dinner service wasn't the time or place. One of them needed to be a leader here. Needed to be strong for the sake of their business. And that person was clearly not going to be Tina.

She shook her head, irritated with herself for lingering out here for so long. There was work to be done.

"I'll figure something out," she said, before reluctantly turning and walking back toward her responsibilities.

She didn't know how she got through dinner service. But it was another quiet evening, and the last patrons left at eleven. The kitchen had taken final orders at ten thirty, and by the time the customers left, most of the kitchen staff had already headed home. Libby and Agnes were the last to leave the kitchen at just after eleven.

She bade the slightly younger woman good night and watched as Agnes met up with her good-looking husband, who was waiting at reception, and greeted him with a tired hug. The man, Dr. Mandla Ngozi, was the local pediatrician and Clara's doctor. Libby smiled and waved at him. He waved back before escorting Agnes out.

Libby threw back her shoulders and went to the office for Charlie and Clara. The baby was already bundled up in her cute little dinosaur hoodie, a gift from her uncle Harris. Tina was in the office, but after one quick look over at the desk, where the other woman sat staring up at her with mute pleading in her eyes, Libby diverted her attention on Charlie.

"You ready?" she asked the teen. Libby would be driving the girl home tonight, an arrangement she had cleared with Daff and Spencer Carlisle.

"I am," Charlie said with her ready smile. She gathered her backpack and books and waited while Libby grabbed Clara's bag and picked the baby up.

"Night, Ms. Jenson," Charlie called as she bounded from the room.

"Libby, please." Tina's soft, imploring voice halted Libby's movement for a moment.

"I'm exhausted, Tina," she admitted quietly. "It's been a hell of a day. I need to get Charlie home. And then I just have to switch off from all of this for a little while."

"I'm so sorry."

Libby sighed, her shoulders drooping. There was no mistaking the remorse in Tina's voice. But she honestly did not know what to do about that now, and part of her resented Tina for making what should have been a positive experience for both of them so damned stressful.

"I know that, Tina."

"Can we—" Clara's fretful little cry interrupted whatever Tina had been about to say, and she paled at the sound.

Again that extreme negative reaction to Clara's presence.

"I have to go. Good night." This time Libby turned and walked away without a backward glance.

The house was freezing. Clara was fretting; she needed a change and a feed, but Libby had to take care of the heating first.

"Okay, sweetheart," she murmured after putting Clara's baby seat down on the makeshift coffee table. She looked around for the air conditioner's remote, figuring the fastest way to warm up the place would be by blasting heat from the air-conditioning unit. The place had no central heating, and the old radiator heater, which had been left behind by the previous owner, had died last night.

She found the remote with a triumphant whoop, and when she turned the heat on, the air conditioner sputtered for a moment before running with a sickly whir. But at least it was working. Thank God for small miracles.

"Okay, bath time for you, munchkin," she told Clara, keeping her voice cheerful even though she felt like bawling her eyes out. Her day didn't look like it was going to improve much now that she was home.

For the first time, she looked around the shabby place and worried that she had bitten off way more than she could chew. The plumber still hadn't come to fix the pipes. The hot water worked . . . until it didn't, and—she sighed as she walked into the kitchen and stared at the wet floor in dismay—it was now apparent that the roof leaked.

Awesome.

"Just *awesome*," she repeated out loud, opening and closing cupboards to look for a bucket. She knew she had one. She had bought it just last week. She finally found it in the bathroom and carried it to the kitchen to place beneath the leak.

Clara was screeching by now, and abruptly overwhelmed, Libby stood in the middle of the kitchen, staring at the water dripping into the bucket. She covered her face with her hands and inhaled deeply, trying to keep it together.

"I'm coming, baby," she called soothingly, heading to the bathroom to fill the baby bath with warm water. She placed the pink-and-white plastic bath into the ancient claw-foot tub beneath the tap. The faucet sputtered when she opened it, and the water that emerged was a little brown with rust at first, before running clear. She held her hand beneath the stream, and thankfully, the water warmed after a moment.

"Thank God," she muttered before heading back to the living room for Clara, who was not a happy little camper right now. "Oh, sweetheart, I'm so sorry." Libby could hear the despair in her own voice as she lifted her baby into her arms. She carried Clara into the bedroom to remove her clothing.

The air conditioner was starting to heat the small house quite comfortably, which Libby was grateful for. She wrapped her plump, naked baby in a fluffy towel before heading back to the bathroom. The adorable, comfortable baby bath—a gift from Clara's paternal grandparents—was nearly full, and Libby tugged it away from the stream of water before reaching over to close the faucet.

Nothing happened.

"No, no, *no*," Libby moaned. "Please, come on!"

The spigot just kept turning without tightening, and the water continued to run. Clara's cries were escalating now, and feeling increasingly frazzled, Libby wasn't sure what to do. She glared at the relentless flow of water resentfully, attempting to rock Clara while not at all sure how to deal with this latest in a seemingly endless list of problems.

A loud knock sounded on the front door at that moment, and Libby bit back a juicy curse word at the intrusion. She knew exactly who that was. Seeing him again was inevitable, but of course he *had* to choose the absolute worst moment to show up. She'd been expecting him all day, and he came knocking after eleven at night. Closer to twelve, actually—it was way too late to be bathing Clara, she knew. But Clara was overdue for a bath, and Libby hadn't had much time to do it that afternoon, not after dealing with various crises at the restaurant.

She shook her head and swore softly beneath her breath. Then, still clutching a snugly wrapped Clara to her chest, she made her way to the front door. A quick glance through the peephole confirmed the identity of her unwelcome visitor, and for a brief moment she considered ignoring him, before bowing to the inevitable. Might as well just rip the Band-Aid off the wound.

She unlocked the door and swung it open to glare at her soon-to-be ex-husband furiously.

# Chapter Six

"It's late, Greyson," she stated unnecessarily, and he nodded.

"I know," he said in his usual quiet way. "I'm sorry. But I figured you'd be busy earlier."

"I'm busy now," she said pointedly, still rocking Clara, who absolutely refused to be soothed. Greyson's gaze dropped to Clara before shooting back up to Libby's face. The look had been almost furtive and reminiscent of the way Tina avoided looking at Clara.

He kept his eyes pointedly fixed on Libby's face after that one swift look down, and she frowned.

"We need to talk," he said softly. Libby had always found the quiet way he spoke appealing. The cadence of that deep, mellifluous voice was always gentle. He rarely raised his voice. Even at the hospital, she recalled now, when he'd been accusing her of the most horrid crimes against their marriage, his voice had remained soft and controlled.

"I don't want to talk to you," she said, feeling more and more ruffled. This was *not* how she had wanted their first real discussion about their failed marriage to go. She was supposed to have the upper hand, she was supposed to be in her comfort zone . . . instead he looked calm, unruffled, and she felt like she was splintering into a million different pieces.

"I'm aware of that, but you know we have to."

She chewed on her bottom lip before stepping aside to allow him in, only then seeing that it was still raining and that his head and shoulders were damp. She closed and automatically locked the door behind him. He brought with him the smell of rain, wind, and brine, combined with the delicious, familiar scent of the expensive aftershave he wore.

He moved into her living room, and the place immediately shrank around him. He had that effect on every room he entered. In the past it had made her feel safe; now she just felt claustrophobic. Her gaze raked over his body in confusion.

He looked different.

"You're wearing jeans," she said, knowing she sounded as shocked as she felt. She had never believed she would see the day Greyson donned jeans. Yet here he was, wearing ripped jeans, trainers, and a fleecy gray *hoodie*. He still looked like Greyson, with that perfect carriage and flawless hair, but also fundamentally different. Aside from the uncharacteristic clothes, his jaw was blue with stubble, and he had dark shadows beneath his eyes.

"It seemed appropriate. No point wearing suits here."

"I didn't think you owned jeans," she said and then felt stupid for harping on about this. There were rather more pressing concerns at hand.

"I didn't until this afternoon. This is my first pair," he muttered. "My first hoodie too. Uh . . . why is . . . why is *she* crying?"

He kept his gaze glued on Libby's face when he asked the question, and for a second Libby had no idea to whom he was referring, since he never looked down at the wailing infant. Why wouldn't he look at her?

"She's hungry. And uncomfortable."

"Why uncomfortable? Is she . . . ," he asked, and Libby's eyes were drawn to the movement of his Adam's apple as he literally swallowed down whatever he'd been about to ask.

"Is she what?" Libby prompted him.

"Is she okay?"

"Why won't you look at her?" Libby asked curiously, fascinated by his seeming inability to look at the baby.

"I wasn't sure . . ." He halted again before blinking rapidly. An expression of shocking vulnerability fleetingly crossed his handsome face before he asked, his voice even quieter than usual, "Can I? *May* I?"

Libby's head tilted to the left as she tried to figure that out. "Can you what?"

"Look at her?" His voice shook, and her brows met.

"I think you should," she said, keeping her own voice quiet. She watched as—after receiving her go-ahead—his gaze dipped to the baby's wet face before darting away again. His eyes tracked back to the angry, sad little visage as if irresistibly drawn to it and lingered a little longer. This time the blue gaze lifted to Libby, and his face took on an expression of bemused wonder before he looked at Clara again, this time taking in his fill.

"She looks like you," he said, his voice dusted with the same wonder she had seen on his face.

"So I've been told," Libby said curtly, not wanting to be moved by his reaction to the baby. "I have to bathe her, but—"

*Crap!* She had completely forgotten about the running faucet and dashed into the bathroom, vaguely aware of Greyson following her. She swore furiously when she saw that the tap was still merrily flowing into the unplugged bathtub. Clara's bath was waiting, and Libby was tempted to just wash the baby despite the broken tap. But it would be too messy.

"Why's the water running?" Greyson asked from the bathroom doorway, and Libby swore again, immediately feeling crowded by his larger-than-life presence.

"The faucet's broken. Fix it, will you?" She very much doubted Greyson, who wasn't any kind of handyman at all, could repair the problem. Still, she took a perverse pleasure in saddling him with a dilemma she *knew* he couldn't resolve.

"Meantime, I think I'll feed Clara and give her a wipe down. I'll bathe her in the morning instead." Libby liked to list things. Sometimes verbally, usually on paper or on her phone . . . it helped her remain goal oriented. Whether with long-term or immediate goals, a list kept her on track.

She took Clara into her bedroom and pointedly shut the door behind her, leaving him to sink or swim. She didn't particularly care which.

Greyson stood beside the bathtub in the cramped bathroom and stared at the doorway through which Olivia had just exited. He heard another door shut, and the sound of the baby's wailing became more muffled behind the barrier of the closed door.

They were both so beautiful. With her golden-brown skin that seemed to glow from within and her silky black curls, Clara definitely looked like her mother. But Greyson couldn't deny those dark-blue eyes.

*His* eyes.

His throat closed up, and he sat down on the side of the bath as he struggled to regulate his breathing. His fist clenched, and he thumped his thigh with leashed violence. He despised himself for what he had done, and everybody else did too . . . rightfully so. But he wanted to be a part of that baby's life. And he wanted Olivia back.

And Greyson, usually the man with a plan . . . had no idea how to get what he so desperately wanted.

He turned his attention to the gushing faucet and stared at it for a long, blank moment.

How the hell was he supposed to fix this? He didn't have a clue. He dug his phone out of his pocket, wincing a bit at the unfamiliar snugness of the jeans. He should probably have gone for something a little roomier. He wasn't sure how comfortable he felt in this unfamiliar garb, but he had wanted to seem more amiable. More like Harris, who appeared to be everyone's buddy.

Greyson knew he wasn't the most approachable of men. Especially not in the three-piece suits he enjoyed wearing. And yes, sometimes the suits felt like armor—a well-made suit was a formidable weapon in any successful man's arsenal. It inured one to the petty shit.

At least that was how Greyson always felt.

He felt naked in these clothes.

He shook his head, dispelling the foolish thoughts. Clara's heart-breaking cries had finally died down, and he could hear the faint, comforting hum of Olivia's voice as she spoke to the baby. He longed to go into that room and sit with them. Watch the baby feed. Watch his wife soothe and cuddle their child.

But he wouldn't be welcome. He had *this* task, and he was grateful for it, because while he didn't have a single damned clue how to solve this problem, at least she hadn't kicked him out.

Besides, he had a secret weapon: his phone and the world's most powerful internet search engine at his fingertips. He found a temporary solution in no time, but he needed a wrench, and because he had stupidly left the brand-new toolbox that he had bought for just such an eventuality back in his crappy room, that meant disturbing Olivia.

He left the bathroom and stood uncertainly outside her bedroom door, slicking back his still-rain-damp hair nervously before lifting his fist to rap on the door.

Her voice went silent, and there was a long pause before she responded to his knock.

"What?" she called, and he stared at the scarred wood of the barrier between them.

"I need a wrench," he said.

"Under the kitchen sink," she replied without hesitation. He nodded, then felt foolish because she couldn't see him.

"Thanks."

He moved to the kitchen, not seeing the bucket in the middle of the floor until the very last second. He swore and swerved to avoid it. The roof was leaking. This place was a bloody disaster. He hated the thought of Olivia and Clara living like this but knew that his stubborn wife would never consider allowing him to buy her a better place.

He found the wrench amid a mishmash of other mysterious tools. He wouldn't be able to explain the function of most of those under threat of death and dismemberment. He made fast work of closing the faucet after that and was inordinately proud of his accomplishment as well as the fact that he'd barely made any mess at all.

He heard the bedroom door open and sensed Olivia's presence at the bathroom entryway before she spoke.

"You fixed it," she said, her voice flat. He turned to face her, noticing that she had changed from jeans and a sweater into a pair of black yoga pants and a comfortable-looking slouchy white top that slid off one shoulder. Her soft, wavy black hair was swept away from her face in a high, sloppy bun.

He swallowed audibly at the sight of her. He remembered the first time he'd recognized her beauty. She'd been sixteen, and he'd been home from college for Christmas. Before that he'd never seen her as anything more than a pesky kid, but that year, he'd finally seen the exquisiteness in that delicately boned, heart-shaped face with its rounded, high cheekbones and wide, whiskey-colored eyes, framed by long, thick black lashes and accentuated with sweeping, perfectly arched brows. She had the prettiest button nose, almost too cute for the rest of the beauty in that face, but it matched the adorable dimples, which gave her smile an impish quality. Then there was her mouth, that full, luscious mouth that tasted like honey and kissed like heaven. He forced back a shudder as he recalled those gorgeous lips closing over his length and . . .

*Jesus* . . . this was not the time or place for these thoughts. But seeing her again stirred up so many memories. She was a contradiction in so many ways. Tall but delicate, she had the rangy athleticism of a long-distance runner but moved with the grace of a ballerina. Back when she'd been sixteen, he'd taken one look at her, still a schoolgirl, before turning around and walking out of his parents' home. He'd spent more time away from the house that vacation than at home with his family.

After that he had gone to great lengths to avoid her. Even after she'd reached adulthood, it hadn't felt appropriate to want the daughter of family employees. It wouldn't have been an equal partnership. He would have felt like *that* guy. The one who took advantage of his family's wealth and power to coerce the girl he wanted into sleeping with him.

But when he had seen her again last year, knowing that her parents had retired and she was an independent, career-oriented woman capable of making an informed decision about sleeping with him, all bets had been off. He had wanted her, he had known she wanted him, and that was it. He'd gone after her, he'd gotten her, and then he'd wanted to keep her.

He cleared his throat, aware of her staring at him in puzzlement when he didn't respond to her statement.

"I didn't fix it," he denied. "I merely closed it. It needs to be replaced."

She shut her eyes and shook her head tiredly. "Add that to the growing list of repairs, then." Her voice was heavy with exhaustion.

"Where's, aah . . . where's the baby?" he asked.

"*Clara* is in her baby seat, in the living room," she said, emphasizing the name pointedly. "She's been fed and changed and will probably doze off soon. Now's the time for you to say your piece and get it over with."

She turned and headed back to the living room, where she curled up in an easy chair and watched him as he followed and tentatively perched on the edge of the sofa. His eyes were drawn to the cooing baby, whose seat was on a small table, as she clumsily swept her chubby hands at the bright mobile dangling above her. She was making happy little sounds, gurgling and bubbling like a cheerful brook.

"What do you want, Greyson?" Olivia asked pointedly, and he looked at her, stunned by the directness of her question.

"You. Clara." Perhaps not the most appropriate of responses, considering the frigidity of her expression.

"You can't have us, so what's next?"

"Olivia, I know I fucked up," he said, and she nodded.

"You did." She didn't give him anything more than that.

"I'm trying to fix it."

"You can't."

"Olivia . . ." He tried hard to keep the misery he was feeling from seeping into his voice, but he wasn't sure he was successful.

"Greyson," she began in an unemotional, perfectly reasonable tone of voice. "This was no small thing. You don't get a do-over on something like this. And I'm not just talking about the night of her birth—I'm talking about the *months* and *months* of disinterest and absolute contempt before that. It was like being married to a ghost. You were never there. You couldn't have made your lack of anything resembling affection or concern for me, or *her*, any clearer. I don't want you in my life any longer, and if I could get away with it, I would prefer not to have you be a part of Clara's life either."

"For years I believed . . . I thought . . ." He shook his head, feeling ridiculously inarticulate, as he tried to clear his mind and formulate his thoughts. So much rested on what he said here and on how he said it. "I didn't think I would ever be a father, Olivia. I'd resigned myself to that, and . . . but here she is. So perfect. So absolutely, gut-wrenchingly beautiful, and against everything I'd ever thought possible, she's mine."

"No. She's *mine*," Olivia corrected him, her voice steady and cold, and he flinched in response to her words.

"I was okay with not having children. I'd had more than ten years to come to terms with that fact . . . but I'm not okay with it anymore. I have a daughter. I want to get to know her. To spend time with her."

"You have a daughter? How sure are you of that? What if you decide tomorrow that's she's not yours again?"

He deserved that; he knew he did. He absorbed the blow and gritted his teeth as he fought back the resultant swell of pain. "I know she's mine."

"How? You said you didn't have tests done. Why are you suddenly so certain?"

Did she know about the accusations he had aimed at Harris? Greyson couldn't be sure. He peered at her closely, not certain how to respond to her questions. He felt like he'd been dumped in the middle of a minefield and a step in any direction could lead to catastrophic consequences.

"I just am."

"That won't cut it, Greyson. We might as well stop talking right now if you're going to continue dissembling."

"Just . . . something Harris said," he said, still hedging, but at least this answer was within the same realm as the truth.

"What did he say?"

"He, um . . ." Greyson lifted his fist to his mouth and cleared his hoarse throat before continuing. "He said she had the birthmark."

"And that was enough for you?" she asked in disbelief. "You couldn't check that *before* coming into the room that day and blowing my life, and what was left of our marriage, to hell?"

It wouldn't have mattered, not when he'd thought his own brother was the father. But telling her that now would only make things worse. Greyson was staggered by the breadth of his stupidity. Everywhere he turned, he was confronted by yet another one of his dumb mistakes. So many missteps and bad decisions.

"Let's leave that for a moment and go even further back," she said, folding her arms over her chest, and his stomach roiled, knowing where she was going next. Yet again, he had no excuse. Nothing but sheer selfishness and stupid masculine pride.

"How could you marry me believing you were unable to have children? Don't you think that was something I deserved to know *before* I made my decision?"

Libby couldn't tell what Greyson was feeling. His face remained completely expressionless. He was the most frustrating man, and it made her want to scream. How dare he come in here with his half truths and his prevarications? Did he think she was so stupid that she was incapable of seeing through his deceptions? He might have a killer poker face, but she knew when he wasn't being honest. And she was getting sick of it.

"I have no excuse, other than I wanted you too badly to risk losing you."

"Yeah, no. That's *definitely* not gonna cut it," she said with a disbelieving little laugh. "I have no idea what alternate universe you're from, Greyson, but that's not how relationships work. You should have given me the opportunity to make my own decision. Stripping me of that power was almost as bad as accusing me of cheating months later and rejecting your own child. You're lucky I'm willing to talk to you at all, because quite frankly, you don't deserve any face-to-face time with me. I should have let my lawyers deal with this, but I'm affording you more respect than you deserve and way more than you ever gave me."

"I know." That was it. Just two words, emerging on the quietest of voices. It suddenly occurred to her that he hadn't uttered one word of apology for his actions four months ago, and she wondered about that. Was he too proud to apologize?

"Why did you want to marry me?" she asked suddenly, remembering the way he had pushed for marriage. He'd asked her often; it had been flattering how eager he had seemed to marry her. "I know it wasn't because you loved me. But I thought you—" She stopped speaking abruptly, not about to embarrass herself by admitting she'd hoped that he would eventually come to care for her in a more romantic sense.

She shook her head and continued with something a little less revealing, "At first I believed it was because of that broken condom, that you thought I was pregnant. But then two months passed without any sign of pregnancy, and you were still asking, and I wondered if it was out of some sense of misguided duty."

"Why did *you* marry me, if you didn't think I loved you?" he retorted, bringing the focus squarely back to where she would prefer it not to be. For the first time she heard a hint of defensiveness in his voice. How interesting. Why would he be defensive about this, when there were so many other, more serious issues on the table? She raised her eyebrows at him in disbelief.

"Are you seriously answering a question with a question right now?"

"I'm interested in hearing your response," he said, and she snorted in confounded amusement.

"I *don't* care. I asked you first."

"Will you answer my question if I answer yours?"

"Why are you hedging?" She was completely exasperated with this frustrating topic and couldn't keep the scowl off her face.

"It was time to get married and settle down," he said. "And I figured you were someone I'd known for years, we got along, and we were great in bed together. I thought it was a good fit."

*A good fit.* Such a Greyson thing to say. So damned logical and emotionless. She said nothing in response to that, and he held her gaze.

"Well?" he prompted her, and she lifted her brows.

"Well, what?"

"Why did you marry me?"

"Since it's not relevant to this conversation, it's not something I care to discuss right now." Especially since the truth was humiliating. She had stupidly allowed her infatuation to flourish into deeper and more real feelings for him. Then she had convinced herself that he would eventually come to love her.

They'd had two months of something resembling a real marriage, and even then, he had rarely been around during the first month. With him working such long hours, she had seen him only late at night, when he'd stumbled into bed to make love with her. The second month had been better; he'd been around more, and just when things had seemed to be settling into a pleasant routine, she had told him about her pregnancy. And that had been the end of that.

It had hurt so much when he had distanced himself. When he had moved in to another bedroom with only the flimsiest of explanations. His lack of interest in her pregnancy, his absence and coldness. All of that had hurt like hell, and she would be *damned* if she allowed him to see that now.

"I can fix that faucet in the morning," he said, changing the subject unexpectedly. Libby couldn't help it: she snorted at the thought of Greyson properly fixing something. He looked affronted by her amused response.

"What's so funny?" he asked softly, and Libby shook her head.

"I'm sorry. It's nothing. But you don't have to do anything; I'll have the plumber come in tomorrow and have it fixed."

"On a Sunday? That's going to cost the earth."

"That's my concern, not yours."

"Let me take care of the problem, Olivia," he demanded, sounding way too much like his old bossy self.

"How do you propose to do that, Greyson? By throwing money at it? That's how you fix all your problems, isn't it?"

His lips thinned seconds before he ducked his head, frustratingly hiding his reaction from her. He was always so good at disguising his visceral reactions, and back during those first couple of months of their marriage, Libby would have done anything to get a rise from him. Now, while it irritated her, she couldn't afford to care much anymore. What was the point in trying to figure him out anyway? Their marriage was over. She would leave it to the next woman to try and read Greyson.

Someone else could attempt to get under his skin, provoke him into honest responses, coax him into sharing himself. Libby had a child to raise.

Alone.

She swallowed painfully at the near-constant fear that resurfaced whenever she found herself faced with that reality. She wasn't sure she could do this alone. Not while trying to simultaneously restart her career and keep a restaurant afloat with very little help from the best friend who was supposed to be her partner.

Abruptly overwhelmed and feeling more than a little terrified, Libby pushed herself to her feet and walked toward her sleepily gurgling baby, ostensibly to check on Clara but really just to take a moment to compose herself.

"I meant I could attempt to fix the plumbing myself." Greyson's stiff voice spoke from behind her left shoulder, and she screwed her eyes shut and inhaled deeply in an attempt to calm her nerves while formulating her response.

"I'm pretty sure you have no clue how to fix the plumbing, Greyson," she said, giving his suggestion the curt, scathing dismissal it deserved.

"I solved the faucet problem earlier, didn't I?" he pointed out, seeming frustrated with her.

"It doesn't take a genius to figure out how to turn off a faulty tap." Okay, so maybe she was being bitchy, but she wasn't feeling very generous right now. Having him so close made her feel like her skin was wrapped too tightly around her body. "I would have done it if I hadn't been so preoccupied with Clara."

"There are other problems with this place, Olivia. Like the leaking roof," he said. His doggedness was starting to seriously annoy her.

"You should leave," she said, injecting a fair amount of additional frost into her voice.

"But . . ."

"Greyson, I don't need you for anything. Not anymore. I was curious about what you had to say, but I can't say it's blown my socks off."

"What about Clara?" His eyes, which had often flitted toward the baby during their conversation, drifted back to Clara and for an instant revealed such naked yearning it almost had the power to soften Libby toward him.

*Almost.* But not quite.

"Truthfully? I'd rather she never knows you. But I know you'll come in with your money and your lawyers and take what you want anyway. So I'm willing to discuss the matter with you."

"Now?"

"No. I'm exhausted. Clara and I should be getting to bed."

"Of course," he said, huffing a resigned little sigh. He pushed himself to his feet and joined her at the coffee table, his gaze fixed on Clara, who shifted her big blue eyes to the stranger standing beside the familiar figure of her mother. She stared at him fixedly, her mouth forming a pout and her forehead wrinkling. It was the face she made when she was deciding if she should cry or not.

"She has my eyes," he whispered, his voice filled with reverence. Libby didn't say anything in response to that. Clara kicked vigorously at the sound of his voice, the pout fading from her lips as she decided to reward the dark, pleasing timbre of his voice with a gummy smile instead.

Greyson's mouth widened as he responded with a delighted grin of his own. The smile was very similar to—if more toothy than—his daughter's. Greyson didn't smile like this often—usually they were pale, close-mouthed imitations of this gorgeous grin—and it completely transformed his face, taking it from austere and coldly handsome to breathtakingly beautiful in an instant. He looked approachable, warm, and eminently likable.

It was probably a good thing he *didn't* smile like this often. Because people would too easily be deceived into thinking he was a nice guy.

Cold and austere suited him. It accurately reflected the man beneath the handsome face and perfect body. Libby, who had been graced with a few of these rare smiles during their first two months of "courtship," had allowed herself to believe in its warmth rather than the more usual sternness of his features. She had been convinced there was something more there.

More fool her.

Watching him now, Libby tried hard to maintain a neutral expression, but she would have to have a heart of stone not to be affected by the sight of father and daughter meeting for the first time. And it looked like love at first sight. It made Libby feel like punching something when she thought of the time that had been wasted because of Greyson's stupidity. They could have been a family; father and daughter could have properly bonded even before birth. Greyson had robbed them of that opportunity, and it was lost forever.

"Would you like to hold her?" she found herself offering, surprising even herself with the question. His eyes jerked up to meet hers. They were wide with panic, hope, and what looked like longing.

"I-I'm not sure. What if . . . I mean . . . I've never held a baby before." His voice, usually so confident, was halting and unfamiliar in its timidity.

"You'll be fine," she said, bending to unclip the seat's safety harness. She picked up her happily cooing baby and held the active, wriggling bundle close.

"Cradle her the way you would a rugby ball," she instructed him.

"I've never held a rugby ball in my life," he said coolly, back to his usual arrogant and aloof self in an instant. Well, almost. His eyes were still trained on Clara, and his hands curled and uncurled restlessly as if he itched to reach for her.

"Seriously?" she asked in surprise, a little taken aback by his statement. "Not even at school?"

"I played lacrosse and tennis. And dabbled in cricket a bit," he said, and she cleared her throat. She remembered that. She used to watch him play. He had been a fantastic athlete, of course. He'd been fantastic at everything, studies and sport. Greyson had seemed incapable of doing anything less than perfectly.

"Well, just do what I'm doing. It's pretty instinctive. You'll manage." Because Greyson always did. Aside from their marriage, Libby was pretty sure he had never failed at anything. Which explained his staggering arrogance. She wished that, just *once*, he'd be bad at something. Just to take his ego down a notch or two.

Well, he didn't look arrogant now, just nervous and a little terrified. It was an expression she had never seen on his face before, and Libby found that she liked it. And that made her feel like even more of a bitch. Clearly the anger and resentment she harbored toward him ran much deeper than even she knew.

She shoved her roiling thoughts and confusion aside and gently placed Clara in his nervous hold. He watched intently, his expression tight with concentration, and she carefully withdrew her arms. His eyes widened when he realized that he was holding the gurgling baby without any help from her, and his grip instinctively tightened. Clara didn't like that and immediately started crying.

The look of utter panic on his face when Clara let loose with her high, thin cries was quite comical.

"Shit! What do I do?" he asked desperately, instinctively rocking from side to side.

"Well, keep that rocking movement going, and maybe let up on the death grip a tiny bit. You wouldn't like being held in a stranglehold either." His arms loosened fractionally. "A little more, Greyson."

"But what if I drop her?"

"You won't. She's not a slippery eel. You have her in a secure position; you just need to relax." He loosened his hold, and Clara, seemingly comforted by the proximity of her mother's calm voice and the more relaxed embrace, stopped crying. Her tear-drenched wide eyes searched the unfamiliar face above hers, and her forehead wrinkled in displeasure. Greyson's forehead was wrinkled in an identical frown of confusion and misgiving. They so resembled each other that it brought a reluctant smile to Libby's lips. Her fingers itched to dig out her phone and take a picture of them, but the device was still in her bag, and she didn't want to be taking pictures of Greyson. No matter how damned adorable he looked holding his daughter for the first time.

She watched a tentative smile replace the frown on his face, a smile that widened to reveal even white teeth and deep grooves in his lean cheeks. He had eyes only for Clara, who still looked a bit doubtful about this large stranger who was holding her. Libby suspected that it was only because she was standing right beside Greyson that Clara wasn't crying. Although the baby still looked undecided about whether or not to launch into fresh tears.

She was so beautiful. Greyson had never once imagined that it would feel this *right* to hold her. In the time since her birth, he'd pictured reconciling with Olivia, pictured Clara growing up, envisioned her playing with her toys, with the puppy he'd get for her, dressed in tutus, princess gowns, or perhaps something less traditionally girly. Maybe she'd want to be Buzz Lightyear. Who knew? He'd imagined her laughter, pictured her smile, her adorable curly hair springing wildly in every direction as she played and laughed and danced.

But he had lacked the imagination for this. He had never considered how it would feel to hold her. His parents hadn't been very tactile people, and Greyson had always kept his more physically demonstrative brother at a distance.

But now that he held his daughter in his arms, close to his chest, now that he could feel her weight, her warmth, the sweet softness of her, he knew that he didn't want to be the type of parent his own had been.

He wanted to know this child, cuddle her and hug her as she grew up. He never wanted her to doubt that she was loved.

She was both heavier and lighter than he would have thought. And if he had ever given any consideration to what it would feel like to hold a baby, he would have expected less movement and more . . . limpness. But she was alive, moving, restless. He could tell she was tense and wary of him. And that surprised him too. She didn't know him, so she didn't trust him. He would never have believed a four-month-old baby capable of such instinctive intelligence.

Maybe it was just this one. Maybe she was a prodigy. Well, considering that her mother was a culinary genius, it wouldn't surprise him.

His kid was a genius. He liked that.

He stared at Clara, his smile so wide it actually hurt his cheeks, and Clara stared at him. Her frown was back. And it reminded him of Harris. Only about a thousand times cuter.

"Do I look this pissed off when I frown?" he asked, keeping his voice low so as not to startle Clara.

"Well, she didn't get that black look from me," Olivia said. And Greyson wondered if she had deliberately phrased it in a way that would allow her to avoid actively acknowledging him as the father. He bit back a soft sigh. This visit hadn't gone as planned. They hadn't really resolved anything . . . but he didn't care. At least he'd received this unexpected bonus. And he'd take this over almost everything else.

He very carefully lifted Clara close enough to drop a kiss onto a chubby, still-tear-wet cheek. One of her flailing little fists grabbed hold of his earlobe and tugged.

"*Jesus.* Ouch," he muttered, cringing in pain but trying not to react because he didn't want to startle Clara. Olivia made a muffled sound of amusement and reached over to loosen the baby's death grip on his lobe. "How the hell is she so strong?"

"Baby power," Olivia said in a wobbly voice.

"Does she know her name?" he asked curiously before, without thinking about it, injecting some falsetto into his voice and directing his next comments to Clara. "Hey, Clara. You're so pretty. Do you know your name? *Claaara.* Pretty Clara. My gorgeous girl! My gorgeous, clever girl."

He was immediately embarrassed by the babble of high-pitched nonsense that had gushed uncontrollably from his lips and clenched them shut before anything even more ridiculous could escape. Olivia made a choking sound, while Clara's already-big eyes got impossibly wider. They flooded with tears, and she immediately started crying again. More high, piercing cries that just about broke his heart.

"God. I'm sorry," he said, not sure if his apology was for Clara or Olivia. He attempted to rock her like he had before, but she was writhing in his arms. Undecided before, she now knew she didn't want to be there, and she wasn't prepared to be soothed into compliance.

"What do I do?" he asked Olivia again, hating the fact that he didn't know. That he was so terrible at this.

"She's tired," Olivia said, reached for Clara. "Give her to me, she needs to get to sleep."

His hold on the baby tightened possessively as every cell in his body protested the idea of letting her go. Olivia's eyes went cold as she recognized the movement for what it was.

"Hand my baby over, Greyson," she demanded frigidly, and Greyson reluctantly relinquished his hold on Clara. Olivia looked completely resentful of what had been an involuntary reaction on his part. Her eyes were shuttered and her entire body tense.

"Olivia," he tried, wanting to explain that he hadn't meant anything by it. But she wouldn't look at him as she cuddled the still-crying baby close to her chest. Greyson's own arms felt empty, and he longed to pluck Clara from Olivia's hold to soothe her. But he knew if he did that it would only make her cry more—she didn't know him. He was a stranger to his own daughter, and he hated it. Hated himself because he knew the situation was entirely his own fault.

"Time for you to go, Greyson," Olivia said coldly, marching toward the front door and unlocking it. There was an odd metallic crack, and Olivia swore furiously beneath her breath. Greyson joined her, and they both stared at the broken key in her hand. He tried the door; it was unlocked. A quick look confirmed that there were no other latches or locks on the door. And no security gate.

"You can't lock the door," he stated unnecessarily.

"Thanks for the news flash, Captain Obvious," she retorted with childish sarcasm.

"You can't stay here if you can't lock the door."

"And what do you propose I do? Check into the nearest hotel? Share your hotel room, maybe?"

"I'm not staying at a hotel. It's fully booked."

She looked curious for a moment, and for a second he thought she would ask him where he *was* staying, but she tamped down her curiosity.

"Nothing stopping you from leaving, Greyson. You're not locked in."

"I'm not leaving if you can't lock the door behind me."

"This town is perfectly safe."

"Do you *really* want to take that risk with Clara?" The question made her hesitate, and she swallowed as her eyes dipped to Clara's crying face.

"If anybody wanted to break in here, a simple lock wouldn't keep them out."

"No, it wouldn't, and that's something that needs to be addressed at some point as well . . . but that simple lock was better than nothing. I can stay. I want to stay. It's that or you find somewhere safer to sleep tonight."


Libby was still looking at Clara and knew that even though the odds of anything happening were minimal, she had to place her baby's safety first. She briefly considered contacting Tina, but after their tense exchange that evening, she was very reluctant to reach out to the other woman for help.

Greyson staying here was ridiculous. There had to be another solution.

"I'll call Harris. He'll let us stay with him."

"That suits me fine. Since I'm sharing the house with Harris."

He was? That was news to her.

"Fine. Harris can stay with us here."

"Why disturb him, when I'm here already?" Greyson asked between clenched teeth. But Libby couldn't get the image of him tightening his hold on Clara out of her head. She may have made an error in allowing him so close without a lawyer present. Clara was a living, breathing child to him now. And Libby would have to be blind not to have seen the love bloom in his eyes when he'd held his daughter for the first time.

She knew she was courting disaster if she allowed him to spend any more time than necessary around her and Clara, but the stupid key had snapped, and she didn't have a spare. Until she had the lock replaced, there was no way she could lock the front door.

She chewed at her lip while she gently rocked Clara. The baby's cries were diminishing, and she was starting to drift off, suckling on her tiny fist.

"It's not like you'd be much protection against a determined evildoer," she pointed out, giving him a scathing once-over. Or at least she hoped it was scathing, because while he was lean, he was well built and looked capable of taking apart most bad guys with his bare hands, and she couldn't stop her eyes from lingering on some of the more pleasing aspects of his impressive physique.

"You know I have a black belt in Krav Maga."

"I did *not* know that." She kept her tone even, determined not to be impressed. But *damn*, from what she knew about the discipline, that was quite an achievement. "One of the very many things I don't know about you."

"It probably didn't come up," he said, sounding uncomfortable.

"Like the fact that you thought you couldn't have children?" She couldn't resist the completely unrelated barb. But it would take a bigger person than Libby to resist the allure of the opening he'd given her.

He didn't respond to that, his face expressionless and his eyes blank and frigid. Libby sighed before shaking her head impatiently.

"You can sleep on the sofa." She walked away without further comment, heading for her room.

She placed Clara in her crib and quickly went through her closet for some stuff before going back to the living room. Greyson was on the sofa, toeing off his trainers.

She still couldn't get over the fact that he was wearing trainers. And *jeans*.

She dumped clean sheets, a pillow, and a thick comforter on the sofa next to him.

"If you use the toilet, jiggle the handle after you flush, or the cistern won't fill. Oh, and open the kitchen cold-water faucet really slowly—if you don't, your shirt will get soaked."

"Anything else?" he asked. She tilted her head, trying to figure out if she detected sarcasm in the two words. In the end she decided that she didn't really care and shrugged.

"Lots, but those are probably the things that will affect you most directly tonight."

"Please let me fix up some stuff around the place. It's for both you *and* Clara. You'd be free to focus on her a lot more if you didn't have to worry about faulty plumbing." The kitchen light chose that moment to brighten with a loud hum and then flicker. He glanced at it before focusing his gaze on her face. An ironic smile flirting with the edges of that too-beautiful, too-cruel mouth, he added, "And faulty electricity."

"I may borderline loathe you, Greyson," she admitted, and he winced at her frankness. "But you *are* Clara's father, and I would hate for you to electrocute yourself trying to repair something you have no clue about."

"Then allow me to hire someone to fix it for you?"

"Sorry, Mr. Moneybags, I refuse to allow you to pay for a single thing in my home."

"Then let *me* fix it. I can fix it."

She shook her head, and a half-amused, half-despairing laugh bubbled from her lips. She should let him, just to watch him fail. It would do him a world of good to be terrible at something for once.

"Good night, Greyson," she said, hoping she sounded icy enough.

"Sleep tight, Olivia," he responded in that disturbingly quiet voice of his.

*Olivia.* Nobody else called her that, which she was grateful for because she didn't care for her name. Yet whenever Greyson said it in that darkly gentle way of his, it sent a frisson of pleasure shooting up her spine. She had always loved that he called her that. Because he was the only one who did, it felt special. Intimate.

*Of course, I don't feel that way anymore,* she reminded herself. She didn't care what he called her.

# Chapter Seven

Greyson woke up with a stiff neck, a sore back, and a surly disposition. To say he had slept badly would be putting it mildly. The sofa was too short and too narrow to adequately house his tall, broad frame, and any movement had had the potential to send him tumbling to the carpeted floor. And he sure as hell didn't want to wind up on that carpet. It was stained and looked like it hadn't had a decent steam clean in years.

Greyson would be the first to admit that he was mildly germophobic. Well, it wasn't so much germophobia as a revulsion to anything less than a clean living space. He knew some people would probably call it snobbery. But if that meant wanting to exist in a clean environment, then okay, he was a snob! Truth be told, this entire little trip to the Garden Route was severely testing his boundaries. The place he shared with Harris was truly revolting, and now Olivia's house was less than ideal too.

He knew from living with her before that she liked to keep things neat and tidy too. She wasn't borderline OCD about it like Greyson, but she wasn't a messy person. Which likely meant that living here, with the house in its current state, couldn't be too pleasant for her. And all he wanted to do was make it a little less unpleasant. For both Olivia and Clara. He reached for his phone, placed within easy reach on the small table in front of the couch. He wasn't sure what purpose it was meant to serve, footrest or coffee table. It seemed like a random thing to just plonk in the middle of the living room.

He checked the time on his phone—just after seven in the morning—and went through his messages. There was one from Harris.

**Where are you?** Nothing more than that, but the three words conveyed a level of concern that Greyson wasn't sure he deserved. He felt like an ass for not telling his brother he wouldn't be back last night. It would have been the considerate thing to do.

**At Olivia's place. I didn't mean to worry you.**

**Not worried.** His brother's response was brisk and to the point, and Greyson felt curiously let down by it. Until his brother's next message: **Okay maybe a little worried. I was concerned you'd skipped out on me without paying your half of the rent.**

Greyson's lips tilted at the lame little joke. It was better than nothing.

**I'm good for it.**

**What do you mean you're at Libby's? Why are you there? Are you saying you slept there?**

**I slept on the sofa. I think it did my back in.**

**Good.** This time the unsympathetic reply startled a quick laugh out of Greyson. **Anyway. Got to go. I have a coffee date.**

Greyson didn't bother to reply to that and put his phone back on the coffee table–footrest–hybrid thing. The other room was silent. He was thankful for that because Clara had cried three times last night, startling him out of a sound sleep every time. It must have been exhausting for Olivia. He didn't know how she did it. She had not once lost her patience. Her sweet voice had remained soft and crooning each time, and Greyson had been filled with so much admiration for his lovely wife. She was an amazing mother. Kind, attentive, and loving. He had found himself wanting to relieve some of her burden. If things had been normal, maybe he would have rocked Clara to sleep or changed her nappy. Anything other than uselessly lying in the other room and listening to her cry.

He sat up and bit back a groan at the various aches and twinges that seemed to awaken with the movement of his body. Screw this crappy couch—it was a goddamned torture device.

He contemplated the closed door of Libby's room again. She'd probably be up in an hour or so to get ready for work. Since she hadn't explicitly stated that she wanted him gone before she woke up today, he was going to overlook the possibility that it might have been an unspoken expectation. He needed a shower to ease some of the aches from his body, and he wasn't going all the way back to Harris's place for that.

He quietly padded to the bathroom and contemplated the tub shower for a second. It was going to be cramped. The showerhead wasn't tall enough to slot Greyson beneath it, but he'd have to make do. He wondered if there were any special tricks to the shower, like with the toilet and kitchen tap, but then shrugged and figured he'd soon find out.

He was wearing only the boxers he had slept in and quickly shoved them down and off. He checked the water, and thankfully it was hot and the water pressure perfect. He used her soap, and the familiar fragrance of vanilla and honeysuckle wafted in the steam and surrounded him. It smelled like Olivia, and it made him hard.

He groaned at the erection, his first in months. He hadn't been aroused in so long. It was like his sex drive had died the day she'd walked out on him. Before that, during her pregnancy, even while he'd thought she'd cheated on him, he had seen her increasingly lush body and had wanted her. Every time he'd found himself in her presence, his cock had swelled and strained, forcing Greyson to will it away with the reminder that she'd betrayed him with someone else. Probably with *Harris.*

It had been as effective as a cold shower . . . but now, surrounded by what felt like her essence, nothing could deter this erection, and he fisted himself, pumping up and down for a few strokes before groaning again and swearing. He forced himself to let go. He wasn't going to jack off in his wife's shower like some creepy pervert.

He turned the water to cold and manfully refrained from yelling when the water doused both his libido and his will to live with a deluge of ice that he felt right down to his bones.

*"Jesus,"* he swore viciously. It was beyond cold. But at least it succeeded in getting rid of that damned inconvenient hard-on. His teeth were chattering when he stepped out of the shower and folded the tiny towel around his waist. Where were her large towels, anyway? This thing was so small it left a gaping slit over his thigh, and his dick and balls were on display with every step he took. He opened the bathroom door tentatively and cast a look down the hall. Thankfully, her bedroom door was still shut. Great—he didn't wish to be harangued because he couldn't find a towel large enough to accommodate him.

He crept out of the bathroom, back to the living room, where he had left his clothing in a neatly folded stack on the coffee table. He had just bent and reached for his jeans when the bedroom door opened, and he froze, glancing over his shoulder to the stunned face staring fixedly at his ass and his junk, which he knew had to be on prominent display to her horrified gaze.

She made a funny, squeaky little sound of dismay before her hand flew up to her mouth in shock. Her eyes were still on his tackle, and he shook himself out of his horrified reverie and cautiously stood upright again. Keeping his back to her while still watching her over his shoulder. All that staring had a predictable effect on his dick, and the erection was back.

*Fucking fantastic.* She was never going to believe that he hadn't planned this. Especially if she happened to catch a glimpse of his raging hard-on.

"I grabbed a shower," he explained unnecessarily. "It was quick; I'm sure there's plenty of hot water available. You don't have any adult-size towels in there, by the way."

He had to say the last thing . . . wanting to explain himself but knowing she wouldn't be receptive to it. At least this way he could let her know that he had looked for other towels.

"Just . . ." She waved a frantic hand in his general vicinity. "Get dressed, okay?"

"Yes. Of course." He reached for his jeans and hoodie again, trying to do it without bending.

"I'm going to get changed," she said, her voice still unusually high. She retreated back to her bedroom, and he could hear the sounds of quiet rustling around in there. He tugged his clothes back on, foregoing underwear because he didn't have a clean pair; he felt very unlike himself, going commando like this. He wasn't sure he liked it. But he had no other alternative.

He moved to the kitchen, got the kettle on, and tried not to wince at the unfamiliar sensation of the rough denim against his sensitive male bits. It felt fucking weird. Maybe with a different fabric he could get into the no-underwear thing, but definitely not with denim.

He scrounged around and found cooking implements. He got some scrambled eggs going and had bread in the toaster before she finally exited her bedroom again.

"What are you doing?" she asked in horror.

"Making breakfast. I figured you'd be too tired after last night. And, uh . . . maybe you eat at work . . . ," he concluded awkwardly, suddenly comprehending that that was probably exactly what she did and feeling stupid for not thinking of it before. It was humbling being around her lately; he always felt wrong footed and like everything he said or did was dumb, inappropriate, or just plain insensitive. He felt like he was walking on a tightrope and a wrong move could send him tumbling into the void.

"It's Sunday. MJ's is closed on Sundays."

Well, okay. He could work with that. He nodded and gestured toward the stove top. "Then you're going to need to eat."

"I can prepare my own breakfast," she said, and he nodded. Of course she could—she was a brilliant chef. But he remembered that she absolutely loathed cooking for just herself, and back in London—when they had been dating—they would often order takeout. Greyson had once attempted cooking for them . . . it had been a disaster. This breakfast was only his second attempt at cooking. How hard could it be to scramble eggs and put bread in a toaster?

"I know, but I've already finished most of it, so why don't you have a seat?"

"Greyson, the last time you cooked for me, I nearly died of food poisoning."

"That's an exaggeration," he said, his brow lowering in consternation.

"Well, I probably *would* have died of food poisoning if I had eaten that raw chicken."

"It wasn't *that* raw," he said defensively.

"It was bleeding on my plate," she reminded him. "It turned the lumpy mashed potatoes pink."

Back then they had both laughed at his failed attempt at cooking. She had kissed him and thanked him for trying. Then they had ordered Indian food and spent the rest of the night making love. That was the night she had finally said yes to his marriage proposal.

"Eggs are easier," he said confidently. "I was too ambitious that night. I guarantee a salmonella-free breakfast today."

She pursed her heart-shaped lips before shrugging. He kept sneaking glances at her as he worked. She looked absolutely stunning, as usual. She could wear a sackcloth and look gorgeous. Her figure still retained some of her pregnancy weight, but it suited her. Her breasts were fuller, her hips seemed rounder, and despite the innate athleticism of her willowy body, she looked *lush*. He ached to touch her, to explore those fuller curves, her plump breasts . . . she looked like an earth goddess, with the frayed silk of her wavy black hair billowing around her face and all of that golden, glowing skin that he knew would be satiny soft to touch.

She was wearing a short, long-sleeved lacy white dress—the contrast against her skin was fantastic—combined with a faded denim jacket and heavy-duty combat boots. She loved those boots. She liked working in them and had once told Greyson that they were the comfiest shoes she owned and perfect for standing for long hours. He hid a grin at the sight of the frilly socks peeking over the tops of the boots.

He had always enjoyed her quirky dress sense. The combination of hard and soft suited her to a T.

"Something's burning," she said, her voice interrupting his mooning thoughts.

"Shit," he swore. He leaped for the toaster and pushed the button that would eject the slices. The bread popped from the appliance, and he managed to catch one piece, swearing when it burned the tips of his fingers. The other slice landed on the floor. And that was fine because it was burnt to a crisp.

"What the *fuck*?" he couldn't stop himself from exclaiming, raising his voice a notch. "I'm sure I had it on medium." He checked the dial, and it was definitely on medium. "Did the toaster come with the house?"

"Yes," Olivia said, her voice tiny and almost contrite, and yet he was sure he detected amusement threaded through the regretful tone in that one word. "I *do* have one of my own."

"Why the hell didn't you tell me?" he asked, a little exasperated.

"Well, I didn't know that one was broken," she confessed. "I mean, I haven't really made toast since living here."

"Where's your toaster?" he asked, his voice a surly grumble. He bent to pick up the other slice of toast from the floor and chucked both in the dustbin.

"Cabinet next to the oven. It's still boxed. I don't think it's worth the effort. I could just have normal bread."

"I'll decide if it's worth the effort," Greyson stated, then hid a wince at the imperiousness of both his words and tone of voice. She raised her eyebrows, looking seriously unimpressed with him, and folded her arms over her chest, nodding her pointed little chin at him.

"Go for it," she invited him, and fully committed now, Greyson turned to fish out the brand-new four-slice toaster. He removed the eggs from the stove top, not wanting to burn those as well, and shoved the skillet into the oven before focusing on the toaster once more.

He had to use a knife to slice through the tape, and the first one he used was too blunt, so he exchanged it for a butcher knife, nearly cutting himself in the process. After that he had to deal with the weird soft bag thing wrapped around the device. It stuck to the metal of the toaster, and Greyson had a hard time extracting it from the bag. He then battled his way through seemingly endless plastic wraps and ties, as well as the weird tiny cardboard housing that seemed to have been jerry rigged around the plug, before finally exultantly holding the unboxed toaster aloft, curbing the instinct to throw back his head and utter a triumphant war cry. He felt like a conquering hero until he happened to glance at Olivia. She was sitting at the kitchen table with her cheek resting in the palm of her hand, watching him with an enigmatic curve to her lips.

Mona Lisa had nothing on the mysterious little smile gracing Olivia's mouth. Was she laughing at him? Probably. He couldn't even open a bloody box without fucking it up.

"Toast coming right up," he promised, hoping the eggs weren't too cold by now.

The toast was blond, so pale it was just warmed bread, really. It turned out Greyson, in his haste to get breakfast served, hadn't checked the settings. Libby kept her amused grin hidden when he swore a blue streak at the sight of that underdone toast.

Because Greyson so rarely swore, hearing all those f-bombs dropping from his lips was quite entertaining. He also never failed, and this breakfast was just one miserable fail after another. The eggs were cold—expected, what with him taking twenty minutes to open up that box—and congealed. She took a polite bite, then wrinkled her nose and lifted her napkin to her lips to discreetly spit out the mouthful she'd just chewed: it was sickeningly sweet.

Greyson, who had been silently brooding on the other side of the tiny kitchen table, his festering glare flitting from eggs to toast and back again, took a forkful of eggs into his own mouth before spitting it back onto the plate.

"What the fuck?" he exclaimed, his nose wrinkled in disgust. "What in the actual *fuck*?"

Libby bit her lips to keep her laughter at bay.

"I think," she said in a distinctly wobbly voice, "maybe you used sugar? Instead of salt?"

He glanced over at the stove, and the glare deepened even further.

"Why the hell is your sugar next to the stove?"

"If you look closely," she said, an acerbic bite in her voice, "you'll note that it's placed next to the kettle, right between the tea and coffee. And if you squint, you may be able to make out the letters on the surface of the glass."

He scowled at the huge black letters on the glass, prominently spelling out the word *sugar* as clear as day.

He shook his head and shoved the plate aside.

"At least the coffee is good," she said, taking a cheerful sip from her mug, and he glowered at her.

"You made the coffee," he reminded her, and she sent him a grin over the top of her mug.

"I know," she said. He focused his scowl on the steaming black liquid in his own mug.

"Grab a couple of bowls and some cornflakes from the cabinet behind you," she offered him quietly, not because she felt sorry for him. Never that. She was just . . . hungry. And since he was here, she might as well share with him.

His eyes lit up at her words, and he jumped up to do her bidding. She got up, too, heading to the refrigerator for milk and fruit.

They didn't speak again until both had a large bowl of cornflakes garnished with fresh berries and bananas placed in front of them.

"Does she—uh, Clara—usually sleep this late?" he asked after swallowing down his first spoonful of cornflakes.

"It varies. She was more restless than usual last night; I think it exhausted her."

"You're really good at this," he said, sounding almost shy.

"What do you mean?" she asked, genuinely confused.

"Mothering. It seems to come naturally to you."

"Thanks," she said self-consciously, her cheeks heating at the compliment. "I'm a wreck most of the time. I call my mother every day for advice, and I'm always terrified I'm going to do something horribly wrong and mess her up for life."

"Nothing you do will ever compare to my colossal fuckup," he muttered, crunching his way through another spoonful of cereal.

Libby kept her focus on her bowl, reluctant to acknowledge his words. Right now, this situation with Greyson was one of those moments she was afraid would negatively impact Clara's life. Her baby would grow up shuttling between two households, not knowing what it was like to live in a stable home with both her parents present. And maybe, because she would never know any better, that would be okay. But it was so, so *far* from what Libby had wanted for her child.

And Libby felt like she was at the crossroads now. The decisions she made about Greyson during this messed-up period of her life would forge the framework for Clara's childhood. It felt like a huge and terrible responsibility, and she resented Greyson for putting her in this dreadful position.

A tiny whimper sounded over the baby monitor, and Libby tilted her head, waiting to see if it would lead to anything more. Another whimper, followed by a soft inhalation, and then a thin little cry.

"Aaaand she's awake," she said. She got up immediately and made her way to the bedroom. Clara's cute little face was screwed up, and Libby grinned at how truly tragic she looked. "Oh, sweetie. It's okay, Mummy's here. Are you hungry? *Pee-ew!* Maybe we should change that nappy first, you little stinker."

She heard dishes rattling in the sink and threw a quick glance over her shoulder through the open bedroom door to see Greyson clearing off the kitchen table.

"You don't have to do that," she called while nimbly undressing Clara.

"I made a mess; I should clean it up," he said, barely raising his voice despite the fact that she was in a different room.

"No, what you should do is leave. We're fine now. Thanks for staying last night, but I'll find someone to change the lock today." She truly just wanted him gone from here. She recalled the disturbing sight of him nearly naked after his shower, bent over with that tiny towel doing *nothing* to cover his behind . . . or the rest of him. Seeing him like that, the firm, sculpted planes of his butt, the impressive heft of his penis swaying between his strongly muscled thighs . . . it had sent a shudder of awareness through her body.

And she had felt a disturbing awakening of senses that had been dormant for too many months. She didn't want to feel that way around him, didn't want to be sexually aware of him. Not again . . .

not anymore. This marriage was ending; all that was left to decide on was the formalities.

"I can change the lock," he said confidently, snapping her out of her disturbing thoughts, and she shot him a derisive look over her shoulder. She thought of his incompetence in the kitchen. He had sounded confident then too. The man really had no sense of his own shortcomings. He needed a serious reality check. And yes, it was petty, but Libby wanted to be around when he tumbled from that lofty perch of self-assurance.

"Okay." It was hard to stay focused with the stink Clara had created wafting up to Libby's nostrils, but she managed to get the word out almost cheerfully.

She had her eyes on Clara's cute tush as she ran a baby wipe over it and so didn't know Greyson was in the room until his voice had drifted to her ear from just over her left shoulder. "What did you say?"

She jumped and then glared at the man standing just behind her. And why was he standing so damned close? And in such an awkward spot? "Move over there so that I can see you without getting a crick in my neck, would you?" she instructed him, pointing to the head of the bed, the soiled nappy still in her hand. Greyson reared back comically before doing as she had instructed, giving her a wide berth. He had a pristine, neatly folded white handkerchief pressed over his nose and mouth as he stared at Clara in abject horror. The baby had stopped crying and was now happily gurgling, her fat, dimpled little legs kicking as she tried to catch her toes. She was naked and completely oblivious to the foul stench she had created.

"How the hell can something so small produce a smell that huge?"

"This isn't too bad. It can get much, *much* worse," Libby said.

"Seriously?" he asked, sounding truly appalled, and Libby tried hard not to grin. He was staring down at Clara with something close to fear in his eyes, and it was hilarious.

"Uh-huh," she said, grabbing a nappy-disposal bag from the changing table on the other side of the bed. The small room was very cramped with Libby's double bed, Clara's white crib, and the matching changing table all squeezed into the tiny space. She had managed to get only one bedside table in. The other one was stowed in the living room and serving as a coffee table for now.

"Did you mean it? About me changing the lock?"

"You might as well make yourself useful," she said with a shrug, then gave him an assessing look. "In fact, since you're just hovering there, doing nothing much, can you open that faucet again and run her another bath? Not too hot—just lukewarm is fine. I'll feed her while you're doing that. I don't usually feed her before bath time, but our routine is shot to hell with my working hours being the way they are, and then she didn't get her bath last night as planned, and . . ." She stopped talking, feeling like a failure and not wanting to reveal much more of the hopelessness she felt. Fearing he'd use it against her if they ever got into some kind of custody dispute. She didn't trust him at all. She knew he wanted Clara, and after witnessing his reluctance to let go of the baby last night, she wouldn't put it past him to fight dirty.

And maybe it wasn't wise to have him constantly around, but aside from wanting to see him fail, she also felt she should begin to subscribe to the "keep your enemies closer" school of thought. But she had the very real fear that while she was waiting for him to fail, he might be around to see *her* fail. Fail at her job, at her friendships, or as a mother. She would hate for Greyson—of *all* people—to witness any of that. The terrifying possibility was nearly enough to change her mind about allowing him to "fix" things around the house.

Nearly.

"You shouldn't be so hard on yourself," he said, in response to her earlier statement. His words succeeded in drawing her from her dark thoughts, and she tilted her head, curiously waiting for him to continue. "You're doing an amazing job, despite the shitty hand you've been dealt."

"The hand *you* dealt me, you mean?" she asked, and his eyes shut for an instant before he nodded.

"Yes." He thrust his hands into the back pockets of his jeans and swayed restlessly back and forth on his heels for a couple of moments. "I'll get the bath organized."

"Thank you."

He nodded in response and left the room abruptly.

Libby sighed and shut the door behind him, picking Clara up for her morning feed. The baby would be transitioning to solids soon, and Libby planned to have her fully weaned by six months old. She treasured this wonderful closeness with her serenely suckling daughter. Libby would miss it, but because of her work and the fact that Clara spent half of every weekday in day care, it would be best to get her onto formula. Libby found that she was producing less milk than during the first three months as well, and she wasn't sure if that was because she'd mentally resigned herself to transitioning Clara to formula sooner rather than later, or if it was because she was already breastfeeding less. Perhaps it was the stress of going back to work. She knew pregnancy and breastfeeding were different for every woman.

The duration of Clara's feedings had shortened over the last couple of weeks, and she now seemed content with a quick suckle on each breast. Dr. Ngozi had told Libby it wasn't anything to worry about because Clara was growing and gaining weight.

She had just shifted Clara to her left breast when a soft knock sounded on the door. She reached for a towel and used it to cover herself and her feeding baby before calling for him to enter.

The door opened tentatively, and Greyson's head appeared first. He assessed her state of undress before stepping farther into the room.

"The water has been ready for about ten minutes. I was wondering if I should add some more warm water to it, since it was pretty lukewarm to start off with."

"Yes, please, she's nearly done," she said, and his eyes dropped to the mounded towel. The soft snuffling noises Clara made when she suckled were the only sounds in the room, and Greyson's gaze never moved from the gently shifting towel.

"How often do you feed her?" he asked, his voice hushed.

"About six times a day. I'll be adding solids to her diet soon. Possibly this week. She's drinking expressed breast milk at day care, but I want to start supplementing that with formula." She paused before grimacing. "Sorry . . . that's more information than you asked for."

"I don't mind. It's stuff I *want* to know. Stuff I *should* know."

Clara's mouth went slack, and Libby, with practiced ease, slid her bra and top back into place beneath the towel before lifting Clara to her shoulder and gently patting her back.

Greyson was watching the circular motion of her hand intently. "Why do you do that?" he asked.

"Burping her. When she gets a little more active, sitting up by herself and moving around more, I won't have to do this for her anymore. I feel like we're nearly at that point. She's constantly trying to roll over, and she lifts her head like a champ. She's growing so fast."

His eyes flickered with something resembling sadness or regret before his lids swooped down and he ducked his head to hide his reaction from her.

"I should get back to Harris's. For my tools," he said a moment later, bringing his carefully blank eyes back up to hers.

"Tools?"

"I, um, bought some tools yesterday because I thought you may need some help fixing things around here."

Well, wasn't *that* overconfident of him?

"That seems a little presumptuous, don't you think?"

"Not really, I just like to be prepared."

"Of course you do," she said, finding it hard not to sound caustic. But at the same time not really caring if she did. He cleared his throat, and his eyes roamed around the room as he seemed to search for something to say.

"Did you know that Harris rented the house next to Martine's?" he asked abruptly, and Libby felt her eyebrows shoot straight to her hairline at that bit of information. Tina hadn't mentioned that at all.

*Then again,* she thought bitterly, *Tina hasn't exactly been a font of information lately.*

But Harris hadn't mentioned it either. Maybe the subject had just not come up? But it seemed like an odd detail not to mention.

"That's weird," she said. "Were there really no other places available?" She couldn't imagine Tina being too thrilled about it.

"I'm starting to wonder if he didn't do it deliberately," Greyson said, and Libby blinked.

"Why would he do that? They hate each other."

"I think the hate is one sided. Harris has never felt any animosity toward Martine."

"How do *you* know that? You and Harris don't exactly confide in each other."

"I just do," he said cryptically, and Libby was tempted to question him further but didn't want to have a cozy gossip with him. She didn't want to encourage such familiarity.

Greyson couldn't stop watching Olivia with Clara. Her gentle stroking of the baby's back mesmerized him. Despite her modest claims to the contrary, there was a naturalness to her mothering that was beautiful to see. And Greyson wanted to watch and encourage and assist and hold them both close and never let them go again.

But he didn't have that right. It killed him not to follow his instinctive inclination to claim them and protect them. He wanted to be a father . . . something he'd never dreamed possible. He wanted to be a husband—something he'd been horrendous at for the most part.

He wanted a second chance.

But he didn't deserve one, so he had to settle for second best. He just didn't know what second best entailed yet.

"I'll go. I'll be back in about an hour. I think the hardware store is open until eleven on a Sunday; I'll pop around there for some stuff."

"I'm paying for whatever you're buying," she stated, her voice brooking no argument. That didn't stop him from trying to argue.

"That's not necessary; it'll just be a few things."

"You pay for anything, and you can forget about the handyman routine," she warned.

Check. And mate. There was no arguing with that. He hadn't made any secret of the fact that he was desperate to make himself useful. But she could take that away in a second.

He shut his mouth but couldn't stop himself from glaring at her.

"If you call in a professional behind my back, so help me God, Greyson . . . there will be hell to pay."

Not keen to find out how much more hell she could dish out, Greyson dipped his head in surly acquiescence. He was a reasonably intelligent guy—a renowned problem-solver and troubleshooter. He could do this.

"Whatever you want, Olivia," he agreed softly. "I'll add that warm water to her bath. Then I'll head out."

She didn't say anything in response to his words, just kept her focus on Clara. Greyson waited for a moment, but she had already dismissed him.

So now he knew how *that* felt. It was a move he had used on so many others; perhaps it was poetic justice to have the old freeze-out practiced on him for a change.

He turned away and left.


Clara was bathed, changed, and on her back swatting at the little safari animals dangling from the mobile above her playpen.

It was still pouring outside, and Libby had emptied the bucket beneath the leak twice in the thirty minutes since Greyson had left. Her only solace was that no other leaks had sprung up overnight.

The air conditioner sounded even worse than it had last night, and Libby feared the thing was on its last legs. No surprise, really—*everything* in the house seemed to be on its last legs.

Her phone chimed, and she reached for it, swiping at the screen to check her messages. It was from Greyson.

I'm buying a new handle for the front door, also adding two dead bolts.

She grimaced, thinking of the cost.
One is fine, she typed back quickly.

Two is better.

I want one, Greyson!

FINE!

She shook her head, swiping to check the rest of her messages. Her shoulders fell when she realized that Tina hadn't messaged her. Then again, Libby wasn't sure if she would have responded if she had messaged.

But at the same time, after the way they'd left things last night, Libby had expected more from the woman who was supposed to be her best friend. An explanation, more of an apology . . .

*Something.*

She sighed, tempted to send a message and find out if Tina was okay. She couldn't help recalling the misery in her friend's eyes, along with the dejection in her voice, just before Libby had left last night.

Tina was profoundly unhappy, and Libby recognized that it was an unhappiness that had been building over the years. The other woman rarely made the effort to go out and only ever went to family events, which meant she wasn't meeting new people. It was frustrating to watch. Libby had always been the more gregarious of the two, but she couldn't recall Tina being this bad when they were kids.

After Libby had returned from London last year, she had been keen to spend more time with Tina. But Libby was honest enough to admit that during her first two months of marriage, she had been wholly preoccupied with Greyson. And then, when she had discovered her pregnancy, which had been swiftly followed by Greyson's emotional abandonment, it had been all about Libby. But Tina had been there, to hold Libby's hair back when she puked, to hold her hand during doctors' appointments, and then to simply hold her up after Greyson had flipped her world upside down.

Libby knew that Tina deserved more than the cursory and dismissive discussion they had had yesterday. But she needed to curtail her mother-bear instincts the next time she and Tina spoke. Libby knew she tended to be selfish . . . but she would have to curb that inclination, because something was fundamentally wrong in Tina's life. It had taken Libby way too long to recognize that fact.

Decision made, she was lifting her phone to send Tina a message when it chimed again.

The back door needs a dead bolt as well.

"God!" This again.

It doesn't. It has a perfectly serviceable lock.

It's flimsy.

GREYSON!

FINE!!!

Greyson had always been so calm and emotionless—she couldn't remember ever finding him *aggravating* before. But he was like a dog with a bone about this handyman stuff. He was taking it so seriously, when Libby knew he didn't have a gnat's chance in hell of fixing anything in this place.

His persistence was annoying. But kind of endearing too. And she wasn't sure how the hell something could be annoying and endearing at the same time. It was bizarre how Greyson, the most logical man in the world, completely defied logic right now.

Her phone chimed again. Irritated, she lifted it, ready to blast him for his crap.

The grocery store is still open. Do you need anything while I'm out?

Oh. That was kind of sweet and considerate. She did a quick inventory of her kitchen.

I'm out of milk. Full cream. And Clara needs nappies. Hold on I'll send you a pic. She went to her room and took a picture of the nearly empty bag of disposable nappies, then sent it to him.

Anything else?

No. Thanks.

Coolio.

Coolio? That was weird and uncharacteristic. But that seemed to be the new normal for Greyson lately.

Libby decided to rearrange her kitchen to her liking, hoping it would feel more familiar when she was done with it. It wasn't a great kitchen, small, with very few surfaces to work on. Not her dream chef's kitchen by any stretch of the imagination, but it was *hers*, and it was better than nothing.

Clara was starting to squeal, high-pitched happy sounds, and Libby glanced over at the baby. Clara was clumsily reaching for one of the soft toys Libby had scattered in the playpen. She kept missing it, and her squeals were starting to take on a frustrated edge. Abandoning the kitchen for the moment, Libby walked over for a closer look—always very interested in Clara's every move. The baby's head lifted at Libby's approach, and she blinked up at her mother before gifting Libby with one of her wide, dimpled smiles.

"Hey, sweetheart, you wanna play peekaboo with Mummy?" Libby asked in a deliberately excited voice. One that Clara usually responded to. It made Libby recall the ridiculous voice Greyson had used while talking to Clara the night before, and she found herself involuntarily grinning—and then chuckling—at the memory.

Clara slapped her plump starfish hands on the floor of the playpen, kicking her legs in reaction to the voice, and Libby picked her up. She carried Clara over to where she already had a play area set up—a thick, clean comforter spread on the carpeted floor, strewn with more soft toys. She placed Clara in the secure, padded floor seat that helped sit her upright. The cute, bright seat had been yet another gift from Clara's paternal grandparents, one that Libby was finding more and more useful. Clara seemed to love it, her hands constantly grabbing and exploring the attached toys. And because it allowed her to sit upright, she could watch the world around her with increasing fascination. Libby found it especially great for peekaboo.

She knelt in front of the seat and smiled at the baby, who watched her animatedly. Using one of the clean spit-up towels she kept close by for emergencies, Libby started a rousing game of peekaboo with Clara.

"*Wheeeere's* Mummy?" she asked in a gradually rising voice, hiding behind the little towel. Then she dropped it with a high-pitched "Here I am!"

It never failed to elicit the most jubilant sound imaginable from her gorgeous daughter. A contagious, chortling laugh that lit up her beautiful face and shook her round little body.

The game never got old . . . for Clara. But Libby was starting to flag after her tenth miraculous reappearance from behind the towel.

The front door opened in midreveal, and Greyson walked in to the sound of Clara's burbling laughter. He stopped dead on the threshold and simply stared, the expression on his face revealing shock, pleasure, and pain. So much pain. Much more than such a joyful sound should ever be responsible for.

# Chapter Eight

"I didn't know she could laugh," he said, his voice low and gruff with emotion. Libby swallowed with difficulty, reacting to the shocking vulnerability in his eyes more strongly than she'd thought possible. Part of her felt she should be happy to see him hurting like this . . . but she couldn't find it within herself to revel in his misery.

"Close the door, will you? It's cold," she said softly, and he seemed to come out of whatever daze he was in and stepped farther into the house, his hands filled with grocery bags, which he put down before shutting the door. Clara was groping for the towel in Libby's hand, and she let the baby have it. She absently lowered her eyes to Clara and gasped when the baby clumsily lifted the towel to her own eyes and then squealed with laughter, creating her own adorably awkward version of peekaboo.

"Did you see that?" she asked Greyson, her voice hushed. He knelt on the floor next to Libby and made a sound of affirmation, still looking dazed. They both watched Clara fixedly, waiting for her to repeat the action. Libby's breath caught when the towel went up again, and then she exhaled on a shuddering sigh when it went straight into Clara's drooling mouth and the baby proceeded to gum the flannel fabric contentedly.

"She's been giggling and laughing for the last month or so. She gets really into peekaboo," Libby explained huskily, and Greyson cleared his throat.

"I see. She seems really smart."

"I think she is. Very precocious. I wish she'd slow down a bit. I want to enjoy this part a bit longer."

Greyson's eyes were stormy as he nodded his agreement. He had missed out on so many milestones already. And she knew he was thinking of those. These firsts were so precious, and Libby knew that if she were to miss out on any of them, the loss would be immense.

Clara's eyelids were starting to droop, and they both watched as she drifted off. Libby reached out and supported her lolling head while unhooking her from the seat. She picked the baby up and gently deposited her on her back in the middle of the thick comforter. She covered the baby with a light blanket and scattered a few light cushions in a wide protective circle around her.

"Is that safe?" Greyson asked gruffly, and she looked at him with a quick, involuntary smile.

"Safe as houses," she replied in a hushed voice.

"Is the floor warm enough? Is the carpet clean?" Fastidious Greyson couldn't disguise the wrinkle of his nose at the last question, and she knew he found the carpet less than acceptable. Which, she had to admit, was a fair assessment.

"There are two thick blankets underneath the comforter. She's fine."

He nodded curtly, still looking skeptical, his gaze not shifting from the contentedly sleeping baby.

"How did we make something so damned perfect?" he asked softly, the awed words barely loud enough for Libby to hear. But she did hear them, and they made her irrationally angry at how easily he was able to claim Clara now. After four months of zero contact following that first vehement denial.

So easy for him. While she still had no idea what had triggered this change in him. The huge chasm between the way he had been that last night in hospital versus his behavior now was completely unbelievable to her. She shook her head, not trusting herself to speak to him just then, and headed for the kitchen to continue her reorganization of the room.

She knew he was watching her, but he wisely refrained from saying yet another dumb thing. He picked up the grocery bags and brought them to the kitchen. She eyed them askance before glaring at him.

"That doesn't look like just milk and nappies."

"I brought a couple of steaks, for dinner."

"Dinner? You assume you're staying for dinner?" she asked flatly. It wasn't even close to lunchtime yet, and he was thinking about dinner?

He had the grace to look embarrassed by the question. "I may be here awhile, what with the door and the plumbing and the roof . . ."

"Greyson, I'm not letting you anywhere near the roof."

"But . . ."

"Look, I may be pissed off with you, but I don't want you dead. And in this weather, if you fall off that roof—and let's face it, you'll fall off the damned roof—you'll kill yourself!" Besides, he couldn't suffer if he was dead! And Libby bloody well wanted him to suffer. Ugh, she was turning into a monster . . . but she wouldn't be human if she didn't want to punish him for the pain and confusion and loneliness he had inflicted on her for so long.

She didn't want him dead! Greyson could barely contain his jubilant grin at that. Still, why was everybody assuming he was so damned useless at physical labor? When he had picked up his toolbox earlier, his brother had been equally disparaging of his handyman abilities. And of course the other man couldn't resist adding a few more dire warnings about not forcing himself into Libby's life.

But maybe she was right about the roof. At the best of times, Greyson had a thing about heights. He couldn't imagine being up there in slippery conditions, with the howling wind . . . he shuddered at the thought.

"Fine, I won't attempt the roof. Today."

"Ever."

"We can discuss it later."

"It's not up for discussion."

"I think I'll fix the bathroom faucet first. I don't want to make any loud noises in case it wakes Clara."

She nodded, and he turned to the front door, intending to go back to his car to pick up his toolbox. Her voice stopped him in his tracks.

"Greyson?"

"Yes?" He turned to face her. She looked so damned gorgeous with her hands planted on her hips as she glared at him.

"You're cooking your own damned steaks."

"Damn it!" Not even the internet could save Greyson from this disaster. He had no idea what the hell he was doing. He had managed to find and turn off the water mains and removed the hot-water tap from the bath. The guy at the hardware store had said that it was probably a bad washer that needed replacing and had given Greyson a quick explanation on how to replace said washer.

Unsure of the size needed, Greyson had bought all the sizes—sneakily ringing up only one on the receipt he had handed to Olivia. The rest he had paid for separately. He knew he was treading a fine line . . . any dishonesty, no matter how harmless it seemed, would be ill received by her right now. He knew that, but at the same time he tried to rationalize it to himself. She only needed one washer, and so she only had to pay for one. Not knowing the size had been on him, so it should be his expense.

Whatever—that was the least of his concerns right now. He had managed, with the help of several YouTube videos, to replace the washer and had even—after a lot of sweat, swearing, and even spilled blood, thanks to the fleshy part of his left palm getting scratched on some sharp edge or the other—gotten the tap screwed back on. But it wasn't working. He had switched the water back on, and nothing. Not one drop.

There was a sharp rap on the bathroom door, which swung open without further warning. Olivia looked like she was about to say something, but her eyes narrowed when she saw his bare chest.

"Why are you always half-naked in my house, Greyson?" she asked, her voice peppered with annoyance and wobbling slightly. Her gaze seemed glued to his chest, and she swallowed heavily after asking the question.

"Sorry . . . I was hot in the hoodie and needed my T-shirt to mop up some water."

"I have old towels you could have used. You didn't have to ruin a brand-new shirt."

"It was already ruined," he admitted reluctantly, and she tilted her head in that damned appealing quizzical way of hers.

"What do you mean?"

He lifted his hand to show her the bloodied makeshift bandage wrapped around his palm, and she gasped before surging in from the doorway and coming to stand right in front of him, grabbing his hand in both of hers.

"You foolish man," she muttered. "*What* did you do?"

Greyson didn't reply, his eyes focused on the top of her downturned head as she unwrapped the bandage he had devised from a torn strip of his T-shirt. He hissed slightly when the cloth pulled against the dried blood on the edges of his cut.

"It's bleeding again. Did you even rinse it?"

"Uh . . ." He forced himself to focus, his head swimming with both the scent of her and the pain in his hand. "No water."

She lifted her face unexpectedly, nailing him with that whiskey-colored stare of hers, and he inhaled a shuddering breath at the beauty in those eyes.

"Which reminds me! *Why* is there no water, Greyson?"

He barely heard her question, his eyes lost in hers.

"God, you're so damned beautiful," he said beneath his breath. He lifted his free hand to trace the silky curve of her cheek with his knuckles.

"Don't," she said quietly, one of her hands releasing his injured one to halt the movement.

"Olivia. I've missed you so much."

"No, I think you mean you've *missed* so much. *So much*, Greyson. That first kick, when I felt her and knew she was in there and alive. The first ultrasound, when I heard the incomparable rapid whooshing of her heartbeat. It was . . . it was so indescribable."

"I know. I *know*, Olivia. And it kills me to have missed all of that."

"You don't understand what it did to me, Greyson. You don't know . . ."

"Tell me," he invited her, and she shuddered and closed her eyes, tears—which he had seen shimmering in that golden gaze—overflowing to streak down her cheeks. Greyson made a dismayed sound in the back of his throat and clumsily wiped at the moisture. The first tears he'd seen from her since that night in the hospital. Those tears still haunted his nightmares, and these would torment his waking hours. He hated making her cry. He fucking despised it.

She shook her head in response to his invitation and rested her forehead on his naked chest, just a few centimeters above his heart. He palmed the back of her head, his fingers entwining in the thick, soft curls of her hair. He kissed the top of that honeysuckle-scented head, and she lifted her tear-drenched face to look at him. His hand moved to cup the curve of her cheek, and before he could think of what he was doing, his lips dropped to hers, claiming her mouth in a hungry kiss. A kiss that offered comfort and asked for the same in return.

She made a soft sighing sound and hooked her arm around his neck while her mouth blossomed beneath his, opening up to his gently questing tongue. His other arm curved around her waist, and his fist clenched in the fabric of her dress, just above the swell of her behind. He dragged her close, until he could feel her every curve outlined against him.

His beautiful wife; he had missed her so much. Missed holding her, kissing her . . . loving her. He couldn't seem to get her close enough, and she appeared to feel the same way. As the kiss intensified, she undulated against him, her pelvis grinding against his hardness.

He was suddenly grateful for his lack of underwear: it gave him room to grow, so to speak. His erection lengthened and thickened. With her thrusting against him and the rough denim rubbing his sensitive length, he already felt close to bursting. From just this kiss.

It was a sublime kiss, but he hadn't ever come so close to losing control over his libido before, and certainly never over a kiss. But this was Olivia. His Olivia. His wife, the mother of his child, and he . . .

She planted her hands on his chest and forcefully shoved him away. His head jerked up, and he stared down at her in bewilderment. Her cheeks were flushed with pink, and she had her hands clamped over her breasts.

"I—" he began, wanting to apologize. *Needing* to apologize. That had been so way out of line. But she beat him to it.

"Oh God, I'm sorry," she said, and he frowned in confusion. What did she need to apologize for? This was all on Greyson.

"It just happened." She was still talking, and she shook her head before uttering a miserable, *"God."*

Greyson glanced down to where her hands were still covering her breasts, and he felt his own cheeks go red.

*Shit.*

"No. It's my fault. I shouldn't have . . . uh . . ." He wasn't sure what exactly could have caused the spreading damp patches beneath her hands. Possibly arousal. But he couldn't apologize for turning her on. Not when he felt as horny as a fucking teenager himself. He didn't even care. He wanted to kiss her again, touch her, do so much more. And if that was evidence of her arousal, then fucking bring it on.

He was ready to reach for her again when his eyes fell to her dress, and he froze. Her beautiful, unspoiled lacy white dress. All that innocent perfection . . . covered in blood. His blood.

Just another example of Greyson destroying every perfect thing that he touched.

"Your dress," he said, his voice weighted with misery, and she looked down. Her eyes widened in horror at the sight of all that red on the previously perfect white of her dress.

"Greyson, that cut is really bad," she said, her voice urgent and seemingly unconcerned with the state of her pretty dress. "Give me a minute to change, but rewrap your hand. I'll be right back."

She turned and exited the room, leaving him feeling a little forlorn and a lot lost. He wanted her back—having her close made him feel anchored. Without her, everything was a confusing mess, and all he could see was the bright red on that pristine white. He felt sick to his stomach and fought the urge to retch.

He had ruined it. He had ruined *her*. His perfect, beautiful Olivia.

### Fifteen months ago

*Blood.*

Why was there blood? Greyson stared down at the patch of blood on the snow-white sheets in complete confusion. Olivia had just gone to the bathroom, and he had sat up to watch her leave. His eyes had remained glued to the perfection of her naked ass until she had shut the door between them. That was when his gaze had dropped and he had seen the blood on the sheets of his king-size penthouse-suite bed.

They had just slept together. Her body had responded to his every practiced move with predictable ardor, and Greyson had . . . well, he had *loved* it. She had made him feel more, experience more, than any other woman before her, and he had reveled in it. There was something powerful, so damned powerful, about finally bedding a woman he knew had wanted him for years. A woman *he* had wanted for almost the same amount of time. A woman whom he had considered off limits for way too damned long. It had really gotten his rocks off, and he couldn't wait to have more of her. To try more *with* her.

She had been so damned receptive to his every touch—Greyson was already borderline addicted to her. The smell of her. Taste of her. *Touch* of her. Her softness, her heat, her tightness. *God,* her tightness.

His gaze remained fixated on the red splotch. Trying to make sense of it. It didn't belong there . . . he couldn't figure it out.

He looked down at himself, and then he saw it . . . more blood. Down there. On his still-erect shaft. It caused a shudder of primitive alarm to jolt down his spine until he realized that it wasn't *his* blood. It was hers.

Olivia's.

She exited the bathroom. Her smile was radiant. Perfect.

*So fucking innocent.*

*God! Damn it!*

She crawled back into bed with him and snuggled up to his chest. His arms closed around her automatically. This perfect woman. This beautiful woman. He should have left her alone. He wasn't deserving of the gift she had given him.

Maybe she didn't even consider it a gift. Maybe he was making too much of it. But damn it! He'd known her for too long to not think of it as such.

## *Present day*

Greyson was still lost in the past when she joined him in the bathroom again. She had changed her dress, exchanging one pretty frilly thing for another. This was another long-sleeved lacy dress, a little longer than the previous one. In a light buttery yellow. She had tied up her hair and had a first aid kit under her arm.

"Sit down," she commanded as she entered the small room. Greyson, seeing the familiar stubborn glint in her eyes, knew better than to argue and sank down on the side of the bath.

She tenderly lifted his hand and unwrapped the bloodied scrap of gray fabric. She glowered down at the ragged gash on his palm, while he took one queasy look before diverting his gaze. His palm was a mess, and he couldn't really stand to look at it.

"How did you do this?" she asked, sounding completely grumpy.

"Not sure," he confessed, keeping his gaze fixed on one of the tiny pearly-white buttons on the bodice of her dress.

"You'll need a tetanus shot. It doesn't look deep enough for stitches, but you may need some antibiotics. It *would* be nice if we could give it a proper clean, but without water . . ." She shrugged eloquently, and he grimaced.

"I'll have it back on soon," he promised. "I couldn't work on the tap without turning off the water."

Only he didn't know why the water wasn't back on.

"You can't go back to messing around with the pipes after I bandage your hand," she said sternly. So bossy. She'd been bossy even as a child. His mother had often called her impertinent, complaining that "the girl" probably believed she was a Chapman, she was so demanding.

His mother, while always so aware of appearances, had harbored a genuine fondness for Olivia. But that hadn't stopped the older woman from resisting the prospect of Greyson's marriage to Olivia. Citing their upbringing and backgrounds as prohibitively different.

But appearances had rarely mattered to Greyson when it came to Olivia. He had always wanted her, but once he'd finally had her, he hadn't cherished her. He had allowed distrust and jealousy to cloud his relationship with her. And his relationship with his brother.

"My hand's fine," he said. He could be as stubborn as Olivia when he wanted. And he wasn't about to fail at the first obstacle. He was going to prove to her that he could do this. That he could be useful to her. To Clara.

"I like the name, by the way," he suddenly admitted, and she lifted her eyes to his and tilted her head. He loved how she could ask a question with just that head tilt. He elaborated in answer, "Clara."

Her eyes shuttered. "I don't care. You didn't have any interest in helping me choose a name for her, so I picked one I liked."

"You chose it as a dig at me," he said, keeping his voice light. Once he had seen that first picture of the baby, the name hadn't mattered.

No. It *had* mattered. It had mattered because it had been so damned right.

"But it suits her," he continued. "It's pretty and sweet and perfect, just like her."

She shrugged, a quick, birdlike rise and fall of her narrow shoulders. "Like I said before, I don't care. Your feelings on the matter are completely moot."

Well, hell. That stung.

He cleared his throat. There was silence while she dug around in her medical kit for whatever it was she needed. She muttered bad temperedly beneath her breath while she worked, words and half sentences that just eluded comprehension. She had had the habit for as long as he'd known her—her entire life. She grumbled to herself all the time. Happy, sad, angry, or just concentrating. Sometimes it was a list of things she needed to do. Other times it was like this . . . irritated little words and sounds that made no sense to anyone but Olivia.

He had always found the habit endearing. Even now, when he knew she was probably cursing him beneath her breath, it was cute as hell.

She gently wiped away the blood with some wet wipes, pausing for a long moment when the cleanup revealed the white gold of his wedding band. She stared but didn't comment on it. Greyson had noticed that she no longer wore her ring, a feminine version of his.

They had had a rushed civil ceremony, nothing traditional, wanting to present family and friends with a fait accompli rather than having everyone weigh in on the subject of their nuptials. The only bit of tradition to the ceremony had been the exchange of rings, which they had chosen together.

Greyson hated that she no longer wore hers. But he couldn't blame her for removing it. He had abandoned her at the time when a woman needed her husband most.

He hissed in shock and pain when something cold, wet, and really bloody astringent came into contact with the wound. It served as an effective distraction from his roiling thoughts, and he yanked his injured limb out of her grasp. "*God.* What the hell was that?"

"Don't shout. You'll wake Clara," she warned, grabbing his hand again and dabbing at it some more with a wet cotton swab. Whatever was on the swab smelled sharp and surgical and burned like a son of a bitch!

He cringed when she daubed it all over his cut, his eyes watering at the vicious sting of it.

"Satan uses that shit to torture lost souls in hell," he ground out from between tightly clenched teeth.

Olivia shot him a narrow-eyed look. "It's antiseptic, you big baby," she said. "Clara fussed less when she got her first shots at a mere two months."

"Why does an infant need shots at such a young age?" he asked in horror, momentarily diverted from his own discomfort. He hated needles and couldn't imagine his tiny daughter being stuck with one.

"Her first vaccinations," Olivia replied, her head down again as she thankfully set the bottle of antiseptic aside to pick up the gauze. "She's due for her second dose next week."

Greyson didn't say anything but wondered how she would take it if he asked to accompany them on that doctor's visit. He filed the information away for later. She had allowed him a lot of leeway today, and he knew asking for anything more would be pushing it. He would save that particular request for a different day.

She placed a square cotton pad on his palm over the wound and wrapped it securely in gauze. Her movements were sure and efficient.

"Something tells me you've done this before," he said.

"Lots of little accidents happen in restaurant kitchens. I'm certified to perform first aid and CPR," she said, and he nodded a bit dazedly. He knew her very well, better than she realized, but she was right—there was so much they didn't know about each other.

He tended to withhold himself from others. He hadn't believed that she needed to know more than he wanted her to. But hearing about her first aid certification, he wondered how much more he didn't know about her, and he was greedy—*desperate*—to know everything.

For the first time he understood how frustratingly elusive he must have seemed to her. He kept people at a distance, deliberately parceled out only the most basic information about himself. And he hadn't seen the need to be any different with Olivia. He'd reasoned that she'd known him her entire life, and that was more information than most other women had ever had about him. He'd thought it would be enough.

It wasn't.

And he now recognized that even if he hadn't fucked everything up with his stupidity, if he had continued keeping the most important pieces of himself from her, their marriage probably would have failed anyway.

Because he had expected so much more than he had been willing to give.

"Done," she said, releasing his hand. He immediately missed her soft, gentle touch on his skin and swallowed painfully, trying to alleviate the dryness in his throat.

"Thank you," he said hoarsely, lifting his hand to inspect her neat dressing. He folded his fingers, forming a loose fist, wincing at the painful pull of his skin. "I'll fix the water and then, when Clara's awake, fit the bolts on the door. I'll change the lock tomorrow. I don't think I can do it today."

"I don't think you can do *any* of those other things today. Not with that hand," she argued.

"I'm fine."

"Greyson, don't be . . ."

"I can do it, Olivia," he said softly, and the rest of her argument petered out into a soft sigh.

"What are you trying to prove?" she asked, her voice tired.

"That you can depend on me."

"I don't want to have to depend on you. I don't need you, Greyson. I can do this on my own."

"I know you can," he said. "But you shouldn't have to."

"No, I shouldn't. But I'm going to."

"Olivia, I want . . ."

"Stop." She held up a hand, palm out, effectively halting the rest of his words. "You're not a part of this family. You removed yourself, along with your wants and needs, from the equation. What you want? It's no longer relevant."

"I'm sorry," he finally said, and her eyes flickered with an emotion he couldn't quite place before she lowered her hand and crossed her arms over her chest.

"For what?"

"That this is so hard," he said after a moment's thought, and she sighed, the exhalation from her nostrils short and irritated.

"Wrong thing to be sorry about, Greyson. Care to try again?"

Not certain what she meant or what she wanted, he stared at her. Afraid to talk, knowing that he'd only say the wrong thing again.

His silence didn't help, and she shook her head before casting her eyes to the ceiling as if seeking divine intervention.

"Fix my water, please," she said after a long moment of strained silence. She turned and walked away, leaving him staring miserably at the empty doorway.


Libby checked on Clara when she returned to the living room and found that she was still sleeping soundly. She dragged out her laptop and sat down on the sofa, ready to start planning next month's dessert menu. She wanted MJ's to be renowned for fantastical and delicious desserts. She wanted to have a full evening every week dedicated to desserts. A chef's tasting menu of only desserts.

This was a revised dream. Originally Libby had wanted to own and operate her own dessert bar, but she now wanted to spend as much time as possible with Clara. Working at MJ's was a way for her to achieve both dreams.

But she couldn't concentrate. Her thoughts were jumbled and confusing. She should have told him to leave. Should have insisted he go. Why was he still here? She knew he would have gone if she'd insisted, but she couldn't bring herself to say the words.

Maybe it was the glimpses of vulnerability she had seen in his eyes and on his face. That was new. He was so far out of his comfort zone that it was ridiculous. With the clothes and the damned toolbox. She still couldn't get over the toolbox. Typical Greyson—he didn't do things by half measures. He had bought the biggest, heaviest, most professional-looking toolbox he could find. And Libby was pretty damned sure he didn't have a clue what most of the tools were for.

She shouldn't have allowed that kiss. Or reciprocated. But it had been so long since she'd felt his mouth on hers, and she'd be a liar if she said she hadn't missed it. She was only human; she had weaknesses, and Greyson had always been her biggest one. And it was *so* much worse now that she knew how it felt to be held, touched, and kissed by him.

Her hand drifted up, tracing the curves of her lips as she recalled the heat of his mouth on hers. Her nipples beaded, and she groaned and flushed when she recalled the reason their kiss had stopped. She had read about sexual arousal sometimes resulting in a letdown reflex but hadn't really thought about it after that. Since she hadn't been particularly concerned about being sexually aroused anytime soon.

Her body was still something of a mystery to her after giving birth. There was the unfamiliar weight of her breasts. The swell of her stomach had gone down a lot, thanks to her natural slenderness, but it still retained a poochiness that she wasn't sure would ever go away. And the fading silvery stretch marks streaking down her abdomen felt like battle scars, which she wore with pride.

There was so much about herself that she no longer understood or recognized. But that surge of arousal—the need and urgent desire—that she had felt when she had kissed Greyson had been so welcome and achingly familiar.

Until her breasts had leaked, plunging her back into confusion and reality.

"Damn it," she muttered to herself. "Get it together, Libby. He's going to fix the water, and you're going to send him on his way. And that will be that."

She inhaled a deep, shuddering breath and scrubbed her palm over her face before forcing her attention back to the computer screen and going to work.

Greyson tentatively emerged from the bathroom nearly an hour later. Clara was awake, and Libby had set aside her computer in favor of playing with her baby. She was sitting on the sofa, holding Clara up in both hands and blowing raspberries on the chuckling infant's round tummy, when Greyson walked in.

He was a mess. His hair was in disarray, and his face and still-naked chest were gleaming with sweat. He was absently patting at his chest and under his arms with his hoodie. Yet another uncharacteristic thing for the very fastidious Greyson to do. But then he followed that up by carefully folding the hoodie and placing it on the wide arm of one of her easy chairs. If she wasn't so distracted by his utter sexiness, Libby would have laughed at the quintessentially fussy Greyson move. Something familiar amid all the unfamiliarity.

His jeans rode low on his narrow hips, exposing his sexy Adonis belt. He looked positively drool worthy, and both Clara and Libby froze when he entered the living room. They stared at him, one with a baby's avid curiosity and the other with a woman's sincere appreciation of a fine male form.

Libby blinked self-consciously, willing herself to look away and back to the baby, who was still dangling in front of her. Libby lowered Clara into her lap, turning her to face Greyson, at whom the infant was still staring in wide-eyed fascination.

Greyson's eyes dropped to the curious baby, and a wide, genuine grin parted his lips for a few seconds. The expression was gone all too soon when he refocused his gaze on Libby.

"Water's working."

"Is it?" Libby asked in frank disbelief. She couldn't help it: she got up, Clara in her arms, and went to the kitchen to check. After a few sputters, the water flowed without any problem at all.

"Wow, Greyson, that's"—*unexpected*—"great. Thank you."

"It's a temporary fix. I did what I could."

"It's more than I was expecting," she replied honestly, feeling terrible for underestimating him. While *also* feeling annoyed that this was yet another thing Greyson the Great could do.

He winced, ducking his head and avoiding her eyes while rubbing the back of his neck as if to relieve tension or muscular strain. Libby tilted her head, trying to assess his body language. He lifted his eyes to hers again, and she couldn't quite read the expression in them.

"I didn't *quite* do it alone," he admitted softly, looking embarrassed. Her eyebrows rose, but she didn't say anything, silently inviting him to say more. "I looked for some solutions on Google."

Libby huffed a quiet laugh. How like Greyson to consider that a failing.

"Everybody uses the internet to seek answers sometimes, Greyson," she said, feeling magnanimous now that he had admitted to needing help. He swallowed, his Adam's apple bobbing with the motion. Momentarily diverted by the movement of his throat, Libby's gaze snagged on that strong, tanned expanse of flesh, and she was seized by the almost uncontrollable urge to kiss him there, then lick him to taste the salt and musk of his skin.

She was so distracted by that unwelcome compulsion that she missed the first part of his next statement.

". . . didn't work."

"Uh. What? Sorry, I didn't quite catch that," she said self-consciously, and he cleared his throat.

"None of the so-called answers I found worked."

"But . . . the water's running."

"No . . . before this. The original fix I found on the internet was the reason the water stopped working."

"I see," she said. When she didn't see much of anything at all. What was he getting at?

"Nothing I googled could help me fix what I broke . . . so I had to call an expert."

*Oh.*

"I see," she said again. Leaning back against the kitchen sink and absently tugging a strand of her hair out of Clara's grasp.

"A twenty-four-hour plumber. She talked me through what I needed to do to get the water running again. But like I said, it's a temporary fix. You'll need to get someone in to look at the plumbing."

"A *professional*, you mean?" she asked pointedly, and he grimaced and nodded in reply.

"I'm sorry," he apologized quietly. His second *I'm sorry* in under two hours. That had to be a record for him. "I thought I could fix it."

"Once again apologizing for the wrong things," she said beneath her breath, and he looked taken aback by that response. She cleared her throat before asking another question. "Is the problem worse than it was before?"

"No. I just got the water back on. But the underlying problem remains the same. I can't tell you what that is because . . ." He shrugged. "Well . . . I mean, I'm not a plumber, am I?"

The question was almost defensive, and Libby bit her lip to stop herself from laughing.

"That's what I've been saying all along," she reminded him.

"I'm paying for the plumber I called, since it was my mistake that needed resolving."

"Yes, you are," she agreed, pushing herself away from the sink and walking back to the sofa. He remained standing in the kitchen but turned to face her.

"No arguments?" he asked, sounding relieved, and she rolled her eyes before sitting down and tickling Clara, who dissolved into chuckles.

"Why would I argue? I'm a firm believer in the whole 'if you broke it, fix it' philosophy."

"That's what I'm trying to do," he said, his voice thickening, and she lifted her eyes from the laughing baby to the man still standing in her kitchen. "I'm trying to fix what I broke, Olivia. I'm trying to fix us."

"Greyson," she said, her voice laden with regret. "We were broken from the start."

"I don't believe that. I *refuse* to believe that," he said fiercely.

"Believe what you want, but you know it's true," she said with equal ferocity. Clara stopped babbling and stared up at her mother uncertainly, and Libby gentled her tone. "Thank you for being honest. About the plumber."

She knew how much that must have cost his pride, and it did mean a lot that he had been truthful over something he could easily have hedged about.

"I'm trying to be different. Worthy. A good father and husband."

"Greyson, please . . . *stop*," she said on a broken whisper. "You still have the chance to be a good father."

"But not a good husband?" he elaborated, and she sucked her lower lip into her mouth, her gaze not faltering from his intent stare. His shoulders sagged, and he cleared his throat before turning away quickly.

"I'll get that dead bolt on the front door," he said over his shoulder.

"You don't have to," she said, and he stopped, his back to her. He just stood there, not saying a word. The defeated droop of his shoulders and head got to her. She screwed her eyes shut, biting the inside of her cheek hard, before continuing, "Not now. Why don't we have some lunch or something? You can give your hand a break and spend some time with Clara."

He turned, the movement so swift it nearly unbalanced him. *"Really?"* he asked, the expression on his face boyishly keen and hard to resist.

"Greyson, this isn't easy for me. You hurt me. You hurt *us*," she said, dipping her chin toward Clara. "I don't know how to . . . to move forward. How to forgive you. I don't think I ever can. But Clara, she's innocent in this, and I don't want her hurt. You have to promise me. *Promise me* you won't hurt her. You won't make her love you and then abandon her."

*Like you did with me.* Libby blinked fiercely, forcing her tears to remain at bay as she determinedly bit back the revealing words. They remained unspoken, and she hoped he wouldn't find them lurking between the lines. She had never told him she loved him. Had never really known if she did. But she knew now. His betrayal had hurt as much as it did *because* she loved him.

"I'm so sorry you think I'd do that."

She sighed impatiently, and he halted. "Another apology for the *wrong* thing," she pointed out, and he made a soft sound of distress in the back of his throat.

"I promise you, Olivia," he continued quietly. "On my life. On *her* life, which is more precious to me than you would ever know . . . I will never again intentionally hurt her. Or you."

"I don't matter," she said, and he shook his head.

"You do."

"No. I don't. Clara is all that matters. You don't hurt her, Greyson. You love her and protect her."

"Of course," he said. "Of course I will, Olivia. How could I not?"


Greyson stared at them, his daughter and the wife who no longer wanted to be his wife, and once again felt the urge to wrap them both in his arms and never let them go. Olivia, so fierce and beautiful and proud, didn't want to need him, didn't want to want him . . . and he couldn't blame her for that.

But he still had one small glimmer of hope. Fifteen months ago, sex had been the driving force behind their relationship. It had brought them together and kept them together. For a time.

In the end it hadn't been enough to build a foundation strong enough to support a marriage. They had needed more than just great sex. They had needed commitment, respect, understanding, trust. Mutual admiration—what some would call love. Those fundamental building blocks had been missing, and their marriage had crumbled at the first real test. But the sex . . . it had allowed them the opportunity to try.

And it could again.

Greyson wasn't one to make the same mistake twice, but after that kiss he knew she still desired him. He saw how her eyes lingered on his body. Yes, she still wanted him. And if that was all he had to work with, he would damned well use it again. But this time, he'd make sure they added the other essential ingredients into their relationship. He'd make their bond so damned unbreakable even an earthquake would not be able to shatter it.

They had great, almost irresistible chemistry, and they had Clara. He could make this work. He *had* to make it work.

# Chapter Nine

"I'll get lunch started. You're definitely not staying for dinner, so I think we can put those steaks to use now," Olivia said after a long, fraught moment of silence.

"Wait, I thought you said I should prepare the steaks."

She laughed at that and shook her head. "I'm starving, and after what you did with breakfast, I'd rather you didn't set foot in my kitchen again," she said.

Jesus, he couldn't seem to get anything right today. She got up and padded toward him. Before Greyson knew what she intended, she deposited Clara into his unprepared arms. He clutched at the baby, terrified of dropping her, and Clara immediately began to fret in his tight hold.

"What are you doing?" he asked on an urgent whisper. "She's going to cry again."

"I'll be busy in the kitchen, and it's your job to entertain her. She likes peekaboo, tickles, and tummy raspberries. And she *always* likes being swooped."

"Swooped?" he asked, forcing the word past his suddenly dry and closed-up throat.

"You know? When you lift her above your head and then kind of lower her a bit faster?" She demonstrated with an up-and-down motion of her hands, accompanying the gesture with a whooshing sound. Clara stopped fretting and chuckled at her mother's actions. Olivia grinned and, wrapping her hands around Greyson's forearm, leaned in to kiss the baby's adorable nose.

"You like that, don't you, Clara girl?" Olivia looked up at Greyson, still touching his bare arm. He was excruciatingly aware of her soft hands on his skin, but she didn't seem as affected. Instead she was smiling at him. A sweet, unforced, genuinely warm smile, filled with all the love and affection she felt for Clara.

God, she could move mountains with that smile.

"Just play with her, Greyson. You'll both be fine."

"What if I drop her?" he asked, panicking when she removed her hands from his arm and turned away. He felt abandoned, even though she was still in the same room.

She looked at him over her shoulder, responding to the frantic question with just one word. "Don't."

Greyson's eyes dropped to Clara, who was staring at him with wide blue eyes. Her rosebud mouth puckered into a pout, and her eyes filled.

*Shit.*

He loosened his tight hold on her and forced a smile. The movement of his lips temporarily stopped the onslaught of tears, and her head tilted in the same quizzical way her mother's often did. The familiar gesture in this brand-new little person delighted him, and his smile widened.

Her arms thrashed, her legs kicked, and she cooed. Returning his smile with a gorgeous one of her own. Gummy and drooly and perfect.

He exhaled slowly.

"Okay," he whispered, his words for her ears only. "Okay, honey. We've got this, right? You're going to be a good girl for your daddy, right?"

More cooing and smiling.

"God, you're so perfect," he said, still keeping his voice down. An emotional lump formed in his throat. His eyes burned as he gazed down into the face of the child he had so carelessly and callously tossed aside. He had nearly lost her. Could still lose her . . . but he had this moment. So generously gifted to him by a woman who had every right to hate him.

"I love you, Clara," he whispered and kissed her soft cheek, his nose nuzzling the powder-scented silky black curls at her temple. "I love you so much. And I'm sorry I wasn't there for you. Daddy's so sorry."

Libby watched him covertly, not wanting him to feel like he was under scrutiny. She wanted his interaction with Clara to be as natural as possible. After a few moments of just holding the baby and cuddling her close—whispering words meant only for her uncomprehending ears—he gingerly made his way to the comforter on the floor. He kicked off his trainers before padding to the center of the comforter and sinking into a cross-legged sitting position. They made quite a picture, the big, bare-chested man, wearing nothing but a pair of jeans and socks, holding the tiny, curly-haired little girl so protectively close to his chest.

He slipped his hands around her torso, his big palms folding around her back, and lifted her until he had her dangling at eye level in front of him. Clara kicked happily, her arms waving as she blew spit bubbles and charmed her father with her smile. He grinned back and dropped an affectionate peck on her wet mouth before blowing raspberries into her cheek and neck. Clara rewarded him with a squeal and high-pitched giggles, prompting him to do it again and again.

Satisfied that they were okay for now, Libby left them to it and bustled around the kitchen getting their lunch ready.

When she looked up again, Greyson was flat on his back with Clara held straight above his face. The baby squealed and tried to grab his hair, but he lifted her until she couldn't reach, and she kicked and squealed even louder. Until he lowered her again, and she made another grab for him. That continued for a while, and Libby was openly smiling at their antics. She didn't once fear for Clara; the baby was absolutely safe in those large, strong hands.

Libby started on the salad and vegetables, and by the time lunch was done, she realized that it had gone quiet. She looked up, and her heart stuttered in her chest.

They were both asleep. Clara was on her tummy on Greyson's broad chest, her cheek resting between his pecs, a tiny fist curled up next to her face. Greyson had a hand on the baby's back to keep her in place, and his head was turned to the side, facing the kitchen, and Libby wondered if he had been watching her work before falling asleep.

Libby swallowed convulsively a couple of times before clearing her throat. She had never been more confused in her life. She didn't know what to do and wasn't sure who to talk to about this. Her parents would listen but offer little advice. They had always encouraged her to make her own decisions and rarely argued against them. Even when she had married Greyson, and she had known they didn't approve. And then when she had left, they had wanted her to stay with them but hadn't pushed hard when she had refused.

There was always Harris. But Harris was already caught between a rock and a hard place with this situation; she didn't want to make it any worse for him. And then there was Tina . . .

Thinking of Tina made her eyes automatically seek out her phone, which she hadn't looked at all morning. She picked it up, and sure enough, there were a couple of messages from Tina. Feeling a swell of relief, Libby opened them up.

I'm so sorry about yesterday. I want to tell you about it. I want to explain. I do love Clara so much. But it's really hard for me to talk about.

The message made her frown. It was becoming imperative to have a proper talk with Tina. She had to figure out if there was a way to help Tina get through whatever this was. Not just for the business's sake, not even for their friendship, but because Tina appeared to be floundering and clearly needed help.

I hope you're making him unclog drains and plunge toilets. I love you. Chat later.

That was more like the irreverent friend she knew and loved. It made her chest ache, the thought of how much she could lose if she and the other woman didn't talk about whatever was going on with Tina. She wanted her best friend back.

Libby sighed and ran a tired hand over her face. She looked over at Greyson and Clara again and walked over to the comforter, where the man she had once loved so fiercely was sleeping with their daughter securely tucked against his bare chest. She lifted her phone and couldn't resist taking a few photos. Satisfied, she put the phone on her improvised coffee table before sinking down to her haunches and tucking her dress modestly beneath her thighs.

"Greyson," she whispered. He was sleeping soundly, his mouth slack and slightly open, with soft little snores escaping on every third breath. His jaw was black with a two-day growth of beard. The look was unfamiliar but attractive on him, making him look a bit piratical. Especially with the narrow planes of his face.

She allowed her eyes to run over the rest of him. He was still toned, taut, and beautiful, but his weight loss was a lot more evident now that she wasn't distracted by his piercing eyes or the overwhelming force of his personality. It was easy to miss it because he was a big man, but he had definitely lost a significant amount of weight.

She wondered about that, wondered about those months without contact. What had he been doing? Clearly not eating properly.

"Greyson." She added more volume to her voice, and he started, which woke Clara. And Clara was grouchy when she didn't wake naturally. She immediately started crying. She lifted her head and saw Greyson instead of her mother, and her cries escalated into shrieks. The man who had been her best buddy just half an hour ago was now a terrifying stranger to her.

She kicked, and Greyson's hold slipped. Clara slid slightly to the side before Libby reached out and plucked the baby to her chest. She sent Greyson, who looked devastated at Clara's reaction, a quick smile.

"She's cranky when she wakes up. Don't take it personally," she said. "And she's hungry and"—she took a delicate sniff and wrinkled her nose—"oh *my* . . . a little stinky." She directed her next comments to Clara. "Time for another nappy change, you noisy little stinker."

She straightened, and Greyson got up, too, immediately towering above Libby. He was hovering anxiously.

"What can I do?" he asked, and she gave him a speculative look.

"You really want to help?" she asked, and he nodded a little desperately. "Well, get your hoodie on—enough with the soft-core exhibitionism—and join me in the room."

He eagerly did as he was told and was in the room behind her seconds later. Libby already had a towel spread out on the bed, and Clara was on her back, her face red and angry, while she waved her fists and legs in futile rage, shrieking all the while.

"I'm going to stick the food back in the oven. You get her out of the onesie and take the dirty nappy off. I'll show you how to put a fresh one on when I get back."

"Wait. *What?*" He looked horrified by her demand, and Libby savored that look for a moment before grinning—she knew there was probably a hint of evil in her expression—and leaving him to it.

Maybe it was cruel, but she'd had to learn a lot of this stuff on her own. It would do him good to at least try.

"But she's crying." His voice floated from the room behind her, and she bit back a chuckle.

"Babies do that. Parents don't get to hand them over when they start crying," she tossed back at him over her shoulder. "You'll be fine."

"Yes, but will she?" he called back, his voice escalating. He sounded terrified. It was the first time in all the years she'd known Greyson that he'd ever raised his voice above normal speaking range.

"You won't break her, Greyson." God, she hoped not.

She kept a close ear on proceedings as she deliberately lingered over putting the food in the oven. She heard him frantically trying to shush Clara, then utter a swift, heartfelt prayer. She waited a few moments, and then . . .

"Oh my *God*. Oh fuck. Sweet Jesus, what the fuck did you eat, baby girl?"

Libby heard him retch, and she covered her mouth with her hand as she fought back her laughter.

"*Olivia!* I think she's sick. Christ, this can't be normal."

Libby took a deep breath, lifting her eyes to the ceiling as she strove to keep her laughter under control. Another deep breath, and she threw back her shoulders and walked into the room, where Greyson was still gagging and holding a soiled nappy at arm's length. Clara was no longer crying; she was staring up at Greyson—her toes in her hands—chortling at his antics.

Compressing her lips and biting back her giggles, Libby reached for a disposal bag and held it open for him.

"Put it in here," she instructed him. He dropped it as if it were toxic waste, and Libby knotted the bag quickly before handing him the wipes. He took them from her, then looked down at Clara, back at the wipes, and at Libby. He did that a few times before shaking his head.

"I don't know what you want me to do with these," he said, sounding confused and a little helpless.

"You can't just put a new nappy on that stinky butt. You need to clean it."

He blanched. His eyes dropped to Clara's naked tush and then back up to Libby's gaze.

"Oh man, that's not right." He looked like he was about to retch again. "Don't I get gloves or something for this job?"

He was so unintentionally entertaining that Libby wished she were filming this.

"Stop being such a drama queen, it's just poop."

"She's not even on solid foods yet. How could this come from just milk? Maybe it's something *you* ate? Are you sure she's not sick?"

"You're stalling, Greyson. That bum's not going to wipe itself." She probably shouldn't be enjoying this as much as she was, but seriously, it was cute and hilarious.

He swallowed, and looking like a man approaching the guillotine, he pulled a fistful of baby wipes from the packet and approached Clara cautiously. His arm was outstretched as if he were wielding a crucifix instead of mere wipes.

He was thwarted by Clara's flailing little legs.

"Grab her feet with your free hand and hold them up and out of the way."

He did as he was told and closed his eyes before wiping in the general vicinity of the mess.

"You're not watching what you're doing."

"It's seriously gross," he said, his voice back to its usual quiet tones but filled with revulsion.

"Uh-huh," Libby agreed unsympathetically. Clara, not happy with being restrained, was starting to pout, her lower lip trembling and her eyes filling.

Greyson sighed, his face softening as he stared down into Clara's sad face.

"Okay, stinky butt, no need to cry," he murmured gently. "I'll get you cleaned up in no time."

He was still tentative about it, but faced with the threat of tears, he did a pretty decent job. By the time he had put on the fresh nappy, after several failed attempts, he was flushed and grinning like an all-powerful conquering hero.

"That's not bad for my first attempt, right?" he asked, seeking praise.

"Fourth attempt," Libby corrected him, pointing to the pile of discarded nappies.

"Third," he bargained. "That second-to-last try doesn't count, since she peed while I was putting it on."

"Hungry?" Libby asked him, and he wrinkled his nose.

"I don't know, I still have that awful stench stuck up my nostrils. I'm not sure I'll ever be able to eat again," he said. They both looked down at their freshly powdered, primped, and preened daughter. She was watching them in that serious, thoughtful baby way and sucking at her fist.

"Well, Clara's hungry," Libby said. "I should feed her. Do you mind getting the plates out of the oven? The food's probably gone a bit dry by now. I'll join you in a few minutes."

Lunch was *nice*. Greyson could think of no other word to describe it. The meal itself was spectacular. Then again, even though it had sat in the oven for a while, it had still been prepared by an exceedingly talented chef. Perfectly cooked medium-rare steak with roasted sweet potatoes and cilantro pesto—it was mouthwateringly delicious. No surprise there.

What *was* surprising was how comfortably companionable the meal was. In the past, before her pregnancy, their meals had always been fraught with sexual tension, the food just fuel to replenish lost energy and prepare them for their next athletic bout of sex. They hadn't talked much, and on the occasions he had spoken, it was invariably about work. His or hers. It didn't matter; it had been filler. The real talking had been done with their eyes and their seemingly careless touches. Promises and intentions made clear through long, speaking glances, with the occasional brush of her hand over his or his arm against hers.

Today felt different.

"This restaurant is quite a big undertaking for both you and Martine," Greyson said, taking a sip of water. She had offered him wine, but he was still abstaining and would probably continue to do so long into the foreseeable future.

"It's exciting, but I'm not sure how invested Tina is in the venture. She seems to be half assing it," Olivia said, her eyes downcast. She was twirling her fork restlessly.

"What do you mean?" Greyson prompted her, and she lifted her shoulders before spearing a perfectly golden potato almost aggressively.

"I don't know, she's making silly and unnecessary mistakes. We had an ad announcing the relaunch, but it never got emailed to the newspaper. It somehow got stuck in her outbox and didn't send. She also mixed up the banner delivery dates. We designed this awesome relaunch banner to hang in the window, along with flyers to put under windscreen wipers and distribute to local businesses . . . and she gave them the wrong dates. How do you get something like that wrong? Sometimes, I feel like she's her own worst enemy. But I've put a lot into this as well, and I don't want to fail. It means too much to me. But what's the point in me working my butt off if . . ." She stopped talking abruptly, her cheeks reddening. Her shoulders sagged, and she sighed.

"I sound like such a bitch. Slagging off my best friend," she said softly. "Things have been a little tense between Tina and me lately."

"How so?" Greyson asked, hating how miserable she looked.

"It's nothing," Olivia said, clamming up. Which frustrated Greyson. He wanted to know what was bothering her, wanted to be her confidant and offer advice on how to make things better. He hated feeling like a voyeur, his nose pressed up against the glass and his breath steaming up the window as he stared in on her life. Forced to remain outside in the freezing cold while it was happy and cozy and safe inside with Olivia and Clara.

He wanted to be someone to whom she could entrust her innermost thoughts. He had never been that person, had never wanted to be that person . . . but now he looked at her and wanted to know *everything* about her.

"You can tell me," he urged, and she laughed, the sound a little bitter.

"I'd rather not," she replied, lifting the fork to her lips and biting the potato in half.

"Would you tell Harris?" he impulsively asked, then immediately wished he could retract the question. Her head whipped up, and she stared at him curiously, chewing slowly while she pondered that question.

"Harris is easy to confide in," she finally said.

"And I'm not?" Hell, where were these questions coming from? It felt like he had zero filter between his brain and his mouth, and that was terrifying for someone like Greyson. He usually had control over every syllable he uttered and every movement he made. But today . . . he barely recognized himself. He had never in his life—not even when he had been a kid—rolled around on the floor before. And yet today, with Clara, it had felt completely natural. And he had loved every second of it.

"No," she replied, after taking a moment to consider his question. "You're not. Not easy to confide in or talk to or be with."

Jesus, that was more elaboration than he needed. Whatever asshole said not to ask questions if you weren't prepared to hear the answers was a smug, know-it-all bastard.

"I can change," he said, hating the edge of desperation in his voice.

"I don't think you should," she said with a shake of her head. "Not for me. When you attempt to change something so fundamental about yourself, it should be for you or someone you love."

He blinked, having no real response to that.

"You're my wife," he reminded her faintly, and her small smile was bittersweet.

"Not for much longer, Greyson," she said gently.

He swallowed. A few minutes ago, he had been marveling about how *nice* this fucking meal was, and suddenly it felt like he was swallowing razor blades and breaking bread with an adversary.

And he *hated* it.

Clara, who had been napping in her playpen, thankfully chose that moment to wake up and cry. Greyson cleared his throat and pushed his half-eaten meal aside.

"I'll get that dead bolt on," he said. "I'll change the lock tomorrow."

She nodded, getting up to tend to Clara.

After a few stops and starts with the unfamiliar drill, the dead bolt was fairly easy to install. And half an hour later, he stood back and surveyed his accomplishment with pride. It was on straight—who knew how awesome levels could be?—and it was working. And when Olivia came over to look—Clara was snoozing in her playpen again—Greyson felt like he had conquered the world.

He wanted to beat his chest and roar.

"Not bad," Olivia said, sliding the bolt in place. "Thank you."

"I didn't even have to use Google for this one," he boasted, his eyes on her profile, and her lips twitched and hiked up at the corner.

"Progress," she said lightly.

"Damned straight."

"Greyson . . ."

He turned toward her, and she did the same; they were standing chest to chest. So close he could feel the heat coming off her, inhaling the familiar scent of vanilla and honeysuckle. He went rock hard, a visceral reaction to the scent, the closeness . . . the husky sound of his name on her tongue. His breath caught as he saw her eyes flare and spark as the awareness hit her. The answering heat in that gaze was all he needed.

"Olivia," he moaned and was embarrassed by the uncontrollable huskiness of his voice. He stepped closer; she did the same, and when he leaned down to kiss her, she met him halfway.

His hand found the curve of her neck, his mouth welcomed her tongue, and his pelvis rocked against the inviting cradle of hers. He turned them until her back was to the door and he was plastered against her front, one hand still caressing her throat, the other braced flat against the wood of the door above her head. He rocked his hardness against her softness and moaned at the unbearable friction. He felt out of control. An unfamiliar, heady sensation. He never lost control, but he felt like he was about to come, hot, hard, and ready for her. Too damned ready.

She gasped into his mouth and hiked up one leg. He dropped his hand from the door and grasped the crook of her knee, pulling the leg up even higher, before sliding his hand down the silky expanse of that long, toned thigh. He grabbed hold of her firm ass, his fingers digging in as he pulled her closer. His mouth left hers and traversed down her jawline to her sensitive neck, dropping suctioning kisses en route to the scented little nook below her ear. An area he knew could make her knees weak if he touched and kissed it in *just* the right way.

She sighed when first his lips and then his tongue caressed her there, but she squealed when he took a gentle nip at the flesh and then nuzzled it with his nose—loving the scent of her arousal mingling with the warm vanilla and honeysuckle—and then with his beard.

*"Oh."* Her breath left her in a single soft, exhaled moan, and her head flew back and thumped against the door. Greyson regretfully left the little secret cove of sensation and meandered down the column of her neck to the swell of her breasts, kissing the fuller mounds reverently.

Not sure if it was okay to touch the way he wanted to touch, he erred on the side of caution and moved back up, leaving a necklace of kisses on her décolletage before finding her hungry mouth again.

The hand he had on her behind moved up to cup one of her breasts gently, exploring the new shape behind the thick padding of her bra. Her nipple was so hard he could feel it burning into his palm like coal, despite the layering between her skin and his.

"Is this okay?" he asked against her mouth, and she moaned her assent. Despite her clear enjoyment of his touch, he did not want to risk a repeat of what had happened to her earlier and instead moved down to the swell of her stomach. Her contours there were also new, but he loved the fuller mound of it. He knew that that was where their baby had rested and had a violent longing to go back and do what he should have done then. Feel Clara moving in Libby's womb, talk to his unborn baby and reassure her mother.

He felt tearing regret at the loss, but his hand had a life of its own, not caring about his remorse or pain. Instead it crept under her skirt and found the lace of her panties.

She arched into his touch, and thus encouraged, his hand slipped down the front of the lace and found her sopping, swollen slickness an instant later. He gently grasped the full bud of her clitoris between the knuckles of his first and middle fingers and rolled it in a firm massaging motion.

She cried out, her arms clamping around his neck. Her grip was almost painful as she tried to drag him even closer.

"Oh my *God!*" She sounded shocked, almost horrified, and she buried her face in his neck as she pushed herself against his hand and shuddered against him. Her orgasm was fast and powerful and left her limp in his arms.

He was as shocked as Olivia. She had always been extremely sensitive and receptive to his touch, but this was way faster than usual. She had gone quiet in his arms, still shuddering intermittently, her breath coming in harsh sobs, but she was no longer urgently moving against him or kissing him.

"That was such a mistake," she whispered into his ear, and he screwed his eyes shut.

"We still have *this*, Olivia. It was good between us before. It can be good again."

"I admit we have some serious chemistry, but . . . ," she began to say, her face still in his neck, before she paused and then sighed. "Uh . . . do you mind moving your hand?"

The request was so polite that for a second, he had no idea what she meant. Until she wriggled against him. He flushed and withdrew his hand from her panties. He stepped away from her in the same motion.

"Whoa," he cried in alarm when she wobbled, and he grabbed her arm to keep her steady. She found her footing immediately, and he loosened his grip and reluctantly let her go.

Her eyes dropped to the front of his jeans, which did little to conceal his erection.

"Sorry," she said with a grimace. "That can't be pleasant."

"It's not. But it won't kill me."

She didn't say anything in response to that, merely smoothed her hair back from her face. "You should go. Thank you. For the door and the plumbing . . . but please just leave."

"Olivia, we still have this spark between us. We can—"

"It's just sex, Greyson. It's always been just sex between us," she interrupted fiercely.

"We made it work before."

"You know that's not true," she said tiredly. "It didn't work. It never could. Because without the sex, what else did we have? Just lies and distrust. Our marriage was doomed to fail, and our relationship—such as it was—should have remained sexual until it burned itself out and we both went our separate ways."

*What the hell is wrong with me?* Libby despaired. Why was it so hard to resist him?

"You know that you're sending me some very confusing signals, right?" he asked gently.

"I know that," she admitted, her voice exasperated and filled with regret. "You don't think I know that? I'm confused too. I know I don't want you in my life anymore, but for some crazy reason I still want you in my bed. I'm only human, and we've always been really great together, and I can't stop thinking of that."

And it didn't help that he was suddenly so much sweeter, more approachable, and more appealing than before. Her head and heart couldn't agree on how she felt about him. Her head told her she hated him and should keep him at a distance. Her heart said he was the father of her child and he was trying to make amends . . . and then her horny body joined the conversation and said, *Hey, guys, let's sleep with him. That'll be fun and awesome and cool, right?*

Ridiculous.

"You still want me in your bed?" he asked, his face lighting up. Jeez, how like a man to focus on that detail.

"Yes, but it's not going to happen."

His face took on a frustratingly neutral expression before he nodded. "You're right, I should leave. But . . ." She tilted her head, waiting for him to continue. "Can I come tomorrow? To replace the door handle?"

"You can come in the morning or evening, after Clara and I have left. The door will obviously be unlocked . . ."

He nodded, and before she knew what he was going to do, he walked to the playpen to stare down at the sleeping baby.

"I'll see you soon, baby girl," he said quietly, shoving his hands into his pockets as he watched her. He turned his head unexpectedly and snared Libby's eyes with his intent gaze.

"Thank you," he said, his voice holding a gruff note of sincerity. "For today. It meant everything."

He strode to the front door, brushing past Libby on his way out, and departed without another word. Leaving Libby with the overwhelming and confusing compulsion to call him back. Fortunately, she curbed the impulse, closing and engaging the newly installed dead bolt before she was once again tempted to throw caution and common sense to the wind.

Harris wasn't at the house when Greyson got back. Which was odd, since his car was parked out front. Stranger still was the fact that Martine's Lexus was missing, leading Greyson to conclude that either Harris had gone walking in this terrible weather, or—more likely—he and Martine were off somewhere together.

Intriguing.

Martine had very good reason to never want to speak or spend time with Harris. Greyson didn't think either of the other two was aware of exactly how much he knew about what had happened between them ten years ago. In fact, Greyson had put out several fires in the immediate aftermath of their encounter. Another fact he knew neither Harris nor Tina was privy to. He doubted they would have appreciated his intervention.

He was on everybody's shit list these days, and even though he had had the best of intentions, they probably wouldn't have anything positive to say about his involvement in the matter.

He clenched his fists as he blindly stared at the shabby interior of the house. His eyes fell to the table and the remnants of a shared meal. Two place settings, two empty wineglasses. His eyebrows rose.

Even more interesting.

Greyson sighed heavily, and his shoulders sagged. He had too much else on his mind to spend time speculating about what could possibly be happening between Harris and Martine. Whatever was going on wouldn't end well—of that he was sure. In fact, Greyson wasn't sure there were any happy endings in sight for any of them.

He briefly considered cleaning up after the other two, but his hand was throbbing, and he was developing a headache, and he just . . .

*Fuck it.*

He felt defeated.

He should be with them. He shouldn't be here in this shitty house, wearing these unfamiliar clothes, feeling sweaty, grubby . . .

Helpless, hopeless, and so fucking alone.

He sank down onto the sofa and covered his face with his shaking hands. He allowed himself a moment . . . two . . . three . . .

*Stop this!* the stern inner voice of his conscience commanded. It was the same voice that had finally penetrated his alcoholic haze three months ago, the voice that had clamored, *This is wrong!* in his head when he had accused Harris of the most reprehensible offenses . . . the voice that had *constantly* urged him to convince Olivia to marry him. Every time he'd been with her, every time they had made love, it had been there: *Marry this woman. You have to marry her.*

It had gone completely silent when she had announced her pregnancy. And then had flared back with a vengeance after Clara's birth. Demanding he look at her, pick her up, hold her close.

Turned out his conscience was a damned sight savvier than Greyson. He should probably listen to it more.

To take his mind off his inner turmoil, he dug his phone out of his jeans pocket and checked his messages quickly. One from his mother, telling him they were going to renovate the kitchen. He shook his head. His mother always kept them informed about random crap like that. It was her way of staying in touch with her sons. He had no doubt Harris had received a similar—if not identical—text.

His father had sent a dad joke. These had become more frequent since the old man's retirement two years ago. No real content, just dumb memes and terrible jokes. His parents were as dry—and boring—as toast, and Greyson knew he took after them. But he did not see anything wrong with keeping one's emotions under lock and key. It was neat and efficient. Harris was the overly emotional one in the family, and it had been tiring to keep up with his many moods during their childhood and early adolescence. And then that thing with Martine. Shit, Greyson would never have gotten himself into a similar situation.

But Olivia . . . she had always incited more feelings than he knew what to do with. First as a kid, trailing after them, always wanting to play whatever games they were playing. Harris had happily roughhoused with her, while Greyson had observed grimly from the sidelines. Always with a nervous knot in his stomach as he watched his careless brother carry the petite little girl around on his shoulders or back. Fearing that Harris would drop her, hurt her . . . break one of her fragile bones. But for all his rough-and-tumble ways, Harris had never dropped her. That fact had not prevented Greyson from placing himself within catching distance, just in case.

And then in his teens, when he'd been more of a loner and she had trailed after him like a lovesick puppy, it had been embarrassing and annoying, but he had allowed it to carry on for the longest time. Not wanting to say anything because he didn't want to hurt her feelings. It had gone on for two years before he had told her to back off. But he had been overly harsh, and he could still recall the wounded look in her large eyes and the clumsy way she had bolted away on those long, coltish legs. At fourteen she hadn't yet come into the willowy grace she now possessed. No, that had happened somewhere between the ages of fourteen and sixteen. Greyson had missed the transformation, which was why it had been so damned jarring seeing her again when she'd been sixteen. She had been the same lovely Olivia Lawson, but with an appealing added sensuality, grace, and beauty.

He recalled walking into the house, greeting his parents, looking up, and spotting her standing with *her* parents. And he had literally stopped breathing. She had been smiling, the familiar wide, generous smile that he knew so well, but it had never before made him want to kiss her. He had glowered at her, not understanding his reaction—or maybe understanding it too damned well—and her smile had dimmed, replaced with uncertainty and hurt.

That was one of the few occasions he had actually appreciated Harris's spontaneous exuberance. His brother, after planting an enthusiastic kiss on their protesting mother and hugging their father, had surged toward Olivia and lifted her up in a hug, swinging her around in the process. Her previous uncertainty had disappeared in the face of all that unrestrained affection, and she had giggled happily.

But that day was also one of the first—of many—times he had felt pure, unadulterated envy at how easy it was for Harris to hug Olivia and touch her and kiss her. After Harris had finally put her down, Greyson had offered her a tight smile and greeted her parents politely. Immediately following that, he had fabricated a flimsy excuse and left the house. Afterward he had avoided her for nearly ten years, until he'd seen her again at that party. A party that he had known she would be attending.

He shook himself out of his memories, refocusing his attention on his phone. None of the other messages were pressing, and he opened up his favorite app, an adult coloring program, which held his attention for a while. He found the process of adding color to otherwise lifeless pictures soothing and could lose himself for hours before he finished one to his liking. No one knew about his escapist little hobby. It was a great stress reliever.

# Chapter Ten

Greyson was up later than usual the following morning. After confirming that he had indeed been out with Martine, Harris had clammed up last night after Greyson—looking for any excuse to make conversation with his brother—had pushed a little too hard for details. Harris's responses had been curt and impatient. And Greyson had retreated to his room, acknowledging that attempting conversation with Harris on the matter was a futile endeavor. But sleep had been hard to come by. Greyson had tossed and turned for most of the night.

Now he had overslept and was up late, and when he stumbled blearily into the living room, it was to find Harris sitting at the kitchen table, his laptop open in front of him. There were files and sheaves of paper spread out on the table.

"What's going on?" Greyson asked, unsuccessfully attempting to stifle a yawn. Harris "caught" his yawn and executed a jaw-popping one of his own. He dropped the Montblanc pen, which Greyson had given him for his birthday five years ago, on the table next to his laptop and leaned back in the rickety kitchen chair to stretch before doing a few shoulder and neck rolls.

"I have to call the office in Perth later. We still have a problem there," Harris said on another yawn. He was referring to the embezzlement scam in Australia that had cost the company $10 million earlier in the year. Greyson had gone to Perth just before Libby's due date, conveniently placing himself out of the country for Clara's birth.

He had been such a coward.

"What do you mean, we still have a problem?" Greyson asked, trying to force the memory of missing Clara's birth to the back of his mind.

"Not sure, and I won't know until I've spoken with Norm Fisher in accounts. We have a Skype meeting in about forty minutes. I'm going over the financials he sent me last night. And some of the old reports from when you went in March."

"Want me to sit in on the meeting?"

"That would probably be the easiest and best way to keep you in the loop." Harris nodded. He glanced down at Greyson's bandaged hand, and a frown flickered across his brows. "What happened to your hand?"

"I cut it. It's not a big deal."

"You cut it playing handyman, didn't you?"

"I'll shower and change," Greyson said, choosing not to respond to that. He really wasn't in the mood to hear an *I told you so.*

"Why? It's just a Skype call," Harris asked.

Greyson shook his head in response to his brother's question. Harris was wearing a fleece hoodie with a random number printed on the front, jeans, and no shoes. Granted, Fisher wouldn't see anything but their heads and shoulders, but Greyson wasn't about to let one of the company employees, especially a high-ranking one, see him unshaven and underdressed.

"I won't be long," he said, not bothering to answer. "You can brief me on the financials later."

"Whatever you say, boss," Harris muttered, refocusing his gaze on his laptop screen. And Greyson hovered for a moment, wanting to respond with an equally pithy comeback. But he wasn't great with one-liners and found himself standing there just long enough to make things awkward, before clearing his throat and turning toward the bathroom.

Greyson felt horribly overdressed when he walked into MJ's with Harris three hours later. Their Skype meeting had run long and had frustratingly confirmed that they definitely still had a problem in Australia. They were hemorrhaging money. After a month or two without any suspicious activity, it looked like the person or persons unknown were back to their larcenous ways.

Dumb. It was only a matter of time before they were caught. They didn't even recognize how much rope they'd been fed with which to hang themselves. Fisher had been expertly reeling them in and felt certain he would be able to identify them within the week.

After their meeting, Harris had nonchalantly suggested they head to MJ's for brunch, and Greyson had immediately agreed. Harris had quite unequivocally stated that he would drive, and Greyson, eager to spend time with his brother, had agreed to that as well. Even though he absolutely *loathed* being driven by anyone. He didn't trust any other driver to get him to his destination safely or on time. On the occasions when necessity called for him to use a driver, he found himself constantly on edge. And even though he had never said as much, Harris knew that about him and usually let Greyson drive.

Not today. Greyson wondered if it was yet another means of castigation.

He hadn't given Greyson enough time to change, and now he felt conspicuous in the three-piece, pin-striped, navy Armani suit that he had worn for the Skype meeting.

No sooner had they set foot in the restaurant than he was accosted by a small, pale, redheaded virago. She looked pissed off as hell, glaring at him from beneath that vibrant, curly fall of hair. Martine was small, but her hair always made her seem larger and louder than life. It was a ridiculous contradiction—she was such a quiet, unassuming, and shy woman. Well, usually. Today, she looked ready to tear him limb from limb.

"Martine," he greeted her quietly, preempting what he was sure would be yet another rude demand to know why he had dared set foot anywhere near her friend. She didn't return his greeting; instead she shocked him by clamping her hand over his forearm and tugging him toward the back of the restaurant.

Recognizing that protesting would only antagonize her further, Greyson allowed himself to be dragged away. This confrontation was inevitable. Martine was Olivia's best friend, and she clearly felt that gave her some right to comment on Greyson's relationship with his wife. And while Greyson had never had a best friend, he understood that this was the kind of thing one did for one's dearest compatriot.

"Try not to kill him, Tina," he heard Harris say as she led him away. His brother's voice was quiet, but he could hear an underlying tremor of amusement in the words.

"I'll just stay here and order for us," Harris continued in a louder voice. Yes, he was definitely amused. Greyson sighed softly and passively followed Martine into a tiny, untidy back office. Once there she immediately turned to confront him, planting her hands on her hips and glaring at him.

"What do you want, Greyson?" she demanded to know, and he schooled his features into passivity.

"Lunch. But I suppose we're doing this instead," he said, maintaining an even tone of voice. Her face went bright red, which clashed horrendously with her hair.

"What the hell are you doing here?" she asked angrily, her voice lowered to a fierce whisper. Knowing that she meant the town and not the restaurant, Greyson chose not to misunderstand, figuring it best to just lay his cards on the table. He hated how everybody seemed to think they had to know his business, but he understood that this was the price he had to pay for his cruel stupidity.

"I'm here for Olivia. And Clara."

"You don't deserve them," she said coldly, and that uncomfortable bit of truth infuriated him. Like he didn't know that already. Why did everybody just assume that he wasn't aware of that reality?

His defensive anger made him tap into the icy well of control he kept reserved for just such occasions. It helped him keep a handle on the messy emotions that tended to interfere with most other people's higher brain functions. This way he always knew what to say and how to react.

"And you don't have the right to an opinion in this matter," he said. "It's between my wife and me."

*Shit.* So much for controlling his higher brain functions. That was probably one of the dumbest things he could have said. She paled dramatically, losing the unbecoming red flush, and Greyson braced himself for what was to come.

But when she finally spoke, her voice was admirably quiet and contained just the smallest hint of a tremor.

"The mere fact that I was there when she needed me and you weren't gives me the right to an opinion, Greyson," she said, and he swallowed again, his throat tight as he *barely* stopped himself from nodding at the veracity of that statement. "I was at almost every doctor's appointment. I was there when she heard *your* daughter's heartbeat for the very first time. I held her hand and cried with her. Where the hell were you, Greyson?"

He had no answer to that, but she did.

"You had an important luncheon with a potential investor—that's what Libby told me. She smiled when she told me, always trying to be *so* brave. But I could see how heartbroken she was. She asked them to record the ultrasound; she was so sure you'd want to see it. Did you ever watch it?"

He hadn't, of course. Not then. Only months later, after Clara's birth. After his recognition of the truth.

But that evening after the missed appointment, Olivia had arranged a special romantic dinner, after which she had intended for them to watch the first ultrasound together. She had been so excited, telling him she knew how disappointed he must have been to have missed the appointment. So she had tried to turn it into an occasion . . . for him.

Greyson, however, had taken one look at the romantic table setting, with candles, red wine for him, and sparkling water for her . . . and hated it! He'd resented her so much for trying to force him to participate when he had tried to make his disinterest so clear.

He had pleaded exhaustion, with no further explanation, and left the dining room. Part of him taking pleasure in the disappointment he saw in her eyes, and the other part just feeling numb and betrayed. He had moved out of their bedroom that night, the baby and imagined adultery more tangible to him after that ultrasound. Continuing to share a bed with her would have felt like a total farce to him.

He couldn't remember what bogus excuse he had given her. Whatever it had been must have left her so damned hurt and confused.

He clenched his fists and bowed his head and allowed more of Martine's words to crash into him. Needing to know, wanting to experience some of the pain Olivia must have felt at the time.

"Then there was the day she fell in your penthouse. Where were you *that* day, Greyson? When she started bleeding and was terrified she would lose the baby? She tried to call you, and it went to voice mail. Over and over again. Harris was in Johannesburg, and she didn't want to scare her parents, so I rushed over and found her crying, too scared to move, too scared to call an ambulance, because she didn't want to hear that she'd lost her baby."

Greyson was fighting for every breath, feeling brutalized and bruised. His knees felt weak, but he fought to stay upright. He had to listen and hear and *know* . . .

The day she'd fallen . . . she had called him five times, and each time he had dismissed the call. He had been irritated by her persistence. He recalled that much. Because he'd been so fucking *busy* being fitted for a new tuxedo.

When he had eventually listened to her voice mails, the anxiety and fear in her voice had caused a knot of sick guilt to form in the pit of his stomach. Guilt and fear. She had sounded so terrified he had panicked. Fearing that she had hurt herself badly, he had rushed to the hospital, absolutely petrified that she would die.

But when he had gotten there, it was to find her laughing and surrounded by her parents and Martine and other friends. She had seemed fine . . . and after allowing himself a moment of absolute relief, he had turned and walked away before anyone had spotted him. He had resented her so damned much for making him worry. For making him think she was in danger when she was fine and happy and glowing and beautiful.

The baby hadn't even crossed his mind. He felt sick with horror at that realization now. What a selfish bastard he had been. What a hateful fucking asshole. She could have lost Clara, and he hadn't given the awful possibility a moment's consideration.

He had gone back to see her hours later, once he'd had his emotions under strict control. And she had been so fucking happy to see him. He clearly remembered the words she had spoken when he'd walked into that hospital room. That radiant, relieved smile and those words: *Greyson, I've been so worried about you.*

She had been worried about *him.*

He felt a sob rise up and lodge in his throat and stumbled backward. Martine was still talking, quietly, fiercely . . . so damned magnificent in her defense of her friend.

So many words . . . so much he had deliberately missed out on. Decorating the nursery, buying toys and clothes, and speculating about the baby's personality. Martine had been there for that. Harris had too. Olivia's parents . . . *his* parents. Everybody but him.

And then after Clara had been born, her first milestones. The time she had cried nonstop all night and Olivia had panicked. She and

Martine had rushed to the hospital with Clara, who had had an ear infection.

And then he heard about all the times Olivia had cried and tried to hide it from her friend . . .

Greyson was sitting down. He didn't know when his knees had given way, but he was staring up at Martine mutely.

There was no defending himself from this.

Saying Libby was livid when she heard from Harris that Tina had accosted Greyson and dragged him off to the office would be an understatement. She was so furious she couldn't see straight.

*How dare she?* Just when Libby was striving to feel a little more understanding and sympathetic toward Tina, she went and did something like this. On Saturday there had been all of that oddness over Clara, and now she was intruding in Libby's *marriage?* It was completely out of bounds.

She was so angry she could barely focus on her conversation with Harris. He had persuaded her to sit down at the table with him, and she had done so because she needed to get her temper under control before confronting Tina. But Harris's words were starting to penetrate.

And she resented him for being so damned sensible.

"Answer me this," Harris continued, his voice quiet. "How many friends do you have?"

What the hell kind of question was that? Libby shook her head and shrugged. "I don't know . . . a few."

"And since coming here? Have you made any new ones?"

"Yes, of course."

"Of course," he repeated with a gentle smile. "It's easy for you—you're sweet and warm and genuine, and people are drawn to you."

She shrugged again, not sure where this was going. "Maybe."

"Tina has *one* friend, Libby. You," he was saying quietly, and the words made her feel defensive, guilty, and resentful. It wasn't Libby's fault Tina had no friends. The other woman isolated herself from people. She didn't make any effort to be sociable.

"Well, that's her own fault," she said defensively. "She could have more if she wasn't so distrustful of everybody she met."

Libby felt small and mean and petty as soon as the words left her lips. It didn't help that Harris—who had a historically terrible relationship with Tina—looked disappointed in her. Tina had been bullied horribly when they were younger. More so than Libby. Libby was tougher; she could handle the mean kids, but Tina had taken every slight about her weight to heart. And the kids in their school had said terrible things about Tina and her body, often to her face.

"People haven't given her much reason to trust them in the past, Bug. You know that." Why did Harris have to be so damned reasonable?

"I've been through the same experiences," she said stubbornly. "I overcame them."

"Your experiences haven't been the same," Harris said. "You had supportive parents; you had *me*. You had Tina. And once you went to university, you had so many new experiences, made new friends. Tina only ever had you."

"You don't even like Tina. I don't understand why you're talking like this," she reminded Harris. Tears welled up in her eyes, and she swiped at them self-consciously. Because he was right: Tina had been lonely. Libby had known that, but she had been preoccupied with her own life and goals. And then later with Greyson and Clara.

Her friendship with Tina had been one sided. She knew that. Always skewed toward what was going on with Libby, and that had been selfish. But it had been so easy to overlook anything going on in Tina's life because she had been so secretive and closed off since returning from her gap year. Libby had noticed, but she had never really asked Tina about it because she wasn't sure she would have received a straight answer from the woman. It had been easier to pretend things were still the same and hope that Tina would find her own way out of her funk. Clearly that had been the exact worst thing she could have done, because now Libby wondered how far back she would have to go to find out why Tina was the way she was. Something had gone tragically wrong in her friend's life, and Libby had been too damned preoccupied with her own concerns to recognize that fact.

"I like Tina," Harris said, shocking the hell out of Libby. "I've always liked her. But *I'm* the reason she and I could never be friends and never got along. If she hasn't told you about it, then I can't. But whatever caused this rift between you, it's making her"—he paused, and his hand moved toward his chest and grasped something through his shirt—"sad. It's making her so sad. And I have to tell you I'm finding it . . . *difficult* to see her sad."

*Wow.* Forgetting for a moment what Tina could possibly be saying to Greyson, Libby stared at Harris in absolute wonder. How the hell had she missed this? How could she not have any idea what was going on with her two best friends? It made her feel like a complete jerk. Okay, she had been out of the country for a significant portion of time over the last few years and hadn't often seen Harris and Tina in the same room together, but to her it had always seemed so black and white . . . Tina had once worshipped Harris, but something had happened to sour her feelings toward him. Whatever it was had caused a massive rift between them. One neither of them would discuss. Libby now acknowledged that—partly due to her own shortcomings as a friend—Tina hadn't shared anything real with her for a long time. But Harris . . . he talked to Libby about pretty much everything. Yet his relationship with Tina, or lack thereof, had always been off limits. Not that he'd explicitly stated that, but he tended to change the subject whenever Libby even attempted to broach it. In the end it had been easier to just go with it.

Another mistake . . . Libby was starting to recognize that she had made plenty of those in her dealings with both Harris and Tina over the years. She should have pushed them both for answers. There was real history here, and it bothered her that she had no idea what the hell had happened between them. Worse, that she was only now even realizing that it must have been something huge for it to have affected them both so deeply.

She decided to tell Harris about Tina's reaction to Clara, testing the waters, wanting to see how well he truly knew Tina. Perhaps he could help her shed some light on why Tina was the way she was around the baby. But Harris merely looked confused by her claim that Tina seemed to hate kids.

"She adores Clara," he said, his voice brimming with certainty. Libby wanted to believe that, she really did. But as she tried to explain Tina's puzzling behavior to Harris, it just seemed to baffle him even further.

"I don't know what's going on, but there has to be a reason for it, Libby. Talk to her."

His staunch loyalty toward Tina was staggering, and Libby nodded dazedly. "I will, Harris. Of course I will. She's my best friend, and I do want to figure this out . . ."


The stream of quiet, vehement words staggered to a halt, and Greyson, whose head was spinning with the recognition of so many lost moments, didn't register it at first. It was only when he heard Olivia's voice that he finally fought his way through the suffocating waves of guilt, despair, and absolute desolation.

His head whipped up as he desperately sought reassurance that Olivia did not hate him as much as he currently hated himself, but she was staring at Martine. She looked distraught, her eyes shining with unshed tears, and Martine appeared equally distressed.

Greyson leaped to his feet, nearly losing his balance when his knees almost refused to support him. Martine looked at him, and he could see sadness and, if not regret, then dismay in her gaze. It seemed like she was about to say something to him, and Greyson tried not to grimace at the thought of even more from Martine.

She was small, but she packed a hell of a wallop. Greyson didn't think he could survive a second round with her. But Olivia asked her to leave, and Martine nodded before glancing at Greyson again. Her expression was troubled, but she said no more. She and Olivia exchanged a few more words before Martine left the room.

"Greyson?" Olivia sounded wary, and she was watching him uncertainly. Greyson wondered why she appeared so alarmed. Surely he didn't look that bad? Or maybe he looked like he felt . . . like he'd been run over by a freight train. "Tina shouldn't have been that . . . uh . . . *blunt.*"

"How much did you hear?" he asked hoarsely. His voice shocked him. He sounded like he had eaten nails for lunch.

"I think she was up to the time I nearly dropped Clara, freaked out, and rushed to the hospital. We went to the emergency room so often and for so many trivial things I was on a first-name basis with most of the staff." Her voice was light, inviting him to share in the joke, but all Greyson could think of was how genuinely frightening each of those "trivial" things must have been for her.

"I should have been there," he said, and she chewed on her lower lip for a few seconds before nodding.

"Yes, you should have." Nothing else. Her voice lacked accusation, resentment, hatred . . . all of the things she should have been feeling. Instead she stated it as simple fact.

He should have been there. But he hadn't. No denying the former, no changing the latter.

He looked completely shell shocked, and it concerned Libby somewhat. He hadn't been himself at all these last couple of days, but this was worse. He seemed staggeringly vulnerable, and maybe it should satisfy her to see him suffering, but it didn't. It just saddened her.

From what she had heard, Tina had let him have it with both barrels. Telling him exactly what he had missed out on by being such a prick, and it had hurt him. All of Libby's residual anger and resentment toward Tina had evaporated when she had witnessed her friend defending her so fiercely. And she had promised the other woman that they would have that talk later. Hopefully it would help her understand what was going on with Tina and get their friendship back on track.

But first, Libby had to deal with the wholesale devastation Hurricane Tina had wreaked on the Island of Greyson.

"Olivia," Greyson said, his voice so soft she had to strain to hear him. "I did and said so many things I regret. And I don't know . . . I have no idea how to make it right again. I wish I knew how to fix it. Tell me how. Please. What would make you forgive me?"

"Greyson," she said, her own voice equally soft and laced with sorrow. "I don't know the answer to that question. I wish I did. I wish I could stop being so angry and sad. I wish we could be a family . . ." She shook her head and dislodged the tears that had been threatening since she'd walked into the office, heard Tina's words, and seen the impact of them on Greyson's face. He made a soft sound of distress and ineptly reached over to wipe her tears from her face with his thumbs.

"Don't cry," he pleaded, stepping toward her, his palms cupping her cheeks. "I'm not worth your tears, Olivia. I'm not. I never was."

A sob hitched in her throat. "I just wanted so much more for us, Greyson," she said, her voice choked with tears.

"Me too," he sighed, wrapping his arms around her and tugging her toward him. He gathered her close, until she felt safe and secure in his warm hold. Her own arms went around his waist, and she rested her damp cheek on his chest, just appreciating the quiet comfort of this moment.

"I want you to have a fair shot at a relationship with Clara," she said thickly, putting her palms on his chest and pushing herself far enough away from him so that she could stare up into his face. "And I think the best way to do that is if you looked after her in the evenings while I'm busy here."

He paled, and Libby could tell the notion terrified him. Her offer had been stupidly impulsive, but it felt completely right. She needed a sitter; he needed to spend time with his daughter. It was the ideal solution.

"If that's what you need," he said without any hesitation whatsoever, despite still looking like a deer trapped in headlights.

She stepped completely out of his hold and wet her lips before nodding.

"Yes," she said, digging around in the pockets of her chef's smock for a tissue and thankfully finding one. She wiped her nose before continuing, "I think, because it's hard for Tina to work in her office while Clara's here, it would be best if you watched her at my house."

"But what about feeding her?" he asked, and she shrugged.

"I've started weaning her. I'll start alternating formula and breast milk until she's fully transitioned to formula. I'm sure she'll adjust in no time at all."

He looked doubtful but nodded anyway. "I'll be happy to look after her in the evenings, Olivia," he said solemnly, and she smiled.

"And it's only on weeknights; I have a sitter for the weekend. I mean, I don't know how long you intend to stay in Riversend, but . . ."

"There's no time limit," he interrupted firmly, and that made her speculate, for the first time, how he could uproot his entire safe, predictable life like this. After their whirlwind courtship, once they had been married and starting their lives together, it had soon become very apparent to Libby that Greyson was a creature of habit. He ate at the same times every day, had the same little rituals and habits that had to be done in the same way at the same time. He even read the newspaper in the same order every morning . . . and the mere fact that he read a physical newspaper every day, instead of catching the news online, was very much an insight into the type of man Greyson was. His was an old soul, and he did not like his routine disrupted too much or for too long.

His pursuit of Libby had been an anomaly. Very much out of character for him. She knew that now and wondered about it.

For him to have come here was anomalous too. He was out of place here, off balance, and yet . . . he did not look in any hurry to get back to his routine. He was wearing one of his more familiar suits today, but even with the suit, he still had day-old stubble, his hair was a mess, and there appeared to be a coffee stain on the pristine white cuff of his shirt. And his red silk tie was ever so slightly wrinkled.

Everything was *off* about him since he'd arrived here, and it was both refreshing and disturbing to witness.

"How can you stay away from the office for so long?" she asked curiously.

"I can work from anywhere, and Mrs. Pegg is keeping the office from devolving into chaos." Mrs. Pegg was his executive assistant.

"Okay, well, if you're sure you want to do this—"

"Of course," he interjected hastily.

"You start tonight, six thirty. At my place."

"I'll be there. That reminds me: I haven't fixed the door handle yet. I had a meeting this morning. I'll do it tonight."

She nodded. "Well, I should be getting back to work," she said, and he made a murmuring sound of agreement. He was still shaken after his run-in with Martine and needed some privacy to process everything she had told him.

They left the office, and Olivia headed toward the kitchen, while Greyson reluctantly made his way back to the table where Martine and Harris were seated. They appeared to be having a very friendly conversation, and knowing how his brother felt about Martine, Greyson was loath to interrupt them.

He also would rather avoid Martine for a while, not keen on having another confrontation with the woman. He would make it quick and easy on everyone, merely tell them he was leaving and be on his way. He was sure they would be relieved to see the back of him.

Tina was worked up about the childcare arrangement Libby had made with Greyson. The two women were back in the office because Tina had stormed into the kitchen earlier, and Libby had once again abandoned her station in the kitchen to finally have that private conversation with Tina. This was so damned unprofessional, but it was probably best for the restaurant if they cleared the air between them sooner rather than later.

"Tina . . . ," Libby began hesitantly after her friend protested Libby's decision to move Clara off site during dinner service. She tried to find a way to frame her concerns tactfully, but in the end she could be nothing but blunt. Tact had never been Libby's forte. "I can't overlook the fact that you're uncomfortable around her. I know she's just an infant, but babies can pick up on stuff like that. She's so tiny; I don't want her to fret over things she can't possibly understand. That I, quite frankly, don't understand myself."

Tina swallowed, the clicking sound her throat made as loud as a gunshot in the silence that followed Libby's statement.

"I-I . . ." She swallowed again, and Libby waited, desperately wanting to understand what was going on with her friend. "I want to be different. I love Clara. But . . ." More hesitation, and Libby tried to remain patient, even though she wanted to take Tina by her shoulders and physically shake the words from her. But this—whatever *this* was—seemed to be exceedingly difficult for Tina.

"I once had a baby," Tina whispered, and Libby reeled at the words. The air left her lungs on a gasp of dismay. The profound shock of her friend's unexpected statement made Libby's head whirl in confusion.

A baby? When? How could she have had a baby without Libby ever knowing about it? Her eyes remained riveted on Tina's pale face; her friend looked sick and on the verge of hyperventilating. Libby was about to slide an arm around her waist and lead her to the sofa when Tina spoke again.

"He died."

Libby froze, her eyes wide. Tina's green eyes were shimmering with tears, but the expression on her face remained resolute.

"I don't understand," Libby murmured. She didn't know what she had been expecting to hear, but this wasn't it. This was huge, this was . . . she shook her head. How could Tina keep this from her? Why would she? "You had a baby?"

"A boy." Tina's voice cracked, but she forged ahead regardless. "He was two months old when he died. SIDS."

"But . . . *when*? When did this happen? How did I not know about this? Why didn't you tell me?" Libby was confused, upset . . . a little angry that the friend in whom she had confided practically all her secrets could keep one so life-changingly huge from her.

"I was eighteen. Just out of high school, and as you know, my parents sent me to Scotland for my gap year. But in reality, they didn't want anybody to find out that I was pregnant. I was supposed to have the baby, give him up, and come back home and go to college. Carry on as usual. You know?"

Libby nodded bleakly at the tacked-on question, even though she knew it hadn't really required an answer. She sank down onto the sofa, and Tina followed suit. Her body angled toward Libby as she continued to speak, her voice strangely detached, her expression remote.

But her words were devastating, and as Libby listened, her shock and anger faded, and her heart broke for this woman who was trying so very hard to pretend that she was okay.

When it was more than evident that she was broken.

"I didn't want to carry on as usual. I wanted to keep him," she was saying, and a bitter smile lifted the corners of her lips. "But my parents wouldn't have that. They were determined that I should give him up for adoption. I refused. I kept him. He was mine. And I loved him. But one day, I went to wake him from his nap, and he wouldn't open his eyes. He was gone. Just like that."

Libby had a hand over her mouth as she tried to choke back the sobs that threatened, and Tina, obviously noticing her distress, absently patted Libby's knee, as if to comfort her. How like Tina to worry about what Libby was feeling while speaking about what had to have been the worst moment in her life.

"I'm so sorry, Tina. Oh God."

"It's okay. It happened nearly ten years ago. But I've had some . . . issues. I couldn't stand the idea of working with mothers-to-be, delivering babies . . . it wasn't the right fit for me anymore. But I couldn't seem to find anything to fill the void afterward. I was a little lost. And then, in the last year or so, everybody started getting pregnant. Conrad and Kitty"—her oldest brother and his wife—"you. Then Kyle and Dumi were talking about adopting." Kyle was her middle brother. "I didn't know, not until after you had Clara . . . how hard it would be for me to be around babies. But I'm trying to fix it. I love her so much. I want to be the best aunt I can for her and for my brothers' children. And I'm so, *so* sorry if I've been weird. I never meant to hurt you."

Libby couldn't help it—she was sobbing by now. Proper ugly crying, and she reached over to drag her friend into a hug. She sometimes found it hard to spare a tear for herself, but for Tina, she had many. Her friend's heartbreak was so much worse than anything Libby had ever experienced, and her lost baby deserved Libby's tears.

"You should have told me. *Why* didn't you tell me?"

"It was complicated," Tina whispered, trembling in her arms.

"Tell me why," Libby invited her. "What was so complicated that you felt you couldn't tell your best friend about this?"

"Well, for one thing, you were only sixteen, and it just seemed so wrong to burden you with something so *adult*. And Libby, I was embarrassed. You always seem to have it together. Even when we were kids, you were gorgeous, smart, well adjusted. Vivacious and kind. And so, *so* talented. It's a little intimidating being your friend sometimes. You always seem so . . . perfect."

Libby stared at Tina uncomprehendingly. Harris had said something similar earlier, about how popular Libby was and how easy it had always been for her to befriend people. Why did everyone seem to think she was this flawless woman who had her shit together? Her life was a mess, her marriage had fallen apart, and most days she had serious doubts about her ability to be a good mother. Now two people had told her, in the space of an hour, how easy she had it. What the hell was that about?

How could her two best friends not see how riddled with insecurity and doubt she was? Granted, Libby was awesome at the whole "fake it till you make it" thing, but she would have thought Harris and Tina would know her better.

"I'm not perfect," she said, trying to keep her tone neutral, because Tina was already fragile.

"I know that," Tina replied, her voice wobbling. "I do. But you have to admit, Libby . . . you're the most normal and well adjusted of all of us. And you were always so *good*. Everything was always black and white to you. No shades of gray. Something was wrong, or it was right. I was afraid you wouldn't understand, because I knew *you* would never have stupidly gotten pregnant. I felt so dumb. Just another teen-pregnancy statistic."

"Well, you weren't the only one responsible, Tina," Libby said, deciding to let the whole "perfect" thing slide for now. There was a lot for her to think about and examine later, but this wasn't about her. It was about her friend. "The father had some accountability as well."

"I know. But I was on the pill, and I thought we were okay."

"Who was the father?" Libby asked, the question only now occurring to her. She had been so focused on Tina's story she hadn't even thought about the other party. Tina shifted uncomfortably and moved out of her embrace. She diverted her gaze to the floor, and Libby frowned, not liking her furtiveness.

"That was the other thing . . . I didn't want to tarnish one of your dearest friendships. And because of the circumstances surrounding our, um, sexual encounter, I didn't really want him to know about the pregnancy. I was scared if I told you about it, you would confront him."

"Who? Who are you talking about?" Libby asked, even while a niggling suspicion formed in the back of her mind.

Tina chewed on her thumbnail for a moment before sucking in a deep, bracing breath. She released the breath on his name. "Harris."

And Libby's insides froze.

*Of course.* It explained so much. Tina's animosity toward the man, for one thing. Her avoidance of him, for another.

"Harris?" Libby repeated, her voice flat. These revelations had her absolutely reeling in shock.

*Harris?* How could he do something like this? Even at twenty he had always seemed like a decent man. A dependable man with scruples and a good heart. But she couldn't reconcile the image she had of the man she thought she knew with the type of guy who would sleep with an eighteen-year-old and then abandon her.

Everything Libby had once believed about the people closest to her had been a lie or an elaborate facade. Every single thing she had thought she knew about Greyson, Harris, and Tina lay in ruins around her. These people she had once assumed were so perfect were all truly flawed, and Libby felt like her worldview had fundamentally shifted.

"He doesn't know about my pregnancy," Tina said hastily, and Libby's focus shifted back to Tina, where it belonged.

"Why not?" she asked, still feeling a little dazed.

"Because . . . our one time together was a mistake."

"Did he take advantage of you?"

Tina's eyes widened. She seemed surprised by Libby's rather old-fashioned question. "*No.* Oh my God. Of course not. You know I had a huge crush on him back then. If anything, I think maybe I took advantage of him. He was drunk or high or something. I didn't know it at the time . . . he seemed so normal. It was only afterward that I realized he was completely wasted. And I felt humiliated. Like he needed, I don't know, alcohol or whatever to find me attractive." Tina was being very cagey, and Libby knew that she was still not telling her everything. It was frustrating, and she hated that. What other shocking truths could she possibly have to reveal?

"Please don't tell him about the baby. I will. I have to . . . eventually. But he needs to hear it from me. Okay?"

Libby nodded, wanting to know more but letting it slide, because she could see that her friend was at the end of her emotional tether.

"I still think Greyson should watch Clara at my house. I don't want you to feel pressured into dealing with more than you have to, Tina. I understand how hard this must be for you," she said, and Tina looked alarmed by her words.

"Oh, no, Libby. I like having her around here. Sometimes it can get a bit overwhelming, but that's good. I need to learn to cope. Having her around has done so much more good than harm. She and Greyson can stay in the office. Please."

Libby stared at her friend for a long moment but could see nothing but sincerity in her gaze. She nodded. "Okay. But I think you should take tonight's dinner service off. Reliving all of this couldn't have been easy. You can deal with Greyson and Clara in your space tomorrow night. And then you have to promise me you'll let me know if it's too much for you to handle."

Tina gave her a watery smile and bobbed her head in agreement.

"And Tina? You're my best friend. I tell you everything, but it would be nice if you started telling me more as well. How can I be your best friend when I don't know what's going on with you?"

"I'm sorry," Tina said. "I just didn't want to burden you."

"That's what friendships are about. Why deal with the crap the world throws at you solo? When you have a friend who can help you work through it?"

"I'll try to be less secretive," Tina promised, and Libby hugged her again.

"Good. I have to get back to the kitchen. Will you be okay?"

Tina took in another deep breath and gave her a quick thumbs-up and a wide smile. She looked happy and relieved.

Libby returned her smile before leaving the office.

Greyson had fully intended to head straight home, but Harris had convinced him to stay and eat. A decision that had been made easier once Martine had stormed off to talk to Olivia about her decision to allow Greyson to look after Clara.

Greyson was terrified that she would manage to change Olivia's mind, and so he stayed, nervously waiting to hear what the outcome of that chat would be. In the meantime, he was preparing to break bread with his brother for the first time in longer than he cared to recollect.

Harris had once again started in on him about Olivia, but this time—heartily fed up with his brother digging around in his business—Greyson had asked him what the hell was going on with Harris and Martine. Of course, Harris hadn't been pleased to have the tables turned on him, and he had liked it even less when Greyson had revealed exactly how much he knew about what had gone down between the couple ten years ago.

"Why the hell did you make that bet?" Greyson asked his brother, referring to the time when Harris, everybody's favorite good guy, hadn't been so damned good. When he had done something stupid and despicable and downright unforgivable.

It was a question he should have asked years ago. But Greyson had convinced himself it was none of his business, even while he watched Martine disappear from their lives and Harris retreat into himself for a long time after that incident.

A stupid fucking bet, designed to humiliate a vulnerable young woman who had never done anybody any harm. It had been reprehensible, and Greyson had been disappointed and disgusted after learning about it.

And yet . . . it had been so uncharacteristic of his brother, whom Greyson had sometimes caught staring at Martine like he thought the sun rose and set in her eyes.

"That's just it . . . I didn't," Harris said, his voice filled with frustration. "I don't recall making the bet. I remember dancing with her and kissing her . . . after that everything's hazy. I know Jonah and his buddies said some fucked-up shit that I later discovered Tina had overheard. I think Jonah handed me a spiked drink just before my dance with Tina. It's the only thing that makes sense."

Greyson thought about Tina overhearing the details of the bet from a bunch of drunken assholes who wouldn't have been very kind in their comments. It was much worse than he had ever imagined, and he winced at the thought of how much that must have hurt her. He and Harris discussed Jonah Spade, the main culprit behind the awful incident all those years ago. The guy had actually had the absolute gall to try and gloat about the bet to Greyson afterward. Which was how Greyson had learned about it. A few choice threats had seen to it that Jonah Spade never discussed the matter with anybody ever again. And Greyson had frozen him out of their circle of friends shortly after that.

He had never discussed the matter with Harris, but he should have, because when he listened to Harris, it became apparent that Jonah Spade and his cohorts had drugged his brother that night. Greyson should have done more than threaten that bastard. He had needed his ass kicked, and while Greyson didn't believe in violence merely for the sake of it, he had been well into his Krav Maga training by that time and could have done some well-deserved damage to that bastard's smug face.

Harris was telling him about the fact that Jonah Spade now had a comb-over. Which was hilarious because the guy had *loved* his hair.

"No shit?" Greyson said, smiling. "Remember he always carried that comb around with him?"

"The gold-plated thing? Yeah. He was so proud of that retro pompadour. Kept running that tacky comb through it."

"Wonder if he still has it," Greyson speculated.

"He would be getting some real use out of it now." Harris's voice wobbled. He made eye contact with Greyson, and they both started laughing. The moment of shared humor was so welcome and refreshing that Greyson felt a surge of hope that maybe he and Harris could repair their relationship. But he knew they could not do so without Greyson doing something that was long overdue.

His brother needed an apology. A proper apology.

# Chapter Eleven

Libby's morning had been both physically and emotionally draining, and she just wanted to put all of that out of her mind for a while. After picking Clara up from day care and doing some shopping, she went home for a change of clothes before heading to the community center. The kindergarten had been handing out pamphlets introducing a new mummy-and-baby-yoga afternoon class, and Libby was keen to check it out.

She needed to relax and wanted to keep her thoughts away from the Chapman brothers and Tina for a while.

The tiny community center was quite busy for a random Monday afternoon. Old ladies were seated in a circle, gossiping and crocheting. Sam Brand, Lia's fiancé, was sitting and gossiping along with them. He was not crocheting but was happily chatting with the silver-haired women.

A group of teens was tucked away in the farthest corner, practicing some type of martial art. Every so often Sam Brand would look up and call out to them. He appeared to be their instructor.

"Hi, Mrs. C.," Charlie Carlisle called from the midst of the group, waving enthusiastically. Libby smiled and waved back. The girl went back to rolling on the mat with a couple of bigger boys—and soundly trouncing them, from what Libby could tell.

"Hey, Libby," a voice called from the stage, and Libby looked up to see Lia McGregor. "Are you and Clara here for the mummy-and-baby-yoga session?"

"Yes," Libby called back, and Lia beckoned her over. Libby joined her on the stage. There were three other mothers with babies present. Lia hugged her enthusiastically, and Libby grinned. The other woman was so friendly and sweet.

"We're the smallest group, so we got stuck with the stage," Lia explained when Libby joined them. "I'm the instructor. I'm not an expert at the mummy-and-baby stuff. I usually just do yoga in the privacy of my own home. But Aisha, my boss, thought this would be a good idea for some of the new mums, and I volunteered to instruct it, with a doll as my substitute baby. So we're all learning as we go along."

"I'm sure it'll be great," Libby said.

"Hello, Clara." Lia tickled the wide-eyed baby under her chin, and Clara giggled. "Come on, let me introduce you guys to the rest of the group."

Libby felt much better by the time the class ended. It had been fun, and while Lia claimed to not be an expert, she had been a great instructor. Everybody had had a wonderful time, and Clara had giggled her way through most of it, charming everybody in the community center in the process. And Libby had come out of the experience a few friends richer.

Lia had mentioned Daff's baby shower coming up on Sunday, and she'd surprised Libby by saying that she had already invited Tina and urged Libby to come.

Libby arrived home feeling relaxed and ready for a shower, but tension immediately crept back into her body when she spotted the car outside her house.

Greyson.

Libby parked her car in the driveway, cautiously stepped out of the vehicle, and turned to face Greyson, who had come up to the driver's side of the car. He was back in jeans and a hoodie. An ensemble that she was starting to get used to.

"I just wanted to give you the keys," he hastened to explain. "To the house. I fixed the lock."

"Oh . . . well . . . thank you," she said quietly. He dropped the keys in her hand.

"I'll see you later, then," he said.

"Do you want to say hi to Clara?" she asked, and his eyes lit up.

"May I?"

"Of course," she said, and he rounded the car and opened the door, leaning in to unclip Clara's car seat belt. The baby gurgled and cooed at him.

"Hey, Clara. Hey there. Come here and give your daddy a kiss." He lifted her out of the seat, looking a lot more comfortable holding her than he had just two nights ago. He planted a kiss on her chubby cheek and held her close for a quick hug. He smiled at Libby, another of those increasingly common wide and generous smiles.

"I think she recognizes me," he said proudly.

"Seems that way," Libby said noncommittally, not wanting to tell him that Clara had been in a singularly good mood all afternoon, dimpling at any random stranger who had paid her any attention.

Libby lifted Clara's baby bag from the back seat, and Greyson walked them to the front door before giving Clara another squeeze and kiss.

"Daddy loves you, baby girl," he murmured into Clara's ear while Libby unlocked the front door. "I'll see you later. We're going to have so much fun."

He handed Clara over carefully and thrust his hands into his jeans pockets. His shoulders were hunched against the strong, cold wind that had kicked up earlier in the day.

"You'd better get her in out of the cold," he said, stepping away from them. "I'll see you later."

"Yes. Thank you for fixing the door."

"With a little help from the internet," he said with an ironic smile, and she found herself smiling in return.

He looked like he wanted to add something more, prolong their contact somehow, but she nodded and turned away from him. She shut the door so she wouldn't find herself inviting him in.

Allowing him to spend time with Clara was one thing, but letting him creep beneath her defenses was another matter entirely. She had to be careful.


*Fuck! Fuck! Fuck!*

Clara wouldn't stop crying, and Greyson was desperate for solutions. He had tried her bottle, of course, and that swooping thing she liked. Tickling and tummy raspberries only made the crying worse. She refused to be appeased in any way, and Greyson felt like a complete failure as a father. She had started crying about fifteen minutes after he'd arrived at the restaurant for babysitting duty, and it was now nearly half an hour later, and she hadn't let up at all.

He had queasily checked her nappy—clean—rocked her, sang to her, played with her, laid her down, picked her back up . . . nothing helped. He was starting to worry that maybe she was sick. Especially after she'd spit up the small amount of milk he had managed to get her to drink.

He was wearing jeans and a dress shirt, trying to mix his old wardrobe with his new. And he now had baby puke on the shoulder of his white Armani shirt. Not that he cared about that—he just wanted Clara to be okay. To stop crying. He was pacing up and down and bouncing her awkwardly in his arms.

"It's okay, darling," he said, sounding frazzled even to his own ears. "It's all right. Don't cry. Please don't cry. Daddy's here."

"Greyson."

Greyson lifted his gaze, startled to hear his name coming from the doorway. His eyes met Harris's. His brother was watching him, concern and shock evident on his face. Greyson had never been happier to see another human being in his life before.

"Harris! Oh, thank God you're here," Greyson said, desperate for help, not even wondering why his brother was there in the first place. "She won't stop crying. I think she's sick. Do you think she's sick?"

Harris took Clara from him, easily cradling her in the crook of his arm. He tested Clara's temperature with the back of his hand while Greyson hovered anxiously, waiting to hear the verdict.

"She doesn't feel feverish." Clara stopped screeching at the sound of his voice and started sucking on her fist, her pretty blue eyes fixed on her uncle's face. Harris looked at her and smiled, and Greyson's heart sank to the floor.

"Oh my *God*, she hates me." Of course she did. Everybody else seemed to hate him these days—hell, Greyson even hated himself—so why should Clara be any different?

"She doesn't hate you," Harris said, his voice low and soothing. Okay, so maybe Harris didn't hate him. Not anymore. Not since their talk this afternoon, when he had finally accepted Greyson's apology and plea for understanding. "You were tense and panicking. She probably picked up on that."

"I can't do this," Greyson said urgently. "You have to help me."

Harris laughed at him. "No way. You seemed confident you could handle this. So handle it. Libby is literally a stone's throw away if you need her. You'll manage."

"No. Damn it. She'll never let me near Clara again if she thinks I can't cope." Why couldn't his brother see how dire Greyson's situation was? Harris looked way too relaxed and amused for Greyson's liking.

"Greyson, you're able to run a multimillion-dollar organization without blinking an eyelid; you can handle one tiny female."

Was Harris being serious right now? Did he even *know* Olivia?

"No, I can't! You know I can't," Greyson protested. "She fucking up and left me before I had a chance to even recognize what an idiot I was. She defies handling."

"I . . . uh . . . I meant the baby."

"Oh." Of course he meant the baby. Greyson felt foolish for leaping to the wrong conclusion, an emotion exacerbated by the laughter he could see in his brother's eyes.

"Now take your daughter. I have a date to get back to. Call Libby if you run into trouble—she won't think less of you. It'll show that you're more concerned for Clara than you are about your ego."

*A date?* Momentarily diverted by that revelation, Greyson was about to ask Harris about that date, but the other man kissed Clara, gently transferred her back into Greyson's arms, and walked away. Clara immediately started crying again, sending Greyson spiraling into panic.

"Harris!" Greyson called, needing the other man to come back and help him handle this situation, but Harris laughed at him and callously shut the door.

"Okay, Greyson," he muttered to himself. "Okay, you can do this."

He forced himself to relax his hold on Clara. He sat down on the sofa and held one of her rattling toys up in front of her eyes, hoping to distract her from her tears. She blinked at the rattle for a moment, sucking in a breath and quieting down for a few precious seconds. But the respite was all too brief, and her face scrunched up before she released her breath on another angry screech. Her tiny fists balled and flailed in frustration.

"I don't know what to do for you, sweetheart. I'm sorry. I'm so sorry." He kissed her wet cheek, heartbroken that he couldn't make this better for her and terrified that she was ill and his stubbornness in not asking for Olivia's help could be wasting precious time. Finally he conceded defeat, his concern for Clara outweighing his pride and his fear that Olivia would lose trust in his ability to take care of the baby.

He dug his phone out of his pocket and sent a message to Olivia.

I'm sorry. Clara won't stop crying. Not sure what to do.

The "read" notice came up a few moments later, and she started typing her response.

Be there in a sec.

Greyson's eyes and face registered relief and fear when Libby walked into the office two minutes after receiving his text. Clara was screaming her head off, and Greyson was pacing up and down the tiny confines of the office, awkwardly rocking her.

"I've tried everything," he said as soon as he saw Libby. He sounded on the verge of tears himself. "She refuses the bottle, and she doesn't need to be changed. I'm sorry."

*Once again apologizing for the wrong thing.* Libby shook her head but didn't say the words out loud this time.

"You didn't do anything wrong," she said, hoping the reassurance in her voice would convince him of that truth. It didn't seem to help;

he still looked sick with guilt. "I mixed some formula in with the breast milk. Maybe she doesn't like the taste of it."

She took Clara from him, and the baby's screeching diminished somewhat as she recognized her mother's hold and immediately started rooting around for a nipple. She gave a frustrated scream when she was thwarted by the barrier of her mother's clothing.

"Okay, sweetie. I know what you want, but you're going to have to drink that botty," Libby murmured and held out an open hand to Greyson, silently demanding the bottle. Greyson leaped to get it to her. Clara turned her face away from the rubber nipple, clearly adamant in her refusal to drink it.

"Maybe you should breastfeed her," Greyson suggested. And Libby sighed.

"I don't think she'll get much joy there. I pumped before coming to work tonight. And since I'm not producing as much as I did before, there's not much in there . . ." She tried the bottle again, and Clara refused, her entire body arching in Libby's hold. "One of the reasons I mixed in so much formula was because I had so little milk for her tonight."

"And that just happens?" Greyson asked. "It just dries up?"

"I think because I haven't been breastfeeding her as regularly as before, my body has started producing less milk." She heaved a huge sigh as she stared down into Clara's desperately unhappy face before shaking her head and setting aside the bottle. She unbuttoned her smock with one hand, then slid the tank top she wore beneath it down one shoulder and unzipped her soft nursing bra. Greyson's eyes widened, and he turned away, giving her privacy.

"You don't have to do that," Libby said quietly. "It's not like my boobs are a mystery to you."

"I didn't think you'd want me to watch."

"I didn't at first. But breastfeeding is the most natural process in the world; you might as well see how it's done," Libby said, and he turned around just as Clara latched on to her nipple. She watched his throat work as he swallowed. He sank down onto the wobbly desk chair Tina kept for visitors, his eyes glued on Clara's face as she fed.

"Does it hurt?" he asked after a moment of silence.

"She has started biting down a bit lately. I think she's on the verge of teething. She's been drooling a lot more, and everything goes into her mouth." Libby stroked a hand over Clara's silky hair. The baby was making soft, contented sounds . . . but it wasn't long before she started to fret again. Libby transferred her to the other breast.

"You're both so beautiful." Greyson's unsolicited compliment brimmed with reverence, and Libby lifted her gaze to his. He looked sincerely appreciative, his eyes soft and warm. "I should never have let you go."

"You didn't let me go," Libby corrected him. "I left."

"It was my fault you left."

She didn't respond to that statement of fact, and after a short awkward silence, Clara made a frustrated sound and started crying again. She turned her face away from Libby's breast.

"I'm sorry, baby," Libby murmured against her wet cheek.

"What happened?" Greyson asked while Libby set her clothes to rights.

"No milk. She's going to have to take the bottle." She reached for the bottle again, but Greyson leaped from his seat and beat her to it. He looked determined, as if he had made his mind up about something. She tilted her head as she tried to figure out what that might be.

"She's not sick or anything?" he asked, and Libby shook her head.

"Just hungry and hating what's on the menu. My baby is clearly a food critic."

He smiled at her words. "Okay, well, then you should probably get back to work. I can handle this."

"Greyson . . . ," she began, not doing anything to disguise her doubt.

"You're going to continue attempting to get her to accept the bottle, right?"

"Yes."

"I can do that."

"She's going to keep crying," Libby warned.

"And I'm going to keep trying. I guess we'll see which of us is more stubborn."

Libby grinned at his statement. She was almost certain that the clash of wills would be a draw.

"Are you sure?" she asked, and he nodded decisively.

"Now that I know she's not sick, just hungry and stubborn, I feel more confident."

Libby shrugged and got up, handing the writhing and crying baby over into her father's semicapable arms. She had a moment's hesitation, feeling a little nervous about leaving them like this, but she really needed to get back to work . . . the restaurant actually had a decent crowd tonight.

She dropped a kiss on Clara's head and impulsively reached over to squeeze Greyson's forearm reassuringly. "You're doing really well. I'm glad you contacted me when you weren't sure what was going on with her."

He smiled and looked relieved. "We'll be fine," he assured her, and Libby nodded before exiting the room. Hoping she was doing the right thing.


Greyson didn't message her again, and not wanting him to think she didn't trust him, Libby didn't send him any messages either. But she could not wait for dinner service to end—she was dying of curiosity. She and Agnes were the last ones out of the kitchen as usual, and she waved the other woman and her husband off before locking up behind them and finally heading to the office. There were no sounds coming from behind the closed door, and she opened it tentatively before popping her head around and peeking in. Her hand flew to her chest, and her breath escaped on a soft whoosh at the picture that met her eyes.

Greyson was sprawled on the tiny sofa, one long leg flung over the armrest while the other was bent at the knee, with his large foot planted firmly on the floor. Clara was asleep on his chest, and he had a hand lightly resting on her back, holding her securely in place. His other arm was flung to the side, his knuckles grazing the carpeted floor. An empty baby bottle was standing upright beside his hand. His head was resting at an awkward angle on the other arm of the sofa.

His eyes met hers when she walked in, and he gave her a lazy smile of greeting.

"Looks like you won," Libby whispered, and he grimaced dramatically.

"Barely," he rumbled quietly. "I think in the end hunger and exhaustion got the best of her. She drank the formula, but she made it clear that she hated every drop of it."

"I think I'll reward her with some mashed banana tomorrow morning. Adding solids into her diet may aid the transition."

He nodded. He looked so exhausted he was practically cross-eyed. She pointed at him before noting, "That can't be comfortable."

"It's not, but I'm too terrified to move in case it sets her off again."

"She looks out for the count," Libby said, before moving forward and gently lifting the limp baby from his hold.

Greyson gave a relieved groan and sat up slowly. "God, my body is one huge ache. You guys need a comfier sofa in this office."

"How long were you in that position?"

"About an hour," he muttered, his hand going up to massage his nape.

"Next time make yourself more comfortable. Once she's fed, she's usually sleepy and super cooperative."

"Noted," he said. "You all done?"

"Yes, we're the last ones here."

He pushed to his feet and stretched with a huge yawn. He picked up his laptop case—which looked like it had remained unopened for the evening—and waited while she strapped the sleeping baby into her infant-carrier car seat. Then he took hold of the handle.

"I can do it," she said, and he shrugged.

"I'm already doing it," he pointed out. She rolled her eyes before grabbing the baby bag and her purse. She switched off the light, and he led the way to the front of the dimly lit, empty restaurant.

"This is kind of eerie," he said, his quiet voice sounding unusually loud in the silent space. "If I weren't here tonight, would you be here alone?"

"Tina and I usually leave together."

"Tina's not here."

"She usually is."

"But she's not here *now*," he emphasized.

"But you're here now," she said logically, and he made a frustrated sound in the back of his throat.

He followed her to her car, which was parked beneath a lamppost directly across from the restaurant, and handed her the car seat. He watched closely while she clipped it in. She moved to the driver's side and opened the door before turning around to face him.

"Thank you, Greyson. For being there tonight."

He looked inordinately pleased with her words. "Anytime," he said with a beaming smile. "Thank you for trusting me."

She nodded in response to those words, not sure what to say.

"Good night, Olivia."

"Night, Greyson."

He lingered, his eyes dropping to her mouth. It was obvious that he was thinking about kissing her . . . and Libby was thinking about *letting* him kiss her. For a long moment they both stood there, suspended in the moment, before Libby shook her head impatiently. She turned away abruptly and climbed into her car. He stepped back and watched her pull the door shut.

His own car was parked a few meters away from hers, and he walked over and climbed in. His headlights went on, but the car didn't move. She sighed, recognizing that he would not leave until she did. He would probably follow her home to make sure she got there safely.

She buckled herself in and started up her car, and sure enough, as soon as she pulled away from the curb, he did too. He followed her all the way home and then stopped and waited until she and Clara were both safely inside. She went to her front window and waved at him to let him know they were okay, and he waved back before driving off.

It may have been a little overprotective, but oddly enough, Libby couldn't bring herself to feel anything but a reluctant sort of affection toward him. She would have to have a heart of stone to remain unaffected by his quiet determination to prove himself capable and willing to be better.

"Clara, baby," Libby sighed as she unbelted her still-sleeping daughter from her carrier. "What am I doing? Your daddy is a dangerous man. Mummy needs to stay far, far away from him."

Greyson woke up tired but optimistic the following morning. Optimistic because he felt like he had made real progress with both Clara *and* Olivia last night. And tired because he had awoken to the sound of horrendous screams just after one a.m. For a disorienting second, he'd been confused and thought it was Clara crying. But after fully waking, he'd realized that the bloodcurdling sound was coming from next door. He'd jumped out of bed and rushed to the other house, afraid that Martine was being attacked.

Harris had opened Martine's front door wearing nothing but a pair of boxers. His brother had been pale and looked like he'd seen a ghost, but he had reassured Greyson that Martine had just had a nightmare.

Judging from Harris's state of near undress, things had been going pretty well between him and Martine before that nightmare.

Greyson got up and groaned. His mattress was lumpy, and it added to the aches he had already picked up on that damned sofa last night. It was just after six, and the winter sun hadn't risen yet. He stretched, working the kinks out of his shoulders and back, and dragged on some sweats. A session at the gym would do him a world of good. When he left his room, it was to find Harris already seated at the kitchen table, staring off into space, despite having his laptop open in front of him.

"Hey," Greyson greeted him, and Harris jumped, his eyes leaping to Greyson's.

"Morning," Harris replied. "How was the babysitting last night?"

"It worked out in the end, no thanks to you," Greyson grumbled, and Harris's lips lifted in a small grin. "I'm guessing your date was with Martine?"

Harris actually blushed before nodding.

"It seemed to end well. Despite the nightmare," Greyson ribbed, and Harris lifted his shoulders self-consciously.

"I'm not so sure it ended well," Harris said after an awkward pause. "She refused to talk about the nightmare and then sent me home. So . . ." Another lift of his shoulders.

Greyson considered his brother's words while eyeing the full coffeepot for a moment, longing for some caffeine but not sure he wanted to risk poisoning himself with that swill.

"It tastes like shit," Harris said, correctly interpreting his longing glance.

Greyson grimaced before focusing his attention back on Harris. "So what are you going to do?"

"I'm not sure where I stand with her today. We had an amazing evening, but after the nightmare—she has the same nightmare regularly—she said . . ." He paused, and his throat worked as he seemed to struggle with his next words. "I'm a trigger. For the nightmares."

*Shit.* That was bad. No wonder Harris looked so damned torn up about this.

"Do you want to . . . I don't know . . . *do* something today?" Greyson asked, not sure his brother should be alone right now and wanting to be there for him. But this was new to him. Being supportive in a proactive way.

Harris looked somewhat diverted by his question. "Do something like what?" he asked.

"I don't know, something. I'm off to the gym, if you want to join me, and maybe we can drive to Knysna afterward? Check out the sights."

"That sounds tempting," Harris said, looking genuinely interested, but then he shook his head. "But I want to stay for the sunrise . . ."

Greyson hadn't been so wrapped up in his own concerns that he hadn't noticed that Harris and Martine had shared a few sunrises together since their arrival. Comprehending that Harris was hoping it would offer him the chance to talk with Martine after last night, Greyson nodded. But he had actually looked forward to spending some time with Harris, no matter how impulsive the offer, and felt curiously let down by the other man's refusal. "I understand."

"Rain check?" Harris asked, and Greyson offered him a tentative smile.

"Of course."


The gym was empty when he arrived. Spencer Carlisle was there, working on the weights. He lifted a hand in greeting when he saw Greyson.

Greyson dipped his chin in acknowledgment and did a few stretches before picking up a jump rope. His warm-up was fast and vigorous, and when his heart rate was up and his muscles loose and limber, he moved on to the heavy punching bag suspended from the ceiling, starting with basic punches and kicks before moving on to his more specialized training.

He lost himself in that for a while, enjoying the physical exertion and the outlet for his anger and frustration with himself over the last few months. He hadn't trained enough since Clara's birth. First sinking into a pit of despair, then nearly drowning in a seemingly endless well of alcohol, and then, after clawing his way free from that near disaster, burying himself in work and repairing the parts of his life that were more clearly salvageable.

It felt good to do something physical again. Beating and kicking the shit out of that bag was therapeutic and helped him get his thoughts back in order. He lost himself in the soothing, violent rhythm of what he was doing. When he finally ran out of steam and became aware of his surroundings again, he was hugging the bag, his breath heaving in and out of his lungs in huge gasps. His muscles were on fire, his legs and arms felt like jelly, and his still-bandaged injured hand hurt like a son of a bitch—but luckily wasn't bleeding. Yet Greyson felt invigorated.

"That was some workout." The quiet voice with its slow and measured cadence came from somewhere to his left, and he swung his head in that direction to see Spencer Carlisle putting away his weights.

"I needed to—to blow off some steam," Greyson panted, fighting to get his breath back.

"It work?"

Taken aback by the man's abbreviated question, Greyson blinked and nodded. "Enough." Greyson liked that he could just throw the word at the guy. No unnecessary extra details required.

"Good."

Greyson waited, but when nothing more seemed to be forthcoming from the big guy, he pushed himself away from the bag, happy that his legs seemed able to support him again. He made his way to his water bottle and took a thirsty gulp, then picked up his towel and mopped up the sweat on his face, across his shoulders, and under his arms. Harris always liked to joke that Greyson didn't possess sweat glands. A jibe at how neat and controlled Greyson usually liked to keep all aspects of his life. He didn't like messy, not in his surroundings, on his person, or in his personal life. But since everything else was fucked . . . a bit of good, healthy sweat thrown into the mix couldn't do any harm. Besides, Harris had never seen him practice his Krav Maga. It required strength and discipline, which appealed to Greyson, but it always left him wrung out and sweaty. And usually sporting a fair number of bruises all over his body.

"What discipline?" Spencer asked. Greyson's eyes lifted to his, and the man jerked his head toward the punching bag.

"Krav Maga. Black belt." Greyson really liked this guy. He liked his lack of social graces; it encouraged Greyson to abandon all his hard-earned social and conversational cues and just shrug and grunt and gesture.

Spencer's brows lifted, and he whistled appreciatively. "Need a sparring partner?"

"You offering?" Greyson asked, his voice colored with surprise. The guy was huge and looked strong, but he didn't move like a fighter. A fact that was confirmed when Spencer snorted good naturedly and shook his head.

"Wife's brother-in-law, Sam. Former special ops," he clarified, and this time Greyson's brow flew up.

"I'd be interested," he said, starting his cooldown stretching routine.

Spencer left him alone while he did that, going back to setting the gym to rights. A few more people wandered in, all of them staring at Greyson curiously and greeting him with nods and waves. The reticent

Spencer got warmer verbal greetings, which he returned with grunts and slight waves.

Greyson was ready to leave when Spencer approached him again.

"Football match Saturday night. After seven. We need players."

"I'll think about it," Greyson said noncommittally. It really depended on whether Olivia needed him to babysit or not. "If your friend wants to spar, tell him I'll be here in the morning."

"Hmm."


Greyson was at the kitchen table that afternoon, checking his correspondence, when Harris strode into the house. He slammed the door behind him and glared at Greyson, clearly in a mood.

"Your *wife's* looking for you," he said, sounding even more pissed off than he looked. Olivia hadn't seemed too pleased with Harris after her chat with Martine yesterday, and that must have carried over to today. He couldn't remember Olivia and Harris ever being at odds before, and it wasn't as satisfying as he had once thought it would be.

Harris looked distressed, and Greyson didn't like that. He knew that Olivia probably felt equally distressed, and that bothered him. A lot.

"Does she know about the bet?" Greyson asked.

"Not according to Tina."

"Then why is she so upset?"

"I don't know. She says I used Tina, but she should know me better than that. I think they're hiding something from me. Something that gives Tina nightmares and makes Libby look at me like I'm some fucking monster."

"What do you think it is?"

Harris shook his head, looking lost. "Your guess is as good as mine at this point." His voice was heavy with misery.

"I'm sorry, Harris," Greyson said.

"Yeah, well, maybe I deserve this."

"You don't," Greyson said matter of factly. "You were as blameless as Tina that first night, and you've been trying to make things right since then. You don't deserve this at all."

Harris blinked rapidly and cleared his hoarse throat before ducking his head self-consciously. "Thank you." He lifted his head again and met Greyson's gaze unflinchingly. "Seriously, Greyson. Thanks for that. I . . . it means a lot."

Greyson cleared his throat, too, and flushed at the sincerity he could see gleaming in his brother's bright eyes. "Anytime, Harris."

There was an awkward pause before both men looked away abruptly.

"Uh . . . so you said Olivia's looking for me?" Greyson changed the subject, and Harris looked relieved.

"I assume so," Harris said. "She asked me if I'd seen you today."

Greyson frowned and dug his phone out of his jeans pocket. "Shit, the battery died," he said. He put the device on charge.

"I'm going to make a few phone calls and do some work in my room," Harris said. Greyson nodded absently, waiting for the phone to charge. He hoped Olivia didn't have an emergency. It had been careless of him not to check his phone. What if Clara was ill or Olivia wanted to talk? What if he'd blown an opportunity to spend time with them today?

Harris retreated to his room, and Greyson barely noticed. When the phone finally had enough battery power to make a call, he contacted Olivia, not bothering to check his messages.

She answered almost immediately, and she sounded fine, thank God. And not at all upset.

"Olivia, Harris said you were looking for me."

"Greyson, hey. Thanks for calling. You didn't have to—I would have been okay with just a reply to my message."

"I'm sorry, my battery died. I called as soon as it was charged."

"Oh. Okay. Well, I was hoping you could start watching Clara an hour earlier tonight. At my house. Tina wants to have an important meeting before dinner service tonight, and I thought it would be best if Clara stayed home."

"Yes. Of course," Greyson said eagerly. "I'll be there by five thirty."

"Thank you."

Greyson felt optimistic after that phone call, excited to be spending extra time with Clara and heartened that Olivia seemed to trust him a little more every day. He couldn't focus on work after that. He dug the childcare book he had bought before coming to Riversend out of his briefcase and made himself a cup of tea before retreating to the sofa and finding the chapter on weaning.

He was totally engrossed in his reading when the front door slammed open and Martine walked in. She didn't appear to notice Greyson on the sofa, and before he could open his mouth to greet her, she stalked purposefully to Harris's door and opened it.

"We don't have much time," Greyson heard her say before she slammed the door shut behind her. Greyson's jaw had fallen to his chest, and he was still staring at the closed door when the groaning started.

A little horrified and a lot amused, Greyson wasn't sure what the hell to do. This was a bit awkward, to say the least. But at the same time, considering how miserable Harris had been an hour earlier, he was happy for his brother.

The moaning and groaning were starting up in earnest now. The walls in this place were way too thin. Greyson considered his options. He could stay and hear his brother and a woman he had known for most of his life getting it on in the other room, or he could head out to the porch in the icy cold, or . . .

He tilted his head; the sounds were muffled and a lot quieter now. This wasn't too bad. He didn't feel like a voyeur any longer—it merely sounded like someone had left the television on in the other room. If he concentrated really hard, he could pretend that was what it was. Just the TV.

He turned his attention back to the book, and after a few minutes, even the soft pretend TV sounds faded completely into the background, and he went back to reading about baby feeding habits.

He was jarred out of his comfortable reading zone by the sound of raised voices. He lowered his book and watched the bedroom door in concern as the argument escalated. The door opened abruptly, and Harris, visibly distraught, exited. He went straight to the front door and left. The engine of his car started up seconds later; Greyson sat up in alarm, and when Martine exited the room, she appeared to be as devastated as Harris had seemed. She turned to close the bedroom door quietly behind her.

"What the hell is going on?" he demanded to know.

She jumped and turned to face him, her face paler than usual. "Oh my *God*. How long have you been sitting there?"

"If you're wondering whether I heard you and my brother having sex, the answer is . . . kind of. The argument that followed was a lot louder, hence unmissable. Then he storms out of here and drives off without a word. Like I asked before, what the hell?"

"You shouldn't eavesdrop."

"I live here. If you want privacy, move your liaisons next door . . . although that's not much better. The walls are paper thin."

Martine's eyes dropped to the book on his chest. "That's a baby book," she said, stating the obvious.

"I know."

"Why do you have it?"

"Because I'd rather not continue being a shitty father."

She just stared at him mutely for a few moments before the wind seemed to leave her sails completely, and her shoulders fell.

"I have to go. Tell Harris . . ." She paused. Greyson watched her struggle to find the words to express whatever it was she was feeling and felt a surge of tenderness toward the woman who had been so horribly wronged all those years ago.

"Martine, for what it's worth," Greyson said, hoping to make things a little better for her and possibly Harris, "my brother would never intentionally do anything to hurt you. Not ten years ago and not now. That ridiculous bet was so out of character that it makes me question the circumstances surrounding it."

"You knew about the bet?" She sounded sad and humiliated, which hadn't been Greyson's intention.

"Only after the fact. Jonah Spade spoke of it to me precisely once, and to my knowledge he has never, and will never, speak of it again. He was also ostracized from our group immediately after that."

"Does Smith know?" She looked absolutely terrified at the prospect of her brother—and Harris's best friend at the time—knowing about the incident, and Greyson clenched his fists, quelling the urge to get up and give her the hug she so clearly needed. But he wasn't a hugger and would probably freak her out if he suddenly got all affectionate on her.

"Of course he doesn't, Tina," he said, imbuing his voice with the warmth, love, and tenderness he felt toward her. Using the nickname because he wanted her to know that he considered her a friend, even if she didn't feel the same way about him. "I can guarantee Jonah Spade and his cohorts would all have been permanently injured if Smith ever got wind of it. And quite frankly, even though Harris sometimes annoys the hell out of me, he's still my brother, and I dread to think what Smith would have done to Harris if he ever found out. It was selfish of me, but that's one of the reasons I quashed any and all potential rumors."

She crossed the distance between them before he could react and then completely shocked him by bending and dropping a sweet, affectionate, and sisterly kiss on his cheek.

His face went hot, and his eyes widened in shock, but he felt outlandishly pleased by the gesture.

"Thank you, Greyson." She turned and left before he could respond, but he didn't really have a response for her. Instead he traced his cheek with a bemused finger while a foolish grin settled on his lips. He and Tina had rarely spent one-on-one time together in the past. And while he had always felt a brotherly kinship toward her, he knew that she didn't feel any particular warmth toward him. He had always attributed that coldness as some kind of overflow of what she felt toward Harris.

But today, it felt like she was finally starting to see him as someone separate from his relationships with Harris and Olivia. And that felt satisfying. It felt like Greyson was getting at least one relationship right while he was here.

# Chapter Twelve

"Any trouble tonight?" Olivia asked when she returned home that night. Greyson, who had been dozing on the couch before she walked in, felt disoriented and confused by her question.

"What do you mean?" he asked, then cleared his sleep-roughened throat. He massaged the stiff nape of his neck and stared down at his wife, who looked as tired as he felt.

"With Clara?" she prompted him.

"*Oh.* No. She protested a little when it came to the bottle, but she took it with less fuss than last night. We played a bit, and I washed and changed her. After that we settled down to watch some TV together . . . nothing bad," he hastened to add. "Some reality show about baking. I thought she'd want to learn some skills so that she could be a fantastic baker like her mum someday. She fell asleep during the program, but I learned some fascinating things about the history of lamingtons."

Olivia rewarded him with a smile and toed off her shoes with a relieved groan before padding into the bedroom. Greyson didn't follow her but heard her softly talking to Clara through the baby monitor, which he had placed on the coffee/bedside table. He moved to gather up his laptop, phone, and baby book. He knew he could google some of the stuff in that book, but there were things in there that would never even have occurred to him to look up or think about.

Olivia stood with her shoulder braced against the bedroom door-frame and watched him pack.

"I started her on solids today. She loved the mashed banana. Her face was a revelation," she said with a laugh, and Greyson felt his stomach tighten. He would have loved to see that.

"Wish I'd seen it," he said, his voice wistful.

"Me too," she said unconsciously and then grimaced when she realized what she had said. "You're going to miss some things, Greyson. I am too. You'll witness things that I won't and vice versa. That's the nature of the beast, I'm afraid."

"I wish it were different."

"It's not."

"So what was your meeting about?" he asked curiously, thinking it prudent to change the subject.

"Tina has hired a marketing-and-PR person. She wanted me to know about the marketing strategy they've come up with for MJ's."

"That's a good move. The place needs help. It's been close to empty every time I've been there."

"Yes, like I said before, Tina's been half assing it . . ." She paused for a moment before shaking her head slowly. "That's not entirely fair. This business is new to her, but she *is* trying to make it work. And Daff, the PR consultant, has lit a fire under her butt, and Tina looks a lot more motivated now."

"That's good."

"How's your hand?" she asked. The question was unexpected, as was the action that followed it. She reached for his injured hand to inspect the dressing that he had meant—but forgotten—to remove that morning after the gym.

"Better," he said, unable to properly breathe while she had his hand so tenderly grasped in both of hers. Her thumbs gently probed at the fleshy part of his palm through the dressing, but he barely felt a twinge.

He swallowed when one of her thumbs swept up to his wedding ring and traced the smooth surface of the gold.

"Why do you still wear this?" she asked. Her voice was husky with some undefined emotion, and Greyson couldn't get an accurate read on her mood.

"Because we're still married. Why don't you wear yours?" He shouldn't have asked. It was a foolish question, and he knew exactly what her answer would be.

"Because I don't feel married," she responded, saying what he had known she would. Thankfully she didn't elaborate on his flaws and his stupidity again but left it at that.

"I'm sorry," he whispered, and she stepped even closer and placed a quelling index finger over his lips, silencing anything else he might want to add.

"Again. Wrong."

Greyson knew he was apologizing for the wrong things. He knew what she wanted, but how the hell did Greyson apologize for something so damned disgraceful he couldn't even forgive himself for it? *I'm sorry* wouldn't even begin to cover it. And when he found the right words, or when the people in charge of such things created new ones to adequately describe his remorse and shame, *that* was when he would apologize.

The front of her body was pressed against his, so damned warm and tempting. Her beautiful eyes were entangled with his, and her lips, moist and juicy and enticing, were right there, within kissing distance . . . and *fuck*, he wanted to kiss her so damned badly. He wanted to do that . . . and more. But he couldn't. He no longer had that right, and he wished he had the strength to step away from her, but he couldn't do that either. So he remained standing there, close enough for her to feel his arousal, for him to inhale the wonderful scent of her, to feel her heat and her every breath.

*"Please,"* he heard himself begging. Wanting her to do what he could not. "Step back, Olivia."

"Do you want me to?" she asked, remaining exactly where she was.

He groaned. "You *know* the answer to that."

He thrust against her helplessly, and she let go of his hand and reached up to palm his nape instead.

"If we do this, we do it on the understanding that it's just sex. Simple, uncomplicated sex."

He swallowed, not sure how to respond to that. But she seemed to take his silence as enough of a response and went onto her toes to kiss him. Her other hand joined the first on his nape, the fingers of both hands burrowing into his hair and drawing him closer.

Greyson's arms swept around her slender waist, and his hands flattened against her back as he dragged her even nearer, wanting her as close as he could get her. She pulled her head back, and he protested the separation. Her pupils were fully dilated, only the tiniest sliver of amber remaining around them. Her lips were swollen from their hard kiss.

"And we don't do this without a condom."

He had condoms; he always had condoms. He used to carry them before his marriage and had never removed them from his wallet. They were pretty old by now, but he was sure they were good. They *had* to be good because he had nothing else. He used to keep the condoms as precaution against disease. Now there was the added risk of pregnancy.

He nearly laughed at that thought. Idiot. There had *always* been the risk of pregnancy. But he had never trusted a partner enough to have condom-free sex before Olivia. He was so fucking lucky he was health conscious, or who knew how many other kids he'd have scattered around the world by now.

"I have condoms," he confirmed out loud, and she smiled.

"Good," she said before lifting her mouth for another kiss.

Libby didn't know why she was doing this, why she wanted this. She just knew that when she had come home tonight, she'd been tired and tense and bracing herself for an exhausting night trying to soothe Clara to sleep. But she had come home to peace and silence. And Greyson . . . looking so damned disheveled and approachable and dependable. The latter was an illusion, she knew. Reinforced by the fact that he'd fed and clothed their baby and managed to get her to sleep.

Her concerns about the tiring night ahead had evaporated, but the tension remained. And there *he* stood, a six-foot-one, gorgeous, tried-and-tested remedy to stress. And Libby wanted what he could give her. She wanted the sweet oblivion and the powerful release. She *craved* it.

And she didn't see why she couldn't have it. Not if they were clear about the boundaries. This could be uncomplicated, and it was just a one-off thing. Almost exes with benefits, so to speak.

That was a thing, right?

Well, if it wasn't, it should be.

Greyson's shock seemed to be wearing off, and he was beginning to assert himself a bit. His tongue was finally joining the party, and his hands were starting to do more than just hold her close. They were on the move, reacquainting themselves with all his favorite spots on her body before moving on to Libby's erogenous zones. His mouth began to roam, nip, suck, bite . . . and she opened herself up to him.

His hands tugged at her clothing, and she happily helped him drag her long-sleeved lacy top up and over her head. The top fell to the floor at their feet, but neither paid any attention. Greyson was too busy staring at the flesh he'd revealed, and Libby was too busy staring at his face. He looked hungry.

No . . . *ravenous.*

And it made her so much hotter.

His hands went to her bare shoulders, and they both inhaled sharply when his flesh met hers. Libby arched into his touch, wanting his hands to do *so* much more. He growled, the sound shockingly primal. It was like nothing she had ever heard from her usually civilized husband before. And it was a huge turn-on.

His hands curled around her shoulders, and he turned her so that her back was to his front. He yanked her against him, one arm wrapped around her waist while his uninjured hand lifted her skirt. Before she knew it, that hand had found her panties, had burrowed beneath them. And while he ground his hard crotch up against her behind and panted heavily into her neck, his fingers found her sopping core.

Libby cried out, and her thighs instinctively clamped around his audacious hand, but that didn't stop him. He maneuvered her toward the sofa, and before she knew it, he had her bent over the back of it. Her hair tumbled around her face, and she felt an overwhelming sense of anticipation and mystery because she couldn't see what he was doing.

He removed his fingers from her painfully distended clit, ignoring her protest. But he had bigger plans. He knelt behind her and used both hands to tug her panties down over her thighs to her knees. His palms went to her naked behind, one on each cheek, and she braced her hands on the annoyingly soft sofa cushions, trying to lever herself up so that she could have a little more control over the situation, but she couldn't. She soon forgot all about her discomfort at being sprawled ass up over the back of the sofa when his tongue found her.

"Oh my *God*," she keened. This was an entirely new situation for her. Her senses were heightened because she could only feel what he was doing, and he was doing it incredibly well. She parted her legs, as far as the panties at her knees would allow, but it was enough to allow him greater access. The ravenous man had finally found his banquet, and he was *feasting*.

She came twice in quick succession and was still trembling after the second orgasm when his mouth left her and she felt him stand up behind her. She heard him fumbling around for something and once again tried to push herself upright to see what he was doing. But she had absolutely no strength left and could do nothing but wait. Anticipation building with every sound he made.

The sound of his zipper, the rustle of fabric, his low, desperate moan, the crinkle of foil . . . his fingers found her, dipping into her molten core as if checking her readiness. And she was *so* ready for him despite how fast and crazy and confusing this was.

He hooked an arm around her torso and helped her upright. Libby turned her head to *finally* look at him. His face was a study in fierce concentration, beads of sweat popping up on his forehead. She dropped her hands to the back of the sofa, thrusting her behind toward his straining erection.

It was animalistic, and the sound he made was unlike anything she had heard from him before. He dropped his palms to her hips and crouched slightly, adjusting his stance to allow for easier entry . . . and then he was there. The broad tip of him cautiously pushing into her.

He was breathing heavily, huge gasps of air sawing in and out of his lungs as he fought for control. In between the gasps, he was uttering low, desperate words of profanity. Words she rarely heard from him.

It was so different from their past sexual encounters, when he had been mostly silent, just the occasional hitched breath and soft exhalation of air.

This was like being taken by a stranger. If not for the familiar size and girth of his penis inching its way into her channel, Libby would have had to look around again to be sure this *was* the same man she had married.

He lost patience with his slow entrance about the same time that Libby did, slamming into her while she thrust back eagerly. When he was finally fully sheathed, they both remained still for half a second before instinct took over.

Their coupling was fast, primal, and over in just a few strokes. Libby came hard and fast, and when she clenched tightly around him, he lost it completely. His next few thrusts were quick and deep before he came . . . *hard.*

He wrapped both arms around her torso and held her tightly against his fully clothed chest while he emptied himself inside her. He was making harsh, desperate sounds into her hair and shuddering almost uncontrollably.

His hold on her gentled, and he turned her around to kiss her. The embrace was tender and completely at odds with the wild sex that had just preceded it.

*"Christ,"* he groaned after lifting his mouth from hers. It was the first truly coherent thing he had said since their initial kiss.

They were both mostly clothed—her skirt was hiked up around her waist, and her panties were now bunched around her ankles. She was still wearing her bra.

Greyson's jeans and boxers were shoved down around his thighs, but other than that he remained fully clothed.

Libby felt distinctly wobbly; her knees kept buckling, and if not for Greyson's hold on her, she would have fallen. He removed and set aside the condom before clumsily shuffling them around the sofa. He sat down and dragged her onto his lap. Libby was still quivering in the aftermath, and he wrapped his arms tightly around her.

"Th-that was intense," she stammered, resting her head in the comfortable nook beneath his jaw.

His breathing still came in harsh gasps, and he made a strained sound in response to her words.

"And quick," she continued.

"I'm sor—"

She lifted her index finger to his lips to stop the imminent apology. "Don't apologize again," she commanded him, and she felt his lips quirk beneath her finger.

"I lost control," he admitted, and Libby's brows rose to her hairline as she absorbed that statement. Greyson losing control was one thing, but she couldn't quite believe that he had admitted to it.

She lifted her heavy head from its comfortable position to stare into his troubled eyes.

"Did you?" she asked, and he averted his gaze. His jaw tightened, and his throat convulsed as he swallowed.

"You know I did. I didn't mean for it to happen like that. I imagined us on the sofa. Making long, slow love . . ."

"I didn't want that," she inserted hastily, and his eyes dropped back to hers. He looked unsettled.

"What?"

"I'm happy it happened the way it did. We were both satiating a need, Greyson. Taking the edge off, so to speak. I didn't want tenderness. I wanted exactly what you gave me; a quick, satisfying orgasm."

"Too quick."

"Just right," she corrected him. She knew the loss of control disturbed him. She was used to much longer sessions with him. Where every kiss and caress—while earth shattering—had always felt a little rehearsed. This fast and messy encounter with him had seemed so *honest*. Maybe because, for once, he hadn't hidden his responses from her. It had been raw and elemental and pretty damned amazing.

She wriggled in his lap, feeling uncomfortable and constricted in her bunched-up skirt. But he started to harden in response to her movements, and she smiled lazily at his reaction. She kicked her panties off, and before he could react, she sat up and turned to straddle his lap. Her hands settled on the back of the sofa on either side of his head, while her knees sank into the soft cushions next to his thighs.

"Though I wouldn't be averse to another session," she said breathily, sliding her wet furrow over the hard, eager length of him.

He made a helpless, harsh sound as she ground against him, and his hands reached up to grab her head and tug her down for an almost brutally hard kiss.

Libby broke the kiss with a triumphant laugh, reaching down between their bodies to grasp his hardness in her hand. She caressed the eager, hard knot of nerves between her legs with the glans of his penis, and they both moaned in reaction to that.

"Olivia." His voice was loaded with gravel, and the sexy sound of it sent a shudder of pleasure down her spine.

"Not slow and not sweet, Greyson. Hard, like before," she asserted, and his breath seemed to catch in his throat.

"*Fuuuuck.*" The word emerged from his throat as a long, low moan, and she smiled approvingly into his strained face.

"Exactly."


"Great workout," Sam Brand said between gasps two mornings later. He was grinning down at Greyson, who lay flat on his back, after Brand had felled him with a move Greyson had never seen before.

"You're good," Brand went on to say as he held his hand out.

"Not as good as you," Greyson muttered as he took the man's hand and levered himself up.

It was the second morning he had sparred with Brand, and after having his ass handed to him the day before, Greyson had handled himself better this morning. The man had found it marginally harder to beat him now that Greyson had a better idea of what Brand could do.

Greyson's fighting skill came from years of practice in gyms, with the best instructors. Brand's came from military training and real-life hand-to-hand combat. It was revelatory pitting himself against someone like Brand—the man fought dirty and employed moves that Greyson would love to learn.

"Yeah, but for a civilian you've got some great instincts," Brand was saying. He reached for a towel and mopped the sweat from his face and neck. "You want to help me teach a couple of my self-defense classes?"

The question stunned Greyson, who stared at him in slack-jawed astonishment. Brand was chugging from his water bottle and fortunately didn't see Greyson's reaction.

"Self-defense classes?" Greyson repeated, his features schooled into impassivity when Brand looked at him again.

"Yes, I teach a class twice a week at the community center. And I took over a friend's class at the youth-outreach center as well. There has been a fair amount of interest in the lessons at the community center. And I could offer two extra classes a week if I had another instructor. And I could divide my class into older and younger age groups at the youth-outreach center."

"Sounds like quite a commitment," Greyson said. "I have to take care of my daughter on weeknights."

"We could shift the kids to Saturday afternoons. And have a mid-morning class for some of the ladies during the week."

Greyson considered the man's suggestion. He didn't know how long he would be in Riversend, but it looked like Olivia was here for the long haul. He had come here with the intention of bringing Olivia and Clara "home" . . . he nearly laughed at the memory of his own arrogance. Olivia had created a home for her and Clara in this town, and Greyson knew he was going to have to start permanently restructuring his life if he wanted Olivia and Clara to be a part of it.

And he wanted that more than he had ever wanted anything else in his entire life. He felt hopeful for the first time in months. He was loving his time with Clara, not finding the thought of being alone with the baby at all daunting anymore. And Olivia . . . God, she had always been a breath of fresh air in his otherwise stale life, and that hadn't changed at all.

He had been starting to lose hope. But since they had resumed intimacies two nights ago, he felt so much more optimistic. Granted, she didn't want to spend the night with him. Last night and the night before, after several bouts of crazy, out-of-control lovemaking, she had sent him on his way. But he finally felt like things were heading in the right direction for them.

That meant staying in Riversend for now, starting to establish roots, and trying to figure out how to conduct business from here.

"Sure, I'll be happy to help out once we've figured out the logistics," Greyson said, and Brand grinned.

"Fantastic. Thanks, mate."

Greyson nodded and grabbed his gym bag and towel. "Same time tomorrow?"

"Looking forward to it. Hope I didn't leave too many bruises," Brand said tauntingly.

"I'll survive."

"That was amazing," Libby moaned in sincere appreciation on the third night of her renewed sexual relationship with Greyson. They were both curled up on the sofa, which had seen quite a workout over the last three nights. By unspoken mutual consent, neither of them had ever attempted to move their encounters into the bedroom, where Clara lay sleeping. For Libby, it was simply because she didn't *want* him in her bed again. It would complicate matters. Start to feel less casual and more meaningful. She wasn't sure why Greyson had never suggested moving to the bed, but she figured it had something to do with waking Clara. He walked on eggshells around the baby once she was asleep, and their vigorous bouts of sex were anything but quiet lately. Greyson had become increasingly noisy, but Libby could tell that every moan, groan, and gasp were reluctantly conceded. He started off quietly, but by the time he entered her, he was always quivering with need and almost sobbing in relief. He had managed to claw back some semblance of control after that first night, but it was still very different from what they'd had before.

And Libby loved it. More than she should. His intensity and focus added a dimension to their sex that made it incredibly difficult to resist him. Not that she was resisting anymore. But she *was* trying very hard to compartmentalize. It was temporary. They knew that . . . and once they divorced, it would be over.

He was quietly stroking her hair while they both cooled down and the sweat dried on their naked bodies. She felt goose bumps rise on her flesh as her body temperature returned to normal and the cold started to seep in.

"You're cold," he said, wrapping his arms tightly around her in an attempt to warm her up. Libby sighed in contentment, enjoying his heat, snuggling close to his naked chest. She closed her eyes, wanting to rest for just a few minutes before sending him home.

When she woke up, she sensed that hours must have passed. She was still in his arms, but he had managed to drag Clara's playtime comforter over them. She felt warm and comfortable and reluctant to move.

He was limp beneath her, snoring slightly, and she lifted her head to stare down into his slack face. He was so damned gorgeous it sometimes hurt to look at him. She wished things had been different. Wished he had never had the mumps and never been misdiagnosed, never made those accusations . . .

But wishing was futile. And those things had happened. He had betrayed her and hurt her, and he had abandoned her. When she had needed him most.

And she kept losing sight of that.

His eyes opened, and he smiled at her. A sweet, loving smile that made her stomach clench and her heart stutter.

This was so dangerous. She had to stop gambling with their emotions, and she needed to end this.

For all of their sakes.

"You should leave," she told him tightly, and his brow furrowed. "Are you okay?"

"Fine. Just . . . I'm tired. I should get to bed."

"I could . . ." He swallowed, and she could see his next words coming before he said them. "I could stay."

"No, Greyson. You can't."

"Why not?"

"Because I don't want you to." Only she did want him to, and that was messing with her mind so badly.

He looked like he wanted to argue, but he swallowed whatever he'd been about to say and nodded curtly. She moved off him, standing up and wrapping the comforter around herself while she watched him hunt for his clothes.

When he was finally dressed, he turned to face her again.

"I know I'm not good at—" He stopped in midsentence, looking frustrated with himself as he shook his head impatiently. "I wish I could . . . I—"

She waited, intrigued, as he shook his head again, a confused frown marring his brow.

"I'll see you tomorrow," he finally said, and she was tempted to push him about whatever it was he'd *really* wanted to say. But she nodded and watched, her arms crossed over the slipping comforter, as he grabbed his leather messenger bag and left.


Greyson spotted Olivia the following morning as he was leaving the gym. It was a clear morning—no rain for a change—and she was across the road, pushing Clara's stroller.

Greyson was confused by their appearance. It was nearly ten on a Friday morning, and Olivia was usually at MJ's by now and Clara in day care.

"Olivia," he called, dashing across the road to intercept them. She seemed surprised to see him, and her pretty amber eyes were wide with curiosity as she watched him approach.

"Greyson? What are you doing here?"

"I was at the gym," he said. He eyed Clara, who was crying as if her heart were breaking. "Oh no, what's this, angel? Why are you crying?"

He leaned over the stroller, and her adorable face screwed up further as she cried even harder.

"She's been crying since we left Dr. Ngozi's office," Olivia said.

"Dr. Ngozi?" Greyson's blood turned to ice at her words, and he felt genuine fear as his gaze flew up to meet hers. But Olivia didn't look frightened, merely a little impatient. "Why were you at the doctor's? Is Clara sick? Why didn't you call me?"

"No, she's not sick. She had her vaccination. But she didn't take it very well this time."

"Her vaccination," Greyson repeated, his voice flat. She had mentioned that Clara would be going for her second dose this week, and he had meant to ask her if he could join them. But with everything that had happened between them this week, he had hoped that she would at least mention it to him. "Why didn't you tell me?"

"It never occurred to me," she said, sounding distracted. Her eyes were on the crying baby as she moved the stroller back and forth in an attempt to soothe Clara.

"It never occurred to you that I might be interested? That I might have wanted to come as well?" The cold fury in his voice finally snagged her attention, and she gaped at him incredulously.

"It wasn't necessary for you to be there," she said, her voice going as cold as his.

"It would have been nice to be given a choice."

"You're her *babysitter*, Greyson. Not her dad, not yet."

"What the *fuck* does that mean?" he yelled. He couldn't help himself, and he sensed more than saw several heads turning in their direction. Greyson wasn't one to make scenes; he hated drawing attention to himself with vulgar public displays, and raising one's voice was the absolute worst way of drawing attention to oneself. But for *fuck's* sake, how the hell was it okay for Olivia to state that he wasn't Clara's dad?

"It means exactly what it sounds like," Olivia replied, the level of her voice rising to match his. "You've changed a few nappies, bathed her *once*, looked after her a few times—you haven't earned the right to be her father yet. Just because you've graciously decided to acknowledge your biological contribution to her conception doesn't inherently give you more rights. Not after what you did to us."

"This again? How many fucking times are we going to come back to this? Why can't we move on from it?"

"Move on? Are you being serious right now? You waltz into town with your smug, superior attitude, thinking you can fix everything in my life, when my relationship with you—*our marriage*—is what's broken. Fixing a tap or a door, changing a nappy . . . none of that will repair what you destroyed."

"I thought . . . you and I . . ." His words failed him again. Greyson hated how he always seemed to turn into an ineloquent, bumbling, stuttering mess around her. Because he had no defense against anything she had just said. She was right . . . but at the same time, she was so damned wrong. How the hell couldn't she see how much he was changing? Every day, every minute he spent with her and Clara, he was changing. He was adapting, he was trying to be a better man. For *her*. For *them*. But she was blind to that.

Clara was screeching by now, and Greyson felt like howling along with her.

"I have to get Clara to day care," Olivia said, the heat gone from her voice. "And I'm late for work."

"I . . ." His voice broke, and he cleared his throat before continuing. "I can take her. Why don't you get to MJ's? Do you have all her things with you?"

She stared at him for a long, speculative moment, her head tilted and her eyes shining with unshed tears.

"Are you sure?" she finally asked, and he nodded, reaching for Clara and lifting her from the stroller to rock her comfortingly.

"Thank you," she said, all animosity set aside for their daughter's sake. He nodded curtly. She took Clara from him and gave her a little squeeze and a kiss.

"I'm sorry, my darling. I know the mean man hurt you. But you'll be all better soon." She kissed Clara's wet cheek, and a tear slipped down her own as her emotions finally got the better of her. Greyson couldn't tell if she was crying because Clara was upset and she would have to leave her or because of their argument.

"I'll see you later?" he asked hesitantly. He wasn't taking care of Clara tonight; Spencer's sister watched her on the weekends. But Greyson wasn't sure if he should still go around to Olivia's house for the *other* thing.

His heart sank when she shook her head. "I don't think so, Greyson. Not tonight."

"Olivia," he began, his voice miserable. She shook her head, still refusing to meet his eyes as she handed Clara back to him.

"Her bag is stowed beneath the stroller."

She left without saying goodbye.


Libby strode straight into Tina's office after the morning meeting. Her friend had looked increasingly miserable this past week. She had told Libby that she and Harris had had a huge argument, and while she was pissed off with him, she also missed him.

Libby could relate.

"I'm going to divorce him," Libby said without preamble after entering the office.

Tina looked up at her. "Oh?"

"It's time for us to move on with our lives."

"Libby . . ."

"Don't argue with me, Tina," she said, inserting as much firmness as she could into her voice.

"I had no intention of arguing with you; I just wanted to ask if you're sure. He seems so different. Genuinely contrite."

"A contrite man would have apologized by now," Libby said, her voice wobbling alarmingly.

Tina's eyes widened in surprise. "Wait, are you telling me he hasn't apologized at all?"

"Oh, he has apologized for *so many things*, since coming here. But not for accusing me of sleeping around on him, not for his emotional abandonment during my pregnancy, not for the way he treated Clara and me in the hospital that night. I'm not even sure if an apology would make a difference at this point. But he should at least have made one, right? He's still the same entitled, arrogant Greyson Chapman. He expects the world from me, for very little in return. And I'm done. He and I can work out a custody agreement that suits both of us. I want to keep it amicable for Clara's sake. I know he'll want that too."

"I'm so sorry, Libby," Tina murmured, getting up and rounding her desk to hug Libby.

Libby accepted the embrace gratefully, leaning on her friend for emotional and moral support.

"When will you talk to him about the divorce?" Tina asked.

Libby stepped out of the other woman's arms and shrugged. "I'm not sure. Soon."

"You know I'll support you all the way."

"I know, Tina. I love you for that."


The following evening, as Greyson was preparing for his football game with Spencer Carlisle and the rest of his cobbled-together team, his phone chimed.

Hey, I was wondering if you were free for dinner tomorrow night. It was from Olivia.

Greyson felt an anticipatory twinge in his chest. If he were one for fanciful notions, he would probably have described it as his heart leaping. He tamped down his excitement, relieved to hear from her after yesterday's disagreement.

I'm free.

Great. I'm going to a baby shower tomorrow afternoon, but what about meeting after that?

Five?

Sounds good. I'm going to ask Tina to watch Clara, so I'll meet you at Harris's place. Can you ask Harris if he'd be willing to babysit with Tina?

If she was asking Greyson to ask Harris, that meant she was probably still mad at the other man. A year ago, Greyson might have celebrated that fact, but now it disturbed him. Harris had been quiet and depressed since his argument with Martine on Tuesday, and Olivia's continued anger was probably adding to his depression. Greyson had tried to engage with his brother over the past week, but Harris had been uncommunicative. Unusual for him.

I'll ask him. I'm sure he'll be happy to.

Thank you. I'll see you tomorrow.

I'll drive us to dinner.

Not necessary.

Makes no sense going in two cars.

Fine! I'll see you then.

He grinned and sent her a thumbs-up emoji. He was of the opinion that it was a lazy way to communicate. But he felt curiously ebullient after the exchange, and it was an impulsive act.

He stared at the yellow thumb for a long moment after it was sent and, emboldened, threw all caution to the wind to follow it up with a smiley emoji.

He waited for a moment, but while he could tell she had seen it, she didn't respond.

No matter—she wanted to have dinner. That was a good sign. It meant she was willing to talk. Willing to spend time with him away from the usual places.

He panicked for an instant when he realized that he had no idea where to take her. His only options here were Ralphie's and MJ's, both of which were closed on Sundays.

He would figure it out. He'd ask Brand or Spencer when he saw them later. They were both in relationships; they would know of good places to take a woman for dinner.

"What is this place?" Libby asked in horror the following evening. She'd known they would have to head to a neighboring town for dinner and had been expecting Knysna. But he'd driven through the center of Knysna toward the long road that cut through the tidal estuary. And then toward the island at the other end of that road.

He had parked outside a cozy-looking lodge situated right beside the lagoon.

"Spencer Carlisle told me about this restaurant. He says the food's great and it's quiet enough for us to talk."

This was definitely *not* what Libby had had in mind for their discussion. It looked *too* intimate and *too* romantic. An opinion reinforced by the table the young waiter led them to. It was situated in a quiet corner, overlooking the dark lagoon.

Maybe he hadn't known how romantic this place would be. Maybe Spencer Carlisle had assumed Greyson wanted to bring her someplace like this. A natural assumption for the man to make. After all, Greyson was a married man asking another married man for his opinion on dinner venues.

But Greyson didn't look at all uncomfortable with his venue choice. Instead he looked a little too pleased with himself.

"According to the online reviews, the food here is terrific," he said, unfolding his napkin and draping it over his lap.

Libby didn't respond to that, reaching for her own napkin. The awkward small talk on the thirty-minute drive here had been uncomfortable enough.

"I'm sure it is," she murmured, reaching for the menu for lack of anything better to do.

"Not as good as your food, I'm sure," he said with a smile, and she returned the smile with a troubled one of her own.

What did he think this dinner was about? After their argument on Friday, surely he had put two and two together? But this was . . . it felt wrong.

The waiter returned for their drink order, and when Greyson asked for the best cabernet sauvignon on the menu, Libby cringed a little inside. He seemed to be pulling out all the stops, and she wasn't sure what to say.

"We were hammered by the younger team last night," he said, referring to the football match Daff's husband had arranged for his at-risk teens. The kids had played against the adult team. MJ's had catered the event. Another of the brilliant new marketing strategies Tina and

Daffodil Carlisle had dreamed up to bolster business. They would be providing refreshments and meals for a few key local events.

"Oh?" she prompted him, wanting to keep him talking while she tried to figure out what the hell was going on here.

"Yes. Six goals to our three. I scored two of those goals, by the way."

Was that a boast? Was he trying to impress her? "That's great."

The waiter brought their wine and asked if they were ready to order an appetizer. Libby picked something at random; her mind was racing, and she wasn't really concentrating on the menu. She mumbled her way through most of the conversation, while he enthused about the restaurant, praised the food, and kept complimenting her on arbitrary things. Her hair, her clothes, her fricking meal choices.

She attempted to bolster her courage with the wine, absently noticing that Greyson didn't touch his wine at all, sipping from his water instead. They were halfway through their main course when he reached for her hand.

She snatched it out of his grasp and hid it beneath the table. Her entire body was trembling in shock and horror.

*Damn it.*

"Greyson . . . you seem to have the wrong idea about tonight."

# Chapter Thirteen

Greyson had already figured out that he'd made a few inaccurate assumptions about tonight. However he had held out some hope that perhaps he could salvage the evening. But Olivia had been uncomfortable and on edge since they'd set foot in the restaurant, and nothing he had said or done had changed that. It was becoming increasingly evident that Olivia was not here to mend fences and start anew.

She reached for her purse, a large "mum" bag. The type that could stash just about anything. He eyed it with trepidation, not sure he wanted to see what she had in there.

She withdrew a folded white A4 envelope and put it on the table between them. Greyson glared at it like it was a coiled snake, and she pushed it toward him. He moved his hands to the edge of the table, not wanting to touch the thing. Not wanting to know what was in it.

"Greyson, take it."

"What is it?" he asked, and she sucked her lower lip into her mouth and nervously gnawed on it. Her eyes, wide and anxious, spoke volumes.

"You know what it is," she said softly.

He blinked a few times before looking away and silently staring out into the darkness. The lagoon reflected the lights from passing boats and homes on the shore. It was beautiful here. Exactly the right place for a reconciliation. But this wasn't that.

This was the beginning of the end.

He sighed softly. He was lying to himself again . . . the end had started nearly five months ago with the birth of their beautiful daughter. No, much further back than that. That evening when she had smiled at him with love, hope, and excitement in her eyes and told him she was pregnant.

She had hugged him, and his arms had closed around her automatically. While she had enthused about their baby—about the type of parents they would be—he had sat there feeling numb, shocked . . . betrayed. *Hating* her. Hating how vulnerable he felt. Resenting the baby and what he thought it meant.

That was when it had ended for them. When, instead of assuming the doctor had misdiagnosed him all those years ago, he had believed his wife had cheated on him. With the only other man he knew she saw on a regular basis.

"Why don't you tell me anyway," he invited her. Wanting to be wrong. Knowing he wasn't. But he couldn't bring himself to touch that envelope, to see for himself.

"I want a divorce," she said. Her voice held the slightest tremor, and her chin was wobbling. "I had the papers drawn up months ago. When I didn't think you were interested in Clara. So we'll have to change a few things. We have to discuss shared custody."

She was being generous; she could so easily deny him custody. He would fight her, and he would win . . . but she could have made it difficult. Instead, she was trying to be reasonable. Trying to be fair.

"I don't want a divorce," Greyson said, keeping his voice level and low. "It won't benefit either of us. We can still have a good marriage, Olivia. We're physically compatible; this week has proved that. We're still fantastic in bed together. And Clara would benefit more from a stable family unit. Two parents and one home."

"Greyson, too much has happened between us. I don't think continuing with this sham of a marriage would be healthy for any of us.

You don't love me. I knew that when we married, but I was foolishly optimistic. I thought we could make it work. That love would grow between us."

"Olivia, last week I asked you why you married me if you didn't think I loved you."

"I didn't *think* you didn't love me, Greyson. I *knew* you didn't," she corrected him, and it felt like she was hedging.

"Why did you marry me?"

"Maybe I didn't think love was that important."

"I don't believe that's true."

"So what do you want to hear, Greyson? Do you want to hear that I was in love with you? That I thought that even though you didn't love me, you cared about me enough for us to make a go of it?"

"Is that true?" he asked past the huge lump in his throat, and she compressed her lips and glared at him mutely.

"What difference does it make anyway? How does it change the ugly reality of our situation?"

"I hate that I hurt you, Olivia. It was never my intention to hurt you. I thought we could have a happy marriage. I still do."

"You're delusional," she said with a curt shake of her head. "You married me under so many false pretenses I lost track of all the lies and deception."

"I was always honest with you," he protested.

"*Really*, Greyson?" she scoffed.

He winced, feeling like a dick for not recalling his biggest deception. But he didn't consider it an actual deception, not when it had always been his intention to tell her about it.

"I was going to tell you about the infertility thing. But it became moot really quickly."

"This is getting us nowhere. Take the papers. Have your lawyers look at them and make revisions as you see fit. I'm not leaving Riversend, but I'm sure—when Clara is a little older—we can have her spend weekends and holidays in Cape Town with you. While she's a baby, she's obviously more dependent on me, so you'll likely see her less, but I'll send pictures, and you can visit and . . ."

"I'm not leaving," he interrupted.

"What?"

"I'm not leaving Riversend either."

"But the company . . ." She looked completely flustered by his statement, and Greyson was feeling petty enough to take great pleasure in her confusion.

"The current arrangement is working fine. I'll just need to reshuffle a few things, perhaps move my PA here and set up an office in town. But aside from a few meetings in Cape Town once or twice a month and some infrequent trips abroad, I can run the business as easily from Riversend as I could in Cape Town."

"But to what end?"

"My daughter is here," he said, offended that she'd even ask. "*You're* here."

"Stop factoring me into your decisions, Greyson. I want a divorce. Don't make it harder than it needs to be."

"Olivia, if you loved me once, maybe you could love me again. Especially if I'm better. If I'm different. I promise you I can change."

"Greyson." Her voice gentled, and that, more than anything else, scared the shit out of him. "You don't have to change. We were too mismatched, never meant to be together. Let's just . . ." She shook her head, and her eyes brightened with tears. "Let's just end this with dignity and grace? Okay? Please?"

"Olivia," he whispered, his chest tight. He felt panicked and so terrified. He was doing this all wrong. But he didn't know what to do or say to make it right. "I'm sorry."

"I know you are, Greyson," she said, still so gentle. "Now please, take me home."

The drive back was conducted in absolute silence. Greyson, who had felt so hopeful on the drive to Knysna, could think of nothing more to say. Olivia kept her head turned away from him, staring out of the passenger window and into the darkness. When he got to the house, he turned to look at her, but she kept her face averted and unbuckled her seat belt.

"Can I . . . do you still want me to take care of Clara?" he asked, afraid of hearing her answer. Her head snapped up, and he could see the gleam of her eyes in the dark interior of her car.

"Yes, of course, Greyson. I never intended to limit your access to Clara."

He swallowed heavily and nodded.

Not his access to Clara, only to Olivia herself.

"Well, I'd better go and see how they all got along. Tina was terrified of looking after Clara tonight, but she really wanted to give it a go. But I figured she would need some support. That's why I wanted Harris to help, but he and Tina haven't exactly been getting along this week. Part of me kind of hoped that putting them in a room together would encourage them to talk about some stuff. Tina has something vitally important she needs to tell Harris. And I was kind of hoping they'd . . ." Her voice tapered off, and she sighed softly, not finishing her sentence.

Greyson nodded again, unable to summon up any interest in what Martine had to tell Harris. Not right now.

"Are you coming in to say good night?" she asked, and he shook his head.

"Give Clara a kiss from me," he said, proud that his voice emerged so evenly. This time she was the one to nod. She grabbed the door handle, hesitated, and turned toward him again.

"I wish . . . ," she began, before sighing. "Never mind. It's not important. Good night, Greyson."

He got out of the car before she did, not following his usual instinct, which would have been to help her out of the car. He needed to get away from her as soon as possible. Before he said or did something to embarrass himself. He hastened to the front door and let himself in without looking back to see if she had followed him up the porch steps.

The door swung shut with a louder bang than he had intended, and he flinched when he heard Clara's wail through the thin walls.

"Shit," he groaned, feeling like an asshole. "Shit! Shit! *Shit!*"

He stumbled to the sofa and sat down in the darkness, hating himself for making his baby cry. For making his wife cry . . . for fucking nearly making his brother cry all those months ago.

Greyson once again felt completely lost and alone, and he wasn't sure how to find his way back home.

He didn't know how long he sat there before the front door creaked open and Harris stepped in.

"Greyson?" the other man called tentatively, and Greyson shut his eyes, not really in the mood to rehash his evening with Harris. He felt like a fool. Just this morning he had bragged to his brother that he and Olivia were going on a date. He had been foolishly optimistic. And now his world had come crashing down around his deluded head.

Harris stepped around the sofa. "Grey?"

A lump formed in Greyson's throat at the sound of that nickname. Harris used to call him that when they were kids, until Greyson had decided that it was too immature and demanded that his brother call him by his full name. He'd been such a smug little asshole. Still was, really. But he loved hearing that nickname on his brother's lips again. It felt familiar, affectionate . . . and he couldn't for the life of him figure out what the hell he had found so offensive about it before.

"Olivia wants a divorce," Greyson said, as unemotionally as he could.

"I just heard, yeah." Harris's voice was teeming with sympathy.

Greyson sighed and dropped his face into the palms of his hands.

"Christ. I could murder a drink right now." The admission made him feel weak and ashamed. But he was never going to lean on that particular crutch ever again.

He lifted his head, wanting to tell Harris that he didn't mean it, but he tensed when he saw his brother's face. Harris looked awful.

"You look like hell," Greyson said, keeping his voice quiet. Not wanting to distress Harris even further . . . but to his alarm, his brother's eyes filled with moisture.

*Shit.*

Greyson got up, his own problems set aside for the moment. His entire focus on Harris.

"What's going on?"

"She had a baby," Harris said, his voice broken and his words absolutely devastating. Greyson didn't need to ask who *she* was.

"Oh my God," Greyson said, his own voice trembling with shock.

"His name was Fletcher." Harris's cheeks were wet with tears by now, and Greyson felt helpless, not sure what to say or do to make this better. "Oh God, Grey. He died. And Tina had to go through all of that alone. While I got off scot-free. How can she ever forgive me for something like that? When I'll never be able to forgive myself?"

Greyson felt his own eyes fill at that emotional outpouring as he thought of the nephew he'd never known about. Lost to them forever. And Martine, the sweet, emotionally fragile girl who had had to endure so much loss and heartbreak at such a young age. He couldn't imagine how agonizing this must be. Having come so close to losing Clara through his own stupidity, he could barely even consider the notion of losing her so definitively. Of never having the chance to hold her again. Harris had never had that opportunity with Fletcher . . . and Greyson felt like a selfish prick when he considered how carelessly he had nearly thrown away something his brother would likely move heaven and earth to have. Even for just a moment.

He wrapped his arm around Harris's shoulders, but when his brother turned in to his embrace, Greyson gave him comfort the only way he could. He held him while he cried.

Dealing with Harris's loss had temporarily shelved Greyson's own crisis. He had comforted his brother, talked to him about Fletcher, about Martine, about where to go from here. Harris wasn't sure of anything except that he had no way of atoning for his part in what had happened so many years ago.

Which was bullshit because as far as Greyson could see, his brother's only fault lay in caring about a girl and acting on a crush. He hadn't intentionally set out to deceive her. And yet he felt like everything that had happened was his fault.

Harris was a much better man than Greyson would ever be. Greyson knew that. His brother was riddled with guilt over something that had happened when he was barely out of his teens. Something that he hadn't been consciously responsible for.

Greyson, in the meantime, had deliberately withheld important information from his future wife and then gone full asshole on her months later when his secrets had come back to bite him in the butt.

He was nowhere near the man his brother was.

Greyson didn't sleep well. He woke up when he heard Harris leave his room—and then their side of the house—at around one in the morning. The door to Martine's place opened shortly thereafter, and he heard the couple's muffled voices quietly speaking for a while before everything went silent. Greyson managed to doze off, but the sound of movement in Harris's room woke him just before dawn.

He got up and went to check if his brother was okay but found him packing his bag.

"What's going on?" he asked, and Harris looked up, appearing unsurprised to see him in the doorway.

"I'm leaving."

"You really want to do that?"

"I don't want to do it, but I think it's best for Tina. She's a wreck, Grey. She has those nightmares. And she couldn't even stand to be around babies until recently. You should have seen her with Clara last night—it was heartbreaking. *I* did that to her. I love her, but I ruined her life. How do I reconcile those two things?"

Greyson shook his head. He was the last one who should give advice when his own life and relationship were so completely messed up.

"I don't know what to tell you, Harris," he admitted with a heavy sigh. "I wish I did."

Harris lifted his bag to his shoulder, and they walked out into the cool morning together, stopping at Harris's rented 4x4.

"Would you do me a favor?" Harris asked.

"Of course. Anything."

"Will you give this to her? To Tina?" He handed Greyson a silver hoop on a leather chain, and Greyson stared at it for a moment before closing his hand around it.

"I'll make sure she gets it," he assured him.

"And can you . . . I don't know. Keep an eye on her, I guess. She tends to close herself off from the world. I just worry that . . ."

"I'll watch out for her, but are you certain you want to do this?" Greyson interrupted, keeping his voice gentle.

"I have to. It's better for her if she's allowed to continue her life without me around to remind her of . . ." He broke off and shook his head before changing the subject abruptly. "Will *you* be okay? After last night?"

Greyson felt a sharp stab of *something* in his chest. He had tried very hard to put his confusing emotions about Olivia's demand for a divorce on the back burner. But Harris's concerned question brought them all surging to the fore again.

He massaged his chest, trying to ease the discomfort that had settled there, and nodded.

"I'll be fine. I'm not going anywhere. I told Olivia that. I'm going to relocate to Riversend."

"Grey . . . do you think that's wise?"

"I don't want to lose them."

"That's not your call, Grey. You can't force her to stay married to you. Is she being unreasonable about access to Clara?"

Greyson shook his head.

"Maybe it's time to focus on being a good father."

Greyson swallowed, hating how right his brother was . . . he didn't want to give up on Olivia, on his marriage. But he couldn't force her to remain married to him. To care about him again. He'd had his chance. And he had fucked it up completely.

"If nothing else," he began, feeling awkward about what he wanted to say, "I'm glad we . . . you and I . . . I feel . . ."

"I know," Harris interrupted. "Me too, Grey."

They had never been the kind of twins to complete each other's sentences or read each other's thoughts, but in that moment, they understood each other completely.

Greyson smiled, and Harris returned it with a crooked lift of his lips.

"Drive carefully," Greyson muttered, spontaneously reaching out to embrace his brother.

"I will. Stay in contact, okay?"

Greyson stepped out of the hug self-consciously and nodded. "You too."

Within moments, his brother was gone, leaving Greyson feeling a pang of loss at his departure.

When a distraught Tina came flying out of her front door seconds after Harris's car disappeared down the drive, Greyson shifted his focus to comforting the woman his brother loved. He had made a promise . . . and he would not let Harris down.


"You're going to have to let me fix this place up, Olivia," Greyson announced when Libby stepped into her house two weeks later.

They had fallen into a routine over the last couple of weeks. Greyson watched Clara every night during the week, initially at MJ's. But this last week Libby and Greyson had decided that it would be easier and more comfortable if he and Clara stayed at Olivia's house. But tonight, he looked seriously pissed off, and Libby wondered what had broken this time. The house seemed to be getting worse. The plumbing still hadn't been fixed, she had regular electrical shorts, and the air con had finally failed. Which had forced her to invest in more heaters and place even more strain on the electrical system.

She dumped her bag next to the door, massaged her nape, and went directly to the makeshift play area where he had left Clara—buffered by some cushions—to sleep.

Libby smiled down at her sweetly sleeping baby. "How was she tonight?" She kept her voice hushed.

"Good," Greyson replied, his voice equally quiet. "She's rolling over more regularly every day."

Libby grinned, delighted. Clara had started rolling over onto her stomach with ease. She was also sitting up with assistance.

"Did you hear me? About fixing this place up?" Greyson asked, his voice a fierce whisper.

"What happened?" Libby asked wearily. She moved to the fridge for a bottle of water. She had a splitting headache; dinner service had been crazy tonight. The restaurant was really gaining popularity, with people coming even from neighboring towns.

"A few of the roof tiles blew off when the wind picked up earlier. It sounded like the roof was being ripped off. When I went outside to see what happened, I found the tiles in your front garden. If it had happened during the day when you were outside, you could have been seriously hurt. As it is, I'm pretty sure the leak in your roof is going to be ten times worse when it rains. I can't have my child living like this, Olivia. You *have* to let me fix some things, for her sake."

"When you say *me*, do you actually mean you?" Libby asked, pausing to take a thirsty drink from her bottle. "Or do you mean paying thousands to have the professionals come in and do it?"

"Which do you prefer?" Greyson asked, sounding wholly exasperated.

"Neither."

"Well, pick one. And stop being so damned stubborn. This isn't for you, it's for Clara. Surely you want better for her? This place is unsafe. One of the heaters tripped the electricity earlier, and I'm concerned about potential fire hazards."

"*Of course* I want better for her."

"Then let me do this. You know that when it comes to custody hearings, any judge will rule in favor of the parent who can provide decent shelter, right? This isn't decent shelter."

Libby's jaw dropped—she couldn't believe he had just said that. That he had actually *gone* there.

"Is that a threat?" she asked furiously.

"No, it's not. It's a fact. I'm offering to *help* you. Because I want what's best for her. For both of you."

Libby watched him as she nervously screwed and unscrewed the bottle cap, trying to assess his sincerity.

If he was threatening her, if he wanted to use this place against her in order to gain full custody of Clara, she didn't think he would be offering to fix it for her. It would work in his favor if he simply left it as it was. But he wanted to make improvements, and truthfully, the house had become an absolute money pit. She had fallen in love with the charm of its location, the gorgeous views, and the proximity to the beach, but so far it had been one problem after the next.

Libby looked at Clara again. Her baby was so tiny and helpless. She depended on her mother to know and do what was best.

"Okay," she said, reluctantly setting her pride aside. She refused to allow this to feel like a failure. This was the best decision for Clara. "Thank you. That would be nice."

"*Ouch*, that sounded like it hurt. I know it's hard to believe, Olivia, but I can be nice sometimes," he said with a slight grin, and she stared at him in wonder.

Was he *teasing* her?

That was new. She allowed her own lips to tilt upward.

"Okay, Mr. Nice Guy . . . please ensure that these renovations are only what's needed. Nothing hugely extravagant."

"I don't consider working plumbing, a waterproof roof, and a safe electrical system extravagance. More your average, ordinary basic necessities. I'll try not to inconvenience you too much and will ask the contractors to keep the work limited to the hours that you're at MJ's whenever possible."

"Thank you."

"Right, I should be off. I bathed Clara this evening, changed her nappy half an hour ago. And she was fed two hours ago. She still has the runny nose, but no fever."

He picked up his messenger bag and made his way to the front door.

"Greyson," she called impulsively. He stopped and turned to face her cautiously.

"Yes?"

"I just . . . I wanted to thank you. For everything you've done these last few weeks. It's been invaluable."

He nodded curtly. "Thank you for saying that."

"It's the truth. I-I'm happy Clara has you in her life."

She was. He was turning into a devoted father. Not just a glorified babysitter. She regretted ever calling him that. It hadn't been entirely fair. He was trying his best and had been since the moment he'd arrived in town. And she could see that he loved Clara; she just wished he would stop trying to turn them into some kind of family unit. He sometimes seemed completely unable to accept the reality of their situation.

She knew Greyson hated failure as much as she did. And for a success-driven man like Greyson, a failed marriage had to be a bitter pill to swallow. Well, if she could deal with it, so could he.

Besides, one of the reasons Libby wanted this divorce was because she couldn't stand the idea of being in a one-sided marriage again. Where all the emotional investment came from her alone. Marriage to him had become a lonely and painful experience. And she couldn't see enough change in him to imagine that continuing with their disastrous union would result in anything but more pain for her. And eventually for Clara. Libby had to protect her heart and—more importantly—secure Clara's happiness.

"Good night, Olivia. I'll see you tomorrow."

"Good night, Greyson." She watched him leave, biting back the impulse to ask him to stay. It was a weakness she fought—and overcame—every night. But she feared that one evening she'd succumb and they'd fall into bed again. She hated how much she still wanted him. Hated how little control she had over her attraction to him. He felt it, too; it was obvious in the way his eyes often trailed over her body, the way his voice deepened and his pupils dilated whenever he was in her proximity. But he never said or did anything to act on the desire she sensed simmering away beneath all that reticence.

The divorce papers were still unsigned. And she hadn't asked him about them. Another weakness. She was afraid to ask him. Afraid that he would sign them . . . absolutely terrified of the moment when their marriage, such as it was, would end.

"Oh my God. Alistair's band is really, *really* good," Tina announced after coming into the kitchen that Friday night, her eyes bright with excitement. Tina had been incredibly unhappy since Harris had left town, and Libby smiled, delighted to see her friend so animated.

After their massive opening-weekend fail, the restaurant was now thriving under Tina's guidance. And they could now count the mayor as one of their loyal patrons. The man's visits had been exciting for all of them. Tina had fully embraced the concept of Libby's dessert tasting menu. And they had just launched a Wednesday dessert night. It was such a success that people were making reservations weeks in advance.

And now Tina's idea to have a live band in on Friday nights was paying off in spades. Alistair was their restaurant manager Ricardo's new boyfriend, and he and his band were their first-ever live act.

Professionally, both Tina and Libby were doing very well. Personally . . . not so much.

"You're right! The band's awesome," Libby responded. "We've been singing along all evening."

"We've got an amazing crowd tonight; they're loving it."

"And they brought their appetites, which is great for us," Libby quipped.

"Yes indeed." Tina's smile widened, and she actually rubbed her palms together in glee.

Libby's phone buzzed in her pocket, and her smile faded when she saw that the text was from Greyson. Immediately concerned that something might have happened to Clara, she sent Tina a panicked look before opening the message.

It was a video clip. Relaxing marginally, she opened it.

"C'mon, angel. Do it again for your mummy." Greyson's encouraging voice could be heard as the wobbly camera focused on Clara, who was blowing little spit bubbles and waving her arms excitedly. The baby was lying on her comforter on the floor, surrounded by cushions and toys. Greyson's large hand appeared in the frame, and Clara's fist grabbed his finger. She greedily tried to tug it to her mouth for chewing purposes.

Not sure what the purpose of the clip was, Libby watched with a happy little grin on her face. Tina, who was craning her neck to watch, had a similar expression on her face.

"Come on, Clara, up you go," Greyson said gently while pulling his hand back slightly. Clara, who still had a death grip on his finger, grabbed his hand with her other tiny fist and pulled herself up to follow his hand. Soon she was sitting upright and still trying to drag his hand to her mouth.

"Okay, let go now, angel. Show your mummy what you can do . . . I swear she did this earlier, Olivia." His voice was a little louder now as he spoke directly to Libby. "Just bear with us."

The phone wobbled when he set it aside, faceup. And Libby and Tina found themselves staring at nothing but the ceiling and part of Greyson's face.

"Give Daddy's hand back, Clara . . . that's a good girl. That's my sweet girl." The phone moved again, and the camera pointed back at Clara. She was still sitting up, but one of his hands was on her arm to support her. He slowly released her, and Libby held her breath as Clara remained upright for about five seconds before listing to the left. The camera jerked, and Greyson's large hand appeared again to shift the baby back into an upright position.

"Oops, sorry, sweetheart. Daddy let you go before you were ready. Let's try that again, okay? Three, two . . ." His hand slowly inched away, and Clara remained seated, fully in control, her wide eyes staring at something above the camera—probably Greyson's face.

Libby's hand crept to her mouth. "Oh, she's doing it, Tina!"

"I can see that. Like an absolute pro."

"Oh, you're a good girl," Greyson crooned. Clara chuckled. She waved her arms again. And immediately lost her balance. They heard Greyson mutter an expletive as the baby began to topple. The phone went flying as he made a grab for her, and the video ended a few seconds later.

Libby and Tina were both laughing at the abrupt ending to the clip, and Libby quickly forwarded the video to her parents, Harris, Chris, and just about every other person on her contacts list.

She followed that up with a message to Greyson.

OMG! I can't believe she did that. Thanks for filming it.

She's been showing off all evening, keeps pulling herself up and sitting for a few seconds before losing her balance again.

That's because she's after the praise and attention she knows she'll get from you every time she succeeds.

Well such amazing achievements deserve applause : )

Naturally.

Libby looked up from her texting to see Tina watching her quizzically, and she self-consciously tucked her phone back into her pocket.

"What?" she asked when Tina continued her speculative staring.

"Oh, nothing . . . I was just wondering if that soppy grin on your face was still because of the clip or because of the texts you were exchanging with Greyson."

Libby's face heated, and her smile faded.

"Stop distracting me in the middle of dinner service and go schmooze the guests or something," she said without heat, changing the subject mostly because she had no idea at all who was responsible for her smile. The clip had made her laugh, but the banter with Greyson had kept the smile firmly in place. She told herself it was because they had been discussing Clara. But she wasn't so sure.

"Have you told Libby about the Harris thing yet?" Martine asked Greyson the following morning. They had fallen into the habit of having breakfast at her place every morning. Well, he had developed the habit of wandering over to her place for some food in the mornings, and she would feed him like the stray that he was. He couldn't cook, and he didn't do brunch, which was all that MJ's offered, and he liked an early breakfast after gym. Which was about the time that Martine breakfasted.

Even though she admitted to being "not the best cook," she was still much better than Greyson. And they now had a standing breakfast date every morning.

"What Harris thing?" Greyson asked. Martine never spoke to him about his marriage, and he had always appreciated that about her. This question—completely without context—confused him.

"That you thought Harris was Clara's father."

Appetite lost, Greyson set aside his fork and stared at his plate of scrambled eggs. He hated the question, hated the reminder of his crazy lapse in reason.

"I don't think it's something she needs to know."

"Do you want her back?"

He continued to glare at his plate resentfully. What the fuck was this? He never asked about her relationship with Harris. He didn't think it was his business. So why did *everyone* seem to think it was okay for them to thrust their noses into his private affairs?

"She's my friend, Greyson," Tina said gently, and his eyes darted up to hers. She looked compassionate, and it made him feel a little less defensive. "And I'd like to think that you're my friend too."

Well. That was really sweet. And unexpected. And meant quite a lot, actually.

"Yes. I want her back," he admitted, his voice low and rough.

"Then you should start from a place of complete honesty. I shouldn't have to tell you that."

Greyson picked up his fork and prodded his eggs. His thoughts were roiling and his chest was tight, while his stomach did crazy, unfamiliar loop the loops. He vaguely recognized the sensation: the last time he had felt this unsettled had been before his final exams in high school.

"I thought," he began, then cleared his throat and dropped the fork onto the plate with a clatter. "I thought . . . if I showed her I was different, that I was trying, that she would . . ."

He shook his head, not sure how to complete that thought.

"Forgive you?" Martine finished for him.

"Yes. Maybe."

"You haven't even apologized, Greyson. I say—and you don't have to do this, but let's face it, what you've been doing isn't working. But I say be honest and let the chips fall where they may. I spent a long time hiding my truth from the people I loved . . . and it got me nowhere. Don't make the same mistake."

"Martine . . ."

She swore beneath her breath and rolled her eyes. "And for God's sake, stop calling me Martine. My friends call me Tina."

The plumbing was finally working! The last two weeks had been rough on Libby. The house had been in constant upheaval, and at one point the water had been off for two days. Libby had been forced to shower at Tina's flat. Greyson had prepared Clara's bottles at his place and had bathed her there as well.

But finally, the plumbing *and* the electricity were up to code. And it had only taken two weeks to get it done. Greyson had wisely brought in top-notch professionals from out of town, thankfully not attempting to do any of the work himself. He had even hired a gardener to get the weeds and overgrown plants under control.

The roof was still leaking because the near-constant wind and rain had made working on it impossible. Which meant that there were still buckets and pots placed under the leaks that seemed to be springing up everywhere.

The night after the plumbing was fixed, Libby wearily let herself into her house. It was late, and the place was dimly lit and quiet. She went to the bedroom and found Greyson sprawled out on her bed. He was fast asleep. Clara was asleep in her crib; the baby had started teething and was constantly crying and miserable. It was exhausting. And Libby could tell that Greyson must have had a rough night of it. He had kicked his shoes off, and his socked feet hung over the edge of the bed. He was wearing track pants and a pale-blue T-shirt. His hair, which hadn't been cut since his arrival in Riversend nearly six weeks ago, was longer than Libby could ever recall seeing it before. It flopped over his forehead and ears.

He sighed heavily and opened his eyes. He stared up at her sleepily before smiling.

"Olivia." His voice was quieter than usual.

"You look done in," Libby said, sitting down on the edge of the bed next to him.

"She wouldn't stop crying. I felt terrible for her. I iced a few of her favorite teething toys, and that worked for a while, but not for long. I gave her some of that teething powder as a last resort. She fell asleep at about twelve."

"She's only been asleep about half an hour, then," Libby said, and he grimaced.

"I put her in the crib and thought I'd sit here for a while, just in case she needed me; next thing I know you're waking me up." He sighed again and sat up. "I'll head home. Try to get some sleep. You're going to need it. I don't doubt she'll be awake again soon."

"Greyson, you don't look fit to drive right now," Libby said. "You're so exhausted you're practically cross-eyed. Go back to sleep. You can leave in the morning."

The words were out before she could properly think them through, but when he lay back down and wearily covered his eyes with his forearm, she couldn't regret the invitation. It would be unforgivable of her to allow him to drive in his current condition.

"Just a quick nap," he muttered, his voice slurring. "I'll leave soon."

Libby watched him for a second before grabbing a tank top and shorts from her dresser. She was desperate for a shower.

She was back in the bedroom less than ten minutes later. Both Clara and Greyson were still sound asleep. And before she could overthink it, Libby climbed onto the bed beside Greyson, crawled under the covers, and switched off the bedside lamp.

It felt like she'd only been sleeping for thirty seconds when Clara's cries awoke her. Libby sat up and was confused to find the light on.

"I'll be right there, Cla—" The words died abruptly when she looked up and saw Greyson with Clara in his arms. He was rocking the baby, his knuckle in her mouth as he whispered sweet nothings in her ear.

"Sorry," he said when he saw she was awake. "I tried to stop her crying before she woke you. I changed her nappy, but she remains inconsolable, as you can see."

"She's probably hungry." Libby held out her arms, and Greyson crossed the short, cramped distance and transferred Clara to her. "Do you have any bottles prepared? I don't think I have much milk tonight."

"Yes, I'll get one." He left, and Libby shifted her tank top to give Clara access to her breast. The baby suckled greedily for a couple of minutes before spitting out the nipple and starting to cry.

"I know, it's okay. Daddy's getting some more for you," Libby comforted her, trying the other breast, but that one had even less to offer.

Greyson returned just as Libby was covering herself up again and handed her the warm bottle.

"Temp's fine," he assured her, sitting down on the bed next to her. Clara latched on to the teat eagerly, but after only a few sips she started chewing on the rubber instead. She turned her head away to cry again.

Greyson got up without a word and left the room. He returned moments later with a cold, damp washcloth and a teething ring. Libby smiled gratefully, took the cloth from him, and wiped the baby's wet, hot little face and neck before Greyson offered Clara the teething ring.

"I'm so fucking knackered," Greyson groaned, curling up on his side to face them. Clara was fretfully chewing on the cold rubber ring. "I had an early-morning teleconference with Harris and a few other executives in Australia this morning."

"Have the bad guys all been caught?" Libby asked.

"Looks that way," Greyson said on a yawn. "Harris is just tying up some loose ends and will probably be jetting back to Cape Town shortly."

"That's good," Libby said. She scooted down and lay on her side as well, Clara on her back between them, still gnawing frantically. Greyson's eyes drifted to the baby, and he smiled sleepily.

"She's such a little beauty," he said, his voice filled with wonder.

"She *is*, isn't she?" Libby said dreamily, lifting a finger to play with one of the baby's silky, soft curls.

"Absolutely."

"At least we got this one thing right." Her words were starting to slur.

Greyson switched off the bedside lamp before draping his arm over her waist and enfolding their baby within a protective cage. He was asleep in seconds, and Clara drifted off soon after.

Libby lay there for a long time, listening to the comforting, familiar sound of him lightly snoring next to her. She had missed having him in her bed. She had missed the warmth of his body, the wonderful woodsy scent of his aftershave combined with the crisp pine of his shampoo. She had missed all of that and more. And in the forgiving dark of night, she found herself wishing she could curl up in his arms and allow him to soothe all the pain and despair and anger of the last few months away.

It had once been so easy to love him. To permit herself to be vulnerable with him . . . but he had taken that vulnerability and stomped all over it.

She had vowed never to let him close enough to do that again.

But in that moment, in the warm, soft darkness, with her baby's snuffling breaths lightly peppered in between Greyson's heavier exhalations, Libby remembered how wonderful it had been to simply trust that he would never hurt her.

She allowed that false sense of comfort and security to wash over her before finally falling asleep.

# Chapter Fourteen

The first thing Libby saw when she opened her eyes the following morning was the flower. A pretty, freshly bloomed purple African daisy. Its petals glistened with raindrops, and it could only have come from her garden.

She sat up and stared at the simple, lovely blossom. It lay on the pillow that still held the impression of Greyson's head.

"Damn it, Greyson," she whispered, hating the sweet unexpectedness of the gesture. But hating herself even more for being so oddly affected by it. It felt like her brain had turned to mush over a silly, tiny romantic gesture that only a teenage girl should have gone so giddy over.

Exhaling on a shuddery gasp, she picked up the hardy early-spring flower.

"Good morning."

She turned her head to look at Greyson. He stood in her bedroom doorway, Clara in the crook of one arm and a bottle in his other hand.

It had been a rough night for all of them. Clara had woken them several times more, and they had groggily taken turns soothing the baby and taking care of her needs. Libby hadn't even considered the appropriateness of having him stay over until now. It was unsettling how seamlessly he had integrated into her and Clara's routine.

"What's this for?" she asked, lifting the flower.

"Happy birthday," he said, his voice rough with sincerity. "I would have made breakfast in bed, but I'm sure you know how that would have turned out."

The statement surprised a laugh out of Libby. With everything that had happened recently, she hadn't given her birthday any thought at all. And she was shocked Greyson had remembered it.

"Thank you," she said, offering him a small smile. She felt a little shy and not at all sure why that was. "How's young miss today?"

"Still uncomfortable, but I've been giving her a steady supply of iced teething toys. She's had some mashed banana and pear for breakfast, but she was more interested in chewing her spoon."

"Thank you for all your help last night," Libby said, idly running her fingers over the daisy's soft petals.

"Least I could do after you so kindly offered to let me stay."

"I should get ready for work."

"Of course." He nodded and started to leave before pausing. "I was wondering if we could have dinner on Sunday. We need to talk."

"Greyson," she said with an impatient sigh. "Our talks never achieve anything."

"It's important, Olivia."

"Fine. But no more ridiculously romantic, highly inappropriate restaurants. I'll cook, and you can come here. That way I won't need a sitter for Clara."

He looked hesitant. "I was hoping for neutral territory," he said, the words emerging slowly and carefully, as if he was afraid of saying the wrong thing.

"Why? Are you expecting our conversation to get volatile?"

"Possibly," he admitted, and her eyebrows flew up in surprise at his honesty.

Extremely curious now, she tilted her head and eyed him speculatively. "We could go to Chris's café. But for lunch. I don't want to do dinner." It was too intimate.

"Your friend? The model? The one you worked for when you first came here?"

Libby wondered if it was possible for one's eyebrows to ascend all the way to the top of one's head. Because that was how high she felt hers had risen.

"Ex-model. And how did you *know* all of that? Did Harris tell you?"

"No. Nobody spoke to me much after you left." He sounded so morose admitting it that Libby very nearly felt sorry for him. *Very nearly.* Until she remembered why everybody had been pissed off with him.

"So how did you know I'd worked for Chris? How did you know I was here in the first place?" Why had it never occurred to her to ask him that before? Harris and Tina wouldn't have told him. His parents hadn't known. They had sent care packages for Clara to *her* parents, who in turn had forwarded them to Libby.

"That's part of what I want to talk to you about on Sunday."

"I think this is something you can tell me now. Since I've asked, and it's a simple question requiring a simple answer."

"Maybe the answer isn't that simple," he retorted. He looked at Clara, and his expression softened. His shoulders sagged in defeat, and he continued speaking without diverting his gaze from his daughter's face. As if he didn't want to see Libby's reaction to his words. "I hired an investigator. Immediately after you left the hospital. It was my last lucid act for a while . . . but I had to be sure you and Clara were okay."

Libby blinked. There were so many conflicting emotions churning around inside of her that she couldn't entirely figure out how she felt about that confession.

"An investigator? Like a private detective? Why? Did you think Clara and I had gone off to live with her baby daddy? Oh my God, did you think *Chris* was her father?"

Outrage. That was the feeling currently fighting for dominance over confusion, uncertainty, and—*weirdly*—hope.

He winced and lifted his haunted gaze to hers. "No. Of course not. I never once thought that."

"There's no *of course not* here, Greyson. When I left, you fully believed that Clara was somebody else's child. So why wouldn't you think it was Chris? Did you have someone else in mind?"

"By the time you left the hospital, I already knew Clara was mine."

"What?" *The fuck?* "That was the very next day."

"Yes."

"I don't understand."

"I want to talk to you about this, but we don't have the time to get into it right now. I'm happy to go to your friend's restaurant for lunch on Sunday. We can discuss it further then."

Frustrated, because he was right—there wasn't enough time to talk about this now—Libby nodded abruptly and got up.

"Fine. Whatever you want, Greyson." She didn't do much to keep the acid from her voice. If his pained expression was anything to go by, her sarcasm was more than evident. He stepped out of the doorway, and she sank down onto the bed, finding it hard to process the information he had given her.

An investigator. Some stranger watching her every move. And she hadn't once sensed she was being observed. The thought gave her chills, and she wondered if Greyson was even aware of how far out of line that was.

And if he was being truthful about knowing he was Clara's father practically since day one, why hadn't he approached her sooner? Why wait four months? Nothing about this made sense.

She had so many questions, and she wasn't at all sure she was ready to hear the answers.


"That was ridiculously childish," Libby told Tina two hours later. The staff had given Libby a smash cake for her birthday, and it had given

Libby a childish kick to wreck that cake. All she had to do was picture Greyson's face as she smashed the hell out of it. Very therapeutic. She and Tina were now in the tiny office at MJ's, changing out of their sticky clothing.

"But fun," Tina said with a laugh, sounding more lighthearted than she had in weeks. That alone had made the entire messy, crazy cake fight worth it in Libby's book.

"Yes," she conceded. "It was fun. Thank you."

"Admit it, you're just happy you didn't have to eat it," Tina quipped, and Libby chuckled. Tina had baked the cake, and she wasn't a very good baker.

"I think *that* was my real birthday present," Libby teased her.

"Shut up, we can't all be master pastry chefs," Tina said with a little pout. She combed her fingers through her thick, damp hair, searching for cake residue. "I get it all?"

Libby cast a quick eye over her friend's hair. Tina had been forced to wet it to get rid of some of the stickiness. "Looks like it."

"Soooo . . ." Tina stretched out the word as she continued to toy with one of her long strands of hair. "I'm thinking of heading to Cape Town for a few days next week."

"You are? Why?"

"I'm going to sell my flat."

"You love that place," Libby said. Tina had been so happy and proud when she had bought that flat; it was hard to imagine her willingly giving it up.

"I love this place more. I want to buy a house here. No point clinging to the flat when I'll never live there again."

"That makes sense."

"And I want to meet Edward"—her new nephew, Conrad and Kitty's baby, born shortly after they had moved to the Garden Route; Libby was happy that her friend was at the point where she would willingly meet a baby—"and Harris is leaving Australia today." Tina didn't have to elaborate for Libby to understand that she meant to see him.

"I know," Libby said with a soft smile. Harris had sent her a birthday text earlier and told her he'd be leaving Perth today.

"He and I have some unfinished business." Tina paused before continuing in a rush. "I'm going to ask Greyson to oversee management of MJ's while I'm gone."

"You don't have to do that," Libby protested, not at all pleased with the notion of having Greyson hanging about, bossing everyone around.

"You're busy with the kitchen, Libby. Ricardo has his hands full running the floor. I need someone here in a supervisory capacity to make sure things run smoothly between the front of the house and the kitchen. You know that. And I thought Greyson would be a good choice because he could watch Clara while he was chilling in my office being a figurehead."

Ha! As if a control freak like Greyson would be content with being just a figurehead. Tina would be lucky if she returned and found her restaurant still recognizable after leaving him in charge.

"Does it *have* to be Greyson?" Libby asked, knowing she sounded petty, but really . . . yeah, she *felt* petty. Especially after Greyson's revelations that morning.

"It won't be for long, a few days max."

"If you *must*. But you tell him to keep his nose out of my kitchen."

"I'll do that."

"When are you leaving?"

"Day after tomorrow." That was on Sunday. She'd have to endure a "possibly volatile" conversation with Greyson before seeing him all day, every day, for goodness knew how long. Tina wasn't being very forthcoming about the exact length of her absence.

But Libby knew her friend still had a lot of personal business to settle back in Cape Town. Not only with Harris but with her parents and brothers as well.

"You do what you have to do, Tina," Libby said, offering the other woman an encouraging smile. "MJ's will be fine."

"I don't know why you decided to drive," Greyson grumbled as he loaded Tina's heavy bag into her car early on Sunday morning. "Flying would be safer and faster."

"I like the drive, and it'll give me time to think."

"Less thinking and more concentrating on the road, okay?"

"I'll drive safely," she promised.

"No speeding."

"That's generally what driving safely means, Greyson. You're turning into a mother hen," she teased him, and Greyson smiled. He couldn't recall being teased much before. But Mar—*Tina*—had started doing so regularly. He quite enjoyed it, even though he had no idea how to tease her back. That had always been his problem. He didn't know how to relax and be comfortable around others.

With Olivia, at the start of their relationship in London, he had felt a sense of belonging. He had been able to relax and laugh with her. But when they had returned to South Africa, she and Harris had immediately fallen into their old, easy friendship. Greyson hadn't been able to see a place for himself within that dynamic. And it had been isolating.

"Well then, drive safely. Take regular breaks in safe locations, and text me when you do."

"Why? So that you can check up on me?"

"That. And so that I won't worry."

Her face softened, and she nodded. "I'll do that."

"Good." He patted her shoulder awkwardly. "I'll see you soon, then."

"Silly," she chided before stepping into his arms for a hug. Greyson stared down at the top of her head before closing his own arms around her comfortable frame. "Thank you."

"For what?"

"Caring."

She stepped out of his arms and smiled at him, her expression tinged with sadness. "Libby told me you guys are having lunch today?"

"I'm going to tell her everything."

"She's going to be angry and hurt . . . but think of it as fresh blood draining the pus out of a festering wound."

"That's"—he wrinkled his nose—"truly disgusting, Tina."

"Yet apt. It'll be fine, Greyson."

"I'm afraid of losing her." It was the most revealing thing he had ever said to anyone. It was more than he'd even admitted to himself.

"Greyson, you've lost her already," Tina said gently. "What you need to focus on is winning her back. And that means being completely honest with her. At the risk of sounding like a total cliché, you have nothing to lose . . . but everything to gain."

She shook her head and laughed. The sound was short and loud and lacked any semblance of humor. "Look at me, doling out advice like some love guru when I can barely get my own shit together."

"I appreciate your insight," Greyson muttered.

"Do with it what you will. I'd better head off; I want to avoid the church traffic."

"Is that an actual thing?"

"It is in Riversend," Tina replied. "There are, like, three churches here. And the mosque."

She gave him an airy wave and climbed into her car. Greyson waved her off before turning to go inside. He paused and stared at the ramshackle old split house for a moment. He'd had every intention of moving out after he'd first arrived, but when Harris had asked him to keep an eye on Tina, Greyson had shelved the idea . . . and this horrid, small, grubby place had started to feel like home. Something he hadn't imagined possible a mere six weeks ago.

He wouldn't want to permanently stay here, but he didn't mind it as much anymore. But with both Harris and Tina now gone, he felt a pang of melancholy and loneliness.

He trudged back inside, sank onto the sofa, and brought up his adult coloring app to kill time until lunch.

An hour before he had to leave for lunch, he set aside his phone, having colored his way through three pictures in the interim. He showered, shaved, and carefully considered what he wanted to wear for this meeting.

In the end he armored up . . . going with what was familiar and safe. He figured he was going to need the extra protection.

"This is quite off the beaten track," Greyson observed when they arrived at the quaint cabin nestled among tall yellowwood trees. The place was aptly named Le Café de la Forêt.

"Didn't your investigator inform you of that fact?" Olivia asked caustically. She dragged Clara's nappy bag from the back seat, while Greyson unbuckled the baby from her seat.

At Olivia's insistence, they had traveled in separate cars. Greyson had chosen not to argue, meekly following her from her house for nearly forty minutes before they arrived at their destination. Her sarcastic question about the investigator didn't bode well for the rest of their talk. She was clearly still upset with him after his revelations on her birthday, and Greyson hated that they were starting such a crucial discussion off on the wrong foot.

The door to the café opened, and a tall, impressively built man with sharp, striking features stepped out.

"Aaah, you brought my little bonbon for a visit," he raved, heading straight toward Greyson and plucking Clara from his arms before he could react. Greyson instinctively moved to grab her back, but the baby was chortling happily, and the man was already at Olivia's side and sweeping her up into an effusive hug.

Greyson stared in mute frustration as this . . . this godlike creature of masculine perfection monopolized *Greyson's* family's attentions and affections for endless moments. Fussing over a babbling Clara and peppering Olivia with questions about the restaurant, her new recipes, how she was doing, how the house was shaping up . . . while not acknowledging Greyson at all.

Asshole.

Greyson stepped forward and deliberately invaded their cozy little cocoon of hugs and kisses. "Greyson Chapman," he interrupted rudely, thrusting his hand out pointedly. The other man, Chris, stepped away from Olivia and thankfully dropped his arm from around her shoulders. He looked down at Greyson's hand for a long moment before shaking it. The action was pointedly reluctant and perfunctory.

"*Oui*, I know who you are," the guy said, his voice cold.

"Greyson and I have important matters to discuss, Chris." Olivia's quiet voice.

"I will happily keep my sweet little Clara occupied while you do that." He kissed Clara's cheek, and the baby gurgled happily in response. "Did you miss your *oncle, ma petite*? I missed you."

"That's not necessary," Greyson protested, hating how at home Clara seemed in the man's arms. How clearly familiar he was with her. "She can stay with us."

"Nonsense, we are old friends, Clara and I. She remembers all those poopy diapers I had to change. And all those times I rocked her to sleep and soothed her when she cried. Not so, little one?"

"She probably doesn't," Greyson said tautly. "Babies only start remembering people they don't see regularly when they're six months old."

"Clara is much more intelligent than your average baby."

Well, there was no way Greyson could argue with that, since he happened to agree with it. He clammed up. He couldn't help resenting the history Chris had with both Clara and Olivia, but he was unable to deny that the man had been there for them at a time when Greyson had been too incapacitated by his own self-pity and weakness to do the job himself.

Chris slid an arm around Olivia's waist and led her into the restaurant, leaving Greyson standing there like a chump. They looked like the perfect little family, and jealousy gnawed painfully away at Greyson's gut.

He glowered at Chris's broad back, seething silently while the man continued to fuss over Clara.

So much for this being neutral territory. Olivia was clearly very at home here, while Greyson felt immediately wrong footed and out of place.

Chris led them to a small, intimate table in a quiet back corner of his tiny coffee shop. The place wasn't very busy; in fact they were the only ones there, and Greyson cast a puzzled look around, wondering why this place was considered so successful when it was this quiet on a Sunday.

His question was answered when Olivia took a similarly quizzical look around the shop. "Chris, the café is closed, isn't it?" she asked, sounding exasperated. "I thought you were open on Sundays."

"I usually am, but this seemed urgent."

"Wait, you closed because of us?"

"No, of course not," he said soothingly, before tossing Greyson a seriously disdainful look. "I closed because of *you*. And of course this little mamsell." The last was directed at Clara, and he tweaked her nose. A gesture that was greeted with a delighted chuckle.

"Chris, that's crazy. You shouldn't have done that," Olivia said. Greyson looked down at the floor, furious. If he made eye contact with anyone right now, he would probably blow a fuse. This was so far out of bounds he wasn't sure how to react. All he knew was that he wanted to take his kid away from the arrogant, ridiculously good-looking douchebag and . . . and steer his wife out of this place where the owner obviously had strong feelings for her. Feelings Greyson wasn't sure were strictly platonic.

"Neutral territory, huh?" he grumbled, unable to prevent himself from lifting his seething gaze to Olivia.

*Crap,* Chris was really going overboard with the protective-friend bit. Libby understood that Greyson had to feel ambushed and felt guilty to have led him straight into it. But she hadn't expected this show of macho alpha male bullshit from her usually easygoing friend. Like she didn't have enough to deal with already. She knew Chris thought he was looking out for her, and part of it stemmed from how emotionally fragile she had been when she'd first arrived here all those months ago. It had kicked his protective instincts into hyperdrive, and he had taken on a big-brother role that seemed to have morphed into whatever the hell this was.

"Chris, *se détendre s'il vous plaît.*"

Her friend glared at her, clearly not happy with her telling him to relax. Greyson raised his eyebrows at her words, and she sighed. She had forgotten he spoke fluent French. Also German, Japanese, Italian, Mandarin . . . and probably a few more that she had forgotten about.

"I will bring your entrée," Chris said stiffly, and Libby bit back a groan. She was getting heartily sick of men and their brittle egos. He turned away, still holding Clara, but when the baby realized he was carrying her away from them, she uttered a protesting cry and reached her arms out toward Greyson.

Libby's mouth fell open. It was the first time Clara had ever reached out to a specific person. Toys and her bottle, yes, but never an actual person. Her eyes tracked over to Greyson, who was staring at the baby's outstretched arms in disbelief.

His gaze flew to Libby's, alight with joy and something that looked very much like relief. The smile that lit his face was an appealing mix of pride, happiness, and absolute vulnerability. As if he wasn't quite sure he could believe what he was seeing.

"She's never done that before," he said, his voice hushed, and Libby couldn't help but return his elated grin.

"No, she hasn't."

The baby was still reaching for Greyson and wriggling in Chris's arms in an attempt to get to her father. Greyson got up to take her, and when Chris relinquished his hold on her writhing little body, she practically launched herself into Greyson's arms.

"Hey, sweetheart. Do you want to stay with Mummy and Daddy? That's okay, my darling. You can sit with us." He held her close and kissed her cheek.

"I will return in a few minutes," Chris said, taking Clara's rejection with a good-natured smile.

"Thanks, Chris," Libby said as Greyson took his seat across from her. He was still talking to Clara and made sure she was settled on his lap, her pacifier in her mouth as she snuggled into his chest, her sleepy gaze on Libby's face. She was absently tugging at Greyson's red silk tie. He was dressed to a T today: three-piece navy-blue suit and red tie with a pair of black wingtip shoes on his feet. He looked like the Greyson Chapman she knew, and—her thoughts skidded to a halt before she could complete the phrase. Well, he looked like the Greyson Chapman she knew.

Familiar, austere, distant.

"So you and Chris—"

"He's just a friend," Libby interrupted tautly.

"Seems to me he fancies himself as more than that."

"You're imagining things," she said dismissively.

"Possibly. Perhaps because I find it hard to imagine any man wanting to be *just* your friend."

"Don't be ridiculous," Libby said, not sure if she found his words flattering or disturbing.

Chris returned with a couple of tall glasses.

"Green apple and lemongrass soda," he murmured as he placed the glasses in front of them. "I know you don't want to be disturbed, so I took the liberty of preparing a meal for you."

"*Merci*, Chris," Libby said with a grateful smile, while Greyson just glared at the man. Chris popped away for a few seconds before returning with beautifully presented scallop dishes.

"Butter-seared scallops with ginger-infused shallots."

He left before either of them could thank him.

Greyson didn't say anything, ignoring his plate while Libby picked up her fork and sampled one of the scallops. She couldn't contain her moan of delight as the flavors sang on her appreciative tongue.

"You should try it," she prompted him, pointing at his untouched plate with her fork.

"I'm not hungry. And let's face it, we're not really here to eat."

Well, that definitely killed what little she had in the way of appetite. Libby set aside her fork and watched as he leaned to the side and picked up his bag. He fumbled around in it with his free hand before removing a familiar-looking A4 envelope from the bag. He placed the envelope in the center of the table between them. His gesture similar to hers when she had given the envelope to him a month ago.

"I signed them," he said, not meeting her eyes. Instead he focused on Clara's face. The baby looked on the verge of falling asleep. "There are a few changes, of course. With regards to, uh, custody, but I'm sure you'll find my requests reasonable."

"Why now?" She forced the question out. Not sure why she was asking. She should take the papers and run. But now that they were there, right in front of her, she was oddly reluctant to even touch them.

"Because you're going to want them after I've said what I came here to say."

"That bad, huh?"

"Olivia . . ." His voice throbbed with misery, and part of Libby wanted to reach across the expanding chasm between them to take his hand. Offer him comfort.

"Worse than the investigator?" she asked, and he swallowed before meeting her gaze head on. He looked absolutely devastated.

"I don't . . . I can't . . ." He shook his head before trying again. "I'm not a very demonstrative man, Olivia. You know that. I've never been one to wear my every emotion on my sleeve. I know you all used to joke that I probably didn't even *have* emotions."

*You all?* The phrase jolted her and made her wonder to whom he was referring.

"We all *who*?" she couldn't stop herself from asking.

"You. Tina." *Tina?* Since when did he use the nickname? "Harris. I've heard the comments. About me."

"What comments?" she asked, although she was pretty sure she knew what he meant. But their adolescent teasing had never seemed to bother him. Reinforcing their belief that he was unflappable and completely emotionless.

"You know . . . the Ice Man stuff. And, uh, Mr. Freeze, I think it was. The Terminator?"

"Greys—"

"I mean, it's okay," he quickly interrupted, which was great because Libby had no idea what she'd been about to say. There was no denying the mocking nicknames she and Harris had come up with when they were teens. But part of it had stemmed from Libby's desire to be noticed by him, to provoke some kind of reaction from him. She had never succeeded, of course. He had remained as cold and aloof as an iceberg. And the first inkling of warmth she'd ever seen in him had been that night at the rooftop party.

"I'll be the first to admit that I'm not great at revealing what I'm feeling. I find emotions messy and needlessly complicated. I've never found it easy to participate, and quite frankly, when you were younger— a teen—it was simpler to keep my distance. Whenever I found myself in your presence, I wanted to do highly inappropriate things. And that would have been . . ." He shook his head. "It wouldn't have been acceptable. You were young and vulnerable. Your parents worked for mine. There was an imbalance of power, and I wanted to stay as far removed from you as possible because you were so very hard to resist."

"What?" Her voice was quiet and confused, and she found herself reeling at the admission that he had wanted her for so long. He had never let on. Not once.

But he did himself a disservice when he said he was cold. She now knew he was far from cold. He was hot and passionate, and there was a wealth of emotion teeming just below the grim surface he presented to the world. She had managed to tap into it, as had Clara, and the more time she spent with him, the more of himself he revealed to her.

"Are you saying you wanted me? *Years* ago?"

"I was always aware of you . . . but when I saw you after I came home from college. The year you turned sixteen. *God.* My world flipped upside down. You were so fucking beautiful." It still jolted her to hear the f-bomb from him, but there was such intense sincerity in his voice that there was no denying he meant every word. "But you were so young. I couldn't allow what I felt to show. I kept myself as far away from you as humanly possible. But you and Harris . . . you were so close, and I-I envied him. I was jealous of his ability to be so at ease with you. I wanted to talk and laugh with you. But Harris was the one you went to with your stories and your laughter and your confidences."

She tilted her head as she absorbed those words. Of course she talked and laughed with Harris . . . they were friends. They were closer than friends: they were like siblings. Greyson knew that.

"When I saw you again at the party," he continued, "I couldn't resist you anymore. You were . . ." He shook his head, seemingly unable to find the words. "I knew your parents had retired. You were independent, career minded, talented . . . and I could finally act on my need for you. After that—knowing I was your first—the thought of letting you go was . . . difficult for me. I started pushing for marriage. I shouldn't have; I should have told you about my fertility concerns. I should have told you so fucking many things, Olivia. But I didn't. I wanted you. And I would do anything to have you."

Clara had gone limp, and he gently shifted her so that she was cradled in his arms. So sweet and unbelievably tender with the baby.

He traced her features with a reverent finger before looking up at Libby, his eyes gleaming with moisture.

"When I heard that I probably couldn't have children, I didn't really care. I was nineteen; kids had been a distant dream. Barely even a dream. At that age, the thought of fatherhood had never occurred to me. It started to niggle as I got older. This awful feeling of inadequacy formed deep down in my gut. I forced myself not to think about it, told myself I'd cross that bridge when I came to it. I considered going for a second opinion, but the thought of being told—*again*—that I was flawed in such a fundamental way was exceedingly disagreeable. I kept delaying it, telling myself it didn't matter to me. But it *did* matter.

"I could never be a father. I could never give my parents grandchildren. And the thought of telling a woman, a potential mate, I couldn't ever give her a child . . . it was humiliating. By the time you and I met up again, I had *almost* convinced myself that it was unimportant. And when I asked you to marry me, parenthood was literally the last thing on my mind. I just wanted *you*."

Libby stared at him, her heart lodged in her throat as she finally began to comprehend just how devastating the mistaken knowledge that he could not father children had been on a proud man like Greyson. As if something like this could make him less of a man. She would never

311

have thought that; most people wouldn't. But Greyson wasn't most people, and Libby imagined this so-called biological flaw had unconsciously eaten at him for years.

"It was only after you said yes," he continued—and Libby forced back the urge to reach across the table and take his hand; it wasn't her place to comfort him; not anymore—"that I realized that I hadn't told you about my perceived infertility. I convinced myself I'd tell you. But I kept delaying the conversation. Do you have any idea how daunting the thought of telling you was? You're beautiful, perfect, talented . . . why should you have to settle for someone who couldn't even give you a child? I didn't want you to think less of me or, worse, feel sorry for me. The thought of you marrying me because you pitied me was repugnant. By the time we married, I'd convinced myself we could adopt, that you'd be fine with that. Then we moved back to Cape Town, and you seemed so happy to be home. You started hanging out with your old friends, with Tina . . . and Harris."

The pause after he said Harris's name seemed significant, and Libby, still not sure where this was going, sat up a little straighter. Greyson seemed so much more vulnerable than she had expected. The words were tumbling from him in almost-frantic haste, and she knew that he was building toward something big. Yet everything he told her was a complete revelation, and she wasn't sure how much more she could take.

"I'd come home, and Harris would be there. He would stay for dinner or a movie; he'd just be hanging out, helping you with the dishes, talking, laughing, playing . . . and I was back to being the third wheel. The Ice Man who just didn't *get* you guys."

Her jaw dropped at that, and she stared at him, feeling sick to her stomach as she *finally* began to get an inkling of what this was leading up to.

"When you told me you were pregnant—"

*"No,"* she said, her voice quiet but vehement as she tried to stop what she knew was coming. Because if he said it, then *nothing* would ever be the same again.

"When you told me you were pregnant," he repeated doggedly, "I felt such anger and resentment and absolute hatred. I felt betrayed by the two people—"

*"No,* Greyson. Don't you say it! Don't you dare say it."

"I'm sorry, Olivia," he said miserably, for once apologizing for the right thing. But the affront was so completely unforgivable that his apology made absolutely no difference. "I'm so sorry."

*"Harris?"* she said, her voice thick with tears. "You thought Harris and I . . . ?"

"It was the only thing that made sense to me. I didn't want to believe it. I told myself it couldn't be true. But I couldn't imagine who else it could be. And then the birthmark seemed to confirm . . ."

"Oh my God," Libby moaned, her hand going to her mouth as the tiny bite of scallop she had swallowed threatened to come back up. "I think I'm going to be sick."

"Olivia . . . I hate myself."

The words—soft, fervent, and heartfelt—made it so much worse, and the tears she had been holding at bay for the last few minutes finally overflowed to forge scalding paths down her cheeks.

"Not as much as I hate you right now, Greyson," she promised on a heated whisper. "Nowhere near as much as that."

"I'm sorry. I'm so sorry."

"I can't," she panted, her hand going to her chest as she fought for breath, "I can't breathe. How could you think such a vile, despicable thing? I mean, thinking I cheated was bad enough, but with *Harris?* With your own brother? I can't comprehend the level of distrust and . . ." She couldn't complete the thought. There were literally no words to describe how she felt right now.

"I didn't want to believe it."

"Oh, well, that makes it all better, then, doesn't it?" She shut her eyes and pinched the bridge of her nose in an attempt to ward off the headache that was starting to form.

"I was tearing myself apart, imagining . . . believing . . ."

"*Stop.*" She held up a hand to halt whatever horrible thing he'd been about to spew forth next. "I'd rather not have whatever the hell it was you'd *imagined* or *believed* imprinted in my brain. What I already have to deal with is bad enough."

He sat quietly while she gathered herself, thankfully not offering up any further excuses.

"So why did you decide you were wrong about . . . about *that*?" she finally asked. "You didn't have a paternity test, and you no longer think you're infertile. Why is that?"

"Harris. He reminded me that he'd had mumps too. And the doctor had given him the same diagnosis. He pointed out that if I believed *he* was the father, then that meant I had to believe that the doctor was wrong. And it naturally follows that if the doctor could be wrong about him, then . . ." He shook his head, not needing to complete the sentence. But Libby was more horrified by the revelation that Harris had known about this all along.

"Oh my God, Harris knows about your disgusting suspicions? Why didn't he tell me?" She wasn't sure how she felt about Harris keeping this from her.

"You can't blame him for that—he urged me to come clean. He felt that this would have to come from me. He . . . he felt the same way you do. I hurt him. I hurt you both so much, and I . . . well, there's no coming back from this, is there?" He said the last with a bitter smile, his eyes falling to the envelope between them.

Libby dropped her palm onto the envelope, and she dragged it toward her.

"Nothing has changed," she affirmed. "This merely reinforces the need for a divorce." She laughed, the sound dark with bitterness and anger. "What's that saying? 'Marry in haste, repent at leisure'? Well, proverbs exist for a reason, I suppose. Yet people just continue to make the same stupid mistakes over and over again."

She picked the envelope up and slipped it into Clara's nappy bag and then nearly laughed again. Right back where it had started. Those papers had been in that bag for so long before she'd finally handed them to him. It was kind of funny that they now found themselves tucked back in with the nappies.

She was focusing on silly little details to avoid thinking about what Greyson had just told her. She didn't know why, but being accused of cheating with Harris felt like a bigger betrayal than his initial accusation. It was so beyond messed up . . . the level of distrust was much worse than she'd believed. And maybe she shouldn't allow it to affect her so much, not when she had already made up her mind that their marriage was over. But this . . . there was no hope for an amicable relationship after this. They would be strangers raising a child together. And she had wanted more for them.

For Clara.

"I thought I was in love with you." She blurted out the words before she could stop herself, and he raised his wretched gaze to hers. He looked completely desolate, but she couldn't allow that to affect her. She wanted him to know this, wanted him to understand what he had destroyed with his distrust and his cruelty. "You wanted to know why I married you? That's why. I'd always liked you. You know that. But after those two months, those crazy, happy whirlwind months . . . even though you still kept yourself apart from me, even though I knew you didn't feel the same way, I was in love with you. I thought . . . perhaps . . . with time . . ."

Her voice wobbled as a sob built, and she clapped her hand over her mouth in an attempt to hold back the anguished sound she was almost sure she would make if she continued to speak. Tears brimmed and overflowed, scalding their way down her cheeks and beneath her fingers.

His face twisted, and his own eyes gleamed.

"Olivia. Please . . . I'm so . . ." He shook his head, and the movement dislodged a tear. A gleaming droplet that tracked down his lean cheek. Libby's eyes followed it, watching in fascination as it reached the rigid line of his jaw, where it teetered stoically, on the brink of falling. He impatiently rubbed his chin against his shoulder, ruthlessly obliterating the teardrop. And Libby blinked, the destruction of that single perfect teardrop bringing her back to the present with a jolt.

"For weeks," Greyson was saying, his voice sounding rough and distraught, "I've been trying to find the right words. The proper combination of sounds that would make you forgive me, that would make up for what I said and did. But those words don't exist. And nothing I could possibly come up with will ever make up for the things I've said and done. How could I apologize when the words are too small, too insignificant, to *ever* properly communicate my regret and my absolute self-loathing? The only words I have to work with are *I'm sorry* . . . and they're so fucking inadequate."

# Chapter Fifteen

She said nothing. And who could blame her? There was nothing left to say. Greyson had known telling her would spell the definitive end to everything he held dear. No matter what Tina or Harris said . . . he had always known that it would obliterate even the chance of a friendship between him and Olivia.

She was distraught, hurt, absolutely furious, and she was completely justified in feeling the way she did.

"Why did you tell me this?" she asked. "I wanted a divorce. Telling me changes nothing and just rakes up so very many negative feelings."

"I was hoping . . ." His voice petered off as he recognized how futile his hopes had been. How stupid and unrealistic. "I thought if we ever stood a chance of resurrecting something of our marriage . . . our relationship. Even our friendship. We shouldn't have something of this magnitude looming between us."

"We barely had a marriage," she scoffed. Her stark words lacerated him, and he flinched. "Our friendship—what there was of it—was completely one sided. And as for a relationship . . . we had great sex. Well, really good sex. It could have been great. It *should* have been great. Those few nights we had here, in Riversend, showed me how great it could have been. But you always held back. You never allowed yourself to lose control. To trust me at your most vulnerable. And *that* was the real problem with our relationship. That lack of trust led to where we are today."

"It's always been hard for me to trust, Olivia. I don't like losing control. But with you . . . it was different. I was different. I was well on my way to trusting you, to giving myself to you completely, when . . . everything happened."

"'When everything happened'?" she repeated scathingly. "When I got pregnant with your child, you mean? When you looked at me and were convinced that the only way that could be possible was if I had cheated on you—with your own brother?"

She looked like she was about to gag and shut her eyes tightly as if to force her nausea back.

"You and Harris . . . ," he began, not entirely sure what he was going to say. "It's so *simple* for you."

She blinked, something in his words making her pause. "What do you mean?" The question was reluctant and forced out through barely moving lips.

"I've never found it easy to be around people. I prefer solitary pursuits. But you were like sunshine in my world. You lit up a room with your smile, with your laughter. You attract people to you. I was drawn to your warm, generous light, and it made me uncomfortable. Because I never knew what to say, or do, around you. Even before I desired you, I found it difficult to interact with you. You were constantly laughing over things that I often found incomprehensible. But Harris always seemed to get it."

She started fidgeting with the edge of her place mat. Greyson was familiar with the habit. It was something she often did—fidgeting with random objects—when she was nervous or trying to figure something out.

"When you were a kid, you used to follow me around, remember?"

"Until you called me a stalker," she muttered, sounding like a resentful teen.

"I allowed it for years before I put a stop to it. I liked knowing you were there. You were always close, and I was getting too used to it, too comfortable with it. I remember once I turned around and you weren't there, and I panicked because I worried that something had happened to you. But you had stopped to pick up a treat from the kitchen, and you came traipsing into the living room, a plate of cookies in hand, sat down with your book, and proceeded to ignore me as usual. Always trying so hard to be unobtrusive. Trying to pretend that you just *happened* to be in the same room I was in. That was when I decided that I needed to put an end to it. I had become too accustomed to your presence, and it confused me. I feared that one day I would have to interact with you, and your sweet little crush would disappear when you discovered that I wasn't interesting or funny or anything like my brother. I didn't want to see the disappointment on your face the day that happened. So I drove you away. And then, when you were older, I kept you at arm's length because it was the only thing that would save my sanity."

"Greyson, I knew who you were. *How* you were. And I loved you anyway. I loved you because of that. You anchored me, and I liked that. I felt safe with you. I *never* wanted you to be like Harris. Why would I? I already have a Harris in my life, and I love him. I always have. He's like a brother to me. A funny, goofy older brother whom I adore and maybe hero-worshipped a bit when we were younger. But I'm not in love with him. That emotion was reserved for you. For the man I thought I knew. You should have trusted me, Greyson. You should have trusted me with your heart and your body and your soul. I would never have betrayed you."

He diverted his gaze down to his precious daughter and felt like a hole had been ripped in his chest. A huge, gaping, bleeding hole . . . a fatal, self-inflicted wound that could only lead to anguish and death. A painful, agonizing death of the soul.

"There's nothing more to be said here, Greyson," she told him, her voice almost gentle. "I'll go and say goodbye to Chris. I'll fetch Clara on my way out."

He nodded numbly, unable to say another word. She was right—there was nothing more to say. She was lost to him. And the family he could have had, the life he had so coveted, was lost with her. All he had left was this wonderful angel, this miracle child, innocent and sweet, who was at the center of all this emotional upheaval.

Olivia left, and he dropped a gentle kiss on Clara's soft cheek.

"Daddy loves you, darling. Always and forever," he whispered. So easy to tell her he loved her. She was the only person in the entire world to whom he had ever said those words, and it still surprised him how very much he meant them.

When she returned, her friend was with her. Greyson got up and gave Clara to her. His reflexes felt sluggish, and he sat down again. Olivia looked exhausted, and he was immediately concerned for her.

"Will you be okay to drive?" he asked, and she nodded.

"Yes. I wouldn't take risks with Clara in the car."

He hated her fucking car. It was almost as bad as her house, and he regretted not insisting he drive them to the restaurant. He would follow them closely to ensure they got home safely.

But as he watched her hug her friend and watched the man make a fuss over Clara, he found himself unable to move. She cast him a troubled look before she and Clara and Chris exited the restaurant, but she did not say another word to him.

Greyson looked around for his bag . . . there it was. Still on the chair next to his. Right where he had put it. His car keys were in the bag. He kept staring at the bag, willing himself to reach for it, to get his car keys . . . to move. *Something*. But he couldn't do any of that. He continued to sit exactly where she had left him.

He heard her car start up, and a few moments later the front door to the café opened, and Chris strode in. The man halted when he saw

Greyson still seated at the table. Greyson sensed his perusal but continued to stare at his bag.

He felt . . . he couldn't . . .

His inability to move or even finish a thought was starting to terrify him. What was wrong with him?

Christién Roche sat across the table from Greyson and dropped a crystal tumbler in front of him. He poured a generous dose of amber liquid—just a shade or two lighter than Olivia's eyes—into the tumbler.

"You're in shock, *mon ami*. Take a drink."

Greyson shook his head. "I don't drink."

"I think . . . in this case, exceptions can be made."

"No exceptions," Greyson said hoarsely. Feeling a little more like himself. He couldn't drink. The last time she had left him, he hadn't stopped drinking for days . . . weeks. He wouldn't do that to himself again. He had responsibilities. Aside from his own work, he had promised Tina he'd manage the restaurant, he had a self-defense class at the community center tomorrow afternoon, and most importantly, he had Clara to take care of. No more self-indulgent benders for him. Never again.

The other guy made a strange humming sound before getting up and disappearing into the back, where Greyson presumed the kitchen was. Greyson reached for his bag. He should leave. She wouldn't be too far ahead of him . . . he should make sure she got home safely. It was his responsibility.

He pushed himself up and was surprised by how leaden his limbs still felt. Chris came back into the restaurant and tut-tutted when he saw Greyson standing. "*Non*, you cannot drive in this state you are in. First drink this."

"I told you I don't . . ." The words died in Greyson's throat when Chris shoved a mug of warm liquid into his hands. "What's this?"

"Sweet tea. Is good for the shock."

Sweet tea. Greyson would have laughed, but he didn't seem to have any laughter left in him. He sank back down and obediently drank his tea. Chris sat and watched him closely, taking an occasional sip of the liquid he had poured into the tumbler for Greyson. It smelled like whiskey.

Well, Greyson would never again underestimate the restorative qualities of a good cup of tea. Warmth started to flood into his limbs, bringing them—and him—back to painful life. Truth be told, shock was better. It kept the emotions at bay. The agony of loss was so much more bearable when one's emotions were muted by the immediate trauma of separation.

"Good, you are not so pale and ghostlike anymore," Chris observed.

"My marriage is over," Greyson said, unable to stop the words from escaping, and then he could have kicked himself for saying them.

"I believe your marriage was over many months ago."

"Perhaps," Greyson agreed stiltedly, still not sure why he was talking to this guy about it. He wasn't exactly a neutral party. "But I had hoped I could repair the damage."

"When you accuse your faithful wife of cheating, the damage is irreparable."

"I don't believe that. I feel if the marriage is strong enough, if the misunderstanding came from a place of genuine confusion and distress, there should still be some hope for reconciliation."

"You do not strike me as a fanciful man. Yet . . . you say many unrealistic, idealistic things. Why is that?"

"I thought I was infertile."

"You did not tell her that."

"I thought we would be happy. That we could adopt."

"You did not tell her that."

"How the hell do you know what I told her or didn't tell her?" Greyson snapped resentfully, and Chris shrugged in that fatalistic French way. Made all the more irritating by the fact he wasn't French.

"I have known Libby for a long time," the other man said, and Greyson glared at him.

"I've known her for longer." Okay, so maybe he was turning this into a pissing contest, but he'd lost so much recently. He could really do with a bloody win.

"This is true. Then you know what she needs, *non*? What would make her happy?"

Greyson found himself unable to make eye contact with the man as he acknowledged to himself just how very unhappy he had made Olivia. In all the time he'd known her, he couldn't recall a time he had ever made her truly happy.

*"Merde,"* Chris swore impatiently, and Greyson's gaze moved back to the man. He looked disgusted. "You are truly a . . . how you say? A buffoon. I've known Libby since she was barely out of her teens. And the girl talks all the time. Talks about her family, her friends. Harrison, Tina . . . *Greyson*. Always Greyson. *You* had the power to make her happy. But you . . . you squandered this power. So easy for her Greyson to make her happy. All he had to do was love her. But you . . ."

Chris waved a dismissive hand at him and gave him a look of such disgust that Greyson felt smaller than a gnat.

"I do love her." The words, soft, unfamiliar, and shaded with a large measure of self-discovery and reverence, fell into the silence.

Greyson did not know or understand why he had not recognized this sooner. Perhaps because the emotion was so unfamiliar to him. He loved his parents and his brother. But he had never been in love.

Only he now understood that he had. He had been in love for years. But he hadn't recognized it as such because it had always been a part of who he was. This love had grown from reluctant affection, to infatuation, to desire . . . to *this* all-consuming, raging, out-of-control emotion that he hadn't even known was there . . . because it had been hiding in plain sight.

"I do," he repeated. "I've loved her forever."

"You did not tell her *that*." There was a pause before the statement was followed by, "Did you?"

Libby pulled over three times on the way home to cry. Part of her was surprised that Greyson hadn't followed her from the café, but a larger part of her was grateful. She didn't want him to see how much pain she was in. And she was happy to have this privacy to get the worst of it out of the way.

When she finally got home, Clara was awake and hungry. Happy for the distraction, Libby spent her time bathing, feeding, and playing with her baby. But hours later, when Clara was asleep again, Libby was left with nothing but her confusing thoughts.

She picked up her phone for the first time in hours and found several messages waiting for her.

One from Tina: Hey, looooong drive. But finally in Cape Town. Happily checked into my hotel and ready for bed.

Another from Harris: Flight just landed. Glad to be home.

Her mother had sent her a typo-riddled message: Spmthin wrpng wiyh new phne.

Followed by one from her father: Ignore your mother's last message. I put the predictive text on for her.

The messages had prompted a small smile from Libby. Her mother couldn't wrap her head around smartphones, and the new phone Libby had sent her for her birthday last week seemed to be particularly hard for her to master. Thankfully her father was a bit more tech savvy.

Libby missed her parents and felt a fierce longing to just pack Clara up and go home to them for a bit. Maybe it was childish, but she always felt like none of the bad things in the world could touch her when she was with them.

There was one more message. From Greyson: Are you home safe?

She stared at it for a while before typing her one-word response.

Yes.

She swallowed down her tears and brought her mother's number up on the screen. Needing to hear the older woman's voice.

"Hello? Libby? Roland! It's Libby." She raised her voice to call for her husband.

"Hello, Mum." She could barely keep her tears at bay, and her hands tightened on the phone as her mother's warm voice enveloped her like a comforting hug. "I miss you . . ."

It was hard to go into work the following morning, knowing that Greyson would be there. He didn't make eye contact with Libby while he gave the expected "carry on as you normally would do" speech to the staff. After that, he retreated to the office, and she thankfully didn't see him for the rest of service.

The morning and afternoon passed pretty uneventfully, but Libby was still a bundle of nerves when she collected Clara from day care. She was desperate for a relaxing session of mummy-and-baby yoga, which had become part of her normal Monday-afternoon routine. She walked into the community center, smile at the ready for the crochet club, who liked to fuss over Clara. Sam Brand wasn't sitting with them as he usually did, and her eyes tracked over to the self-defense class . . . only to see Greyson chatting with the group of teens. He was wearing a pair of low-riding gray sweatpants and a black T-shirt. He had his arms crossed over his impressive chest, and his legs were spread shoulder length apart as he nodded and listened to what a boy of about fifteen was telling him.

It came as a nasty shock to see him there. Why was he here? How could she relax with him just meters away?

Lia spotted her and waved. "Hey, Libby. How're you doing?"

Greyson's head shot up at the sound of her name, and his eyes immediately found her. His gaze raked over her, taking in her black yoga pants, off-the-shoulder top, and high ponytail in seconds. His attention switched to Clara, and a small smile played about his lips as he took in the baby's matching outfit. Libby had even managed to scrape together enough curls for a tiny, loose topknot.

He raised a hand in acknowledgment, and she nodded before deliberately dismissing him and making her way to the stage.

"Hey there, Auntie," Libby greeted Lia with a grin. Daff had given birth to a bouncing baby boy just a couple of weeks ago. He had been nearly two weeks overdue, and toward the end, Daff had been cranky and almost impossible to be around. "When will Daff and Connor be joining us for yoga?"

Lia rolled her eyes. "She's complaining about everything right now. Especially the stitches." Connor had been quite large, and Daff had required an episiotomy. An unfortunate fact that poor Spencer had not yet heard the end of. "When I suggested she join us for yoga, she practically kicked me out of her house. So . . . I doubt we'll be seeing her anytime soon."

The other women laughed.

"Right, time to get started . . ."

"Wait, Lia, you have to tell us," one of the other women, a pretty, blonde single mother named Alix, called out. "Who's the hunk teaching Brand's class today?"

Lia's eyes flew to Libby; she looked like a deer trapped in headlights. Clearly not sure how to answer the question.

Libby had thought most of the town was aware of their relationship. It seemed that Alix was a little out of date with her gossip.

"He's my husband," Libby stated curtly, putting Lia out of her misery. Alix's eyebrows flew to her hairline, and her speculative gaze raked over Libby and then Clara.

"Oh. I thought you were a single mum, like me," she said bluntly, her eyes dropping to Libby's bare ring finger.

"Not quite," Libby said dismissively. Not willing to discuss her personal business any further. Besides, the woman could go fawn over some other guy. Greyson was . . . he was . . .

Her thoughts stuttered to a halt as she ran out of steam.

Greyson was nothing to her. She had no claim on him. And he had none over her.

But he *was* her child's father, and it wasn't okay for Alix to stare at him like a hungry shark ogling her next meal.

Unfortunately yoga did *not* have the desired effect that day. Libby's eyes kept drifting to Greyson. He seemed so at ease with those kids, so knowledgeable in what he was trying to teach them. She had never known he was this adept at his chosen field of martial arts.

Clara picked up on her tension and cried through most of the class, setting the other babies off. In the end, Libby excused herself. Greyson appeared next to the stage while she was rolling up her mat.

"Do you want me to hold her while you pack up?" he asked quietly. Aware of the avid gazes from the other women, Alix especially, Libby nodded and handed Clara to him. She heard the collective sighs from all the females—young and old—in the huge hall when he cuddled Clara to his chest and kissed her wet cheek.

He didn't seem to notice the ovarian meltdown in the room, his entire focus on his daughter.

"Hey, munchkin, why so grumpy?" His large hand stroked her small back in soothing circles as he continued to quietly speak to her. He walked her over to the group of teens, and Charlie ran to them and took Clara from Greyson, making a huge fuss of her while introducing her around to the other kids. Clara, always happy to be the center of attention, stopped crying and stared at everybody in fascination. While Greyson kept a close eye on them, Libby kept an eye on *him*. She packed up the remainder of her things and said a quick goodbye to the ladies, who were only halfway through their yoga session.

She threw her bag over her shoulder and made her way to Greyson.

"Why are you here?" she asked him, her eyes on Charlie and Clara.

"Brand asked me to help him out with a couple of his self-defense classes. I don't usually teach this one, but Brand had a business meeting today. I instruct the ladies' class on Wednesdays and a youth class on Saturday afternoons."

"I didn't know you were good enough to train people."

"I told you—I have a black belt."

"What else don't I know about you?" she asked, her voice soft and speculative and a little resentful.

"I hate carrots," he said, the words hurried and impulsive.

"I've seen you eat them," Libby replied with an incredulous little laugh.

"Didn't say I didn't eat them; of course I eat them. They're healthy. But I absolutely loathe them. Same goes for cabbage and"—he shuddered—"brussels sprouts."

Libby stared at him, a little astounded by these revelations. It was so typical of Greyson to stoically endure something he disliked because it was the right thing to do.

"And then there's this," he suddenly said, digging his phone out of his back pocket.

Libby watched while he scrolled through it. He nodded when he seemed to find what he was looking for and turned the screen to her. She stared blankly at the beautifully colored, complicated-looking mandala on the screen.

"What is this?"

"An app. A coloring app. I like to color things. I find it soothing."

She stared blankly at the beautiful blend of colors, and they all ran together when her eyes blurred with tears. Her lips compressed, and she handed his phone back without a word.

He had always enjoyed jigsaw puzzles, building models, putting pieces together to create a whole. It came as no surprise to her that he enjoyed an activity like this. It would speak to his sense of organization. What did surprise her was the amount of creativity and imagination such a task would require. And Greyson had never struck her as a particularly creative man.

She returned her gaze to Clara and Charlie. The baby had forgotten her tears, clearly feeling familiar and comfortable with Charlie.

"I'll let you get back to your class," she said, and he shook his head.

"Our hour's nearly up."

"Nevertheless, I should get Clara home for her bath and nap."

"Of course. I'll see you both later, then."

"Yes. I'll bring her to Tina's office." Libby hovered for a second longer before striding toward the group of teens to retrieve her baby.

Greyson watched them leave, his throat closing up with emotion. Divulging meaningless little factoids about himself wasn't going to achieve anything. He knew that, but he wanted her to know that he was trying. That he wanted to be less aloof. She had once told him not to change for her. That any changes he made had to be for someone he loved. Olivia and Clara were the two people he loved the most in this world. They were worth changing for. If nothing else, Clara deserved a warm, loving, and demonstrative father. Greyson was trying to be that for his little girl. Trying to be open and approachable with the people who meant the most to him.

He wanted Olivia to know that. He wanted her to know that while he had failed dismally as a husband, he would be the best possible father to Clara. And a reliable coparent to Olivia.

Unfortunately, dinner service did not go as smoothly as Greyson had hoped it would. They were understaffed because of a flu epidemic sweeping through town and had a much bigger Monday-night crowd than usual.

"Olivia?" Greyson called as he cautiously stepped into the bustling kitchen. He had left Clara asleep in her crib and had the baby monitor tucked in his pocket. Olivia looked up at the sound of her name, and her eyes went frosty when she saw him intruding in her domain.

"Uh-uh . . . unless this is related to Clara, I don't have time for it."

It was the first time Greyson had truly seen her in her element, and she was a sight to behold . . . fully in control of her kitchen and staff. Which made what he had come in to say even harder.

"We're understaffed, and as you know, we're being slammed out there. We need a couple of your underchefs to step in and . . ."

"No," she snapped curtly. "They're not waiters."

"It wasn't a request," Greyson said, his voice cooling significantly. This was business, a business that did not belong to him. And Tina had entrusted him to make these hard calls. Olivia knew that.

"I need all my people," Libby maintained stubbornly.

"Chef, I can help out. I finished my—" one of the young underchefs began to say.

"Kenny, we need more cabbage sliced for the slaw," she interrupted the guy shortly, and he practically saluted before rabbiting away to do as she bade.

"That was petty," Greyson said through gritted teeth.

"You're in charge. Figure this out."

"I found a solution," he pointed out.

"One that doesn't include my kitchen staff. I told Tina I didn't want you anywhere near my kitchen."

"You're being a raging—" He shut his mouth with a snap, refusing to complete the sentence, and she folded her arms over her chest, chin up as she glared at him.

The rest of the kitchen staff and Ricardo, who had followed Greyson into the kitchen, were staring at them with wide eyes.

"You." Greyson pointed to a young man, barely out of his teens, standing by one of the industrial-size dishwashers. "What's your name?"

"Vusi, sir."

"What do you do?"

"Busboy."

"Vusi, you've been promoted. Ricardo, find him a uniform."

"I need the busboys," Libby said urgently. "Without them the kitchen will descend into chaos."

"They're here to assist the waitstaff, not the kitchen staff. Besides, I'm letting you keep those guys," he said, pointing to three other young men also standing by the dishwashers. "But I'm co-opting Vusi."

"I don't have any real serving experience, sir," Vusi said as he untied his apron from around his waist.

"Neither do I, Vusi," Greyson admitted grimly. "But I guess it's trial by fire for us both tonight."


He was actually doing it. Libby sneaked surreptitious peeks around the kitchen doors whenever she had a chance, fascinated by the sight of Greyson Chapman waiting tables. According to a few of the other waitstaff, he had dropped a couple of trays and messed up a few orders, but he was so charming and self-effacing the patrons happily forgave him. Especially when he offered them discounts on food and drink.

Libby felt small and mean for her irrational behavior when he had first come into the kitchen to ask for help. It had been a knee-jerk response to seeing him in her domain. And it hadn't been her finest moment. When he had actually picked up the slack himself, it had made her feel awful. Because he had shown true leadership in that moment, proving himself willing to get his hands dirty while helping out their beleaguered waitstaff. While Libby had come out looking— and feeling—like the raging bitch he had so nearly called her.

The first time he'd come into the kitchen to pick up an order, she had snidely asked him who was looking after Clara while he was playing waiter. And he had withdrawn his phone from his breast pocket without saying a word. They both had the baby monitor app on their phones, and they had cameras at Libby's place and in the office. Libby immediately felt silly for asking.

And when she took a moment to go and check on Clara herself, it was to find Lia and Brand in the office sitting with the baby.

"What are you guys doing here?"

"We were just finishing up our meal when we noticed Greyson taking dinner orders. We figured he was probably doing double duty and offered to sit with Clara for a bit," Lia said.

"That's so kind of you."

"That's what friends are for, right?" Lia stated with a wide smile.

"Greyson did me a solid today, taking on my Monday class," Brand murmured. "He offered to stand in for me last minute. Least we can do is return the favor."

"Oh. Well. Thank you," Libby said, a little flustered to recognize that Greyson was making real connections and friendships in town. He wasn't a man to socialize easily, and he definitely didn't have any close male friends that Libby knew of.

It made her think of what he had said yesterday . . . about how easy it was for her and Harris to talk and laugh and joke. Harris had said something similar to Libby a while back. And Tina had alluded to it as well. It was easy for her to make friends and socialize. It wasn't for people like Tina and Greyson. And she didn't always have the patience to appreciate that.

That impatience was something she needed to work on because she was now beginning to comprehend that she tended to project her unrealistic expectations onto others. Like with Tina and this restaurant: she had expected her friend to simply comprehend the ins and outs of the industry. And then, when Tina hadn't immediately excelled at it,

Libby hadn't shown her any empathy or understanding. That did not reflect very well on her as a person or as a friend.

She needed to readjust her thinking and loosen up a bit. Life would be a lot less disappointing if she didn't keep placing people on unrealistically high pedestals.

"She's a darling," Lia said, bringing Libby's attention back to the present. "She's been sleeping for the most part, but it's good practice for when Sam and I have babies."

Brand went white as a sheet at her words, and his faintly panicked expression didn't escape Lia, who laughed and gave him a reassuring kiss.

"When Sam and I have babies, years and *years* from now, I meant to say. We'll be in our dotage by the time he's ready for parenthood," Lia teased her, and Libby grinned. She left the couple and headed back to the kitchen, stopping when the sound of crashing glass brought all conversation to a halt.

"Sorry, sorry! More drinks on me," Greyson shouted from across the room, and the crowd laughed.

"You're just trying to get us all drunk, Chapman," someone called.

"The more you drink, the more you eat, Dr. McGregor. There's method to my madness," Greyson retorted good naturedly, and more laughter followed. Libby watched in shock, not sure who this friendly, bantering man was, because he bore very little resemblance to the quiet, reticent man she had married. This was the man who just yesterday had told her that he had no idea how to laugh and joke, yet here he was. Showing absolute grace under fire and surprising even himself, she was sure.

"You were quite a hit with the crowd tonight," Olivia said hours later, when she came into the office after everyone else had left.

Greyson was slumped on the lumpy sofa, feeding Clara, who was lazily kicking her legs as she contentedly drank from her bottle. He really should gift Tina with a more comfortable piece of furniture for her office. It would benefit only him in the long run, since he was the person who seemed to use it the most.

He stared at Olivia for a moment, slow to process her words. He was beyond exhausted.

"I don't know how many glasses I broke tonight. Tina may well kill me when she returns. That kid, Vusi . . . he's a great waiter. I'm going to talk to Tina about promoting him; he's friendly, efficient, and coped well under pressure tonight."

Olivia sank down onto the spare office chair. "I'm sorry about earlier . . . you were right about the busboys being support for the waitstaff. But I tend to turn into a bit of a rage monster when I feel like someone is trespassing in my kitchen."

"Admit it . . . ," Greyson said on a yawn. "You could have spared one or two of those vegetable-cutting dudes."

"Perhaps," she said with a twitch of her lips. She seemed to be battling a smile. "But when the front of house is slammed, it's usually three times as bad in the kitchen, so I wasn't going to risk losing them."

"I think Ricardo may well go crying to Mummy after our little dispute earlier."

"He did look a little freaked out, didn't he?" Olivia asked with a giggle, and Greyson smiled, not sure what to make of her mood. She seemed relaxed, friendly . . . not as on edge as usual.

"We'd better get out of here; I'm afraid if I don't move right now, I'll never get off this sofa," he said, and she got up and took Clara from him.

"You do seem to be doing a lot lately. Do you even have time for the business?" she asked as she strapped Clara into her carrier.

"Gym in the mornings, important emails and paperwork after that." He yawned again, which set her off. And—adorably—Clara too. "That usually takes me through to lunchtime, after which I help out with the self-defense classes—depending on the day—or take on hours of boring international business calls. I prefer the classes, frankly. But one does what one must. Then it's Clara time. My days are pretty full . . . but I'm enjoying them."

"And you're still determined to stay?" The question seemed non-chalant on the surface, but Greyson mulled it over for a moment before replying.

"I like it here." It was a deceptively simple answer. It was the absolute truth, of course . . . but there were so many complex emotions underlying those four words, and he knew she knew it.

"If that's the case, you're going to need a new house. And you really can't keep driving a rental car," she said after a loaded silence, and he nodded.

"After Tina moves. Harris asked me to look out for her. Can't do that if I'm living elsewhere."

Her face reflected her surprise at the words, and he held her stunned gaze unflinchingly.

Libby tilted her head assessingly. To say that Greyson's response had shocked her would be an understatement.

"Why would he do that?"

Greyson sighed heavily. He was still sitting on the sofa, with his elbows resting on his spread knees and his hands clasped loosely between his legs. He fixed his gaze on those hands, and Libby stared at his bent dark head as she waited for his response.

"We've worked through a lot of stuff, and I regret that he and I were never close. We never seemed to have much in common, and when I . . . when I . . ." He lifted his face, and the despair in his eyes made her flinch in reaction. He looked absolutely ravaged. "He's my brother. I love him. I did and said stupid, unforgivable things, and he made damned certain I suffered for my sins. Do you know he sent me a picture of Clara every single day for four months?"

"He did?" Libby asked on a whisper, sitting down again. Clara had dozed off in her carrier.

"Every day. I began to dread the chime of my phone, while eagerly anticipating it. She was the most perfect thing I'd ever seen, and I loved her fiercely. Those pictures, they saved me in ways you can't possibly imagine. They were the only ray of light during my darkest days. Harris had no idea how much that meant to me . . . he did it to punish me. But it saved me."

"I don't understand," Libby whispered, keeping her voice low, both because Clara was sleeping and because Greyson looked like any loud sound would spook him right now.

"I apologized to him. And I guess, because we're kind of stuck with each other, he forgave me. And we . . . we've become friends, for lack of a better word. He's in love with Tina and concerned about her. She has nightmares, and he asked me to watch out for her. So I'm sticking close to make sure I can keep a promise to my brother. It's the least I can do after everything that has happened."

"When did you start calling her Tina?" Libby asked when he seemed to run out of steam, and his brow furrowed as he considered her question.

"A couple of weeks ago. She asked me to stop calling her Martine."

While Libby had spent her days trying to figure out how the hell she felt about this man, it seemed that everyone around her had gone and befriended him. She wasn't certain what her feelings were about that. But at the same time, when she looked at him, at the lost, vulnerable— almost beseeching—look on his face, it was hard to resent it. Greyson needed friends; he needed to belong. She had never really understood that because he had always seemed so damned self-sufficient.

It was a role *she* had always wanted to play in his life . . . friend, confidante, *lover*. But if she could not be friend or confidante, then she wanted someone else to be that for him. Her mind shied away from the thought of him eventually finding someone to fulfill the role of lover . . . but she knew, with the divorce, that would be inevitable as well. He was a healthy, good-looking man, and if they were going to live in the same town, she was going to have to prepare herself for that eventuality.

For some reason Alix, the gorgeous single mother in her yoga class, sprang to mind, and she immediately shoved that deeply disturbing notion from her mind.

*Hell no!* He'd better not go there. *Ever.*

Her eyes drifted to his clasped hands, to where his wedding band gleamed on his finger, and she was confused by her relief to see it still there. Her own ring was tucked away in a jewelry box. She knew exactly where it was but hadn't looked at it in months.

"We should be going," she said, and he nodded, getting up and lifting Clara's carrier from Tina's desk.

He followed them home as usual and waited while she went into the house and switched on the lights. She watched from the front window as he started up his car and drove off and hated the weak part of her that still wished he could stay.

# Chapter Sixteen

Tina returned three days later. Greyson and Libby had managed to not kill each other during her absence, despite a few more management clashes. Disputes had been resolved with compromises and a bit of grumbling from either side. But they had usually been able to laugh about it at the end of service.

By the time Tina returned, Libby almost regretted the fact that Greyson wouldn't be hanging out at MJ's all the time. The staff liked him, Clara adored him, and Libby had enjoyed the glimpses of a more relaxed, laid-back Greyson. A man who wasn't afraid to offer a small smile here and there, who cracked the occasional dry joke and even laughed a few times.

It reminded Libby of the man who had seduced her at that party so many months ago, the man who had enchanted her, entertained her, laughed with her, and made her feel so special. She had thought he was a figment of her imagination. Perhaps a fabrication designed to entice her into sleeping with him and later marrying him.

That man had disappeared when they had returned to Cape Town. Replaced by the more familiar, grim Greyson who rarely smiled, never laughed, and often stared at her and Harris with that judgmental gaze that had made her feel like a kid being chastised by a parent.

Reflecting on it now, she could see that she and Harris had often behaved like schoolkids giggling about the strict headmaster. Whispering to each other behind their hands and laughing in reaction to his stern glares, turning every interaction into a chummy "us and him" scenario. It had been a silly childhood habit that they had automatically fallen back into after her return.

When she considered that behavior now, in light of his revelations about how excluded he had often felt around them . . . she could see *why* he had felt that way. It wasn't an excuse for his lack of trust or his accusations, but the behavior had been inappropriate. And unfair. It should have been Libby and Greyson against the world. Not Libby and Harris against Greyson.

She was at home after a busy evening service—the first since Tina's return—and thinking about how much she had missed having him around the restaurant tonight. He had stayed at her place with Clara and left as soon as she'd come home.

She picked up her phone and, without really considering the time, called Harris.

"Libby?" He sounded groggy, like she'd woken him from a sound sleep.

"Were you asleep?" she asked, suddenly realizing how late it was.

"Trying to sleep. Not really succeeding."

"Why is my friend so damned miserable?" Libby asked him, thinking about how *sad* Tina had been all evening. They hadn't had much time to talk about it, but Libby planned to corner her tomorrow after lunch service to have a girl talk about what the hell was going on between her and Harris.

"I'm not good for her, Libby. She would be better off without me in her life. Every terrible thing that has ever happened to her is my fault. And this is the only way I can make amends," he said quietly, and Libby bit back a groan. Why were their lives so damned messy?

"I don't agree. And I don't think she'd agree either."

"She'll get over it. We both will. We have to. Our relationship has been painful and destructive. It was never meant to be."

"Harris . . ." Libby wished she knew what to say. She didn't agree with him. He and Libby clearly had strong feelings for each other.

"Anyway," he said firmly, clearly wanting to change the subject. "What's happening with you and Grey? He told me he signed the papers."

That surprised her. In fact, every time she heard that Greyson had confided in someone, it surprised her.

"Does he talk to you often?" she asked curiously.

"It doesn't come easily to him. He always starts a call or message talking about some work thing or the other . . . and then he moves straight on to Clara or his self-defense classes. He told me he was considering taking up surfing. Can you imagine that? Greyson as a surfer dude? And he always finds a way to talk about you, Libby."

The last was said in a much quieter, more serious tone of voice, and Libby swallowed painfully as she considered that bit of information.

"He told me what he believed about us." Just saying it made her feel a little queasy, and Harris made a disgusted sound in the back of his throat.

"Gross, right?" he said with an unamused laugh. "Like I'd want to sleep with a bug like you."

"Shut up," she said with a little huff. "This is serious."

He exhaled heavily. "It's easier to laugh about it. Because I've already gone through the rage and righteous indignation and all the other bullshit negative emotions."

"Why didn't you tell me?"

"Because you were already hurting, and I didn't want to add to that. And because it was Grey's sordid little suspicion, I figured I'd leave the telling to him. If it's any consolation, he looked like he regretted verbalizing it the moment it was out. And he fucking hates himself for ever thinking it."

"Do you think we . . ."

"Yes." The word was out before she had even properly formulated the question in her mind. "We were unfair. He doesn't know how to be close to people. I don't know why. That's just the way he's wired. He has a natural reticence that we just don't get. Tina's the same way. They exclude people until they feel they can trust them enough to let them in. Grey let you in. And we didn't recognize that. Or respect it."

"But we're friends. You're the brother I never had."

"And you're my sister. But we should have been a little more sensitive to the fact that we were ostracizing him. We both love him, and yet we didn't even understand how badly we were hurting him."

"It's no excuse for what he did," she whispered, blinking rapidly as she tried to keep the tears at bay.

"No, it's not. But it does kind of help you understand why he leaped to that dumb conclusion. Not forgive . . . but understand."

She lost the battle against the tears, and they slipped down her cheeks as she struggled to formulate her next words. But she honestly had no idea what else she wanted to say, and she just sat there in silence, her breathing heavy and raspy as she fought to get her emotions back under control.

They had hurt him. Greyson, who had always seemed impervious to emotions like pain and distress and insecurity . . . he had admitted to feeling all of those and more because of the nonchalant manner in which Harris and Libby had continued their friendship without any regard for the considerably changed circumstances of their trio. He had been working long hours, and Libby, between jobs, had sought to fill the void of his absence by spending time with Harris and—to a lesser extent—Tina. Thinking about it now, all she could remember was the many nights Greyson had come home to find Harris and Libby hanging out together. The few times he had come home early, he'd lingered for a few moments and then retreated to his study.

She considered their lunch at Chris's café a few days ago. How he had once again been hovering on the outside of one of her close friendships. She had never made the effort to include him. Not with Harris and certainly not with Chris. As with Tina and the restaurant, she had once again simply *expected* him to know how to join in and take his place by her side. Assert himself, be sociable, friendly . . . amenable.

*God.* What was wrong with her?

"Bug?"

"Yes?" Her voice was embarrassingly hoarse.

"Have you seen Grey take a drink since he's been in Riversend?"

The question baffled her, and her brow furrowed as she tried to make sense of it. "What do you mean?"

"A beer? Glass of wine, perhaps?"

She shook her head mutely, not understanding why he was asking her this.

"I don't know," she said, wiping the heel of her hand across her cheeks. "I'm not sure."

She thought back to the night he had taken her to that ridiculous restaurant. He had ordered the most expensive bottle of wine on the menu, yet he'd spent the evening sipping from a glass of water. She remembered thinking that it was odd at the time.

"I don't think so," she said.

"Ask him why not."

"Harris . . ."

"I have to go, Bug," he interrupted her abruptly. "You take care of yourself and give my beautiful niece a hug from me."

He hung up, leaving her even more confused and confounded than she had been before making the call.


"I was thinking, with the weather getting so much warmer, it would be fun to take Clara to Birds of Eden in Plett tomorrow," Greyson told

Libby one Saturday night about a month later. Charlie had a swim meet, and Greyson had stepped in as weekend babysitter. Their routines were comfortable and established. And what was left of their relationship revolved now around work and Clara. They rarely spoke about anything other than those two topics. Her work, his . . . it was all just small talk. Clara had sprouted her first couple of teeth on her bottom gum and was making delightful *mamamama* and *bababab* sounds. Greyson had been diligently trying to teach her to say *dada* without much success. She was six and a half months old, and Greyson and Libby both agreed that she was streets ahead of most other kids her age.

Coparenting with Greyson was *good*. More than good. He was a wonderful partner, and she relied on him more than she probably should. She wasn't sure how sustainable their arrangement was, but it worked for them now, and she wasn't going to upset the applecart with unimportant details unless she absolutely had to.

"What's Birds of Eden?" she asked absently, watching while he collected his laptop and the adult coloring book she had bought him a week ago. It had been a spur-of-the-moment purchase. One that she had regretted almost instantly. But when she had gone back to the stationery store to return the book, she had instead found herself buying expensive coloring pencils to go with it.

He had been absolutely delighted with the gift, and now, whenever he had a spare moment, she found him hunched over the ridiculous thing, coloring away furiously. And every night he'd show her his favorite picture of the day. It was really . . . sweet.

"Spencer was telling me about it yesterday. It's a free-flight bird sanctuary. A lot of the birds were previously caged or came from abusive backgrounds. They've got tropical birds, bushveld birds, every kind of bird imaginable. I thought Clara would enjoy it."

"I doubt she'd really understand what was happening."

"She'd love the color and the movement, you know she would," he said, and she pursed her lips.

"I think she definitely would," she agreed.

"So should we go?"

"We?"

"I thought it would be nice for her if we all could do something together for a change. She rarely sees us together except when we do our baby handovers. I know it's better for her to get used to it, but I thought we could, just once . . . maybe . . ." He stuttered to a miserable halt. Not sure how to say what he wanted to say.

"That'll be nice," she said gently. "What time do you want to leave?"

His head jerked up, and he stared at her in searching disbelief. "Uh . . . nine?"

"You'll pick us up?"

"Yes. Of course," he said hastily.

"We'll see you then."

He blinked and then grinned.

"Yes. Great. I'll see you then. Uh, great." He swung his messenger bag up over his shoulder and stopped by Clara's crib to drop a kiss on the sleeping baby's cheek.

"Sleep tight."

"You too, Greyson."

She shut the door behind him and waited for panic and regret to hit her. But they remained absent, and when she thought back to his excitement, she allowed herself to smile.


"That was amazing, I mean, I didn't even know birds came in such a vast variety of colors and species," Libby enthused the following afternoon when they stopped for lunch after a morning of spectacular birdwatching. "Okay, I knew it. And I know there are probably thousands more than we saw today . . . but it was still quite a sight to behold."

"A shame Ms. Clara didn't stay awake long enough to enjoy it," Greyson said wryly, and they both looked down at their daughter, who was fast asleep in her stroller. She had stared—unimpressed—at a few birds before dozing off, and she'd been asleep ever since.

"She's too young to appreciate it. We'll bring her back when she's a little older," Libby said with a laugh. "But I loved it."

"I did too."

The morning had been very amicable. They had taken a leisurely stroll through the sanctuary, marveling over the different species of birds, laughing at the antics of some of the primates. Greyson had been relaxed, smiling often and laughing a lot.

Libby had enjoyed his company and often found herself staring at him while he laughed at something one of the animals had done.

He was wearing jeans, trainers, and a T-shirt today. She no longer found it odd to see him dressed like that. Maybe because he no longer looked self-conscious in the more casual attire. He had cut his hair again, and it was back to its regular style. But she found the mix of casual and conservative very appealing. It suited him.

They were at a huge family-friendly restaurant in Plettenberg Bay. The kind of place with a play area for children and a junk food menu. It was noisy and filled with laughter, loud chatter, and crying or squealing children.

Libby reached over and stole one of his fries. It was a habit she had formed in London when they had still been dating—tasting his food without permission—and now she grabbed the fry without thinking.

"Hey." His protest was automatic and playful. "Stick to your salad, woman, and leave my fries alone."

He made a grab for the fry, and she pertly popped it into her mouth. Then she reflexively opened her mouth again, and the fry dropped onto her plate while she fanned her tongue frantically.

"Why didn't you warn me it was scorching hot?" she asked him, her eyes streaming and her mouth on fire. Greyson laughed helplessly.

"You didn't give me a chance, greedy minx. You had it in your mouth before I could warn you."

"It's not funny, Greyson. I burned my tongue." She stuck it out and pointed to the scalded bit.

His face immediately went contrite. "Oh, sweetheart, I'm sorry," he murmured sympathetically, reaching out to gently cup her chin with his hand and adjust her head so that he could have a closer look. They both immediately froze at the contact, and his hand withdrew as they retreated back to their respective shells.

The interaction had been so familiar. So right.

And it had unnerved her completely.

She took a sip of wine in an effort to cool her tongue and calm her nerves while Greyson took a thirsty drink from his tall glass of water.

The water made her remember the strange question Harris had asked so many weeks ago.

She tilted her head and watched him assessingly as he took another sip of water. He caught her gaze and raised his brows. "What?"

"You never minded a glass of wine with lunch before."

"I'm driving," he reminded her.

"I don't think I've seen you having so much as a sip of alcohol since arriving in Riversend."

"Why is that weird? We haven't exactly been in party mode since I got here."

"What's weird is that you seem to be consciously avoiding it. Why?"

"It's not a pretty story," he warned on a heavy sigh, and she laughed grimly.

"None of our stories lately have been pretty."

"When you left . . . after I understood what I'd lost by driving you away . . . I kind of went off the deep end for a bit. I gave the staff time off, tore the penthouse apart, and fell into a vat of whiskey and didn't come up for air again for three weeks.

"I don't remember too much about it. I was a wreck. The apartment was trashed; the only room I didn't touch was Clara's." He shook his head. His eyes had a suspicious sheen to them before he looked away. "I hated myself so fucking much. I hated what I'd done to you, to Harris, to Clara . . . I mourned everything I had missed out on and lost. I tried to stop myself from feeling all of that pain and . . . thought the alcohol would numb it. It didn't. Everything just seemed sharper. I was trapped in a world of memories with only you for company, and you hated me. It was . . ." He shook his head. "Indescribably painful. But I knew I deserved it. When I finally surfaced, it was to discover that the staff had returned, that they had set most of the place to rights . . . but I heard them talking. About how Harris had kept our parents and the rest of the world at bay. He had done damage control at the company, saying I was on a leave of absence and all decisions went through him. He had protected me while simultaneously worrying about my mental, physical, and emotional well-being. It was humbling. I had treated him unforgivably badly, and he had still gone out of his way to take care of me. He doesn't know that I know what he did for me. And I have no way of ever repaying him. Except to make sure that I never allow something like that to happen again.

"My dependence, my weakness . . . it shook me. I don't ever want to go back to that place. That dark, desolate place. It took me a long time to come to terms with how far off the rails I'd gone. I still can't fully believe the magnitude of that meltdown. In the immediate aftermath, after I'd sobered up, I had a hard time coping with my new reality. With your loss and Harris's silent animosity. The world I woke up to was completely alien to me. I was horrified that I could be so weak and cruel and stupid. I told myself you were better off without me, but every picture Harris sent, every update from the investigator . . . they were like lifelines to a drowning man. In the end, the thought of never seeing you again, never knowing Clara, became unbearable, and I had to come to you. I had to at least *try* to fix things."

Libby didn't know how it had happened, but she found herself clinging to his hand, needing the contact and desperate to offer some degree of comfort in return. The soft, rushed words tumbling from his lips, offered to her with a stoicism she could only marvel at, seemed unimaginable. Yet the starkness in his eyes testified to the brutal truth behind his horrifying words.

She had continued on after his awful betrayal. She'd had the support of her family and friends. Her new baby to love and cherish. She had been in pain but never alone . . . never allowed to wallow in total despair. She had emerged stronger, more independent, secure in the love of those nearest and dearest to her.

Greyson had been the author of his own destruction. And it would be so easy to say he deserved every bit of punishment he had received after his lies and distrust and cruelty. But all Libby felt was an overwhelming sense of sadness that he had been so alone. That he had been in so much pain he had verged on the brink of self-destruction.

Even at the times she'd felt like she hated him beyond all reason, she would never have wished such suffering upon him.

He lifted her hand to his lips and kissed her knuckles.

"I'm sorry, Olivia. You deserved better. You both deserved so much better," he said, his eyes lifting to meet hers, and she found herself drowning in those dark-blue depths. His sincerity and regret were unmistakable, and Libby felt immeasurably lighter as she comprehended that she no longer harbored any anger or resentment toward him.

She lifted her free hand to his lean cheek, and her thumb ran over the sharp line of his cheekbone.

"Finally apologizing for the right thing," she said, a slight hitch in her soft voice. "Greyson . . . this isn't easy for me to admit. But I do forgive you. For everything."

She meant the words wholeheartedly. The things he had said and done had seemed so completely unforgivable for such a long time. They had been heinous and painful, but in the end, they had hurt him much more than they had her. After everything she had learned since that day, she could see that his actions—while reprehensible and horrific—were the end result of misinformation, misplaced anger, and misunderstandings. It didn't make it right, but she could understand where it had all come from. And with understanding and sympathy had come forgiveness.

His face seemed to crumple, and he shut his eyes before hurriedly yanking his hand from hers and covering his face with his palms in an attempt to hide his reaction from her and the rest of the lunchtime crowd.

This was an entirely inappropriate venue for such a private discussion, but there was nothing to be done about that. Things happened when and where they were meant to. But in such a busy place, every table was a microcosm, each encapsulating its own tale of joy, sorrow, anger, or apathy. Nobody was interested in anyone else's business, and Libby, Greyson, and Clara may well have been alone for all the attention anybody else paid them.

She sat quietly while he got himself under control. When he finally lifted his emotionally ravaged face back to hers, he graced her with the smallest of smiles.

"Thank you. That means so much to me."

Feeling horribly weepy herself, Libby could only nod. Afraid that if she spoke, she would break down. Because it felt wonderful to forgive him, to move on from all the anger and negativity. But without all that fuel to fire her determination to remain emotionally distant, she felt ridiculously vulnerable and uncertain of what to do next.

She thought of those divorce papers. After he had signed them, she had moved them from nappy bag to nappy drawer. All she had to do was sign them and send them to her attorney, and the deed would be done. But she hadn't signed them yet, and to all intents and purposes, the man sitting across from her was still her husband.

The man she had known and hero-worshipped her entire life. The man she had hated for a brief sliver of time. The deeply flawed, vulnerable, slightly insecure man she now *knew* she still loved with every fiber of her being.

She was so confused. And she didn't know where to go from here.

The half-hour drive home was comfortably silent. Clara was awake and happily diverted by the toys on her car seat, but by the time Greyson brought the car to a halt outside Libby's house, the baby was starting to fret.

They both exited the car, Libby grabbing the baby bag while Greyson unbuckled Clara and lifted her into his arms. She was crying, a nagging sound that told them she was hungry and tired. They didn't speak, but Libby marveled at how in accord they were as they entered the house. It resembled a well-rehearsed dance: Libby went straight to the kitchen for a bottle while Greyson carried Clara to the room. He changed her nappy and gave her a quick wash and powder before putting her in a more comfortable onesie. By the time he was done, Libby was waiting with her formula and a bowl of homemade butternut squash puree.

Greyson put Clara in her high chair and then sat across from them. Libby was very aware of his avid gaze while she fed the baby, who gradually calmed down and happily ate her butternut. She kept futilely trying to take the spoon from her mother to feed herself and then happily guzzled down half of her bottle.

"She was hungry," Greyson observed idly, and Libby made a lazy sound of assent. Clara's eyelids were starting to droop, and Libby took her from the high chair to rock her slightly. It had been an exciting day filled with new sights and sounds, and that, combined with a long car ride and a full tummy, was making her sleepy.

"I should head home," he said, sounding reluctant, and Libby found herself on the verge of protesting. It was that instinctive desire to keep him close that kept her mouth shut, and she nodded, afraid that if she spoke, she would ask him to stay.

"Do you want to tuck her in before you go?" she asked, indicating the sleeping baby.

"I'd like that," he said quietly, getting up to take Clara from her. It was early evening, and they both knew Clara would wake again in a few hours' time, so he tucked her into the bassinet in the living room and ran a gentle finger over her adorable little nose.

He turned to look at Libby and, with the same finger, tenderly brushed a curl out of her face and slotted it behind her ear.

"I'll see you tomorrow?"

She nodded. "Thank you. For today. It was wonderful."

He didn't say anything. His eyes searched hers for a long moment, and Libby was powerless to do anything but stare back. She couldn't quite read the emotions in the roiling depths of those beautiful eyes, but she couldn't bring herself to tear her gaze away either.

When he made a muffled sound, something between a sigh and a groan, and shut his eyes with a shudder, she empathized. Feeling the same helplessness, desolation, and temptation that was evident in the quiet sound.

Greyson shouldn't do it. He knew he shouldn't. But he was going to kiss her. He was physically incapable of stepping away from her in that moment. Of dropping his hand and severing the contact between them.

The tender acceptance he had seen in her beautiful eyes didn't do much to deter him, and with a quiet moan, he shut his eyes and closed the distance between them. He claimed her mouth in the softest, lightest of kisses. When she didn't resist, he deepened the caress and felt a surge of satisfaction when she put her hands on his chest.

He kept the kiss gentle, exploring her mouth and taking his time, feeling like he was tasting her for the very first time.

By the time he brought his hands into play, touching, stroking, caressing, she was moaning softly into his open mouth. Her own hands had fisted in the fabric of his T-shirt, and her pelvis was rocking slowly and rhythmically against his.

It had been a relatively warm early-October spring day, and she was wearing a sweet, short slip dress with ties on the shoulders, and he fumbled with the bows for a few minutes before releasing one tie and then the other. The dress slid—without any attempt from her to stop it—all the way down to pool around her ankles. He hadn't intended for that to happen, but when he lifted his mouth to stare down at her beautiful body, clad only in lacy black panties and a matching black bra, he said a reverent prayer of thanks.

He swallowed heavily and met her eyes.

"Olivia?" He wasn't sure how far he could take this. Wasn't sure how she felt about where it was going, but she hadn't protested and did nothing to hide her body from his avid gaze.

She didn't respond to the questioning lilt in his voice but stepped toward him and eagerly pushed his T-shirt up over his chest. He moaned, happily taking that as the acquiescence he had sought, and helped her, dragging the shirt up and over his head and tossing it aside.

He grabbed her hand and led her into the bedroom, but he found himself helplessly claiming another kiss from her before they even made it to the bed. She closed her arms around his neck and levered herself up, wrapping her firm thighs around his waist and locking her ankles behind his butt.

"Oh God," he whispered, before voraciously eating her mouth. He laid her down on the bed, one hand flat against the small of her back to support her and the other braced on the mattress to maintain his balance. He placed a knee on the bed while keeping his other foot on the floor. He couldn't get enough of her. He had wanted to keep this tender and reverent, but they were both too greedy. Too damned hungry for each other.

Before he knew it, he was licking his way down to her breasts, lavishing attention on each taut nipple. Her own mouth and hands weren't idle, and she was stroking and sucking every inch of his flesh she could reach. Soon she was fumbling with his belt and then his fly, and then she had him in her grasp, and they both groaned at the contact.

"Condom?" she asked tautly, and he made a rough sound of assent, begrudgingly leaving the wondrous hills and curves of her body to kick off his jeans and search for his wallet. When he found a condom, they both hastily fumbled to get it on, and once they succeeded, he tugged her panties off and clambered between her spread thighs.

He sank into her without further delay, having the presence of mind to slow things down enough to make it a gradual entrance, rather than slamming into her without any finesse.

They both sighed contentedly at the contact, and Greyson could only describe it as a sense of homecoming. He was back where he belonged.

After he was fully sheathed, they took a moment to appreciate the tight, perfect fit of their joining, and then he began to move, long, slow strokes. Each one punctuated by a soft, helpless moan dragged from his mouth.

His lips stayed on hers, and his tongue mimicked the lazy thrusts of his body in hers, while his hands were fisted in her long, soft hair. Her hands were on his ass, fingers clenched in the taut flesh as she tried to pull him closer. Urging him, without words, to move faster.

He eventually complied, plunging into her with a wildness that he found hard to temper. When she dragged her mouth away from his and whispered his name, he lost all semblance of control. His hands went to her hips as he reared up and slammed into her.

He was vaguely aware of the wild, keening cry coming from her as she orgasmed. The tight convulsions of her sheath brought on his own climax, and when he came, he cried out her name.

The strength seemed to seep out of Greyson with his climax, and he slowly sank down onto her sweaty, breathless body. He angled himself so that only his head was resting on her chest, between her breasts. And Libby knew he had to be hearing the thundering beat of her heart. She couldn't remember ever having an orgasm that powerful before. Her body was limp, and she wasn't sure she'd ever be able to move again.

The entire experience had been transcendent and so much more emotional than the sex they had had before. Greyson's face was hidden against her chest, and his body was shuddering with what felt like sobs. He was muttering something against her skin, but she couldn't quite hear him over the beat of her heart and her heavy breathing. One of her hands was soothingly stroking his hair, and she made a concerted effort to control her breathing so that she could hear what he was saying.

". . . love you. I love you. I love you so much." It was soft but unmistakable. He was repeating the same phrases over and over again. Libby listened, her hand stilling in his hair, not quite sure if she believed it or if he was aware that he was saying them. Eventually his words started to slur, his head grew heavier, and he was asleep moments later. Leaving Libby even more uncertain about what her next move should be.

They made love twice more before Clara woke up, but Greyson never repeated the phrase. They didn't speak about what the intimacy meant for their relationship, if it changed anything or where they would go from here. They just enjoyed each other's bodies, and after Libby fed Clara, Greyson kissed them both and went home.

It was confusing, and Libby hated not knowing what came next. She was terrified of getting hurt again. He had said he loved her, but she wasn't sure how she felt about that. Or even if she believed it.

She barely slept that night, and by the following morning she had made an important decision. After the staff meeting she went straight to Tina's office. Her friend had been very quiet and withdrawn over the last month. She had confided in Libby that she wasn't happy with Harris's decision to call things off between them. It was clear that the woman was pining for Harris, and judging from Harris's messages, he missed Tina too. The two were obviously in love, and Libby wished she could help them both recognize how right they were for each other.

But sometimes, the past loomed too large to be overlooked. She knew that better than anybody else.

"What's up, Libby? You okay?" Tina asked, her concerned eyes giving Libby a once-over.

"I'm hoping you could give me a week or so off. I'll prep Agnes and the rest of the kitchen staff to handle things in my absence." She knew she was being a coward, running away at a time when she should stay and try to figure out, for all their sakes, what the hell was happening between her and Greyson, but she was so damned exhausted. She just wanted to switch her brain off for a while and not think about it.

"That's fine, Libby. I know things will be handled competently while you're away. I'm more concerned about you. Where are you going?"

Libby gulped, drawing in a shallow breath before exhaling on a soft gasp and burying her face in her hands. She wasn't sure she was doing the right thing, but she needed to think, and she couldn't do that with Greyson always around. She couldn't trust her judgment where he was concerned.

She felt Tina's arm encircle her shoulders in a comforting hug. The other woman led her to the sofa and sat down beside her, bringing Libby's head to her shoulder. The unquestioning support set the waterworks in motion, and Libby found herself in floods of tears as she accepted her friend's consolation.

In the months since she had left Greyson, she had stayed strong, for Clara, for herself. The tears she had shed had been private and rushed. And they had been rare. And when she had found herself overwhelmed or frightened or lonely, when tears had been inevitable, she had allowed herself very brief moments of cathartic crying bouts. This was the first time she'd allowed herself to break. And she had needed it. Desperately.

When she finally managed to bring herself under control, she lifted her head and patted her cheeks self-consciously. But Tina wasn't judging her. The other woman handed her a box of tissues and gave her a sympathetic smile.

"Want to talk about it?"

"I just need a break. I thought I'd take Clara to visit my parents and the Chapmans. I came here to get away from him, but he's just always around. And I've made stupid mistakes. I've allowed . . . *things* to happen." She blushed, thinking about last night. She wasn't sure if that could be counted as a mistake, but that was the very reason she needed to get away. She needed some clarity. "And I can't refuse to let him see Clara; he adores her. But it's not just Clara he wants to see. And I can't . . . I *can't* let him into my heart again."

Except . . . he was already in her heart. He had always been there, and she suspected that that was where he would stay. Probably forever.

"Has he spoken about what *he* wants?"

Libby blew her nose and shook her head, conflicted and confused. He had never made any secret of wanting her back, but Libby wasn't sure she was ready for that. If she would ever be ready for that, after everything that had happened. Their new reality made that almost impossible.

After last night, neither of them had discussed an alternate version of their previous relationship. And that confused her. She should know, she should have an inkling of what she wanted and needed from him. She hated not knowing what her next move would be. The divorce had been a certainty, but she had kept making excuses not to sign those papers. Had shoved them out of sight and out of mind. And then last night had happened, and now she had no idea what she wanted.

Forgiving him was one thing. Taking him back, giving their marriage another shot, was something else entirely.

"You know that man, he's a frickin' closed book. Who the hell knows what's going on in that head of his?" Okay, maybe she was being unfair, given all his recent revelations, but she wasn't quite prepared to go into all of that with Tina right now. "I know he loves Clara, I know he wants me, but that's the extent of it. I'm not settling again, Tina. Never again. Why can't relationships and men and . . . I don't know . . . *life* be uncomplicated? Why does it all have to hurt so much?"

She thought about the words he had said immediately after sex last night. She still wasn't sure if he was aware that he'd said them. And how could she trust that he had meant them? It just seemed so ridiculously far fetched that Greyson would now claim to love her.

# Chapter Seventeen

"What do you mean?" Greyson asked Olivia that evening after he walked her and Clara into her house.

He wasn't sure he correctly comprehended the meaning of the statement she had just made. They had had a phenomenal twenty-four hours. Yesterday and last night had felt like a real turning point in their relationship. He hadn't had much chance to speak with her today, but when she had invited him in now, he'd had high hopes for a repeat of what had happened between them last night.

Instead she had turned to him after they had entered the house and told him she was leaving.

"Leaving to go where?" he asked.

"I'm going to visit my parents for a few days. I wanted them to spend some time with Clara."

"Why now?" he asked bluntly, and her eyes clouded.

"Greyson, things are complicated right now. What happened yesterday . . ."

"Do you regret it?" he asked, certain that he knew what her response would be. And dreading the confirmation of his worst fears.

"No."

The single-word response—the complete opposite of what he had expected to hear—stunned him. And he reeled for a moment as he stared at her uncomprehendingly.

"What?"

"I don't regret it. Not at all. And that confuses me. I need to think, Greyson. And I don't believe I can make sound decisions with you around to cloud my judgment."

"Olivia."

"I have to do this, Greyson. For all our sakes."

He blinked rapidly, trying to dispel the prickling sensation behind his eyes. The thought of her leaving absolutely terrified him. It felt like the progress he had been making with her, and with Clara, would be lost once she left. He couldn't lose them again. It would kill him this time. He was certain of that.

"When are you thinking of going?" His voice was embarrassingly hoarse, and he cleared his throat self-consciously.

"Tomorrow. I was going to make an online booking tonight."

"Don't. I can arrange for the chopper to pick you up."

"That's ridiculous, Greyson. It's an incredible waste of resources just for us."

"It's safer, faster, and more convenient. It would be better for Clara."

"Greyson . . ."

"She's my daughter, Olivia. You're my . . ." He paused, reluctant to even think the word *ex-wife*. "You're her mother. Please let me do this for you."

"Okay, thank you."

"I'll drive you two to the airport."

She nodded, and he was surprised by how acquiescent she was being. Usually she would argue about every little detail, and he wondered why she was being so agreeable. He wasn't sure if this compliance was a good thing, or if she was just throwing him a bone before finally yanking that rug out from beneath him.

He didn't think she had it in her to be that unkind. But despite what she had said about forgiving him . . . the thought of how cruel he had once been to her still loomed large in his head. He found it difficult to imagine her forgiving him for that. Perhaps because he still had such a hard time forgiving himself for it.

He reached out tentatively and caught one of her curls between his thumb and index finger, desperately needing the contact.

"I know you didn't believe me last night, Olivia. And I don't blame you. I wouldn't believe me if I were you . . . but I *do* love you. I have for much longer than I realized. I thought you should know that."

She stared at him mutely, her arms seeming to tighten fractionally around Clara's small body. He grabbed the opportunity to lean in and kiss her gently.

"Good night. I'll send you a text to let you know what time we'll leave for the airport."

He didn't wait for her to reply but left before he could do something embarrassing, like begging her to let him stay.

*He loves me.* There was no misunderstanding his meaning this time. He had looked straight into her eyes and told her that he loved her.

The words reverberated through her mind as she settled Clara down for the evening, while she packed their bags and set her house to rights.

He loved her.

All her life she had longed to hear those words from Greyson Chapman. For so long she had created girlish fantasies around his romantic declaration of love. Reality had been much less florid and far from perfect.

Reality had been a stark collection of words said in a tortured tone of voice, with desperation shining in his eyes.

And yet those unembellished words rang with truth because they were so typically Greyson.

For the man who rarely smiled, barely laughed, and liked to keep his emotions under lock and key, those few words had been the equivalent of a chivalric knight writing a sonnet to his ladylove.

And Libby now had to decide if that was enough to revive a relationship she had nearly given up for dead.

Greyson barely slept, dreading the thought of driving the two people he loved the most in the world to the airport in the morning. After a restless night he got up just before dawn to take a long shower. And he sent Olivia a curt text afterward, telling her to be ready for pickup in an hour.

He wandered aimlessly around the flat for a while before trying to calm down with a coloring project. When that didn't work, he got up to pace again. Finally, after half an hour, he strode to the door. He was just about to open it when the sound of Tina's voice calling his name startled him into yanking the front door nearly off its hinges.

He stopped abruptly, stunned to find his brother cozied up next to Tina on the porch swing. They both looked ridiculously contented, and Greyson was immediately happy for them.

"Yeah?"

"So I'm in love with your brother," Tina said with a huge smile. "And he's in love with me. We're together. We'll probably get married someday. Harris wants the world to know; I thought we'd start with you."

"That's truly fantastic," he said, genuinely delighted for them. "And if I may say so, about damned time. Be happy."

"Yeah," Harris said. He kissed Tina's neck, and she sighed softly. "I think we will be."

"*Right.* I think . . . I'll head out for a drive," Greyson said, not wanting to ruin the moment for them by stating that he was taking Olivia to the airport. They deserved to have their happiness remain bright and untarnished for as long as possible. They didn't seem to hear him, and feeling like an awkward third wheel, he hurriedly left the porch. Leaving them to their privacy.

He couldn't help but be a little envious of their happiness. Things were just beginning for them, but it felt like everything was ending for him and Olivia, and his gut twisted at the thought.

He was unutterably drained, like a drowning man who had been desperately fighting to keep his head above water only to have a giant wave sweep in and pull him under. It felt like all his efforts had been futile and everything from the instant Olivia had so joyously told him she was pregnant had been leading to this moment of ineffable loss.

She was uncommonly quiet when he picked them up. And the drive to the airport wasn't much better. Neither of them could find much to say.

"Harris is back," he remembered, halfway through the thirty-minute drive to Plettenberg Bay Airport.

"Oh?" she asked, and he nodded, grateful to have something to talk about.

"It looks like they've reconciled."

"That's wonderful," she said, her voice brimming with sincerity. "I'm so happy for them."

Greyson nodded again, not sure what else to add to the conversation, and they both petered off into silence once more.

"You should leave your key with me," he suddenly said, his voice overly loud.

"Why?" she asked curiously.

"So that we can finish the renovations on your house while you're gone." And it would help keep him sane and remind him that she would return. She *had* to. She had a life here.

She dug around in her purse and produced the key, dropping it in the coin tray on the dashboard. No argument. At least they had made progress on that front.

They reached the airport much too soon for his liking. The chopper had been fueled and was ready and waiting. It had been reserved for some other purpose, but Greyson had pulled rank. Something he would never have done if it were for anyone other than Olivia and Clara.

"Well . . . thank you for bringing us," Olivia said with a strained smile at the security checkpoint, and Greyson nodded, finding himself quite unable to speak. He was holding Clara, and he gathered her close, hugging her small sturdy body probably a little too tightly and for a little too long. He breathed in her powdery, clean baby smell, memorizing the warmth and softness of her. Clara squirmed and made a protesting sound, and he forced himself to loosen his grip and hand her over to her mother.

He kissed the top of the baby's head and directed his blurry gaze to Olivia.

"Greyson," she said, her voice so quiet it was barely audible above the noise of the airport. "We'll be back soon. I promise."

He nodded, his jaw taut. He couldn't speak. If he tried to talk, he was quite sure he'd break down and bawl like a baby. His whole world was walking away from him. For the second time. And he wasn't sure he could stand it.

She turned to leave, but he couldn't let her go—not like this—and caught her hand in his, halting her movement. She turned back to face him, and he palmed the side of her face before he dropped a hard, desperate kiss on her beautiful, lush mouth. It was over in seconds, and he pressed his forehead to hers.

"I love you, Olivia."

Her hand lifted to where his was still cupped over her cheek, and she gave his fingers a soft squeeze. Acknowledging his words with a small smile.

"Goodbye, Greyson."

She left him standing there with his shattered heart at his feet, helpless to do anything but watch as she walked away from him.

"Hey, I have someone here who wants to say hello to you," Olivia said in deliberately jovial tones, and Greyson grinned at her words. She had been FaceTiming at the same time every evening so that he could speak with Clara, who always reacted with excitement at the sight of him.

"Hello, Clara," he greeted her, inserting the genuine excitement he always felt at the sight of them into his voice. "It's Daddy."

Her head turned at the sound, and her face lit up when she saw him on Olivia's laptop screen. Her plump, grasping fingers reached for the screen as they always did, and Olivia grabbed them before they could do any harm.

"I know, baby," Greyson said. "Daddy wants to give you a hug too. You *and* Mummy."

Olivia didn't react to the latter; she had made it clear that these calls were mostly for Clara's sake. They spoke primarily about the baby, although Greyson would often update her as to how her house was coming along. He had replaced the air con and the carpet in the living room. And he had transformed the tiny second bedroom into a nursery for Clara. It was much smaller in size than the one she had set up in the penthouse during her pregnancy, but he had duplicated the colors and motifs as best he could.

It was a labor of love. Something to make up for, even if it was in only the tiniest of ways, his lack of presence during her pregnancy. He hadn't told her about the nursery—he wanted it to be a surprise—but he had worked his ass off to get it nearly done in the few days she had been gone so far.

Clara quickly realized that he wasn't really there, as she always did. And she lost interest in the laptop after a couple of minutes, grasping for other things on the table.

"How is everybody?" Greyson ventured, despite the fact that he'd been shot down when asking similar questions in the past.

"Fine. Happy to be spending time with Clara. I went to your parents' today . . ." She shook her head; the gesture held a measure of disbelief. "They're so different around her. They practically fought over who would get to hold her."

Greyson chuckled. "They sent me pictures. Told me you were going to the aquarium with them tomorrow?"

She shuddered. "The aquarium on a Saturday—can you imagine the crowds?" she asked with a wince.

"Quite frankly, I can't imagine my *mother* making her way through those crowds. I'm surprised they didn't suggest taking you out on the yacht or something less . . . ordinary."

"Less *common*, you mean," she corrected him, and he laughed. "They suggested their country club, and I told them Clara would probably be bored. Then they *did* suggest the yacht, and I told them I wasn't sure how Clara would react to the unfamiliar sensation of being on water. Your father is the one who proposed the aquarium, and if looks could kill, he'd be dead after the glare your mother gave him."

"He probably paid for it afterward," Greyson said with a chuckle, and she grinned.

"Probably."

They lapsed into a strange, awkward silence.

"Well, I've got to—"

"We're fixing the roof tomorrow," he interrupted her abruptly in an attempt to keep her on the line longer.

"That's fantastic. How did you manage to get the roofers to commit to a Saturday?"

"It's been tough getting anyone out here; every professional in the area has been booked solid for months since the end of winter."

He knew it was a nonanswer, and he hoped she wouldn't pick up on that. Because he didn't want to tell her that he and the guys—he took a moment to appreciate the fact that he had *guys* now—were planning to do it themselves. Spencer had some construction experience, Brand was handy with a hammer, and Harris, who had moved to Riversend and was looking to buy or build a house with Tina, was happy to lend a hand. A few of the bigger teen boys from the youth-outreach program had offered to help out as well. As had some of his football teammates.

"Okay. Well, thanks for arranging that. I should get Clara changed and ready for bed. Good night."

"Good night, Olivia."

She didn't disconnect the call and appeared to be waiting for something. He smiled and leaned toward the camera before ending the call as he always did: "I love you."

The feed ended abruptly after that, and his smile widened. It felt like progress.

"When are you going home?" her mother's quiet voice asked from behind Libby, and she turned away from her computer to stare at the woman. She was in the kitchen, and usually her parents gave her privacy during these calls, but her mother—who had an empty glass clutched in her hand—must have walked in at the tail end of that conversation.

"I'm not sure. Do you want us to leave?"

"Don't be silly; you know we love having you here. But I'm not sure *why* you're here."

"Can't a daughter visit her parents?"

Her mother smiled and took Clara from her before sitting down across from Libby and pinning her with that all-seeing mum stare of hers.

"Anytime. Only this doesn't feel like you're visiting. It feels like you're hiding. I know you and Greyson have had problems. Of course I know that. We all do. When you first married him, I wasn't too sure it would work out. But you've always had a soft spot for him and then a crush on him, and when you returned from London a married woman, you were mad about him. I don't know what he did to break your heart, Libby . . . and I could kill that boy for the pain he put you through. For abandoning his responsibilities for so long. But I've overheard bits and pieces of these calls every night, and that man loves his daughter, and—while I never saw it before, it's clear as day now—he loves you."

"I'm not sure that his love is enough to save our marriage, Mum," Libby confessed in a hushed voice. "That's what I'm trying to figure out. He hurt me terribly, and I suppose I don't know if I *trust* him not to do it again. He broke that trust once, and he's been trying so hard to make up for it. But I feel like it will always be there, looming between us. And I have to decide if I'm able—*willing*—to set it aside and allow myself to be vulnerable with him again."

Her mother placed her hand palm up on the table, and Libby took it, appreciating the older woman's love and support.

"Did he cheat on you?" her mother asked, and Libby's eyes widened in horror at the question.

"*No.*" The word came out more forcefully than she had intended, but the thought of Greyson cheating was almost ridiculous, and she leaped to his defense without thinking. Once she realized what she had done, she felt an immediate surge of resentment that he hadn't done the same for her.

Why couldn't he have had the same faith in her? That felt like the worst betrayal, and that was the demon she found herself battling with.

"He didn't cheat, but he accused me of cheating. He thought Clara was someone else's. He thought Harris and I . . ." She shook her head. Still mortified at the thought.

"You and Harris have always been close," her mother said thoughtfully, and Libby was a little outraged that the woman hadn't immediately jumped to her defense. "Sometimes to the exclusion of everyone else. Even Tina."

"That's no excuse," Libby said, the outrage dissolving. It always came back to this.

"Greyson should have trusted you; he should have trusted his brother. You were always so warm and approachable and loving. It was hard for me to imagine you with someone like Greyson. Hard for all of us, I think. Even for Greyson. You seemed so much more compatible with Harris, while Greyson was always such a closed-off, distant boy. I remember when you were children, you and Harris would come tumbling into the kitchen and try to charm me out of biscuits or treats. Harris would say ridiculously flattering things; you would smile and plead and flutter those eyelashes at me. While Greyson would stand in the doorway and watch. He never begged or charmed. But he wanted to. I could tell it in the way he would lean in through that door, the way his eyes would follow my hands as I gave you the treats.

"He wasn't cold; he was . . . I don't know . . . the only word I can think of is *distant*. Or *reserved*. Always was and probably always will be. When he wanted something, he asked for it, no frills, no fuss, and sometimes it would sound like a demand. It can be off putting, but it's the only way he knows how to be. What Greyson did was awful, and I'm very angry with him for hurting you and not taking care of you the way he should have. And I can't tell you what to do or how to feel. I just know that I never thought I'd see the day that our cold and controlled

Greyson Chapman would spend time making funny animal noises to a baby and telling a woman he loves her."

Libby groaned and buried her face in her arms on the table. What was she doing here? She wasn't sure she was achieving anything except confusing herself even further.

The aquarium was a complete nightmare. So many people jostling to see the exhibits, crying babies, squealing toddlers, stampeding children. The Chapmans spent the morning looking both horrified and terrified, and it would have been comical if Libby hadn't felt the same way.

Clara seemed to love it, though. The noise fascinated her, the gorgeous exhibits held her attention for long moments . . . but thankfully she started to flag after just an hour, and Libby eagerly suggested they leave when Clara started fussing.

Her in-laws jumped at the opportunity to escape, and they were on their way to a restaurant when Libby's phone rang. It was Tina.

"Hey, Tina, how're you doing?" she greeted her friend warmly. Tina had been on cloud nine since announcing her engagement to Harris on Tuesday. And every time they spoke, Libby could hear the lightness in the woman's voice. Harris was the same, and Libby was extremely happy for them.

"Libby." There was no lightness in Tina's voice this time, and Libby sat upright, alarmed by the urgency in her friend's voice.

"What's wrong?"

"The guys were fixing the roof, and . . . I don't know what happened, but Greyson fell. They rushed him to the hospital. I'm on my way there now. Harris called me; he said he's been trying to reach you."

"What do you mean, he *fell?*" Libby asked, feeling hysteria rising in her voice. "Fell from where?"

"The roof, Libby."

Libby swayed as dizziness overtook her. "That idiot. That stupid, stupid man! Why was he on the roof?"

"They were fixing it. There were a few of them. He couldn't get the roofers out until next month, and he wanted the house to be in perfect condition when you returned. He's been working so hard on it." Libby could hear the swell of emotion in Tina's voice; the other woman sounded like she was on the verge of tears. Libby couldn't react with anything other than shock, anger, and panic.

"How is he?" she asked, her voice sounding faint even to her own ears.

"I'm not sure. Harris said he took quite a tumble. He sounded concerned, but I think he was trying to hide it from me."

"Oh God." Libby took a huge gulp of breath, her dizziness increasing. She was aware of her in-laws staring at her in concern. They were in a huge luxury SUV with their new driver at the wheel. "Oh my God. I'll be there soon. I have to make arrangements."

She dropped the call before Tina could respond.

"Greyson is hurt. I have to get back to Riversend immediately. Can you arrange the helicopter, please?"

Truman Chapman nodded and immediately got on the phone, while Constance leaned toward Libby. The older woman's face was ashen with shock.

"Hurt?" she asked, her voice urgent. "How? What happened?"

"I'm not sure. Tina says he fell . . ." She paused and swallowed, feeling a surge of nausea at the thought of the height he must have fallen from. "From the roof."

"The roof?" Constance looked a little sick and very confused. "Why was he on a roof? How high is it?"

"I don't know." Libby's voice was rising in pitch, the way it always did when she was fighting back tears. "About four meters?"

She clutched a hand to her chest as she fought back her dread and struggled to breathe. She was rocking slightly, trying to calm herself but not succeeding. Had he been conscious? Oh God, if he had lost consciousness, that meant he had hit his head. Her rocking increased as she continued to gulp for breath.

She wasn't sure, but she thought she might be having a panic attack. Her chest felt tight, and her breath was coming in shallow gasps. Her dizziness increased as her intake of air decreased.

She felt Constance's hand on the back of her head and was confused by that until the woman exerted pressure and forced her head down.

"Put your head between your knees," the older woman instructed her matter of factly, remarkably calm under pressure. "Breathe in and out slowly. Truman, call Harrison and find out what on earth is going on."

Everything passed in a blur after that. They didn't return to Libby's parents' place; instead they went straight to the Foreshore, where the Chapman Global Property Group's headquarters were located, and rode the elevator up to the roof, where the executive helicopter was waiting. Truman and Constance boarded the chopper with her, and they were airborne in a matter of minutes.

"My parents," Libby said dazedly, unable to fully formulate her thoughts, every part of her desperate to get to Riversend and to Greyson. She shouldn't have left. Why had she left? She loved the fool man, and he loved her. He loved her so much he kept trying to prove himself to her by doing stupid things like attempting to fix plumbing and doors and climbing onto roofs when she had expressly told him not to.

"Truman called your father. They know what's going on."

"What did Harris say?" Libby asked blankly. She hadn't heard the older man's conversation with Harris. She had been too preoccupied with not passing out.

"He said Greyson is having some tests done. He passed out after falling—"

"Oh God, did he hit his head?" Libby interrupted.

"Harris doesn't believe so. He thinks Greyson passed out from shock and pain."

That seemed worse. How much pain had he been in to pass out from it? Libby fidgeted agitatedly with the buckle of her seat belt, and Constance reached over to grasp her hand reassuringly.

"He'll be fine, Olivia. He's tough." The comforting gesture, coming from a woman who was usually as reserved as her son, sent Libby over the edge. Her tears welled up and overflowed. Like their son, her in-laws had trouble being demonstrative. Yet when the chips were down, they were there to offer support and comfort in their own way.

Harris and Tina were in the hospital waiting room when Libby rushed in, followed at a more sedate pace by Constance and Truman. The latter was carrying a droopy Clara. Harris got up to hug Libby tightly and then his parents, taking Clara from his father. Tina stood back shyly, giving Libby a hug before practically hiding behind her. Libby was confused at first until she realized that this was the first time Tina was seeing the older couple after so unceremoniously announcing her engagement to their son on Facebook a few days ago.

"How's Greyson?" Libby asked urgently, ignoring Tina's caginess in favor of more immediate concerns.

"They're taking X-rays of his arm and leg as we speak," Harris said. "He seems to be fine, Bug. He regained consciousness, and he was more embarrassed than anything else."

Libby refused to be reassured until she had seen him for herself. She glanced around the waiting room and for the first time noticed that the room was filled with quite a few recognizable faces. Were they all here for Greyson?

Spencer Carlisle, Lia, Brand, a few familiar teens from the community center. A few more from the restaurant.

"Why are all these people here?" she asked Harris in a hushed tone, her eyes wide.

"We were all helping Greyson out with the roof."

"All these people?"

"I know, right?" Harris said with a grin. "My brother is Mr. Popular in this town. I mean, I knew this place was good for Tina, but it's been bloody great for Grey as well."

"I want to see him," Libby said. She wouldn't be assured that he was okay until she had seen him for herself.

"He'll be back from radiology soon."

He had no sooner said the words than they heard a commotion coming from down the hall. A loud, irate voice that sounded remarkably like Greyson's. But Greyson never shouted. Especially not in public. Libby's eyes widened, and she dashed through the swinging doors for the wards, Harris and Tina in tow.

"*No.* I refuse to let you do it. You lay one finger on it, and I'll sue this fucking hospital and everyone in it for malpractice."

"Mr. Chapman, it has to come off, I'm afraid," a tall older man in a white coat was saying in a calm, no-nonsense voice. "Cutting it off is our best option. I'm sure you can have it repaired."

"What's going on here?" Libby demanded to know in her most authoritative voice. She surged forward, going straight to Greyson's side. He was on a gurney, and it looked like they had been in the process of wheeling him somewhere when this heated exchange had begun in the middle of a crowded hallway.

"Olivia." Greyson sounded both relieved and alarmed to see her there. He looked *awful*, pale and bruised. He was wearing nothing but a hospital gown, and she could see the multitude of contusions on his arms and legs. His left arm looked horribly swollen and discolored, and Libby swayed when she saw it.

"Oh my *God*, your arm."

"It's just a little broken. Nothing too terrible," Greyson said, in a voice that was noticeably taut with pain.

"A *little* broken?" Libby repeated, outraged by the understatement. "There's no such thing as a little break, Greyson. Why are you screaming the halls down? Are they hurting you?"

She turned her fiercely protective glare on the staff, who were all watching her with slightly bemused looks on their faces.

"Uh . . . Mrs. Chapman?" the doctor asked hesitantly, correctly guessing her identity.

"Yes. What's wrong with my husband?"

"We need to remove his wedding band; his fingers are swollen, and the band is cutting off the blood supply to his finger."

"Don't you *dare* touch my ring," Greyson seethed, and Libby's eyes welled with tears at how very much that ring meant to him. He had never removed it, not when he had believed the absolute worst of her and at no point after that. Even after he'd signed the divorce papers, the ring had remained firmly fixed on his finger, and he was now prepared to do battle with his doctors to keep it there.

"Greyson," Libby said, stepping toward him and cupping his jaw with her hands. "Let them do what they have to do."

"Olivia . . . I *can't*. It means too much to me. I can't let them take it." He sounded so incredibly heartsick at the prospect of losing that ring that her tears overflowed, and she leaned down to kiss him.

"We'll have it repaired. Or replaced."

He stared at her uncertainly. "Replaced?"

"Yes," she said, her gaze unwavering. "With a new wedding ring. Maybe an engraved one this time."

He swallowed, his eyes still unsure and his face shockingly vulnerable. "Olivia . . ."

"Let the doctors fix you up . . . and then we'll talk about what the hell you were doing on that roof."

"Love you," he said with a grimace that was trying very hard to be a smile.

She moved her mouth to his ear, kissing his cheek along the way.

"I love you too, Greyson. Now please focus on getting better."


"A broken arm, two sprained ribs, and a twisted ankle," Libby itemized as she glared down at her repentant-looking husband a few hours later. She hadn't been allowed to see him while they'd strapped what needed to be strapped and plastered what had to be plastered.

He was under observation for a few more hours, but the doctor was confident they could send him home soon. He was sitting up in the hospital bed, cradling his plastered arm to his chest. Harris had gone back to the flat he had once shared with Greyson to get him some fresh clothes.

"You're lucky you didn't break your neck. What were you thinking?"

"The roof needed to be fixed."

"By professionals. Instead you got your cronies together and . . . why are you grinning?"

"I have cronies."

He sounded so ridiculously pleased that all the wind went out of Libby's sails.

"You're an idiot." The words carried no heat at all.

"I wanted the house to be perfect for you. There's more rain forecast for next week, and I didn't want you and Clara to be in a house with a leaking roof anymore. Spencer has repaired roofs before, we all watched instructional videos ahead of time, I consulted an expert—we were doing a damned good job before I stupidly lost my footing and fell."

"Oh God, the thought of you falling off the roof is so—"

"Wait, I didn't fall off the roof," Greyson interrupted. "I fell off the ladder. Although . . . falling off the roof does sound cooler."

"What?"

"It's lame, but I kind of lost my balance halfway down the ladder. My arm and leg got twisted in the rungs on the way down, and I hit the ground hard. The ladder added insult to injury by landing on me."

"I was worried sick," she admitted, and he lifted his uninjured hand toward her. She entwined her fingers with his.

"I didn't mean to worry you," he said, his voice gruff. He tried to touch her face and winced with the movement. She grimaced in sympathy.

"Try not to move around so much," she told him.

"How's Clara? Can I see her?"

"She's asleep, and you need to rest."

"About that wedding ring replacement . . . I was thinking." He hesitated, and she waited patiently for him to continue.

"Thinking what?" she prompted him when he didn't continue.

"I was wondering . . . I mean, this isn't ideal, and I should probably wait until I'm a bit more mobile and bit less drugged . . . but I figured I'd ask before you changed your mind about loving me."

"I'm not going to do that," she said.

"You sure about that? You're not just caught up in the emotion of the moment? I mean, a man gets injured fixing your roof, you're going to harbor some tender feelings for him."

"Possibly, but I doubt I would have told Brand or Spencer I loved them if they had been the ones to fall."

"Good to know. So you meant it?"

"Greyson," she said with a soft sigh. "I left because I wanted to be sure about my feelings for you. I didn't want my judgment clouded by your proximity, or great sex, or what a wonderful father you are to Clara. But I missed you *all the time* while I was gone. I think that kind of sealed it for me. I didn't miss you after I moved out of the penthouse seven months ago. I was too angry with you. Every time I thought of you, I was just filled with so much anger and sadness."

"Not this time?" he asked softly.

"Not at all. I kept wondering how you were and what you were doing. I looked forward to our FaceTime sessions. I know I said they were for Clara, but they were mostly for me. Because I missed the sound of your voice, the sight of your face . . . I missed your laugh and your smell and your touch. I missed the way you are with Clara. The way you cared about us and our safekeeping. But most of all, I missed your companionship."

"I missed you too," he admitted. "That's why I was so damned determined to fix the house for you. It kept me sane."

"I know I've been hard on you," she whispered, her fingers tightening around his. "I was just so terrified of allowing you to creep back through my defenses. Because I knew once you broached those walls, I'd have no option but to give you a second chance. After our night together . . . I confess I was running scared. The walls were coming down, and I was so afraid—I still am—of us just making the same mistakes again. Of failing again. After everything that has happened between us, everything that was said, all the ways we've intentionally and unintentionally hurt each other, how can we *possibly* succeed the second time round? When we first got married, I had this vision of us being the perfect husband and wife, building a perfect life together. But nothing was perfect; instead everything fell apart so quickly. I wouldn't be able to cope if it happened again."

His eyes were boring into hers with an intensity that should have made her uneasy, but instead she found herself comforted by his extreme concentration as he listened to her words.

"Refresh my memory," he said after a long pause. His voice was thoughtful, as if he was earnestly pondering some conundrum. "Did I tell you I love you the first time round? Did *you* tell me you love me?

Did we have the most beautiful, intelligent, adorable baby on the face of the earth back then? Did you have the perfect job? Did I have buddies? A friendly relationship with my brother? And were we having the best fucking sex in the history of *ever*?"

Libby felt her lips stretch into a grin after the first few questions, and by the time he had reached the last one, she was snort laughing in relief at the very valid points he had made in the best possible way.

"No. To all of that," she replied, her heart soaring exultantly.

"Do you love me because you think I'm perfect husband material?" he asked, humor fleeing from his voice and expression. Libby sucked her lips between her teeth as she considered his question for all of two seconds before blurting out her answer.

"God, no!"

He winced exaggeratedly at that response. "You could have at least pretended to give it a bit more consideration," he mock protested.

"You're far from perfect," she said, her fingers squeezing around his once more. "And so am I. And I think I kind of love that about us."

"Liberating, isn't it?"

She laughed and was surprised at how wild and carefree she sounded.

"It truly is," she admitted. "You've done so much for me, Greyson. I know that. And I know I haven't always seemed grateful. But I was trying so desperately hard to maintain those barriers. Everything you did for us was so wonderful. I wanted you to know that I appreciate it all."

"You don't have to be grateful, Olivia. I didn't do any of this for your gratitude . . . I did it because I had to. Because I love you. I love Clara. And you both deserve the best I have to offer. Even if my best isn't always that great." The last was uttered on a wry note, and she shared a grin with him before going serious again.

"I'm just angry with myself. I didn't show you how much what you were doing meant to me, how much I appreciated it, and I feel like this is my fault. If I'd said something sooner, maybe you wouldn't have felt compelled to damned near kill yourself trying to prove yourself to me."

"Hey, now," he said soothingly. "This isn't your fault. I was careless."

"I don't know what I would have done if you'd been hurt even worse than this." Her voice was thick with tears, and he made a soft, reassuring sound.

"I'm not, though. I'm fine. Let's not dwell on things that didn't happen and focus on the here and now."

She nodded and used her free hand to brush away a few stray tears.

"I want you to know . . . ," she murmured, once she had herself under control again. "The things you said about Harris and me . . . I've come to understand why you may have felt the way you felt. Our behavior wasn't fair. You and I were married, and you should have been my best friend, the one I trusted with my innermost thoughts. But it was so easy to fall back into old habits with Harris."

"I don't want my dumb suspicions to deprive you of one of your most important friendships, Olivia," he said. "I don't want things to be awkward between the two of you. I would hate that. I was unreasonable."

"And we were unfair."

He smiled, a gentle tilt of his lips. "Well, now that we've established all of that, let's not make the same stupid mistakes in the future. Which kind of brings me back to what I was trying to say earlier. Well, it's more a question than a statement. I was wondering if perhaps you'd consider . . . uh." He cleared his throat, and his hand reached for hers again, grasping her fingers so tightly it almost hurt. "I wanted to know if you would do me the honor of being my wife. Again. If you'd marry me. For real this time."

Libby gaped at him, her jaw dropping as she tried to make sense of his words.

"We are married. For real," she said. Her heart hammered in her chest as the magnitude of his words hit her. She hadn't known how much a proposal would mean to her. It *shouldn't* mean this much to her, it was ridiculous . . . and yet, it felt so perfect.

"I mean, we're divorced, aren't we? And since we didn't do *anything* right the last time around, I thought we could try again. And do it right. You know? An engagement party, all the announcements, a wedding, a big dress. Clara can be our ring bearer. But all of that is just icing. The actual *cake* would be us, loving each other, respecting each other . . . talking, laughing . . . being partners. Parents. Lovers."

"Greyson . . ."

"Please." Desperation seeped into his voice, as if he was anticipating rejection. His grip tightened even more, and Libby tugged her hand from his with difficulty. He looked absolutely gutted when she pulled away from him. But she very quickly reestablished contact by brushing his hair back from his forehead.

"I'm trying to tell you we're not divorced," she said, and this time he was the one who gaped at her.

"What?"

"I never got around to signing the papers."


*She never got around to signing the papers?*

If Greyson hadn't been in so much pain and therefore extremely conscious of his surroundings, he would have wondered if he was hallucinating. What did she mean, she'd never gotten around to signing the papers? He'd thought they'd been divorced for weeks, and all along she'd still been his wife?

That was . . . it was . . .

A little disappointing, actually.

"But the wedding," he said, feeling like an idiot. "The dress and the cake. And . . . would you have said yes?"

"In a heartbeat," she assured him, kissing him, and his lips spread into a smile beneath hers. Okay, maybe it wasn't so bad. Weddings were hard work. Or so he'd been told. But he had hoped to start things off on the right note the second time around.

"In fact," she said, lifting her mouth from his, "I *am* saying yes. To the wedding and the dress and the party. We could do a vow renewal. In a church. I think that would be appropriate."

"God, I love you so damned much," he said vehemently, and her smile widened, her eyes gleaming with unshed tears. "My life is absolute shit without you and Clara, Olivia. Look what happens when you leave me. I fell off a roof—"

"Ladder."

"We've established that roof sounds cooler. Anyway, I'm useless without you."

"Let's make sure you're never without me again."

"Yes. Let's do that."

"Hey, I brought you some clothes, and . . ." Harris's voice faded as he stepped behind the privacy curtain around Greyson's bed. His eyes bounced from Olivia to Greyson and back again before his lips stretched into a huge grin. "Soooo, what's going on here?"

"Olivia's agreed to marry me," Greyson bragged, and Harris's eyes lit up.

"That's fucking brilliant! That's—" He shoved back the curtain and raised his voice. "Guys, Libby's going to marry Grey. *Again.*"

Olivia laughed incredulously when they heard the shouts of approval and squeals from the crowd gathered just a few meters down the hall. Hurried footsteps rushed toward them, and Tina pushed her way behind the curtain as well.

"*There's* my girl," Greyson said when he spotted Clara in the woman's arms. "Did you miss me, sweetheart?"

"You're getting *married*?" Tina was enthusing as she handed Clara over to Olivia, who lowered her so that Greyson could give her a kiss. "That's wonderful."

"We're already married," Olivia said with another laugh. She looked so damned happy, and Greyson couldn't stop staring at her. Unable to believe that this was really his life. His wife. His child.

But it was. This beautiful woman and this lovely child were his, and he felt so damned fortunate to have them. He had come so perilously close to destroying everything and everyone he cared about the most, but somehow—someway—they had found it in their hearts to forgive him. To love him.

Olivia caught him staring, and her smile changed, became warmer, more intimate. In that moment, no one and nothing else existed. Nothing but Greyson, Olivia, and Clara. Nothing but the love they shared and the life they would build together.

It was all he had ever needed and all he would ever want. And this time, he was going to treasure all the gifts he had been blessed with.

# Epilogue

"Come on, sweetheart, come to Daddy," Greyson urged, kneeling on the floor as he encouraged his gorgeous nine-month-old little girl to walk toward him. She took a hesitant step, then another . . . before tumbling toward him at a precipitous speed, her gait ungainly but determined. He caught her just before she fell and swung her up in celebration. She squealed in delight, and Greyson turned to Olivia, a huge grin threatening to split his face in half.

"Did you get that?"

"I did," she laughed, holding up her phone. "And it's on its way to Gammy and Gampa and Gran and Papa."

"Good girl, Piper," Clara said in her high-pitched voice, clapping her pudgy hands as she praised her baby sister. "I knew you could do it."

"Yes, you did," Greyson said, picking the three-year-old up with his free arm and giving her a huge hug as well. "You're such a great big sister."

"Meat's ready," Harris called from the back patio, and Clara squealed, wriggling to be let down. Greyson complied, and the girl went tumbling to her plastic table and chair, her small, scruffy rescue dog, Flopsy—so named by Clara because the pup had "big, flopsy ears"—yapping along behind her.

"Gweat! I'm hungwy," she announced before sitting down and folding her arms on the surface of the table expectantly.

"I know you are, munchkin," Harris said, stepping into the house. "That's why I put a rush on it."

"I hope that doesn't mean it's burnt on the outside and raw on the inside again," Libby grumbled good naturedly, and Greyson chuckled. His wife often gave his brother flack over his grilling prowess, but they all knew that she would rather have Harris at the grill than Greyson any day.

"I think you're mistaking me for my brother, Bug. We may look identical, but I assure you, I'm the better cook."

"You don't look identical. Greyson has a much handsomer nose," she said, waving a dismissive hand, and Tina laughed from her spot on the sofa. She was heavily pregnant with twin boys and didn't move around easily these days.

"That's a low blow," Tina protested. "I think he looks rakish with that nose."

"You'd damned well better," Harris retorted. "Since you're the one who's responsible for it."

"I broke it, I bought it," Tina said with a smirk. Harris sank down on the sofa next to her, his hand going to her huge belly while he whispered something in her ear. She giggled and slapped his hand.

"You're a lech, Harrison Chapman. Propositioning a heavily pregnant woman like that," she said teasingly, and he growled before planting a kiss on her laughing mouth.

Greyson loved their Sunday-afternoon gatherings. It had become something of a tradition in the three years since they had moved to Riversend. A way to unwind after a busy week. MJ's was doing phenomenally well under Tina and Olivia's leadership. Greyson and Harris had successfully set up a division of the company in Riversend and now used it as their home base. They had created quite a few jobs in the town as a result and had quickly made a mark among the townspeople.

Greyson served on the city council and volunteered at the youth-outreach program with Spencer. And Harris had campaigned to bring several winter festivals—including poaching the cheese festival from the next town over, for some reason—to Riversend in order to promote off-season tourism. It was a very successful pet project, and all the local businesses had seen an uptick in winter commerce thanks to those festivals.

And at the end of every week, they touched base with Sunday lunch at Greyson and Olivia's beach house. The original house had been torn down after a year, and they had built a bigger place to suit their needs. Sometimes they went to the hill, where Harris and Tina had built a delightful log house with a fantastic view of both the town and the ocean. Sometimes Sunday lunch was just a family affair, but their friends often joined them as well.

"Why so serious, my love?" Olivia asked, coming up beside him and winding her arm around his waist. She wiped a crumb from Piper's drooly chin before lifting her gaze up to meet Greyson's.

"I was reflecting on how lucky I am and how incredibly happy you make me. Thank you for my life, Olivia."

"I think you mean *our* life."

Greyson draped his arm around her shoulders and kissed the top of her head. "Our life. Thank you for our wonderful life."

# Acknowledgments

So many things get put on hold while I'm writing a story. Thanks to my family and friends for always patiently waiting for their "turn" with me.

Nathan and Lauren, you guys are the best pet sitters and dog distractors in the world. I appreciate you always.

Thanks to my ROSA ladies. I love hanging out with you—our get-togethers are wonderfully motivating, and I am so proud to be a part of our organization.

Rae Rivers, brainstorming with you is always inspiring!

My agent, Kim Whalen, I'm eternally grateful for everything you do.

I'd like to thank my wonderful Montlake team. You're all fabulous, and I cannot imagine doing this without each and every one of you.

Special thanks to my fantastic acquiring editor, Lauren Plude: you're truly amazing, and I hope we work on many more books together.

And to the exceptionally talented Lindsey Faber, I consider myself incredibly lucky to have worked with you on this project. Every single editorial note enhanced and improved these stories. You're a wonder, and I thank you from the bottom of my heart.

# About the Author

*Photo © 2013*

Natasha Anders has been drawing praise and attention as a unique voice in romance since 2012. Her first novel, *The Unwanted Wife*, was a bestselling sensation and remains a consistent favorite among readers. Her 2017 novel, *The Wingman*, the first in her new Alpha Men trilogy, was a finalist for a 2018 Romance Writers of America RITA Award. Born in Cape Town, South Africa, Anders spent nine years as an associate English teacher in Niigata, Japan, where she became a legendary karaoke diva. Anders currently lives in Cape Town.